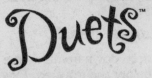

"Don't jump, dear!"

Skyler glanced down from the tree at the crowd gathered below and frowned. They thought she wanted to do herself in! From an oak tree? She pointed at Fluffy. "I'm just getting a cat." *And* she was stuck. "Stupid Fluffy," she muttered.

"Name's Jack, not Fluffy." Skyler jerked her head at the sound of the deep, sensuous voice and promptly bopped her head on a thick branch.

"Hold tight," he said, reaching his strong arms around her. "I'm tryin' to impress my captain."

Skyler blinked. Of course. The new firefighter her brother had mentioned last week. *Another hero.* But she couldn't deny the flutter in her heart as he held her waist snugly and his bold gaze slid down her body.

When they reached the safety of the ground, Skyler gaped up at her gorgeous savior's rugged, muscular body. Way up. There was just so darn much of him to absorb! All that...man. *Whoa, baby!*

He grasped her shoulder, as if to steady her. "Are you okay?"

Light-headed, she nodded slowly, the park starting to spin around her. *Why me?* was her last thought as she fainted dead away.

For more, turn to page 9

Hunka Hunka Burnin' Love

"This is a firehouse, not a dating pool."

Monica stood almost nose-to-nose with Ben, her hands propped on her hips, his arms crossed over his chest. His really broad chest.

The burn of desire in Monica's blood turned to anger, but just barely. She rose up even straighter in her high heels and looked Ben dead in the eye. "How dare you suggest such a thing, Chief Kimball? You barely even know me."

His gaze fell to her lips and she groaned inwardly. *Dammit, what's wrong with me?* She'd never had so much trouble getting a man interested in her before. Ben just looked aggravated, not attracted. And what was that cologne he was wearing? Her stomach trembled; her knees weakened. She seemed to remember being furious with him just a few seconds ago. Where was her anger now?

Heat flashed across his eyes as he glared at her. "I know exactly who you are."

Aha, she thought. *Now we get to it.* Just how much did he know about The Incident...?

For more, turn to page 197

HARLEQUIN DUETS

ISBN 0-373-44159-2

Copyright in the collection:
Copyright © 2003 by Harlequin Books S.A.

The publisher acknowledges the copyright holder
of the individual works as follows:

CAN'T HELP FALLING IN LOVE
Copyright © 2003 by Wendy Etherington

HUNKA HUNKA BURNIN' LOVE
Copyright © 2003 by Wendy Etherington

This edition published by arrangement with Harlequin Books S.A.

® and TM are trademarks of the publisher. Trademarks indicated with ® are registered in the United States Patent and Trademark Office, the Canadian Trade Marks Office and in other countries.

Visit us at www.eHarlequin.com

Printed in U.S.A.

Wendy Etherington

Can't Help
Falling in Love

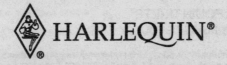

HARLEQUIN®

TORONTO • NEW YORK • LONDON
AMSTERDAM • PARIS • SYDNEY • HAMBURG
STOCKHOLM • ATHENS • TOKYO • MILAN • MADRID
PRAGUE • WARSAW • BUDAPEST • AUCKLAND

Dear Reader,

When I first conceived this book, the tragic events of September 11, 2001 had not yet occurred. But as I finished the story, what was foremost in my mind was the theme I started with: *heroism*. For a romance writer, fictional heroes are our everyday companions and beloved creations. But watching firefighters in Washington and New York, I realized just how real heroes can be.

While these stories are humorous, please have no doubt how seriously I take the issues these characters would face in real life. Local firefighters and police protect my community, just as they protect countless neighborhoods across this country. Find time for these heroes. Support them. Remember them.

Wendy Etherington

P.S. Please come visit my Web site at www.wendyetherington.com or write to me at P.O. Box 211663 Columbia, SC, 29221-1663.

Books by Wendy Etherington

HARLEQUIN DUETS
76—MY PLACE OR YOURS?

To the firefighters and law enforcement personnel
who fought and lost their lives in the tragedy of
September 11, 2001.

Special thanks to Russ Adams, firefighter/paramedic
with the Chesterfield Fire Protection District,
for his patient answers to my constant—
and sometimes ridiculous—questions.

Thanks also to Jacquie D'Alessandro
and Jenni Grizzle, who always have an opinion—
and almost always good ones. And thanks to my
editor, Susan Pezzack, for her terrific brainstorming
skills and her great sense of direction.

1

SKYLER KIMBALL clutched the broad oak tree branch just above her head, stretching her other hand to her nemesis. "Give me a break, Fluffy."

Fluffy, the copper-colored, not-quite-pure-bred Persian sitting barely five feet away, merely blinked her topaz eyes.

"What did you expect, Sky?" she admonished herself. "After two and a half hours of perching in the tree, the animal was just going to fall into your arms? Life's not that easy." Certainly not *her* life.

"I called the fire department, Skyler honey," Fluffy's owner, Roland, called up to her.

"Uh…" Skyler's hand slipped. She hugged the tree trunk as panic bloomed in her chest. "That's not—I mean, maybe we're jumping the gun here, Roland," she yelled down, peering through the thick branches.

Roland Patterson, the owner of the pet store located next to her women's clothing shop, smiled wide, his pale brown eyes twinkling, even from a distance.

And she immediately knew the significance of calling the fire department was not lost on her neighbor. He had a thing for the fire department. Specifically for fire*men*.

For nearly two years, she and Roland had owned businesses on Main Street in her hometown of Baxter,

Georgia. Generous loan terms provided by the city council had given them—along with the bakery, the gym and the florist—opportunities to become part of the city's recent downtown expansion. Skyler loved the independence her shop, Kimball Fashions, had given her, though her protective brothers had argued each and every point of the contract she'd signed.

Brothers who, she reminded herself, would be arriving at any moment with the flamboyant siren, lights and hoopla of the Baxter Fire Department.

She looked heavenward. "Please don't let them bring the ladder truck…please don't let them bring the ladder truck."

The image of her climbing down that long, shaky ladder, with half of downtown staring up her flowery sundress and gossiping about the risqué lingerie no one would have imagined she wore, spurred her to action. She climbed a few branches higher. "Come on, Fluffy," she implored, holding out her hand to the stubborn cat.

Fluffy proceeded to wash her already pristine paw.

The possibility of some panicked individual—Roland came to mind—calling the fire department for such a simple, and clichéd, task as a cat in a tree was the reason she'd scaled the giant oak in the first place. She could handle any crisis. And without her brothers' help. Certainly Fluffy's sudden penchant to spend the afternoon in the park.

In the distance, she heard the peal of a siren. *Yeah, right.*

Briefly, she considered scrambling down the tree it had taken her more than thirty minutes to climb, but one look below at the park's summer green grass changed her mind. She swallowed hard. Had she really climbed so high?

Worse, a small crowd had gathered on the sidewalk. Two elderly women had their necks craned backward as they stared up at her. A couple of kids—was school out already?—danced around Roland chanting, "Jump, jump." Their words caused passersby to grind to a halt. People pointed and whispered. Cars stopped in the middle of the street. When Roland shook his head at the kids and shouted "Stop that right now," they only chanted louder. "Jump! Jump! Jump!..."

"Hells bells." Resting her forehead against the rough tree bark, Skyler cursed her impulsive nature. She'd fought against the "hero" mentality of her family all her life by being planned, controlled and cautious. Her father had lost his life in a fire being the hero, never realizing the financial and emotional strain he might leave behind. Her brothers, Ben and Steve in the fire department and Wes as a cop, strove on a daily basis to live up to his legend, while she, at least on most levels, fought to live it down. She cared for her mother—who'd never fully recovered from the loss of her husband nearly twenty years before—she paid her taxes, attended to her customers, went out every other Saturday night with her friends for girls' night, and fought nervous sweats and panic over her brothers' dangerous jobs.

She had stock to unpack, customers to call about her upcoming sale and books to balance. Why had she decided to take on an ornery feline as her one heroic gesture in *weeks?* If only Roland hadn't cried....

"Don't jump, dear," someone called up.

Skyler glanced down to see one of the elderly women had moved to the base of the tree. "I'm not jumping," she returned. She had no intention of listening to the ridiculous suggestion of a couple of obnoxious five-year-olds.

"Just stay calm. Remember life is so precious."

"Uh-huh."

"You have so much to live for."

Of course…Skyler narrowed her eyes as realization dawned. That lady thought she wanted to do herself in. From an oak tree? In the middle of the park? *Good grief.* Feeling ridiculous for having to explain why she'd climbed the tree, she pointed at Fluffy. "I'm just getting a cat."

"You don't have to make up a story, dear."

Skyler clenched her jaw. "I'm not making—"

"We all love you."

Pushing a group of leaves out of her way, Skyler craned her neck to get a better look at this goofy woman. She'd never seen her before in her life. *We all love you?*

"I'm just here to get the cat." She stepped over one branch closer to Fluffy.

The crowd gasped. The kids chanted louder. "Jump! Jump! Jump!" The lady held up her hand imploringly. "No, don't move."

Then the fire department arrived. In the ladder truck. And the pump truck. And the ambulance.

Skyler sighed, sitting on a branch with her back braced against the tree. "Well, Fluffy, we're getting the full show today."

Captain Benjamin Kimball—her oldest brother—leapt from the passenger seat of the ladder truck, just as Steve, his junior by five years, jumped from the driver's side. Drivers and other firemen scrambled out of the other trucks, all jogging in the wake of their captain. Looking away from the whole, humiliating scene, Skyler absently wondered when the police—and her third brother—would arrive.

Her stomach growled, reminding her she hadn't eaten lunch. Fluffy butted her head against her arm, purring like crazy. She was probably hungry by now, too. Skyler rubbed the ornery feline between her ears. "You know, you could have decided to be friends twenty minutes ago, then we wouldn't be in this mess."

The cat crawled into her lap, flexing her claws as she found a comfortable position.

"Ouch!" Skyler flinched and grabbed an overhead branch to steady herself.

The crowd gasped. The goofy lady squealed. The kids chanted. "Jump! Jump! Jump!..."

"Skyler?" a familiar voice shouted.

Skyler waved her hand in Ben's general direction. "Here."

"You're not planning to jump, are you?"

"Not today."

"Can you climb down?"

"If you really think I should."

"Skyler..." Ben said in his best don't-mess-with-me warning tone—the one he used whenever he was forced to bail her out of some scrape her impulsiveness had driven her to.

"Coming." Skyler planted her feet on a lower branch, using one hand to balance against the tree, while holding Fluffy beneath her other arm. Scooting on her bottom, she managed to move down one branch, but Fluffy panicked at the movement and dug her claws into Skyler's arm. They both teetered. Fluffy hissed, swiped her claw down Skyler's arm, then scrambled onto another branch. Her arm stinging like hell, Skyler swung one leg over the branch she was sitting on, clutching the rough bark between her thighs. Her stomach pitched and sweat trickled down her back. "Okay. That wasn't fun."

"Jump, Jump, Jump!…"

"Shut up already!" she yelled down, past frustration and embarrassment. She examined the inside of her arm, where a thin line of blood had appeared. Glaring up at the cat, she again began her descent. "You're on your own."

Before she could get more than a few feet down, though, she heard the familiar sound of a hydraulic lift. *The ladder.* Again, she leaned her forehead against the tree's rough bark. "Why me?"

The cat hissed.

"You said it, Fluffy."

"Name's Jack, *chère,* not Fluffy. You wanna give me your hand?"

Skyler jerked her head around at the unfamiliar, deep, sensuous voice—and promptly bopped her head against the thick branch next to her. Wincing and rubbing her forehead, she looked down at the man who'd spoken.

She found herself staring into a pair of warm, whiskey-brown eyes, the exact shade of the Jim Beam her father used to drink. Along with those incredible eyes went jet-black hair, an arresting, sculpted and tanned face, broad shoulders, muscular arms, then…

Leaning over to get her fill of her gorgeous savior, she nearly lost her balance.

Quick as lightening, he grabbed her wrist.

Her pulse drummed against his hand. The warmth of his skin seeped into her veins, and she found her whole body heating to his touch.

"Hold tight, *chère*," he said. "I'm tryin' to impress my captain."

Skyler blinked. Of course. The new firefighter/paramedic Ben had mentioned last week at Sunday dinner. *Grew up in a small, southern Louisiana town. Met him at a convention. He wants to move up. A real go-getter.*

Another hero.

Who at the moment was going to save her butt, so she had no business quibbling with him over the dangers of his job.

Still grasping her wrist, he gently tugged her arm. "Come on. I've got you now."

She smiled. That sounded pretty nice. As she climbed onto the ladder it wobbled. She thrust her arms around the fireman's neck, and the heat of his body infused hers. His sculpted face was inches from her own. He smelled pleasantly of sweat, pine and musk, as if he'd applied aftershave that morning, and the scent had melded with his duties during the day. The muscles along his shoulders tickled her fingertips, and for the first time in a great while she found herself tempted by male flesh. Tempted beyond her brothers' tendency toward overprotection. Tempted beyond her staid reputation.

Smiling, he held her waist snugly as his bold gaze slid down her body. "This is my kind of rescue."

Skyler's heart fluttered. It had been a long time since a man had looked at her so brashly—and survived her brothers' fury to tell the tale. Curious herself, she let her gaze rove him as slowly as he had her. He wasn't model beautiful, she decided…he was better. Rugged. Strong. And big. His tanned, muscular arms and broad chest were covered by a white shirt with the Baxter Fire Department logo stitched over his left breast pocket. His black uniform pants glided over his lean hips and thighs as if they'd been custom-made…and she certainly wouldn't have minded being the tailor.

My, my, my. There was just so darn much of him to absorb. All that agility, muscle…and *man.* She dropped her gaze to note he was standing one rung below her, but he still towered over her by several inches. But then, she was a mere five-two, whereas— she observed shamelessly—he was maybe six-four. It was hard to tell with their entwined proximity. Maybe this weird rumbling in her stomach was her weakness for large men.

Then, she remembered. Rescue. The cat.

She pointed toward the pesky feline, still perched several feet above her and looking for all the world like someone had interrupted her late afternoon adventure—and was none too pleased about the censorship. "Don't forget Fluffy."

He glanced over her shoulder briefly, then said, "How 'bout I handle you, then I'll deal with the cat."

Okay by me. She gave Fluffy one last you're-on-your-own glare as the fireman started down the ladder and the crowd began to cheer. When they reached the safety of the ground, and her feet rested on the summer green grass, she gazed up at him.

Way up at him. *Whoa, baby.*

He grasped her shoulder, as if to steady her. "Are you okay?"

Light-headed, she nodded slowly. His smile appeared—bright, charming, confident, maybe a bit reckless, and her throat tightened. As the park began to spin before her eyes, she finally recognized the odd sensation trickling through her body.

Why me? was her last thought as she fainted dead away.

As JACK TESSON scooped the unconscious woman into his arms, he raised his eyes heavenward, deciding some saint up there had finally cut him some slack. Maybe all those years at the hands of the St. Michael's Parochial School nuns had finally paid off. No doubt Sister Katherine, who'd thrown him out at least twice a year, and his grandparents, who'd punished him by making him scrub floors in the restaurant/bar they owned, would say she was the devil's temptation incarnate. Certainly not a woman for "Wild Jack" Tesson.

"Mon Dieu," he whispered, gazing down at her beautiful oval face. Though she looked angelic, he knew from staring up the ladder that her lacy purple underwear was anything but virtuous.

Ben Kimball raced toward him. "Skyler?"

Perfect name for an angel, Jack thought, even as the medic in Jack finally overrode the man. "She fainted." Wait a minute. Skyler? The guys at the firehouse had mentioned her. "Your sister?"

As Ben nodded, Jack realized why those bright baby blue eyes of hers had seemed so familiar. The worried and frustrated version of them stared back at him from his captain's face.

"Let's get her to the truck," Ben said.

As they rushed to the ambulance, they picked up a

trail of curious bystanders, one being Ben's younger brother, Steve.

His expression fierce, Steve ordered, "Get her on a back board."

"She just fainted," his brother explained as they reached the back of the ambulance.

A grin tugged the corners of Steve's mouth. "Naturally." The brothers exchanged a troubled, but affectionate look.

Jack gently laid Skyler on the stretcher Ben pulled from the ambulance bay, pressing his fingers against her wrist and taking her pulse as he did so. A little fast. He fitted an oxygen mask over her face, while Ben hovered, watching his every move. "She's fainted before?"

"Oh, yeah," Steve said, sitting on the back bumper.

Jack pulled a stethoscope from a med kit to check Skyler's heart. As the rhythmic beats reverberated in his ears, she moaned, and he tried to ignore the soft skin beneath his fingers, the tan line along the slope of her breast. He'd worked on patients he'd found attractive before, but never with this level of intensity. Never had one smile and a wide-eyed stare from a pair of baby blue eyes brought him practically to his knees.

He glanced over at his colleagues as he checked Skyler's extremities for injuries, noting a thin cut on her forearm that he cleaned with antiseptic. "Is she pregnant?"

Fists clenched at his sides, Steve leapt to his feet. "She better damn well not be."

Ben grabbed his brother's shoulder, shoving him

back down. "Cool it, little brother. She's not pregnant."

"How do you know?" Steve countered, his eyes narrowed.

"Because you or Wes would have killed the guy by now."

Jack snatched his hands from Skyler's body. Okay. So, he could list an attraction to his boss's sister under the category headed Bad Career Move.

"She tends to faint whenever she gets too excited," Ben explained to Jack. "She has MVP."

"Oh, God!" A man broke from the crowd and threw himself across Skyler's legs. "She's going to die!"

Jack grabbed the guy's arm and lifted him off his patient. His size had always been effective with crowd control, so the small, almost delicate man was easy to remove.

The man gaze up at him fearfully, blinking tears out of his brown eyes. "But, Skyler—"

"Will be fine, Roland," Ben said, looking exasperated as he pulled him away from the stretcher. "MVP is short for Mitral Valve Prolapse. It's a condition where the heart doesn't empty the chamber completely of blood. Stress can sometimes aggravate it."

Roland eyed Ben with a look that Jack could only describe as adoring. "Really? How fascinating."

Ben let go of the man's arm as if he'd just realized he'd grabbed a hot poker.

"Uh, Steve?" Jack said, his voice low.

"Yeah?"

"That guy, is he flirting with Ben?"

"Yep. That's Roland Patterson." The pet store

owner who'd made the 9-1-1 call, Jack realized. *That* explained the other guys' eye-rolling when dispatch had announced their destination. "You should see him whenever Wes is around," Steve continued. "He gets a bigger hard-on for cops than he does firemen."

"No kidding."

"You need to stand back and let the medics work," Ben was saying to Roland as he gestured—as opposed to leading him—to the crowd.

"What about Fluffy?"

"The cat," Jack said when Ben frowned.

Stretching, Steve rose. "I'll check."

He sauntered away just as an elderly woman approached, shaking her head. She handed Ben a business card. Over his shoulder, Jack read *Clovis Crisis Counseling.* "You should encourage her to make an appointment with my office as soon as possible, Captain. Climbing that tree was a blatant cry for help."

"Skyler's not suicidal, ma'am," Ben said, tunneling his hand through his hair. "Just impulsive."

The woman gave him a cagey glare. "Just give her my card." She walked away.

"Damn." Ben braced his hands on the stretcher and stared down at his sister, who rolled her head to the side, obviously fighting her way back to consciousness. "How does she get herself into these things?"

Personally, Jack thought the whole event was kinda fun, certainly the most exciting call since he'd arrived in town two weeks ago. He envisioned "ladder rescue experience" on his résumé, surely an asset when he applied to the bigger fire departments in Atlanta in the coming year. Baxter was going to be a great stepping stone. And he knew he'd learn a great deal from working for Ben. Though the guy could loosen up a bit. Especially when it came to his sister.

Jack glanced at her again, checking her pulse at her wrist to have an excuse to touch her again. Damn, she was beautiful. And tiny. Even her bare feet—with toes painted a shocking orange—were small. She was funny, too, remembering her response of "not today" to her brother's question of whether or not she was going to jump from the tree. Too bad she was off-limits. Of course, a protective family member or two hadn't stopped him before....

Suddenly her eyes flew open, and she bolted upright. Jack found himself practically nose-to-oxygen mask with her.

"What the hell—" She jerked off the mask, glaring at him without recognition, then her eyes went soft, and she smiled. "Oh. It's you."

"Jack Tesson." His whole body rigid with desire, he fought the urge to apply his medical skills to a little mouth-to-mouth and pulled a penlight from his kit to check her pupils. They dilated normally and evenly. "How do you feel?"

She flushed bright red, as if remembering she'd fainted into his arms. Was she as affected by him as he was by her? Or was she just embarrassed?

Before she could answer him, Ben grabbed her hands. "You scared the hell out of me, Skyler. What were you doing in that tree? Risking your neck over a cat?"

"I'm fine." Her eyes darkening, she glanced at Jack. "I just, uh...the heat overwhelmed me for a minute."

Heat, huh? Jack leaned toward her.

"You're not taking your medication," Ben said abruptly.

Jack stepped back as Skyler sighed. What was he doing? Coming on to his captain's sister right in front of him? Not even *he* was that crazy. He began packing his supplies.

"The doctor says I don't need medication," Skyler said to her brother, shaking off his touch. "I haven't fainted since last fall when you and Steve were called to that four-alarm fire in Monroe."

Ben tunneled his hand through his hair. "I can't believe you climbed that tree. You're delicate and—"

"Delicate?" Skyler rolled her eyes, then slid off the stretcher, straightening her sundress. "Please."

"Says the woman I just rescued from a fifty-foot tree branch."

Skyler stuck out her tongue at her brother. "You didn't rescue me. Jack did." She smiled brightly at him.

While Ben scowled, Jack's groin tightened. *Mon Dieu,* she was tempting...

Steve strode toward them with an orange-colored cat tucked beneath one arm.

...as long as no hotheaded siblings are hanging around.

"Fluffy," Steve said. "Safe and sound."

Ben sighed. "Return him to Roland, then let's get this equipment loaded. Another Skyler emergency appears to be over."

Skyler glared at him, and Steve saluted, jostling Fluffy so she hissed. "Yes, sir, Captain, sir."

"Move it, *Lieutenant,*" Ben said to his brother, not looking at all amused.

Sensing this was an old argument about responsibility—and one Jack had seen aimed in his direction by his grandparents more times than he'd like to recall—he turned his attention to Skyler.

Just in time to see her strolling away.

When the crowd of curious bystanders advanced on her, she swung around and headed toward the front of the ambulance. Jack followed, catching up to her as she reached the tree she'd climbed.

"Where the hell are my shoes?"

"What do they look like?" Jack asked.

She whirled as if startled, then she swept out her hands, cocking one hip. "Do you see a big selection of shoes? I'll bet if you spot a pair, they're mine." She turned around, muttering under her breath about men and their general lack of sense/usefulness/reason for living.

Beautiful, tiny, funny, delicate—he had to agree with Ben there, at least in the looks department— independent and sassy. *Laissez les bon temps rouler.* Let the good times roll.

He trailed behind her as she walked around the tree. When he spied a pair of bright orange heeled sandals, he scooped them up. "Yours, *'tite fille?*" he asked, smiling as he held them out to her.

"Thanks." She took the shoes, then slid her feet into them. Straightening, she smiled. The anger was gone from her eyes, replaced by a light full of intelligence and charm. "Ben said you were Cajun. I'm afraid I don't know much French. You'll have to translate."

"Cajun French is a bit different than pure French, anyway." He stepped closer to her. As her head dropped back to meet his gaze, he wondered about the differences in their heights. His size was usually a professional advantage, but women in his past had been both intrigued and intimidated by it.

Skyler swayed on her feet.

Jack grabbed her waist. "Skyler? Do you feel faint?" He pressed his fingers to the side of her neck to find her pulse racing. He was coming on to her, and she was really sick. Damn. He'd worked hard to become a firefighter and paramedic. He had five years of experience. What had he missed?

She blinked, then stepped back. "I'm fine. Just a bit wobbly in these shoes."

He scowled. "You need to see a doctor."

"You were translating," she said.

Not wanting to press on a subject that was really none of his business, Jack let the subject go for the moment. "*'Tite fille* means little girl." Oops. Before she could do more than frown, he added, "Maybe you'd like *'tite femme* better. It means little—" Woman. Big oops. "Uh, I mean, *'tite ange.* Little angel."

She pursed her lips. "That's kind of nice."

The hunger he'd banked surged through his body again. Why was he so drawn to her? His voice dropped an octave. "It suits you."

Laughing, she walked across the grass. "I don't know about that."

They would be back under the careful watch of her brothers in a matter of moments. Jack knew he didn't have much time. "Maybe we could get together for a drink or dinner sometime."

She stopped, looking up at him. "I don't date."

He frowned. Why wouldn't a woman like her date?

She patted his arm as if she understood his confusion. "Sorry. There's just too much darn bloodshed."

2

BLOODSHED WAS AGAIN on Skyler's mind the next day as she unpacked stock in her storeroom. "They shorted me on leather teddies and leopard-print camisoles *again*," she muttered.

Bud's Leather Palace—"the finest quality, direct from Austin"—was in big trouble.

The bell on the front door jangled before Skyler could work herself into a real lather over the mistake. *Fiona.*

She rushed from the storeroom, locking the door behind her. She'd only hired her assistant a month ago, and she wasn't quite ready to trust her with her most intimate—okay, only—secret.

In these A.M.—After Madonna—times, she knew keeping her lingerie inventory secret was a bit archaic, but Baxter's town council was not known for their progression. When she'd proposed a lingerie shop two years ago, the idea had been promptly trounced by the committee, and Mayor Collins, though not much of a traditionalist himself, had bowed quietly to their wishes. Personally, she thought First Lady Collins would look terrific in one of her hot pink bustiers, but she hadn't dared to voice that idea to the people who handed out the business licenses, so, on impulse, Animal Instincts had become Kimball Fashions, and The Secret had been born.

The Secret was held in confidence by a small part of the town—the progressive female part. Skyler knew she needed to bring Fiona into the fold soon. Showing her this month's invoice from Bud's Leather Palace would probably be a good start.

Upon reaching the main showroom of the shop, she saw Fiona Jingle hanging a new stock of mauve dresses on the racks. "Good morning," Fiona said briskly. "I decided to jump right in restocking the sale items."

The contrast of the flowery dresses Fiona held and Fiona—think young Elvira—immediately improved Skyler's mood. "Terrific."

Fiona brushed a lock of long, black hair behind her ear. The bells attached to her earrings, bracelets and waist chain tinkled. With a name like Jingle, Skyler supposed you had to go with your bestowed gifts.

Her young assistant winced at the frilly dresses. "Did you consider my ideas from last week? I mean, some of these women could stand a little figure-flattering black."

"Your ideas were super." Though Skyler had all the leather, lace and satin she could handle in the back room. "In fact, they inspired me to get you a present."

She returned to the storeroom, where she pawed through the boxes. Tucked between three pairs of red leather hot pants and a stack of white leather thong panties, she found Fiona's black leather jeans. Skyler held them up to her waist and studied her reflection in the mirrored wall. She and Fiona were about the same size, though Fiona was a few inches taller, so the pants dragged the ground. But still...

"Hot, hot, hot," she whispered, imagining the cool, tight leather clinging to her thighs. The silver studs running down each side seam glinted seductively in the dimly lit storeroom. Her blond hair would contrast like spun straw against a matching leather vest.

With a rueful smile, she shook her head. "Yeah, right, Skyler. Maybe you could wear them to the church fashion show next month, or the neighborhood block party." She liked her rebellions locked away or hidden safely beneath her clothes. And if sometimes playing it safe got old, well, she always managed to stumble into excitement. Though climbing a tree to rescue a cat had been a first for her impulsive side.

Tucking the pants under her arm, she strode out, locking the door behind her.

As she walked toward Fiona, her assistant's eyes widened. "Where did *those* come from?"

Skyler held out the pants. "I ordered them for you."

Fiona dropped the collection of pastel blouses she held as if they'd suddenly caught fire and stroked her hand reverently down the leather. "No kidding?"

A pleased smile was breaking over Skyler's lips when the bell over the shop's door jingled again.

Jack Tesson, broad shoulders, jet-black hair, whiskeyed eyes and all stood in the opening.

He actually asked me out yesterday was the first thought that popped into her head—after her hormones shouted *whoo-whee,* of course.

She'd often wondered if a man would ever come

along and challenge her brothers, sweep her off her feet and…

And nothing. Rolling her shoulders, she watched him walk toward her, fighting the desire rumbling through her stomach. She'd warned him off yesterday. Why was he here? Smiling at her? That warning discouraged *everyone,* which was fine by her. She didn't need the complication of a man in her life, or warming her bed. And definitely not a firefighter.

The few men who'd warmed her bed hadn't met with encouraging fates, she reminded herself. One had suddenly moved to Florida. One had entered the priesthood—though that story had come from Wes, so she wasn't quite sure about its validity. Then again, the alternative was picturing the guy at the bottom of the lake. Which, according to Baxter legend, was the poor guy's final resting place.

But then Mr. Florida had been something of a deadbeat. Skyler wasn't sorry to see him go. And the priest/lake dweller had slobbered over every female he encountered, so her brothers' intervention had been a frank relief. As the only girl in a sea of testosterone, she'd certainly lived through moments of frustration, but getting rid of and warning off unwanted attention without confrontation by her was not one of them.

However…watching the luscious Jack Tesson stroll toward her, Skyler's usual caution deserted her. The man was really a temptation. A *big* temptation. Her head spun at the thought.

Then she realized she still held the leather pants. How was she going to explain these outrageous things in her conservative shop?

Stopping in front of her, he angled his head. "Mornin', *'tite ange.*"

Her face heated, and the desire in her stomach cruised through her veins. *Not good.* He was absolutely the worst possible man for her. Clearly reckless, adventurous…heroic. Unfortunately, her libido knew what it liked, and it was completely irrational at the moment.

Fiona fared no better. Her assistant's jaw had dropped so low, she was tempted to call an orthodontist.

Skyler cleared her throat and tried to act normal, while frantically wondering how to explain her handful of studded black leather. "Jack, this is my assistant, Fiona Jingle. Fiona, Jack Tesson."

As they shook hands, Skyler puzzled through this attraction. Why did he affect her so strongly? Maybe she'd been working too hard. Maybe she'd spent too much time picking out ostrich-feather and leather lingerie.

Yes. Desperate, she latched on to that excuse. That's it. Her mind, focused on lingerie, had made the natural leap to sex. Then Jack had appeared and *bam*, instant attraction. One man could not so effortlessly create near-panting, cat-rescuing and lust-inducing preoccupation in a woman who'd sworn off men—especially dangerous men.

"You sure got a *diverse* inventory, *chère*," Jack said as he stood between them, his gaze taking in seemingly every detail of the leather pants she held.

Skyler didn't need that kind of scrutiny. Classy as her shop was, it couldn't survive without the lingerie revenue. Jack couldn't be trusted with her secret. He worked with her brothers, he was a virtual stranger, he was a *man*.

Before she could say anything, though, Fiona said, "Oh, no, Mr. Tesson. Skyler special-ordered these for me. We don't carry this kind of thing."

Grinning, Skyler shoved the pants at Fiona. "Why don't you try them on?"

Fiona danced off, but not before giving Jack one last dreamy look over her shoulder. "Nice to meet you," she said, her facing flushing a becoming shade of pink.

"You, too," Jack said, then smiled.

That same smile had sent Skyler into a dead faint yesterday. The fact that her assistant wandered back to the dressing rooms under her own power only magnified her humiliation. Her heart condition had caused occasional problems in the past, but none this embarrassing. Of course, he couldn't possibly know *he'd* caused her to faint. No doubt Ben had explained something along the lines of overexcitability, stress, etcetera, etcetera. No one—and she meant *no one*—had to know the real reason for the fainting.

She stared up at Jack, noting she was within touching distance of his awesome body. His size fairly dwarfed her. How tall was the man anyway?

He reached out, twisting a lock of her long blond hair around his finger. "Your brothers told me they had a baby sister. I never woulda pegged you as her, though."

Skyler snatched her hair from his grasp and stepped back. Those reckless brown eyes had her stomach turning somersaults. "I'm fair, like my grandmother." And if L'Oréal helped with a few well-placed highlights once a month, *he* certainly didn't have to know.

"What about that drink?"

Her eyes widened. "You just don't get it, do you?"

"Get what?"

"Nobody *dates* me."

He frowned. "You already got a *beau?*"

Beau. God, that accent was cute. Maybe they could go out once. No one would have to know. The image of Boyfriend #2's possible fate flashed through her mind. An urban legend, or *glug, glug, glug…?* "No," she said quickly, "I don't have a boyfriend."

"You don't like guys?"

"No. Yes." She sighed. "Of course I like guys."

"You don't like me?"

She let her gaze rove his body—briefly. Her head spun. She took shallow breaths as her heart raced. *Easy, girl.* "I like you fine. I'm just—"

"Scared? Overwhelmed?" Smiling, he stepped closer, his voice deepening. "Aroused?"

All of the above. She felt herself leaning forward, drawn to the heat in his eyes, the confidence in his tone. She didn't need this complication in her life. She didn't *want* to want him. Still, desire stole through her body.

"Aren't you worried about my brothers?"

"No."

With those impulsive Kimball genes vibrating, and on the verge of buckling, she smiled. But the bell over the door saved her from some mortifying fate like fainting or throwing herself into his big, strong arms.

Turning, she saw a young man rushing toward her with a giant bouquet of long-stemmed, red roses. He dropped to one knee beside her, holding out the flowers. "Ms. Kimball, I've come to declare my undying love."

The legend of the Kimball boys is alive and well. Skyler closed her eyes. "Not again."

"Again?" Jack asked from behind her.

"It's a long story," she muttered.

"Skyler, oh sweet Skyler," the boy began. "Your eyes are so blue, your lips are so red. Please don't tell your brothers I'm here, 'cause I'd soon be dead."

Knowing the drill, Skyler accepted the roses, then leaned forward to kiss the guy on his forehead. The imprint of her watermelon-shaded lipstick remained as proof of his mission.

As he rose to his feet, he blushed, the freckles across his nose vivid next to his pale skin. "Thanks."

"What fraternity?" she asked.

"Alpha Kappa Omega."

"Good luck."

"Thank you, ma'am." He whirled, then raced from the shop.

Skyler glanced at the bouquet. At least two dozen. Poor guy. He was probably out fifty bucks. She strode to the counter, retrieving a vase from underneath. After filling it with water from the bathroom, she arranged the roses, then set the vase by the register. Maybe she could give away a stem with each purchase.

Jack leaned against the counter. "You wanna tell me what that was all about?"

She glanced up at him. When she answered his question, despite his assurance he wasn't afraid of her brothers, he'd undoubtedly rescind his drink offer.

He'd probably think she and her family were totally nuts. And maybe they were. Losing their father so young had made them all overprotective.

For the first time in…well, for the first time, she found regret slipping past her defenses. She liked him. His boldness, his simmering energy, his…shoulders. *Que sera sera. Was that a French or Spanish expression?*

"*That* was a fraternity initiation."

Not surprisingly, his brow furrowed.

He really is cute….

But he's got a great job here. Baxter's city council had voted a salary increase for firefighters, police officials and other critical personnel in the hopes of attracting big city professionals. *He's a real go-getter,* Ben had said. He certainly wouldn't and shouldn't risk his job for her. Even if she wanted him in return, which she certainly did *not.* Skyler plus Dangerous Man equals Trouble.

"Bravery is part of most fraternity initiation codes. Since asking me out is akin to near suicide, I've become a symbol, so to speak." When he continued to stare at her in confusion, she drew a deep breath and plunged. "The guys come here with a big production of flowers, declare their undying love, then see how long they can duck out of sight before one of my brothers threatens them. It's all in fun," she said defensively.

"Ah." He leaned his forearms on the counter, bringing his face within inches of hers. "These 'threats' by your brothers, is that the reason you won't go out with me?"

Well, duh! "Isn't that enough?"

His gaze turned hungry. "No."

She goggled. She gaped. This guy wasn't going to be brushed off like the others. And, by damn, if she didn't oddly find herself admiring him for his determination. "Jack..."

"I like the way you say my name, *chère*."

Oh, boy. She swallowed. "You're really nice..."

He winced. "The kiss of death."

"Trust me when I say nice guys are rare. I don't mean you're a sap, or anything, I mean you're gracious and kind and helpful." Heroic, actually, but she didn't know how to say that without sounding idiotic.

"I'm still not sure if you're flattering or insulting me."

He's a guy, she reminded herself. What description would her brothers prefer? Macho, dangerous, virile. The first two she could agree with, the third she could only speculate about, bringing her back to her original intention—to turn him down, for his own good. And hers.

"Be flattered," she said finally. "But my brother is your boss, and if we go out together..."

"I'll be out on my ass."

"Faster than you can say 9-1-1."

The determination in his eyes never wavered.

Yikes. She didn't want to be a challenge. She wanted Mr. Dangerous, Hunky Hero to say okey-dokey and amble merrily on his way.

She already liked him. And liking led to caring. Caring led to love. Love led to loss and deep, dark despairing grief. *No, thank you.*

Again, the door swung open. Roland Patterson swept inside. "Skyler, darling," he called, waving a pad of paper. "You want in on the pool?" He paused at the counter, smiling slowly at Jack. "Why it's Fluffy's savior. How delightful to see you, Firefighter Jack."

Jack nodded. "Mr. Patterson."

Skyler watched Jack's reaction for the usual homophobic nonsense, but he displayed nothing of the sort. Damn. Just when she was ready to put another black mark by his name—other than the job and tendency toward reckless heroism—he had to go and be even more interesting.

"Pool?" she asked Roland to distract herself.

"Frat Boy Survival," he said as if that were obvious, and Skyler groaned. "I saw the *darling* redhead with the roses. Kind of scrawny. I'm giving him twelve hours."

Glaring at Roland, Jack straightened to his full height, leaving Skyler dizzy and Roland gaping. "You're *betting* how long before that kid gets pummeled?"

"Well, uh…" Roland's gaze darted to Skyler for support.

Skyler crossed her arms over her chest. She, too, thought the pool idea was tacky at best, but she also felt obliged to defend her family. "My brothers wouldn't pummel a kid." *Would they?* She'd better keep an eye on them for the next few days, just in case.

"Count me out." Jack glanced at Skyler, then smiled briefly. "I gotta get going." He turned, tossing "see ya, *chère*," over his shoulder before sauntering from the shop.

A deep, heartfelt sigh escaped Roland. "That is one incredible hunk of man."

Her head still spinning, Skyler couldn't nod, but, for once, Roland hadn't exaggerated.

A WEEK LATER, Jack sat in the Leather and Lace bar, sipping a biting glass of whiskey, considering the temptation of Skyler Kimball.

A temptation he should resist, to be sure, though it got harder every day. Hell, *he* got harder every day. Just thinking about those lacy purple panties she wore sent him straight to a cold shower every time. His instinctive reaction to her was inconvenient and stupid, since no matter how beautiful and lust-inducing, she was off-limits.

He'd debated calling her all week, but deep down he knew he didn't belong with *'tite ange* Skyler Kimball. She sold frilly dresses and saved pampered cats. She wouldn't spend her nights with a swamp rat like him. This bar suited "Wild Jack" Tesson better.

The scarred wooden floor looked as though it had greeted many a customer and borne many a barroom brawl. The black vinyl-covered booths were nicked and rubbed down to the Styrofoam padding. The jukebox roared. The bar was long, well-stocked and packed with customers. His grandparents had practically raised him in a similar bar in Louisiana.

Skyler probably didn't even know where this place was. He needed to put her out of his mind. He'd come to Baxter with the intention of earning respect, gaining experience and moving on to bigger things. He'd long ago realized his yearning for success was rooted in his insecure relationship with his parents. He'd never understood why saving whales in Fiji had been more important than raising their son.

Of course, whale-saving had been followed by rain forests, then icebergs, then animal testing in cosmetic manufacturing. He hadn't heard from them in six months, so for all he knew they could be teaching pygmies in Borneo how to rotisserie chickens by now.

"Hey, buddy," the bartender said, nodding at Jack and his nearly full glass. "That's good whiskey. Problem?"

On Friday night, Jack figured the man's clientele leaned toward guys with a heartier thirst. Bikers, blue-collar workers and slick-tied professionals had draped themselves around the place. A half-dozen women were scattered at the tables. All looked ready to start off the weekend with a bang.

"No problem. I gotta work early tomorrow," Jack said to the bartender, a barrel-chested, dark-haired man who could have been any age from forty to sixty.

The bartender polished a beer mug. "Haven't seen you here before. New in town?"

Jack rolled his shoulders, setting aside the problem of Skyler for the moment. "I just signed on with the Baxter Fire Department." He held out his hand, which the bartender shook. "Jack Tesson."

"Gus Saunders. I own the Leather and Lace." He picked up a clean glass, filled it with an amber-colored beer, then sent the mug sailing down the bar. A man Jack assumed was a regular caught the drink, immediately gulping from the glass. Gus grinned. "Quick service saves trouble later."

Jack nodded, recognizing the wisdom of that philosophy. Because of his size and coolheadedness, he'd been designated bouncer at *Grand-père*'s bar since he'd turned fourteen.

"Welcome to Baxter." Gus grinned again. "At least the notorious side."

Just where I belong. Jack toasted him. *"Merci."*

"That accent isn't Georgia."

"No. St. Francis, Louisiana."

"Cajun country?"

"Oui. The bars at home, they're situated along the bayou. Gators discourage the troublemakers. Keeps things colorful."

"I'll bet." Gus waved his hand. "Hey, you know how to cook? Make some of that Cajun stuff—gumbo and crawfish? On the weekends, I bring in a live band and sell food. I think my customers are tired of chicken wings and nachos."

"A noncooking Cajun is only half a person."

"How 'bout next weekend, you make me something Cajun, and I'll give you an unlimited bar tab."

Cooking was his second-favorite activity. And with the lovely Skyler off-limits, the chances of him indulging in his favorite looked dim. "Sounds good to me," he said to Gus.

"Great." Laughing, Gus filled a few orders before returning to his washing and drying position in front of Jack.

As more customers continued to flood in, Jack asked, "You don't have any other help?"

"A waitress and busboy, but they aren't on until nine."

"Need any help?"

Gus sighed. "Always."

"I worked in a bar for years," Jack said, standing.

All he had to go home to was Casey—the freckly-faced, eighteen-year-old frat boy hiding out in his apartment. He'd found the kid hiding under his dorm room bed this afternoon. As if Skyler's brothers wouldn't think to look there.

"I couldn't pay much," Gus said, his expression doubtful.

Jack pushed his glass toward Gus. "How about I work for my drink, for tonight anyway?"

"Deal," Gus said quickly.

Within minutes, Jack commanded Gus's bar, leaving the owner to mix and joke with his customers. The work was sweaty, but honest, familiar and comfortable.

Until a certain blonde strode through the door.

3

JACK ACTUALLY PAUSED with a beer mug raised in the air, on its way to a customer's hand. Skyler Kimball swept inside the bar with a quiet hush, but nearly every patron of the place turned to see the newcomer, as if they knew something innocent and pedigreed had invaded their midst.

"Hey, man, do I get the beer, or what?" his customer asked.

Disgusted with himself and the sudden swelling in his jeans, Jack set down the beer, sweeping away the money the customer offered, then stuffing it in the register without even counting the cash. What was *she* doing here?

From the corner of his eye, he watched her walk somewhat hesitantly toward the bar. Dressed in faded blue jeans and a white T-shirt, she looked sexy, approachable. The jeans hugged her slim thighs and narrow waist, and even under the dim bar lights her blond hair shone like sunlight.

Damn, he wanted her. How could she strip away his resolve to resist her so easily?

Ben wouldn't fire you for just talking *to his sister*, whispered the seductive devil serving as his conscience.

Right. He could *talk* to her. His captain was a by-the-rules kind of guy, he rationalized, and technically only the city council could fire him. Just play it cool, he told himself.

He met her gaze. And the impact of those blue eyes staring into his caused a tremor of need to vibrate clear down to his toes.

He wasn't cool any longer.

She approached him, angling her head and frowning. The two men in front of him jumped off their barstools, scooting them back with a loud scrape across the wooden floor, each holding out a hand for Skyler to take his seat.

Waving their gesture aside, she asked, "What are you doing here?" in such an accusing, frustrated tone, he had to smile. Could this attraction be a two-way street?

"Have a seat, *chère.* I had no idea you'd come collecting my drink offer so soon."

"I'm not here to see you."

Jealousy kicked him hard in the ribs, and he knew he'd been kidding himself about fighting their attraction. He'd taken plenty of risks before. Why should this one worry him?

She accepted one man's offer of his stool with a brief thank-you, but continued staring at Jack suspiciously. "You never answered my question."

Jack forced his gaze away from her glistening pink lips. "Huh?"

"Why are you here?"

"Helping Gus. You?"

"I'm—" She stopped and glanced over her shoulder. "I come here all the time," she said, turning back with a bright smile on her face.

"Uh-huh." He responded to a couple of shouted orders for refills on drinks, trying to picture Skyler

Kimball sidling up to the bar for a whiskey after work. The vision didn't gel.

Looking nervous, she glanced over her shoulder again.

She was up to something. Something she didn't want to tell him about. Of course he was a virtual stranger. Why would she tell him? Her business was none of his business.

He stood in front of her, leaning against the bar. *Be cool, remember?* "So, what'll you have?"

She set her purse in front of her as her gaze danced down the bar. "A beer, I guess."

"What kind?"

"Huh?"

I come here all the time. Right. He didn't mention the slip, but said, "I've got Bud, Bud Light, Michelob, and Coors Light on tap. In bottles, there's—"

She held up her hand. "Whatever you like."

He drew a Michelob from the tap, placing the cold mug in front of her.

After a brief sip, she smiled. "This is better than the last one I had."

Momentarily struck stupid by her smile, he didn't comment. Her parents had named her right. She was an angel who belonged in a pure, cloudless sky. Not being gawked at by a swamp rat, respectable citizen wanna-be like him. But then, there were those nonrespectable panties of hers...

He grabbed a towel from beneath the bar and wiped down the wood. When was the last time a woman had affected him so strongly, so quickly? Since...never.

"Are you moonlighting?" she asked after another sip of beer.

"Sort of," he said, glad to be distracted from his thoughts. "I'm the restless type, I guess."

"Aren't you tired after working a twenty-four-hour shift at the firehouse?"

He shrugged. "Nah. We usually sleep uninterrupted through the night. There's not a lotta action in Baxter."

"Is that what you want—action?"

Something in her tone brought his head up from his cleaning task. Her eyes reflected an odd combination of wariness and curiosity. "Sure. I jumped at Ben's offer to come here, 'cause I want to work in a big city station. With Atlanta so close, I figured this was the perfect opportunity. I sure wasn't gettin' anywhere at home."

"In Louisiana?"

"Yeah. A tiny town just outside Lafayette. St. Francis makes Baxter look like a booming metropolis." He leaned one hip against the bar, smiling as he pictured his grandparents' white cottage on the banks of a tiny stream, brimming with crawfish in the spring and mosquitoes in the summer. "We didn't even have a fire station. Me and another guy—who double-dutied as the undertaker and town coroner—covered fire and medical emergencies with volunteers and occasional help from the sheriff."

She returned his smile. "Baxter used to be like that. My grandfather was the only paid firefighter back then. What about your family?"

"My grandparents still live in St. Francis." He didn't mention his parents. Explaining them could take hours. "They own a bar and restaurant."

Waving her hand at the bar, she said, "That's why you look so comfortable back there."

He shook his head. Comfortable wasn't even a remote possibility around Skyler. The urge to pull her into his arms swept through him. Would she tremble beneath his touch? Would her eyes turn smokey with need? Would she smack the crap out of him?

"Bartender!" a guy shouted from the other end of the bar before Jack could give into the temptation.

"Be right there," he called back. After one last look into Skyler's sensual blue eyes, he strode off to fill the order.

By the time he returned, the devil on his shoulder had convinced him he should ask her to dance. *One dance. What harm could there be? He was good enough for one dance.*

From pretending coolness to jumping into the fire. After over five years, he should be used to it.

Gus approached her at the same time Jack did. "Hello, lovely lady. I've never seen you in here before. Name's Gus. This is my place."

As Skyler shook Gus's outstretched hand, a guilty flush colored her cheeks. Again, Jack wondered what had brought her to the bar.

"I'm Skyler Kimball," she said.

"Kimball, huh?" Gus rubbed his chin, glancing from Skyler to Jack, then back. "Ah, that's how you know Jack here, right? You must be those Kimball boys' younger sister."

Skyler winced. "That's me. The little sister."

Rocking back on his heels, Gus nodded. "Great guys. The one who's a cop…"

"Wes," Skyler supplied.

"He's broken up quite a few brawls in here," Gus continued.

Skyler smiled weakly. "He's usually around when there's trouble."

"One night this crazy guy came after him with a broken beer bottle. Wes never even flinched and had the creep disarmed in seconds. It was incredible."

"I guess. If you call fourteen stitches incredible."

Skyler's gaze dropped to the floor, but Jack had seen the worry in her eyes. After losing her father, he supposed she feared for the rest of her family. She sipped her beer, the haunted look lingering in her eyes. She looked small and alone.

Hadn't he sworn to serve and protect? Well, no. That was the cops. Hmm. Well, in addition to being a firefighter, he was a medic. He'd sworn to heal.

His gaze bounced from Skyler to the dance floor, then back. What the hell. "Hey, Gus, I promised Skyler a dance. Can you take over for a bit?"

"Sure." Gus glanced at his watch as he walked around the end of the bar. "My waitress and busboy should be here any minute. You two have fun."

Jack rounded the bar, then stood just behind Skyler, his hands resting on the back of her barstool. The heat and flowery perfume rising from her skin wound his muscles tighter.

"I never said I'd dance with you," she said in a low tone.

He leaned close to her ear, tendrils of her blond hair tickling his nose. "Will you dance with me, *'tite ange?*"

She turned her head, bringing their faces so close, her breath whispered across his skin. His gaze flicked to her lips. The urge to kiss her kicked through him, but he tamped down the impulse.

"Okay," she said finally, a little hesitant.

Before she could regret her decision, he captured her hand in his, then led her to the dance floor. The postage-stamp-size area forced them close together, though only four other couples were dancing. He slid his arms around her waist, while she rested her hands on his shoulders, stretching to reach.

"How tall are you anyway?"

"Six-six." He frowned and noted Skyler frowned as well. Maybe he intimidated her. She was so petite, delicate...untouchable. What the hell was he doing with her?

Dancing. Just dancing.

Yeah, right. Like her cop brother would believe that. A cop brother who came into the bar often.

Jack bit back a groan—of regret and hunger. Skyler felt wonderful, soft and curvy against his body. He longed to run his hands down her backside, pulling her against his erection.

"I haven't danced in a long time," she said, her sweet breath caressing him through his cotton T-shirt.

He stared down at her, his gaze riveted by the glistening curve of her lips. "Me either."

Her eyes turned smokey, needy. That look had followed him into sleep every night for a week. She might be fighting their attraction, but she felt it.

As awareness danced between them, she fixed her gaze on his lips, then licked hers. And he lost his battle with restraint.

Leaning down, he fit his mouth over hers, moving his lips against hers, memorizing the taste and feel of her in case she never let him touch her again. Her lips trembled, then parted, inviting him inside the warmth of her mouth. He slid his tongue against hers, gliding against her heat, her sweetness. As he pulled her closer, her stomach nestled against his erection, and he groaned into her mouth.

Could he work around the brother problem? Could he bury his insecurity about his past? He had no idea, but he wanted Skyler, all her beauty and spunk and curves. Very little else seemed to matter at the moment.

She leaned back, breathing hard, staring at him oddly. "Oh, hell, not again."

Her eyes dilated. Her MVP? If she fainted again, by damn, he'd drag her to the doctor personally. "Skyler?"

She rested her head against his chest. "Hmm?"

"Are you okay? You're not going to faint, are you?"

"Not as long as you're holding me up."

He was certainly enjoying serving as her prop, but even his libido couldn't override concern for her medically. "Take easy, deep breaths. Concentrate on stabilizing your heart rate."

She lifted her head, looking up at him. "Relax. I'm not going to drop at your feet."

He lifted his eyebrows. She had before.

"Again," she finished, then grinned.

Relaxing a bit, he stroked her hair back from her face. "You know, *chère,* about that drink…maybe you could reconsider—"

Her gaze darted over his shoulder, distracting him. He glanced around, but didn't see any enraged brothers bearing down on him, so he turned back to her.

"Would you excuse me just a moment?" she said before he could continue.

Breaking free of his hold, she strode toward the bar, pulled something from her purse, then crossed to a table occupied by three women who appeared to be the walking definition of "biker chicks." Though everyone seemed to be wearing leather lately, these tough faces, windblown hair, black motorcycle boots and tattooed arms belonged on the back of a Harley.

His body still vibrating from her kiss, Jack narrowed his eyes, starting after her. What was she up to?

"I'LL CALL YOU next week about your order, Flash," Skyler said, then glanced back and saw Jack working his way across the bar. *Damn, damn, damn.* He'd never believe Flash and her "gang" were customers of the shop. What in the world was he doing at a biker bar anyway? Didn't he know the cops and fire-fighters all hung out at The Corner Pub in town? And what in heaven's name had possessed her to kiss him?

"Great. Thanks for finding my wallet and bringin' it way out here," Flash said, punching Skyler's shoulder lightly.

Wincing from the friendly jab, Skyler backed away from the table. "No problem. I—" She couldn't get the words "come here all the time" past her lips again. "I was glad to do it for such a terrific customer. See ya." She waggled her fingers, then spun to intercept Jack before he reached them.

Too late, she thought somewhat hysterically as she plowed into his wide chest. She bounced off the hard muscle and would have fallen flat on her butt if he hadn't grabbed her by the waist. Why did the man have to be so attentive…so "gorgeous and avail-able," as she'd overheard at least fifty times during the week from the stream of helpful gossips passing through her shop. Only Roland was disappointed in

Jack's attributes. "Straight," he'd informed her mournfully.

Once she found the courage to look up, her gaze connected with his. *Big mistake.* Those soulful brown eyes belonged on a child, not a full-grown man. And, heavens, did he have great lips. She wanted them on hers again…and again. Desire trembled through her veins.

"Are you okay, *chère*?" he asked.

And that accent…whew. "Just super," she said, hoping he wouldn't question her further. Their explosive kiss had left her light-headed—which he didn't have to know about—so her biker customers had come as a welcome distraction. But, as usual, she was now questioning her impulse.

"What was that all about?" he asked, nodding to the women behind her.

Living up to those brash Kimball genes was damn overwhelming sometimes. She shrugged. *A girl's gotta do…* "Flash is a customer."

Jack raised one black eyebrow. "Flash?"

She stepped out of his embrace, crossing her arms over her chest. "The brunette in the middle—the one with the blond streaks in her hair."

"*She's* a customer?" He smirked. "Somehow I don't picture her seeped in lace and tradition."

"Maybe she likes lace and tradition."

Both eyebrows darted up. "I'm sure."

Ha! She'd found another flaw. The man was quick to judge, dangerous, way too tempting and…leaving. Atlanta was his future. *The perfect opportunity.* Losing him wasn't just an irrational fear of his job—it was assured.

Well, she didn't want to win him anyway.

With her index finger, she poked Jack so hard in the chest he actually stumbled back, though only in surprise. "Look here, you arrogant, judgmental, luscious—"

Walking backward, he grinned. "Luscious?"

Blood red clouded her vision. "You egotistical, daredevil...*man!*" She drew a deep breath before continuing her tirade. "It's been a really long week, and I don't have the time or the inclination to explain to you the finer points of retail sales management, except to say you *never*...and I mean never prejudge a customer. The woman who walks through my front door wearing ripped blue jeans and a ratty T-shirt may have more money than the queen of England. Flash and her friends have the right to shop anywhere they please, regardless of what any close-minded creep thinks about their purchases!"

Jack's jaw hardened. "Creep?"

Flash appeared at her side. "Problem, Skyler?"

Skyler spared a brief glance at her customer. "No. This is a personal thing."

"Right. A problem." Flash's dark eyes narrowed. She advanced toward Jack, her gang flanking her. "He may look big, honey, but trust me the girls and I can handle him."

"No. Really, I can—"

Before Skyler could finish, Flash swung.

Instinctively, Skyler stepped in front of Jack. The fist intended for Jack's jaw landed squarely against Skyler's left eye.

"Oh, damn," she muttered just before she jolted backward against Jack's chest and passed out cold.

"SKYLER...CAN YOU HEAR ME?" Jack's voice sounded as if it was echoing down a long tunnel.

Skyler moaned, then blinked. She lay on the floor of the bar, with Jack's arm cradling her neck. His handsome face loomed over her, along with Flash, her gang and several other people she didn't recognize.

"Hey, Gus, how about some ice?" Jack suggested.

"Frozen peas are better," someone said.

Flash shoved the speaker. "Where are we gonna get frozen peas, stupid?"

"Hey, babe," the guy next to Flash said, his eyes narrowing, "don't push him."

Flash grabbed the front of his shirt. "Shut up!"

"Uh—" Skyler began, trying to raise her head, but the pounding around her eye forced her to lie back down.

Jack's fiercely concerned face and wide chest suddenly blocked her view of the other people, though she could still hear Flash shouting at someone. "I'm gonna carry you to a booth, *oui?*" Caution darkened his eyes. After her tirade earlier, she could hardly blame him.

She tried to nod, found that hurt, so she mumbled, "Please."

Held next to Jack's firm, muscled chest two times in the same day, she marveled. Maybe her luck with men was changing. *Right.* Punched in the eye and near discovery of her secret. Her luck was changing all right, and not for the better.

Even though proximity to Jack was a bad idea and pain pulsed through her eye, she couldn't help but inhale the smoky, spicy scent emanating from his skin. As she wrapped her arms around his neck, his muscles bunched, and she let him coddle her. An impulse she'd regret like so many others, no doubt.

When he placed her in the vinyl booth, she sighed with regret.

Gus handed Jack a plastic bag of crushed ice. "Try this."

Jack laid the cold pack against her face, and she flinched. "Sorry." He cradled her cheek in his palm. "It'll help the swelling."

"Swelling?" Perfect. She might never look in a mirror again. And how in the world was she going to explain this to her brothers?

Across the room several voices rose in volume, but Skyler had her own troubles at the moment, so she pushed aside the distraction. Now that the initial stinging from the ice had passed, the cold had numbed the area enough for her to think straight again.

She had to get out of here. Immediately. Quietly. Just after she gained the sworn silence of everyone in the bar. The black eye she would no doubt have in the morning would be hard enough to explain— maybe she could go for the old "walked into a door" story—but she couldn't let her brothers find out about Jack's connection to her injury. He'd get fired, or worse, thinking again of Boyfriend #2—the lake dweller. *Glug, glug, glug…*

Leaning sideways, she considered her need to protect Jack only briefly—she shouldn't, *couldn't* care— as she peered around his wide shoulders, hoping to spot a back door.

Instead, she saw Flash shove someone. Flanking their leader, her friends planted their fists on their hips. The men across from them leaned forward, their jaws jutted forward. The antagonists began circling each other. The other bar patrons backed away to watch. Money was exchanged.

Central Casting couldn't have scripted a better rumble.

"I'm taking you to the firehouse," Jack said. "I have meds and—"

Distracted from the alarming scene across the bar, Skyler blinked up at Jack. Then ground her teeth together from the pain of focusing. "I just want to go home." The crowd cheered. God only knew what was happening with the fight. "Now." She scooted by Jack out of the booth.

As she stood, the room spun. "Damn." She held her arm out to balance herself. She was *not* going to faint again.

Jack's strong arm slid around her waist. "Change of plans. You're goin' to the emergency room."

"No." Wesley and Steve knew—and had dated— nearly every nurse in the hospital. "I have Tylenol at home."

Crash!

The sound of shattering glass echoed through the bar.

"What in the hell…" Jack began, obviously noticing the rumble for the first time.

"Terrific," Gus said in disgust just as one of the men tossed a bowl of beer nuts at Flash. She retaliated by pouring a mug of beer over his head.

In one smooth, quick motion, Jack picked up Skyler and deposited her in the booth. "I'll be right back."

Before she could so much as blink—and the blinking hurt like hell—he'd started across the room.

What in the world was he doing? Skyler wondered

in horror as she watched him stride purposefully into the fray. *He's a hero, remember? A reckless, foolish—*

He ducked a handful of pretzels flying through the air, stepped over a puddle of chicken wing sauce, then grabbed the thrower by the front of his shirt, as Skyler stared in fascination. Flash charged toward him on the other side, but Jack merely held her back by grabbing her shoulder.

"Let's all calm down," he said.

A couple of guys in the crowd, not liking the interference, tossed nacho chips—cheese included—at Jack. The chips fluttered uselessly at his feet, but the thick, orangy sauce landed with a plop in his hair.

Skyler winced. That stuff was going to be nasty to get out when it dried.

The room fell silent for a second or two, then all hell broke loose.

Beer nuts flew. Chicken bones sailed. Chips crunched beneath boots. Shouts echoed off the walls. People slid through pools of cheese sauce and beer.

It was a smelly, slippery, icky mess. Skyler debated between throwing herself into the middle as the voice of reason, or remaining safely in the booth and laughing her fanny off.

"Anybody who smashes a glass gets arrested," Gus shouted into the confusion.

Jack disappeared behind the bar for a few minutes, then returned with a mop and a bucket. He stood silently next to a stool, cheese dripping off his head, as if waiting for the melee to die down so he could deal with the mess.

She'd known the man less than a week. How could he cause such a roller coaster of pride and hilarity to race through her?

"Well, well, well. What do we have here?" a familiar voice asked from the doorway.

Flinching, Skyler turned to face her brother.

THE VIEW FROM the Baxter City Jail wasn't bad, Jack reflected.

The simple, tidy room contained just two battered oak desks—one manned by a bored-looking sergeant—a few vending machines and two cells. Other than the recent addition of a hall leading to some new offices, Jack didn't have much trouble picturing the place occupied by Sheriff Taylor and Barney Fife of Mayberry.

Skyler paced the floor in front of him, her breasts bobbing with the movement, her worn jeans hugging her hips and thighs. Full of guilt, he wondered how much her eye hurt and if they could pick up at the kiss where they left off.

Of course they were on opposite sides of the bars, so that might be a bit difficult to accomplish at the moment.

"Don't worry, Jack. I'll get you out of there," she said, holding a fresh ice pack to her eye as she turned, then started across the front of the cell again. "Gus is talking to Wes now. He'll explain how you were trying to help."

Jack clenched the bars in frustration. *Trying* to help didn't seem like much comfort at the moment.

The fighting had ended amicably enough. At the appearance of the police, fighters and patrons alike had blinked innocently, dropped their chicken wings and chips and picked up their drinks as if nothing out of the ordinary had happened.

Lieutenant Wesley Kimball had strolled in with

calm authority, received a rundown of the events from a grateful Gus, then proceeded to take down the names of the ones who'd wrecked the bar owner's property. Gus agreed not to press charges as long as the fighters cleaned up and paid for the food. Wes had even acknowledged Jack's assistance in controlling the situation.

Until he noticed his precious baby sister's swollen eye.

Then Jack and everyone else had been taken straight to jail—do not pass *Go*, do not collect two hundred dollars.

"This is all your fault, man," Mike, one of his fellow detainees, said grumpily.

Jack turned to stare at the man who'd brandished a bowl of beer nuts at him less than an hour ago. "*My* fault?"

"Yeah." Mike's jaw jutted forward. "You had to break up a perfectly good brawl."

"Oh, shut up," Flash said. "This is *your* fault. If you hadn't thrown those nachos—"

"Pipe down in there," the desk sergeant called from the other side of the room.

Flash and Mike turned their backs to one another.

Skyler laid her hands over Jack's through the bars. "They can't hold you if Gus doesn't press charges, right?"

Her bright blue eyes were so liquid with worry he didn't want to tell her the truth. At the very least, the police could charge any and all of them with disturbing the peace, destruction of property, attempted assault, actual assault, criminal mischief, etcetera, etcetera. And, frankly, he was more concerned that her brother was, right at this moment, plotting to pin everything from J.F.K.'s assassination to MonicaGate on him.

He stroked her cheek with the tips of his fingers. "Everything will work out," he said without much confidence.

"I'd back off, if I were you, Tesson," Wes called from down the hall. "Going near my sister was what got you into this mess in the first place."

Jack bit back his reply as Wes Kimball sauntered toward the cells, Gus trailing in his wake.

Skyler ran toward him. "You let Jack out of there right now, Wesley. This is outrageous! He tried to *stop* the fight."

Wes smiled down at her, patting her on the head as he walked by.

Jack didn't think dismissing Skyler was such a wise move—or was going to be quite so easy.

Skyler threw her ice pack on the floor and charged after him. With her red, swollen eye and I've-had-it-up-to-here expression, it looked as though the next casualty in this war would be Wes Kimball. "I'm warning you," she said.

"Not now, Sky," he said, his blue eyes, so like his sister's, radiated anger as he stared at Jack. "Toss me those keys, Sergeant." After unlocking the cell doors, he gestured in the direction he'd just come. "This way, Tesson."

Rolling his shoulders, Jack walked out of the cell. It was time they had this out. His and Skyler's relationship, if they even had one, was none of Wes's business, but he'd dealt with hotheaded cops before and knew arguing would only egg him on. Jack intended to keep a hold on his already strained temper and show this jerk a thing or two about self-control.

His gut clenched as he preceded Wes down the hall, remembering the time his parents had been arrested in an animal rights protest, and he'd driven all night to Dallas to bail them out of jail.

They were halfway down the hall when Skyler joined them. "You're not talking to Jack without me."

Jack was suddenly reminded this was the woman who'd sacrificed herself for him. She'd instinctively stepped in front of Flash's punch, telling him more about her strength and loyalty in one brief moment than he suspected most people learned in a lifetime. No one had ever done anything like that for him.

Wes sighed. "Come on, then. It's time I found out what's going on between you two anyway."

Jack stiffened. He wanted to know what was going on, too. No doubt Wes thought he wasn't good enough for his sister. And Wes certainly wasn't the first.

They all entered a small, somewhat disorganized office with Wes's nameplate half-buried beneath a pile of file folders on the desk. Wes indicated the two chairs in front of the desk for Jack and Skyler, while he sank into his swivel office chair. The position of authority. This was his interview.

Jack laid his arms along the armrests. *Stay cool*. He knew he could do so with Wes in a way he'd never manage with Skyler.

The lieutenant wasted no time getting to the point. "So, what's going on between you two?"

"Nothing is going on," Skyler said immediately, though her gaze darted to Jack's, and he knew she was thinking about the kiss they'd shared on the dance floor.

"You two started a barroom brawl," Wes said.

"We didn't start anything. Flash did, and she was only—"

"Ah, yes. Flash." Wes raised his eyebrows. "The biker chick who claims to be one of your customers."

Comments like that were a bad idea. Jack knew from experience. But after an hour behind bars, he'd let the lieutenant learn that lesson for himself.

"My customers are none of your business," Skyler said tightly.

Jack glanced from Skyler to Wes. What about calling *him* arrogant and egotistical?

Wes sliced his hand through the air. "Whatever. The point is she claims your black eye was intended for Jack. She said he was threatening you."

Skyler rolled her eyes. "Oh, please. He was not."

Though Jack appreciated her support, Wes's eagerness to believe he was really a danger to her pissed him off. He leaned forward. "You really think I'm capable of threatening your sister?"

That suspicious lawman gaze flicked to Jack. "I don't know you well enough to determine anything about your capabilities."

At this rate, he never would, either. Wes Kimball had labeled him a troublemaker based on assumptions, guilt by association. Jack swallowed a tide of anger. "But you trust your brother, don't you? Ben thought I was good enough for this town."

"This isn't about the town. It's about my sister."

Who I'll never be good enough for. "I didn't threaten Skyler. I didn't start the fight. I didn't hit anyone. I didn't destroy any property. Do you have any witnesses who say different?"

"No," Wes admitted, though he obviously regretted the lack of evidence.

"Then this meeting is over." Jack rose from the chair, and he didn't dare look at Skyler. He'd never been arrested over a woman, and he knew one look into her eyes would have him risking much more just to be near her.

Wes stood as well. He was nearly the height and breadth of Jack, but not quite. A difference that certainly didn't please the lieutenant, who rested his right hand on the butt of the gun strapped to his waist.

"Skyler, I need to talk to Jack alone for a minute."

"What for?" Skyler asked suspiciously, gazing up at the two men.

"A little man-to-man thing. You understand." Smiling, Wes gestured toward the door.

"Does it concern me?"

"Yes."

"Forget it."

Wes shrugged. "Fine." He directed his intense blue gaze at Jack. "Stay away from my sister, Tesson."

Before Jack could do more than tighten his jaw, Skyler leapt to her feet. "Wesley Austin Kimball!" She leaned over the desk, her hands planted firmly in the center. "That's the rudest—"

"He's a firefighter, Sky," Wes interrupted quietly.

Skyler's gaze darted to Jack, then back to her brother, and Jack had the sinking sensation his job was a bad thing. Usually, women were impressed by his profession. But then she'd suffered a great loss at the hands of fire fighting.

"It's a brother's duty to look out for his sister," Wes continued.

Skyler pressed her lips together. Then, after a penetrating glance in Jack's direction, she addressed her brother. "You know how much I appreciate your concern, but I can handle this. I don't need you to protect me from Jack."

Wes frowned. "You realize if Ben finds out Jack will lose his job."

Skyler shook her head.

Jack couldn't help but wonder—did that mean he wouldn't lose his job, or Ben wouldn't find out, or there wouldn't be anything to find out?

"Jack and I will work this out," she said firmly to Wes. "I don't want your interference."

Wes continued to scowl and look puzzled as if Skyler spoke a foreign language, and Jack grinned. Confidence surged through him. If he'd ever had doubts Skyler was worth any risk, he shoved them aside.

Until she strode from the room.

"And don't think I don't know about that frat boy with the roses!" Wes called after her.

Skyler slammed the door.

Well, hell. The lady might be interested, but, clearly, he still had a long way to go.

Wes dropped back into his chair and propped his feet on his desk. "Well, 'Wild Jack' Tesson, I ran a make on you, you know."

Wishing he didn't so completely miss Skyler's presence, Jack raised his eyebrows. "Really?"

Wes held up his hands. "All part of the background check when you applied for your job." He paused. "You seem to have a tendency toward barroom brawls."

"I don't have any arrests on my record."

Wes shrugged. "I asked around."

And heard a lot of stories about his out-there parents and his own wild early years. "I was a bouncer in my grandparents' bar. I broke up fights. I didn't start them."

"Just like tonight."

Jack was through pretending to be easygoing. And he was through humoring Wes Kimball. He could understand the guy's need to protect his sister, but not at his expense. Saying nothing, he walked to the door. As he turned the knob, Wes called his name.

He glanced over his shoulder.

Wes held up the arrest report. "Tell you what, Jack ole boy, you stay away from my sister, and I'll rip this in half."

Jack wasn't too worried about being prosecuted, but he guessed Wes could hand his report over to the town council, who'd be less than thrilled to have their newest employee in trouble with the law. But after that kiss with Skyler, feeling the heat they generated, seeing the resolve in her eyes made him realize he had no intention of giving up on her. This little pissing contest between him and Wes wouldn't discourage him.

Their relationship couldn't last, he supposed. He'd be off to Atlanta soon, maybe even before she realized he wasn't good enough for her.

But he had no intention of revealing any of that to Wes. He opened the door. "Keep your report. I'd rather have Skyler."

"WHY IS MY LUCK so rotten, Monica?"

Checking the fit of her black satin bustier, panties, garter belt, stockings and four-inch, rhinestone-studded shoes in the wall of mirrors, the statuesque redhead sighed. ''Skyler, honey, having to spend end-less hours planning the Fourth of July celebration with Jack Tesson is good luck, not bad.''

''Humph. The last time I was with him I got punched in the eye, and he got arrested. What does everyone see in him anyway?'' Skyler asked as if she hadn't spent endless hours fantasizing about the lus-cious firefighter herself.

He'd caught her when she'd fainted, stood up to an entire bar of hostile people, he'd stood up to her *brother*. All to his detriment. No doubt Wes hadn't listened to her request that he butt out of her rela-tionship with Jack and had conspired with the mayor to give him the Fourth of July duty as punishment.

The whole mess had Skyler aroused, irritable and guilt-laden. The only positive thing that had happened over the past few days was the swelling around her eye had finally gone down, and she'd reaffirmed her resolve that interest in Jack was completely counter-productive. He was a firefighter. Dangerous and he-roic. And leaving. Even Wes—who could be *ex-tremely* hardheaded—recognized the mismatch. She, Ms. Paranoid Over Her Brothers' Risky Professions, hot for a firefighter? Absurd. Ridiculous. Out of the question.

''He's gorgeous, sexy and charming,'' Monica said. ''And that accent...whew.''

Okay, so maybe the entire female population of Baxter, plus Roland, had excellent taste, but Skyler fully intended to pretend otherwise. ''Don't let Wes hear you say that. He and Jack nearly came to blows the other night.'' Wes and Monica had been dating for weeks—a record for her brother—and Skyler had hopes she'd finally have another woman in their testosterone-in-surplus family.

"They nearly came to blows over *you*. Isn't that terrific?"

Skyler tugged the lace trim into place, then rose. "No."

"I'd love to have two men fighting over me."

"One of them was my brother," Skyler reminded her friend, though she wouldn't want two men fighting over her under any circumstance.

"Yeah, well, your brother certainly isn't that passionate about defending me."

"Of course he is. He's crazy about you."

"I'm not so sure." Monica stepped onto the raised platform positioned in the center of the large dressing room. The track lighting enhanced her curvy figure and pale skin. She cocked her hip and smiled. "But this will help."

Skyler walked around Monica, eyeing the fit of the racy lingerie with a critical eye. In the pink-and-gold decorated back room—her bold nod to whorehouse-chic—they had complete privacy to conduct the risqué business of the shop. Fiona had the day off, and Skyler had installed the new warning bell so she wouldn't have to lock the door in the middle of the day.

"It's not too tight around the bust?" Skyler asked.

"No, it's perfect."

Finally, Skyler smiled. "It certainly is. Wes is going to flip when he sees you in that."

"I hope so," Monica said, but she didn't sound too certain.

"*Chaud, chère,*" a familiar male voice called from behind them.

Gasping, Skyler whirled.

"Hot, hot, hot," Jack Tesson said, strolling boldly into the room.

Skyler blinked, hardly able to believe her eyes. The man had the worst timing of anyone on the planet. And why hadn't her door alarm gone off?

Some inner protective instinct finally asserted itself. *Move!* it yelled. *Cover this up quick, or the town council will know your dirty little secret by noon, and you'll be out on your backside—leather, lace and all.*

She grabbed Monica by the arm. "Let me handle this," she muttered.

"Can I watch?" Monica asked, then laughed.

Skyler didn't see anything to laugh about. She tugged her friend to a dressing stall, shoving the pink velvet curtain closed.

"Out," she said, pointing at Jack as he hovered in the doorway.

He leaned one exceptional shoulder against the frame. "Oh, I like the view from here."

From behind the curtain, Monica giggled.

Skyler seethed.

Jack held up his hand. "I'm leaving." He backed from the room, pulling the door, though before the latch clicked shut, he stuck his head back inside. "I'm just dyin' to find out about *this* special order, *'tite ange.*" The door shut.

"Ooohhh." Skyler stamped her foot. "That man! My life was perfectly normal until he got here."

Monica shoved the curtain aside. "Your life wasn't normal, babe, it was boring. There's a difference."

Staring at the door, Skyler bit her lip. What did he think? What would he *say?* Was there any possibility of bluffing her way out of this disaster?

"Well, go on," Monica said as she pulled her clothes on over the merry widow. "I'll go out the back while you handle him." She grinned. "And I know just which parts of him I'd handle."

"I need a plan, not sex."

Monica just blinked.

"Even if I did want, think about, or ever consider sex with a man like him"—*whose idea of work is battling through fire-engulfed houses, combating floods and contagious diseases and probably leaping over tall buildings in a single bound*—"I'd have to sneak around my brothers to do it."

Monica danced on one foot as she slipped off one four-inch stiletto heel. "So? You sneak around them anyway with the lingerie." Shoving the shoes in her purse, she slid her feet into sandals—with only a three-inch heel. "Besides, I'm hoping to have one brother completely occupied—at least the moment he gets back from the law enforcement convention."

Skyler started for the door. "That just leaves two."

In the hall, leaning against the wall, lounged Jack Tesson, looking as if he planned to hang out all day.

Avoiding him, Skyler let Monica out the back door, then, stalling further in the desperate hope a brilliant explanation would occur to her, she locked the front door and flipped over the Closed sign. By the time she reached the counter, her hands had stopped shaking, and she was pretty sure her voice would sound normal. Bluff, bluff, then lie and bluff some more seemed the most prudent escape. She couldn't lose her shop.

Jack had moved to sit on the counter, his long legs dangling just inches off the floor. "You got some great merchandise, *chère*." He grinned. "Any more of those black things…'' his gaze traveled the length of her ''…in a bit smaller size?''

Heat stole through her body. The shaking started again, this time in her stomach. ''Uh, no. A one-time-only order for a friend.''

''Right. What about the fancy dressin' room?''

''It came with the building.''

''Come on, *chère*. I saw the boxes. Had to be at least four of 'em shoved against the wall.'' He lifted one black eyebrow. ''Bud's Leather Palace? Lickable Lacies?''

Leather and edible underwear. Skyler let her head drop back. She was caught.

4

"YOU GOT A little business goin' on the side, *chère?*" Jack grinned like the scoundrel Skyler had no doubt he was. "Don't bother me. A little shadiness develops character. My *grand-père* sure didn't get through Prohibition by sellin' Coca-Cola."

Skyler planted her hands on her hips. "There is absolutely nothing shady about my business."

He winked. "Right."

She crossed to the front door, eyeing the new "alarm" with disgust. She'd only been half paying attention as she installed the blasted thing the night before, since she'd been focused on listening to the emergency scanner to keep tabs on her brothers' calls. "If you have to know the story behind my shop, the town council wouldn't give me a business license for lingerie, so I decided to expand my inventory. There's nothing wrong with that."

Jack slid off the counter, then he walked toward her. "But I'm thinkin' you didn't tell the council you were…expandin' your inventory."

Determined to avoid the laughing challenge in his whiskey-colored eyes, Skyler ignored his insinuation and experimentally opened the door. *Ding-dong* sang the chimes. She sighed in disgust.

Jack leaned down and laid his finger beneath her

chin, lifting her face. "Does the council know about your little back room?"

She bit her lip. "No."

"Who does know?"

"Other than me and my customers, you mean?"

"Other than them."

He really did have the most lovely, expressive eyes. Being a big, macho fireman, he probably wouldn't appreciate that comment, though, so she kept the thought to herself. If she pouted and batted her eyes, as she'd seen Monica do a million times to get a man's attention, would he forget all this shop business and kiss her?

"Skyler..." he prompted in a low, determined tone.

"Well, uh, let me think." She pretended to ponder the question. Just how would he use the information he now possessed? He was a hero, so he was honorable. Hadn't he protected her at the bar? There was no reason to think he'd betray her now. Finally, she said, "You."

"Me, what?"

"Other than me and my customers, you're the only person who knows about the back room. In fact, you and Roland are the only men who know."

A look of startled wonder crossed his face, quickly there, then gone. "Why Roland?"

She grinned, thinking of the black mask, cape and leather thong underwear she'd ordered recently for Roland. He liked to play Zorro. "He's a customer," she said simply.

"Why no one else?" he asked.

He meant her family. Monica had asked the same thing many times. But then Monica was bold and sometimes even controversial. Skyler liked peace. "They'd try to talk me out of it, or—"

"Accidentally blabber about it to the town council."

She also *really* liked not having to spell out everything to him. Deadbeat Boyfriend #1 had really been slow on the uptake. "Exactly."

"I'll keep your secret," he said, shrugging.

With great effort, Skyler found the presence to close her mouth. A shrug of those massive shoulders, then *I'll keep your secret.* Simple as that. No dire warnings. No predictions of trouble. No questions about her profit or debt or sales projections.

He was definitely a man. But he was an exotic new species in her world.

"...expanded inventory?"

Skyler jerked herself from her musings, realizing Jack had asked her a question. "What?"

"Am I that distracting, *chère?*"

She flipped her hair over her shoulder. "Of course not."

His gaze danced, but he didn't call her on the lie. "What would the council do if they found out about your expanded inventory?"

She tried for nonchalance, but was pretty sure she didn't quite pull it off. "Probably revoke my business license."

"Imagine. *'Tite ange* Skyler, the leader of a town conspiracy."

She fidgeted. "I'm not...exactly."

"Don' be embarrassed, *chère.* You having a wild side intrigues the hell out of me. It makes me more interested." He stroked the back of his hand down her cheek. "More attracted."

Gulp. This not dating dangerous men rule wasn't looking like such a hot idea. But it wasn't just her libido or her heart she was worried about. Jack's career was possibly on the line. Baxter was *the perfect opportunity.* At least until Atlanta came calling.

Rules were made to be broken, chère. She could practically hear the words glide off Jack's tongue. The question was—how badly did she want Jack's tongue gliding over other places? She leaned toward him, drawn to his energy, even drawn to the danger he represented. What her brothers didn't know...

His gaze swept down her body, heating her intimately. "All this sure explains those skimpy purple undies."

Skyler's face flamed. "What undies?"

"Yours."

"When did you—" She stopped, suddenly remembering Fluffy's rescue from the tree while Jack gazed up at her. She gasped. "You, you...I can't believe you looked! You're a city employee, a civil servant, a—"

"I'm a man."

Skyler didn't know whether to be ticked, flattered or embarrassed. She settled for all three. "Jack Tesson, you and I are gonna go a few rounds if you continue—"

He tapped the end of her nose, distracting her. "Call me by my full name."

"Why would I—"

"Just do it. Please."

She heaved a sigh. "What is it?"

"Jackson Phillipe."

Having no idea why she was humoring the man, but needing to make her point about his bad boy behavior, Skyler went on. "Jackson Phillipe Tesson, you and I are gonna go a few rounds if you continue in this inappropriate habit of doing and saying forward things to proper, Southern-bred ladies."

He slid his hand around the back of her neck, pulled her forward, then kissed her hard on the lips.

Mouth tingling, she stared at him. "What did you do that for?"

He grinned. "You reminded me so much of my *grand-mère,* I had to kiss you."

She knew she'd sounded a bit maternal, but... "Your *grandmother?*"

"She always tried to make speeches about proper behavior, too."

"Tried?"

"Without much success—obviously." His eyes danced. "Now for the reason I came by."

Distracted, she'd completely forgotten to question what he was doing in her shop in the middle of the day. She absolutely could not think straight in the man's presence.

"The other night at the bar was completely my fault." He stroked the delicate skin beneath her eye, regret obvious in his tone. "I can't believe you were hurt because of something I did."

She shook her head. Her impulsiveness and desperation to keep her secret had led to the trouble.

"Oui. I should have protected you."

Again, it occurred to her that this whole hero thing might not be so bad.

"So, I want to make it up to you. How 'bout dinner Friday night?"

A refusal was on the tip of her tongue, but something held her back. She'd always been happy to let her brothers protect her from dangerous men like Jack, but now she suddenly didn't want to play it safe. No doubt this urge was the result of her daring and impulsive Kimball genes.

She also recalled her recent conversation with Casey—aka Frat Boy—who'd told her he broke the record in ducking her brothers because Jack had let him hide out at his apartment. Her heart fluttered at the thought.

One date. What could it hurt?

She looked up, meeting his gaze. "Sure."

A broad smile broke across his face, but then he eyed her oddly. "What's the catch?"

The man was definitely quick. She wanted to go out with him, but she wasn't willing to sacrifice his job in the process. "We can't tell anyone."

He crossed his arms over his chest, managing to go from charming to intimidating in that one move. "Come again?"

"I won't have you losing your job over a simple dinner."

"Ben is a reasonable man. He wouldn't fire me."

Ben *could* be reasonable. Wes, she wasn't taking any bets on, and he could certainly make life hard for Jack. Besides, by keeping this date under wraps she could be daring without being reckless.

"I'm not hiding from your family," Jack said.

"Then I won't go."

Looking exasperated, he sighed. "You're a helluva negotiator, *chère*."

"You should see me negotiate prices with Bud."

"Bud?"

"Proprietor of Bud's Leather Palace."

Laughing, he pulled her into his arms. A pretty

great place to spend a Tuesday afternoon, in Skyler's book. "You're somethin'," he said quietly. "And you've got a deal."

Her heart thumped hard in her chest.

He looked down at her, brushing her hair back from her face. "But I won't lie. I'll agree not to advertise our date in the newspaper, but if one of your brothers asks me directly, I won't deny it."

Skyler bit her lip. She didn't like this contention, but since she only intended for them to have one date—she was attracted to Jack, but she couldn't really get *involved* with him. The loss of her father had ruled so many of her actions for so long, she doubted she'd ever change. Adding Jack to her collection of people to obsessively worry over was a really bad idea.

Jack and his dangerous job wouldn't be hanging around Baxter long anyway. Losing him was inevitable.

But since they were only talking about one date, she figured she could keep her heart safe.

She wrapped her arms around his neck. "Okay. Covert, but no lying. Anything else?"

He pulled her tighter against him, so she could feel his hardness growing against her stomach. "How about wearing a selection from Bud's Leather Palace?"

Skyler thought of the black leather jeans with silver rivets down the seams she'd ordered for Fiona. She couldn't imagine ever having the guts to wear something like that beyond her dressing room, much less in front of Jack.

"I'm kidding," he said, as if he sensed her unease.

"But wear a dress." He kissed the side of her neck, just below her ear. "And the purple undies."

She shivered. God, the man knew how to proposition. He was assuming a great deal about the outcome of their dinner, she supposed, but his tendency to push the limits was part of his charm.

"How about a skirt?" she suggested, not about to give him total control over this date, though he seemed to have commandeered—temporarily, of course—her hormones.

"And the undies?"

Smiling, she waggled her finger at him. "My undies, young man, are none of—"

The alarm above the door jangled.

Skyler jumped away from Jack as if she'd just grabbed a hot frying pan.

Mrs. Markenson—a regular customer and cousin to the mayor—sailed through the doorway, her sixteen-year-old daughter trailing in her wake.

Jack, damn him, discretely stroked her side and whispered, "Relax, *chère*. Your secret's safe with me."

Nothing, absolutely nothing about Jackson Phillipe Tesson was safe.

"Good afternoon, Skyler," Mrs. Markenson said, nodding her perfectly styled and highlighted head of light brown hair. "I need to find something appropriate for the church picnic for Christine." She pushed her giggling, blushing daughter, whose wide blue gaze was riveted to Jack, forward.

"Absolutely." Skyler approached her customers. "I have some trendy new styles for teens."

Mrs. Markenson wrinkled her nose. "Nothing *too* stylish, I hope."

Skyler resisted the urge to groan. More girls in living room drapery fabric—just what the world needed. "Of course not." As they moved toward the back of the store, she took the opportunity to introduce her customers to Jack. The momentary distraction gave her time to wonder what semitrendy top or skirt she had in her back room that would flatter Christine without offending her mother.

"We're so happy to have you in Baxter," Mrs. Markenson was saying. "I'm on the council, you know."

Yes, we know, Skyler echoed. *We also know if you found out about the latest shipment of edible underwear, I'd be out on my purple-undie-clad ass.*

Jack, of course, was smooth as glass. "I'm honored you show such confidence in me, madame."

Mrs. Markenson actually blushed at the French form of address.

"We're planning an exciting Fourth of July celebration," Jack continued.

Skyler frowned. She'd forgotten about his appointment to the same committee as her. How was *that* going to work after she told him they could have one and only one date? As Christine giggled beside her, she waved aside this concern for the moment. Happy customers first. Concern for love life second.

After securing Christine and her mother in a large dressing room with several modest, solid-color dresses and a few skirts and tops, she jerked her head toward the door. "You're distracting my customers," she said to Jack. "Out you go."

"Me?" he had the nerve to ask, eyes all innocent.

She shoved his shoulder. "Yes, you. And don't give me that wicked-but-innocent grin of yours. I have a business to run.'' She held open the door. ''Out.''

He grabbed her hand and pulled her through the opening. ''What grin?'' he asked before producing the distracting expression.

Good grief but he was sexy. She half considered hopping on that sleek, black motorcycle parked at the curb, driving away with him, where no inhibitions existed, and she could ease the hunger clawing at her body.

Wait a freaking minute. *Sleek, black motorcycle?*

She groaned. ''Don't tell me—the motorcycle is yours, isn't it?''

He threw one long leg over the seat. ''Course, *chère*. Wanna ride?''

''No, no—'' it does look kind of cool, her libido prodded ''—absolutely not,'' she said firmly, striding toward him. He looked so perfect, so right, so dangerous sitting astride the bike, she had to suppress a moan of longing. And *of course* he wanted her to wear a dress. Wouldn't that be just like a man to satisfy his prurient fantasies by having her straddle him—she had to fight back another moan—with her dress hiked up to her thighs?

''We can't go out to dinner on *that*,'' she said, her voice high and tight. She hoped she hadn't offended him, but the clash between sensible and risky was overwhelming her senses to the point of irrationality.

''I've got a car, *ange*. We'll save the motor for our second date.'' He kicked the engine over, and the street beneath Skyler's feet vibrated. ''See you Friday,'' he mouthed just before he dropped a black helmet over his head and roared away.

Skyler stomped her foot in frustration. There

wasn't going to be a second date, much less one on that rolling organ donor. As she turned to enter her shop, it occurred to her that she was trying to get a dangerous man to play it safe.

She rolled her eyes. "Oh, yeah, Sky. That'll work."

5

FRIDAY NIGHT, Jack slid into the seat next to Skyler just as the mayor called the Independence Day Committee meeting to order. "What's the emergency?"

"I have no idea," she whispered back. She shrugged her shoulder—bare except for her dress's bright pink spaghetti strap. The rest of the thigh-skimming dress clung to her curves and matched perfectly with her heeled sandals and toenail polish.

Delicious. He considered dropping a kiss on her icy pastel pink lips, but knew public affection was definitely a move in the wrong direction. He focused on positive thoughts. Their date might be a secret, but she'd prepared carefully for the event. Definite good sign. In the past few days, he'd managed to dispel the niggling spark of worry that she didn't want to be seen with him. She was worried about his job. She cared. Her motives were sweet. She wasn't using her brothers as an excuse. She didn't have to remind him of the "good girls" in high school, who flirted with him on Saturday nights, then ignored him during school, where he'd certainly not been a part of their clique.

"Okay, people," the mayor said, rising from behind his desk. "I know it's Friday night, and I know y'all have plans, but we've got ourselves a crisis."

Eyes wide, Jack had a hard time concentrating on

the man's serious tone. Mayor Franklin Collins was
dressed as Elvis—the Vegas years—in a white-
sequined jumpsuit, gold necklaces and huge rings on
his fingers. The First Lady didn't disappoint in com-
plementing her husband. She had the voluptuous figure, exaggerated makeup and headdress of a Vegas
showgirl.

Jack leaned close to Skyler's ear, inhaling the
sweet, flowery scent clinging to her skin before he
asked, "What's with the costumes?"

Before she could answer, a male voice called out,
"Hold on, honey." Roland swished into the room. At
least Jack thought it was Roland. He wore glamour-
girl makeup, a blond wig and a gold-sequined evening
gown, so only the voice was recognizable. The pet
store owner waggled his fingers in Skyler's direction
as he crossed the room.

Jack glanced from the mayor, to his wife, then back
to Roland. He asked Skyler, "Did I miss a dress code
meeting?"

"No." She met his gaze, her blue eyes twinkling.
"The mayor's an Elvis fanatic, and Roland performs
at a local bar on the weekends. His act is a riot, sort
of Ru Paul meets Tony Bennett."

"*These* are the people who voted against a lingerie
shop?"

"No," she whispered back. "The mayor only votes
if there's a tie, which there definitely wasn't. Roland
was my only supporter. The rest of the committee—
led by two Baptist deacons—trounced the idea."

The mayor waited while Roland arranged himself
in his chair, crossing his unshaven legs. "Could we
get back to the problem at hand?"

Everyone fixed their gaze on Mayor Collins. How

they could do so without busting out laughing, much
less not cracking a smile, Jack had no idea. He bit
the inside of his cheek.

"A local band wants to play at the festival," the
mayor announced.

And? Jack waited for the other shoe to drop.

"They're calling themselves The Metal Heads this
year," the mayor said wearily, shaking his head.
"Last year they were The Punk Heads, the year before that The Dixie Heads, before that The Rock
Heads."

A collective groan rippled through the room.

"Not them again," one of the other committee
members said.

"I got rid of them last year," Roland called out.
"It's somebody else's turn."

Before Jack could ask what was so awful about The
Metal Heads and why this was an important enough
crisis to delay his and Skyler's date, the mayor turned
to him to explain. "They've been trying to get into
the festival for the past three years, each year with a
different act and collection of horrible songs."

Roland tapped his red-tipped fingernails against the
arm of his chair. "The year they went country they
planned their opening song to be 'I Shot My Dog
Then Got Runned Over by a Train.'"

Ouch.

The mayor sank onto the edge of his desk. "This
year they can't wait to play 'I Bashed My Mama with
My Guitar Last Night.'"

Double ouch.

Still, this problem seemed easy to fix. Everyone
agreed The Metal Heads were a bad idea entertain-
ment-wise. They could just send them a letter—

thanks for your interest, but after a decisive vote by our committee…blah, blah, blah. Problem solved.

Jack dusted his hands together and rose. "No problem. I'll send them a rejection letter and—"

"Won't work," the mayor said. "Last year, after they got their letter, they camped out on the steps of City Hall for three days and nights until I listened to an entire set of their songs." He shuddered.

"They're really very sweet," Skyler said, looking troubled.

"And desperate," Roland put in.

"You know…" the mayor began, staring up at Jack. The beginnings of a smile crept to his lips.

Uh-oh. Jack had the feeling he was about to pay for his impulsive volunteering.

"You could turn them down, Jack. But in person."

Everyone in the room focused on Jack. Their gazes followed his height and breadth carefully. Obviously, they all thought brawn would come more in handy than brains. The story of his life.

Mrs. Collins clapped her hands, gazing up at her husband adoringly. "Oh, Franklin, you're brilliant!"

Everyone rose, obviously considering the matter settled, chattering about their plans for the night. Within minutes, only he and Skyler stood in the mayor's office.

"I'll help you," she said, laying her hand on his arm. "They sometimes play on the street corners for tips…at least until Wes threatens to arrest them."

Jack glanced down. Her fingertips felt cool and delicate against his skin. Flowery perfume drifted to his nose. He inhaled deeply, and smiled at the heat invading his blood. "Forget The Metal Heads for now." He grabbed her hand, urging her to spin. "Turn for me, *'tite ange.*"

He could see her outfit was actually a top and a miniskirt. Of course, she hadn't worn exactly what he'd suggested. His *ange* was such a rebel. And she had great legs.

"You're beautiful," he said, pulling her close.

She glanced toward the door. "Thanks."

"We're alone."

She smiled, but nervously. "I know."

Setting his jaw, he fought the urge to comment on their "secret" relationship. It was no big deal. He didn't need to claim her. He didn't *need* her at all.

He wanted to stay focused on his career. But Skyler was fun and smart, and the contrast between her "good girl" and "bad girl" sides intrigued him. And the way she was biting her lip and glancing around as if they might be caught touching at any moment just shouted for him to give in to his own bad side.

He cupped the back of her head, leaning close. "We're very alone." Her eyes widened, and before she could give him a reason not to, he kissed her.

Her mouth softened, and a sigh escaped her lips. He slid his tongue against hers, slow and easy, wanting, maybe even needing, to lose himself in her sweetness. Her womanly curves pressed against his body as she gripped the front of his shirt, her fingers clenching and releasing, like an itch she was desperate to scratch. She was going to drive him totally crazy. He wanted her, needed her, absolutely *had* to have her.

Who was he kidding about his career being his top priority? Every time he touched her, he couldn't even remember what he did.

He wrapped his arm around her waist, dragging her closer. Her head dropped back, and he left her lips to trail hot, openmouthed kisses against her jawline. Against his chest, her heart pounded like a freight train. Every inch of his body had hardened, and he was considering the sturdiness of the mayor's desk when she gasped his name.

"J-Jack," she said, her tone breathy and uneven.

He nibbled her lips. "Mmm."

"We shouldn't be—"

He slid his tongue against hers, and she moaned, pulling back.

"—doing this here," she finished breathlessly.

Jack made an effort to tamp down the devil—the one Sister Katherine had fought unsuccessfully to rid him of in his formative years—sitting on his shoulder, urging him on. "Wild Jack" wasn't the kind of man for an angel.

Still holding her against him, he tucked her head beneath his chin and savored the sensation of having her close. He drew deep breaths and fought for control of his body. Why did she have to feel so special, so *right* next to him?

He'd kissed her to prove to her she wanted him in spite of the danger, that he could override her cautious nature, only to confirm for himself that no matter how much he wanted her, he sure as hell didn't deserve her.

He released her, taking a physical and mental step away from temptation. "I'm sorry."

She angled her head. "For?"

In some ways she seemed so innocent—big blue eyes, petite frame, pale hair and skin—but as he watched those eyes narrow he remembered her looks were deceiving. A determined businesswoman resided beneath that angelic package. In addition to scandalous purple panties. Hell. His gaze automatically dropped as he wondered what delights that pink skirt hid. Had she asked him a question?

He tunneled his hand through his hair. "Uh, I just didn't mean for things to get so, um, out of control." *Oh, that was real smooth, Jack.*

"It's not your fault. I wasn't exactly fighting you off." She grinned. "That whole might-get-caught part was kind of fun actually."

He grabbed her hand, tugging her through the doorway and down the hall. "Glad you approve. I've got lots of fun ideas." He led her to the parking lot, and, as he tucked her into the passenger's side of his Jeep, the slit in the back of her skirt bared her thighs to a sweat-inducing height.

Oh, yeah. He had *lots* of ideas.

6

HE TOOK HER to dinner at a rowdy Irish pub. She liked the fact that Jack hadn't felt the need to take her to some hoity-toity place with sleep-inducing harp music in the background, while impressing her with his platinum Visa card. He was attentive and fun, and she'd loved every blasted minute of it. *Dammit.* Weren't great first dates supposed to be followed by even better second ones?

She was pondering this glitch in her "one date only" plans as they stumbled upon The Metal Heads at the corner of Fifth Street and Presley Boulevard. Fitting, Skyler thought.

Over screaming guitars and the singer's screeching voice, she understood little of the song they were performing, but she did catch two lines of the chorus— "My girlfriend dumped me, so I jumped her friend. Now I'm in the hospital nursin' my rear end."

Charming.

If possible they'd gotten worse over the last year. Skyler had been secretly hoping they'd improved, any, so they could find a way to include them in the festival. Maybe they could do an "unplugged" session.

She waved her hands above her head. "Excuse me, guys!" she yelled. "We'd like to talk to you."

Oblivious, they sang on. People passing by shouted at them. "Shut up! Go away! I'm callin' the cops!"

Skyler stood directly in front of the guitar player and cupped her hands around her mouth. "Hellooo!"

He played on, his head banging to the beat of the music.

A loud whistle echoed behind her. She turned to see Jack dropping a twenty-dollar bill in the tip bucket.

You could hear a pin drop in the silence that followed.

Passersby applauded—not for the song certainly, but for its absence.

The four musicians surged forward, surrounding her and Jack. "Hey, man, thanks," the skinny singer with long blond hair said. "It's been cold out here tonight. Like frigid."

"Yeah, man," the sweaty, shirtless drummer put in. "People just don't get it, ya know."

The bassist, who wore sunglasses even though it was past ten o'clock, and the lead guitar player, who wore red leather pants so tight you could tell his religion, just grunted in agreement with their band mates. They looked so much like Def Leppard, Skyler was tempted to ask for ID. They'd obviously researched their genre well. If they lip-synched, they might have a prayer.

"Happy to support our local artists," Jack said—and with a straight face. "I'm Jack Tesson and this is Skyler Kimball, we're—"

"Oh, man," the bassist interrupted.

Four avid gazes roved Skyler from head to toe. "Wanna be our first groupie?" the lead singer asked.

If it was possible to be flattered and disturbed at the same time, Skyler was. "Uh, no. Thanks."

Jack dropped his arm across her shoulders. "She's with me."

Four nervous gazes slid up, way up, Jack's body. "Uh, right, man," the lead singer mumbled.

"We're part of the Fourth of July festival committee," Jack went on. "We'd like to talk to you about performing."

Four pairs of eyes widened in hope. The naked need displayed on their faces was painful to witness. If desire was a talent, these guys were loaded with it.

They couldn't reject them, she realized suddenly. Maybe with a little guidance. And voice lessons. And song writing lessons. And music lessons.

Worried, she glanced at Jack. He met her gaze and smiled. "Don't worry, *chère.*"

He turned back to the band. "I have some suggestions for your act. Let me buy you a beer, and we'll talk."

That cheered the guys considerably. They broke down their equipment, storing it in a purple-and-yellow airbrushed van parked at the curb. Then they walked down the street and into a sports bar.

Once they were settled at a table and the guys had taken their first sip of beer, Jack began. "How important is performing in the festival to you?" He met each man's gaze, but they all just looked at each other and shrugged, obviously uncomfortable.

Finally, the lead singer—who'd introduced himself as Masher—took a fortifying gulp of beer then said, "It would be the total ultimate, man."

A positive sign, Skyler decided, though she had absolutely no idea how Jack was going to pull this off.

"Well then, *mon ami,* you have some work to do."

The bassist—his name was the baffling Golden Boy, though everything about him was dark. Hair, skin, eyes, clothes. Maybe it was an ironic rock 'n' roll thing. Golden Boy snorted as if he was thinking, *I knew there was a catch.*

"Your songs need work." Jack glanced at Skyler, and she nodded in encouragement, though he just seemed to be trying to include her in the conversation. As usual, Jack had everything under control.

"How long did you spend writing the one you were singing earlier?"

Masher angled his head, then looked to Golden Boy for advice. "That one's mine," GB said. "Maybe six months."

Skyler bit back a groan. *Six months* on "My girlfriend dumped me, so I jumped her friend. Now I'm in the hospital nursin' my rear end"?

But Jack nodded as if he'd expected this answer. "It ain't gonna fly, boys."

Golden Boy pouted.

"But I have an idea," Jack continued with such confidence Skyler found herself smiling. His voice was calm and controlled. His brown eyes reflected determination. The man could sell snowballs in Phoenix. *My hero.* She was tempted to sigh and bat her lashes.

Wait just a dang blasted second. My *hero?* She did not want, at all, under any circumstances whatsoever, a *hero.*

Especially one who was leaving. One she could never keep.

"You should be a cover band," he said before she could panic about the direction of her thoughts.

Masher and Golden Boy exchanged confused looks, but the drummer understood. "You want us to sing other people's songs?"

Jack nodded. "Audiences are more accepting of songs they already know. You could get some experience while you work out your own sound." He slid his hand along Skyler's thigh, causing her pulse to hum with pleasure. "Skyler actually gave me the idea."

Startled, she glanced up at him.

"She said you've changed your style several times over the last few years. If you looked like the others as much as you look like a metal band today, you obviously understand about image and performing. All that's left is—"

Musical ability? Skyler thought, suppressing a giggle, while the guys stared in rapture at Jack.

"—practice," he finished. "How often do you rehearse?"

"Once a week or so," Masher said.

Jack shook his head. "Try once a *day*. How many paying gigs have you played this month?"

Masher looked away. "Uh, well…we got that twenty bucks from you."

Golden Boy snapped his fingers. "And we played Masher's granny's birthday party a couple weeks ago. She gave us five bucks each."

"If you work at this, you could be earning a *hundred* bucks each, maybe more."

The guys remained silent a moment, absorbing the possibility of a raise. Finally, Masher said, "If we do this—playin' other people's songs—you'll let us in the festival?''

"We're only two votes on the committee, but we'll do our best to convince the other members." Jack leaned forward. "It's up to you to do the work. We're just offering you an audition."

"Okay, man," Masher said. "We need to take a vote." The guys stood, then ambled to the other side of the bar.

Skyler propped her chin in her hand. "That was pretty ingenious. Do you really think they can do it?"

"We'll see." Jack leaned back in his chair. "I knew some guys like that back home. They wanted to perform at my grandparents' bar. My *grand-père* gave them the same advice. Now they're the biggest hit in south Louisiana."

The man flirted outrageously and helped a hard-working bar owner in his spare time. He owned a motorcycle, but had compassion for four talent-challenged rock wanna-bes. He fought fires, floods and disease, but held her in his arms when she was scared. How was she supposed to fight against that reckless, but gentle contrast?

He squeezed her thigh. "Sorry, *chère*. This isn't exactly how I planned to spend the rest of our date."

The warmth of his hand burned her skin, even through her clothes. "What did you plan?"

Stroking his finger along her leg, he grinned. "How 'bout makin' out in my Jeep?"

She smiled back. He was joking, right? She hadn't made out in a car since she was a teenager, and even then not for very long. One of her brothers always found out.

Brothers?

She glanced around quickly. They were in a public place, touching, talking. Half-empty beer mugs rested on the table. To anyone who didn't know they were on a mission for the committee, this looked suspiciously like a date. The bar wasn't very crowded, and no one seemed to be paying any special attention to them, but Wesley always popped up in unexpected places. She'd told her brother to let her handle Jack, but she doubted he'd listened. And she really couldn't blame him. She'd always welcomed his protection before. Before Jack.

Jack's hand tightened on her leg. When she looked up at him, she noted a glint of anger in his eyes. "Worried about bein' seen with me?"

"Yes," she whispered, brushing his hand off her leg. "This is committee business, remember?"

A muscle along his jaw pulsed. He said nothing.

What is his problem? Skyler thought with a touch of irritation. She was trying to protect *him*. His precious fire fighting career would be over before it began if he wasn't careful.

He looked away. "Right. Committee business." He sounded hurt.

Well, hell. "You know what I mean. The committee can be our cover."

"You got a lotta covers, *chère*. Dates. Lingerie. You ever worry you can't keep 'em all straight?"

She stiffened. "My shop doesn't have anything to do with—"

"You got a deal, man," Masher said, suddenly appearing next to the table, the rest of the band trailing him. "When's the audition?"

Jack stood, shaking Masher's hand, then following through with the others. "How about two weeks from tonight? At the Leather and Lace. You know the place?''

"Sure, man.'' Masher's face broke into a wide smile. "Cool joint.''

"I'll have to check with the owner. I'll call you tomorrow.''

They exchanged phone numbers, and within minutes, the new and improved Metal Heads were strolling out of the bar with considerable bounce to their steps.

Jack glanced at her. "I guess the meeting's over.''

His eyes were distant, even cold. His jawline hard. She'd never seen him like this. He was in a real snit. Well, that was just fine with her. She certainly didn't appreciate him insinuating she liked keeping secrets. If he didn't understand her efforts to protect him, he could just stuff it.

"Let's go.'' She turned, making sure her hair swung out in a wide arc, so he'd have no doubt she was annoyed, then stalked from the bar.

In the Jeep, she felt queasy. The lighthearted, teasing relationship she'd enjoyed with Jack had disappeared, replaced by silence and chilled air. As much as she resented his resentment, she wanted the old Jack back.

This is for the best, her heart whispered. She'd told herself all night this would be their one and only date. If he stayed angry with her, she wouldn't have to explain her one date only theory. Yes, it was better this way. Certainly safer.

By the time he pulled into her driveway, though, she knew she couldn't let anger lie between them. She had to make him understand about her family…and about her.

He got out of the car, then walked around to open her door. When he grabbed her hand to assist her to her feet, she said, "We need to talk."

Crossing his arms over his chest, he leaned back against the hood. "Fine by me."

The distance in his eyes, in his stance was depressing. "I had a great time tonight, but you know as well as I do if my brothers found out we've gone on a date, they'll make your life miserable, possibly get you fired."

He just shook his head. "No, I don't know that."

"Well, I do." How could she make him understand? She paced beside the Jeep, her heels clacking on the driveway. Then she remembered when she'd called Wes the day before, bugging him about arresting a burglary suspect—by confronting him in the man's driveway, alone at night, with no backup. "I give as good as I get, you know," she said, spinning to face Jack. "I don't get in the middle of my brothers' love lives, but I nag them about their jobs, the risks they take. And if the price of being able to do that is a few missed dates then that's okay by me." At least it used to be okay, she started to admit. Before Jack arrived she'd never worried too much about the social life she was missing.

"You're saying I'm too risky."

Hell yes. "No. I'm trying to tell you *I'm* too risky for *you*. Wes has already thrown you in jail." She planted her hands on her hips. "What do you think he'll do if he finds out we went out? It won't be pretty, believe me."

"You know that bossy side of yours turns me on, *chère*." He arched one eyebrow. "Do you *want* that, too?"

Looking at him, leaning against the black, adventurous-looking Jeep, his long legs stretched out in front of him, his shirt pulled tight across his broad chest, those intoxicating eyes focused on her face, she wanted him to put his arms around her more than she wanted to draw her next breath. But drowning herself in their physical attraction wasn't a solution. And she didn't understand why he couldn't be circumspect— for his own good.

This wasn't getting them anywhere. "How long have you been a firefighter?"

"Five years."

"Why did you become one?"

He shuttered his feelings as if she'd flipped off a light switch behind his eyes. Shrugging, he returned with "Seemed like a good idea at the time."

Okay. Wrong topic.

"What does your job mean to you? How would you feel if you couldn't do it?"

"My job is everything," he said softly, dropping his gaze.

She sucked in a breath. She'd suspected as much. *Be careful,* she wanted to plead. *Don't take unnecessary chances. Don't leave a widow, kids without a father. Don't—*

She ground to a halt, rolling her shoulders. "You want to move beyond Baxter. You want to work in Atlanta—the big city, you said. True?"

"Oui."

Swallowing a lump rising in her throat, she fought for the right words to push him away. "You won't be able to make that move without Ben's recommendation." *And I* can't *deal with losing someone else I care about.* Maybe she wouldn't lose him the way she lost her father, but he'd leave Baxter. Lost to her either way.

He was quiet for several long moments, and Skyler waited for reality to settle over him. But, as usual, he surprised her. "I think you're worryin' over nothing. I'm pissed about hiding our date. I thought I could deal with the secret, but I can't." He pushed away from the car, turned away, then back, staring directly into her eyes. "I don't know what's real."

Realizing she was getting what she wanted, yet inexplicably miserable about it, she said, "You don't want to see me unless I tell my family about us."

"I don't want to hide."

"So, this is like, what? An ultimatum?"

He inclined his head. "If you like."

Unconsciously, she'd suspected he wouldn't settle for hiding. And hiding their date was an easy way of hindering the relationship before it even began. Take a risk, while still playing it safe. "I won't risk your career." *Or my heart.*

"Don't you think it's 'bout time your brothers let you lead your own life and make your own decisions?"

She lifted her chin. "I am making my own decision."

He cupped her jaw, stroking his thumb across her cheek. A gesture of regret if she'd ever seen one. "*'Tite ange* Skyler, the great protector." Without another word, he walked around the Jeep, opened the door, then slid inside. As the engine sprung to life, he closed the door.

"See you around, *chère,*" he said through the open window.

"I don't even get a kiss?" she shouted after him.

Of course, being the great protector—especially of herself—she'd waited to yell after his Jeep had already roared down the street.

"COMMITTEE BUSINESS, my ass," Jack muttered to himself as he counted boxes of bandages in the firehouse supply closet.

Why did she want to hide so much? And why did the idea bother him?

He'd hidden relationships before—the prom queen, who hadn't wanted her old man to know about Jack and his motorcycle; a woman in paramedic school, who he'd later learned was married. He'd brushed off these bumps in his love life with a shrug.

But the idea of Skyler being ashamed of him filled him with an anger and pain he didn't want to consider too closely.

"I brought you something."

Skyler?

Jack glanced around quickly, then noting he was still alone in the storeroom, rested his forehead against a shelf. Hell, now he was hearing her voice.

"Steve, get your hand out of that basket this instant!"

That he'd hadn't imagined. He stuck his head out the storeroom door, and saw Skyler strolling through the den, a large wicker basket looped over her arm.

A line of firefighters trailed in her wake. Drooling.

Even as a grin started to tug his lips, he smelled the chicken. Fried chicken. Biscuits, too.

That explained the line. The drooling could either be the food or the candy-apple red tank top and denim shorts barely covering Skyler's curves.

He walked down the hall and fell in behind his

colleagues. They formed a line along the bar separating the den from the kitchen. Skyler batted her brother's hands off the food as she unpacked the basket.

"Hey, Jack, I think we'll move gumbo night," Steve said. "Cool?"

Skyler's head jerked up at his name. She met his eyes, then her gaze danced away just as quickly.

He'd switched his work day with another guy, so she couldn't have known he'd be at the firehouse. He tried, and failed, to tamp down his disappointment at her reaction.

She was running like a scared deer from their attraction. And damned if he knew whether it was to protect him, or herself.

Part of him knew she'd been right the other night. His career was vital to him—a career that would take him away from Baxter. Getting involved in a serious relationship was not a good idea at this point in his life. And he couldn't imagine dating Skyler casually.

But that didn't make him want her any less.

He kept his distance as the food was served, then sat at the opposite end of the table during dinner. Resentfully, he watched her smile and chat with the other guys.

He finally managed to casually brush against her as he carried his dishes to the sink. "Dinner was great, *chère*. Thanks."

She glanced up at him, staring over his shoulder. "You're welcome."

He half smiled, his gaze skimming down her body. "I'd prefer to be *welcomed*."

Her gaze darted to Steve. "Be quiet."

He clamped his teeth together for a moment in an

effort to keep the resentment from his voice. He leaned toward her. "You're much more fun when you're playing rebel. How rebellious are you *underneath?*"

Though her face flushed, her gaze met his, the heat in her eyes unmistakable. Why was she resisting? *How* was she resisting? He was on the verge of grabbing her, of telling her he'd hide in a cave indefinitely, when Steve bumped her aside.

"Sit, Sky," her brother said. "We'll clean up."

"Uh, sure." Skyler backed away, stumbling over a firefighter, then knocking over a chair. "I need to get home anyway. Bye." She grabbed her basket, then fled the room.

Jack watched her go. Wanting her. Wanting her way too much.

AT THE Leather and Lace a few days later, Jack nursed a beer and his temper, reflecting on another awkward encounter with Skyler. He'd sat next to her during another "emergency" committee meeting called by the mayor—where they'd discussed the proper shade of red for the banners for *two hours*— yet, a stone statue could have been beside him for all the warmth she showed.

He had to face facts. His own parents never wanted him. Why did he expect Skyler to? She could have anybody. They didn't belong together. Simple as that.

He slid off his barstool and worked his way through the pack on the dance floor, stopping at the jukebox. After selecting the song he wanted, he returned to his seat, rolling the sweating beer bottle between his palms. He smiled as the chorus of the country ballad rolled through the bar.

The singer knew he couldn't be an angel, hadn't ever claimed to be a saint, and philosophically decided it wasn't so bad learning how to fall.

Completely apropos.

He turned his head as someone's hand slid along his shoulder. He found himself staring at a very attractive brunette. Her dark blue eyes slanted exotically against her olive-toned skin. "Is this seat taken?" she asked in a suggestive, silky voice.

"No." He pulled back the stool for her.

As she slid onto the seat, a whiff of her musky perfume drifted his way. She had slender, mile-long legs, exposed to perfection by a tight cotton skirt.

This is just what you need, the devil chanted in his ear.

Smiling at him, she tossed a curly strand of hair over her shoulder, then ordered a whiskey sour from Gus, who'd immediately appeared in front of his slinky customer.

That woman isn't an angel, the devil nagged. *She's perfect.*

He'd thought of nothing and no one but Skyler all week. Replaying every touch and word they'd exchanged on their date. The feel of her delicate hand on his thigh, the way she'd trembled in his arms in the mayor's office, the feminine, flowery smell of her, the delicious taste of her. He wanted her with a desperation that scared him. He needed a distraction.

"My name's Devlin," the brunette said, angling her body toward him.

The devil on his shoulder clicked its heels. *If that's not a sign, you're blind, Jack ole boy.*

"I'm Jack," he found himself saying. "You come here often?" Oh, *that's* original.

She shook her head, her dark, curly hair falling artfully around her face. "I usually hang out at The Corner Pub." She leaned toward him, her gaze dropping to his chest briefly before returning to his face. "I have a thing for firemen."

He smiled—about to admit he was a fireman until he realized he was wearing a red T-shirt with Baxter Fire Department emblazoned in yellow across the back.

Hot damn, the devil whispered.

Jack ignored him. He was put off by her forwardness. He couldn't even work up mild interest in talking to her, much less touching her. She wasn't blond enough, petite enough. She wasn't Skyler.

He sighed, then said, "It's a great job. Be sure to support us at the next tax increase." He slid off his stool. "I gotta get going, Gus." He tossed a few bills on the bar. "We're still on for next Friday, right?"

"Sure thing, buddy," he returned, scooping his bottle off the bar. "Lookin' forward to it."

Jack strode out, hiked his leg over his Harley, then headed into town, knowing he was fooling himself about putting Skyler out of his mind.

SKYLER SIPPED chardonnay and prayed for escape. How many times had Monica dragged her on her dates? She couldn't imagine Monica really wanted her around, since her friend planned to try out her merry widow on Wes later, but she felt sorry for her, alone on a Friday night. A usual occurrence.

And one she was getting damn tired of.

Why did Jack have to be so exciting, so tempting? Why did he have to care about a struggling band and a scared frat boy? Why did he make her wonder about the social life she was too busy and too careful to indulge in? Why did she suddenly think her warnings about him losing his job were just a cop-out to protect herself, not him? How did he make her forget he'd be leaving, that she couldn't take him or their relationship too seriously?

"Having fun, Skyler?" Monica asked, bumping shoulders. Her green eyes twinkled with mischief.

"Oh, yeah. Absolutely." *I'm the best third wheel in town.*

Scrambling for an excuse to escape, she glanced up when the door opened. And who strolled inside? Jackson Phillipe Tesson, hunk hero of the century. She would have groaned if her whole body hadn't tightened, then fluttered in raw, sexual need.

Holy hell, he's beautiful, she thought, her gaze glued to him as he strolled in black boots toward the bar, greeting firehouse buddies and accepting an open stool in the center of the crowd.

He wore a red T-shirt stretched tight across his chest and faded, low-slung jeans, probably complete with button fly. If only she could get close enough for confirmation of *that* detail. Dizzy, she nearly fell out of the booth, trying to get a better angle to ogle his backside.

"Skyler?" Monica said, grabbing her arm.

"I, uh—" Righting herself, she sipped her wine. "Just tired, I guess."

Stuck as she was in the back of the room, Jack hadn't noticed her, and part of her was glad. She didn't know how to react to him, and continuing to try to purposely avoid him seemed gutless. But with recklessness all but vibrating in her blood, going near him was no doubt a bad idea.

Monica's shrewd gaze drifted from Skyler's face to the crowded bar. "Aha," she said, and Skyler assumed she'd spotted Jack.

Unfortunately, Wes caught on. He glanced over his shoulder, then turned back just as quickly. "Well, well, if it isn't 'Wild Jack' Tesson."

After a long week alternating between congratulating and berating herself on her standoff with Jack, Skyler's temper was stretched thin. "What the hell is *that* supposed to mean?"

"Our newest firefighter has a somewhat unsavory reputation, Sky." He raised his eyebrows. "Surely you knew."

"What a load of crap."

"He was a bouncer at some backroads bar."

"So?"

"He got thrown out of school half a dozen times."

Skyler's temper reached the steam level. How *dare* he put Jack down? "Gee, Wes, how many mistakes did *you* make before you were twenty?"

Eyes narrowed, Wes leaned forward. "He's not good enough for you."

Skyler gasped. "That's a horrible thing to say."

Wes's face flushed, probably with a combination of anger and embarrassment. "I don't think he's *right* for you."

"Big news flash, Wes. That's not *your* decision to make."

"Big news flash, Sky. He's a firefighter." Since Skyler couldn't argue with that bit of truth, she said nothing. "How many times have you told me you want a nice, safe accountant?" he continued. "And how many times lately have you told me you don't have time for a relationship? I'm doing you a favor here.''

Skyler shoved her glass aside and scooted out of the booth. ''Maybe I've changed my mind.''

Wes grabbed her wrist, then grinned. ''Don't storm off and do anything rash, sister dear.''

Skyler lifted her chin. ''As if I would.'' Of course you would, her conscience reminded her. Every, single bad decision she'd ever made resulted from some wild impulse. Except the lingerie shop…

With that confidence urging her, she pulled away from her brother. ''Butt out of my love life, Wesley.''

''Love to.''

As Skyler started toward Jack who was still sitting on the barstool in a circle of other firefighters, his lips parted in a smile. The muscles along his forearm bunched as he wrapped his fingers around his beer bottle, bringing it to his mouth.

She wanted to be that bottle.

When she approached the circle of men surrounding Jack, they stood almost in unison, and while Jack's expression remained neutral, the other firefighters smiled—at first. Then they glanced behind her and around the bar, looking for any lurking Kimball boys, no doubt. Obviously spotting Wes, they each took a giant step backward, while shoving their stools forward, leaving her, Jack and six empty stools in the center of a wide circle.

For the first time, she found herself embarrassed by her brothers. She'd *encouraged* this reaction in people.

Jack, naturally, found the whole scene amusing. ''Join us, *chère*. We got plenty of open seats.''

She smirked at him, wondering if her rebel genes

would be the end or the salvation of her, then sat. The others followed suit, then immediately began conversations and ignored her. Jack, of course, was bold enough to scoot his chair close by her side, hooking the heels of his boots around the stool's legs and letting his knees fall open, so she was practically sitting between the vee of his thighs.

She couldn't resist glancing down. Yep. Button fly. As his spicy cologne and heat enveloped her, she imagined ripping them open—with her teeth.

"To what do I owe this honor?" he asked, close to her ear.

She didn't dare look up at him—she was already light-headed. Instead, she tossed her hair over her shoulder. "Just saying hi to a friend. Is that okay with you?"

"Sure."

She braced her hand against his leg, shifting herself in her chair so she could cross her legs without flashing the men sitting across from her. Damn Monica for making her wear a skirt. Nobody ever looked at her legs anyway. When she finally met Jack's gaze, she noted a touch of anger.

"Is this performance for me or him?" he asked.

"Excuse me?"

His gaze deliberately dropped to her hand resting on his thigh. "Come on, *ange.* You're ticked off at your brother. This performance is for him." He inclined his head in Wes's direction. "You're succeeding, you know. If Wes gets any redder, he's gonna turn purple."

"I'm not performing for anyone," she insisted. "And he's not mad, he's laughing at me. Waiting for me to make an idiot out of myself."

"By?"

She squeezed his thigh. "Being impulsive."

Jack wasn't sure if he was angry or flattered. Her rebel had decided to come out and play. But for how long? How genuine was this public attention? And did he really want to know the answer?

Okay, chère, *I'll play along. Just how far will you go to yank dear brother Wesley's chain?* "What were you two arguing about?"

"How did you—" She smiled. "I didn't think you'd even noticed me."

"I always notice you." Jack laid his hand over hers, sliding her hand up higher on his thigh. The tip of her index finger nearly brushed his erection, growing stiffer by the second. Why did she have to look so damn...hot? In a short jean skirt, she didn't look innocent in the least. And the glitter in her eyes was anything but angelic. What did she have on under there anyway?

"A family disagreement," she said, and he returned his gaze to her lust-inducing face. Her perfect blue eyes were slumberous, even sexier than usual. Did she feel the same heat he did? Did she realize his heart had soared when she'd approached him? Was she as miserable as he was?

Sliding his arm across the back of her chair, he tried to focus on their conversation. Nearly impossible considering the proximity of her hand. Just one inch, *chère.* One inch, and she'd be stroking him.

"Mmm," he said, wondering why the hell they were wasting time talking about her brother.

"No big deal." She clenched her hand against his thigh, and he sucked in a breath, closing his eyes. "I'm sorry about last week, Jack."

He dropped his head back, fought for control. Where the hell was his beer? He needed something to put this fire out.

As if by magic, the bartender appeared, offering another round. Jack could have kissed the man. After guzzling half the bottle, which only made his insides burn more intensely, he noticed Skyler had moved her hand back to her own lap. She stared at him oddly.

"Are you okay?" she asked, leaning close.

What an idiot he must look like. She was putting on an act for her brother, and he couldn't see past his desire long enough to embrace this reality. He forced himself back into the game.

Setting down his bottle, he slid his cheek against hers and whispered in her ear, "I want to know what you have on underneath that skirt."

Flushing, Skyler glanced at the men surrounding them.

The guys, who certainly knew they were there—at least they'd noticed Skyler's legs—couldn't possibly hear their conversation.

He moved her hand back to his thigh. "Tell me, *ange*. The purple ones? Maybe black." He glanced at the turquoise shirt she wore. "Maybe they match your top." She tensed just briefly, enough for him to realize he'd hit the mark. "Mmm. I bet they look delicious against your tan thighs. *Oui?*"

"Jack, please."

"Please…what? Please stroke the inside of my thigh like I am yours?" Anticipating her withdrawal, he covered her hand with his, holding it in place. "It's very bold of you." Even as his stomach tightened at her touch, the resentment he thought he'd banked rose again. "Do I owe this attention to Wes? Maybe I should be thanking him."

She met his gaze directly. "I didn't come over here for Wes."

Though he wanted to believe her, he lifted one eyebrow.

"I wanted to apologize for last Friday night, to prove I'm not intimidated by my family."

He went cold inside. "I won't be a pawn for you and your brothers to move around whenever you want."

"That's not what I meant. Damn." She bit her lip, forcing him to remember how incredible she tasted. "Maybe I've hidden behind my brothers long enough," she said finally.

He wanted to say he didn't know she'd been hiding, but since he'd questioned that very idea earlier, he kept silent. And hoped.

Her eyes darkened as she searched his face. "I'm still worried about you and your future. You're leaving and my life is here. As for your job…" She smiled self-consciously. "That's your responsibility. Just like my personal life is mine—which is what I told Wes. I came over here because I want to be with you."

Relief flooded him. He smiled. "Are you trying to tell me I'm right, *ange?*"

She swatted his shoulder. "Maybe. Not exactly. Okay maybe."

He kissed the side of her neck. "Just couldn't resist me, huh?"

Stroking her fingers up and down his thigh, she stared at him. "No."

He leaned his forehead against hers. "I want you," he said, then he flicked his tongue against her earlobe.

Just as the whine of a siren cut through the noisy bar. A fire truck.

Everyone went dead still. Then a man burst through the front door. "A house on Maple Street's on fire. They need reinforcements."

Jack leapt off his stool. Over his shoulder, he cast her a look of regret, but he was the first one out the door.

7

_____

"I LOOK RIDICULOUS," Skyler said as she glared at herself in the full-length mirror. She wore—believe it or not—black leather pants with silver studs running down the outside seam, black high-heeled sandals—borrowed from Monica—a red halter top with at least an inch of her stomach showing, and rhinestones glued around her belly-button. She looked like a reject from an MTV awards show. Or like she was wearing her naughty lingerie on the *outside* of her clothes.

"You look hot," Fiona returned, sliding on her black trench coat.

Skyler met her assistant's gaze in the mirror. "No. *You* look hot. It's got to be at least ninety outside."

Fiona shrugged, tucking a strand of jet-black hair behind her ear, the bell bracelet on her wrist tinkling. "I can suffer for fashion. Besides, we'll be inside."

"Inside a crowded bar."

She settled her hands on her hips. "So I'll take off the coat if I'm hot. Stop being so cranky and turn for me."

Feeling more ridiculous by the minute, she nevertheless did as Fiona asked. In truth, she was tired of arguing, but the complaints kept her from being so nervous. She supposed the perfect reaction would be if her brothers merely scowled over her outfit and

Jack loved it—at least that was Fiona and Monica's theory.

The three women had bonded last Friday night after the men had deserted them for duty, and Fiona had strolled into the bar during the commotion and literally asked, "Where's the fire?"

This trashy yet trendy ensemble was the result of their spontaneous, soul-baring girls' night. Skyler had finally confessed about the lingerie shop to her assistant. Fiona had actually smiled, then dryly said, "I can't tell you how glad I am that I don't have to put that shred-the-floral-pastels plan into action."

After they'd consumed several bottles of wine between them, Skyler admitted that she had the hots for Jack and that she'd told her brothers that she didn't need or want protection anymore. Monica was too preoccupied—and inebriated—to worry about anything except her belief that Wes was losing interest in her before she'd even managed to seduce him.

Fiona had asserted, and Monica had agreed, that Skyler's brothers wouldn't abandon a lifetime serving as The Boyfriend Protection League with a shrug and a smile. No, Skyler had to *prove* to her hovering family that she was truly ready to pursue a relationship with Jack. And leather was the way to do it.

The gospel according to Fiona.

Waving aside the complications of her family for now, she reasoned she was much more interested in Jack's reaction to her outfit than her brothers'. Between him supervising The Metal Heads' rehearsals and working a double shift Wednesday and Thursday, she'd hardly seen him since the Maple Street fire.

Distance hadn't made her regret her decision, knowing she would ultimately lose him. Distance hadn't given her perspective on her feelings. Distance had only intensified her need. She couldn't work or eat or sleep without thinking about his smile, his strength, the way his mouth felt against hers.

She knew she wouldn't have him long, but she'd come to realize that was better than not having him at all.

"You look perfect," Fiona said. "Let's go." She poked Skyler in the back, urging her toward the door. "Enough stalling."

The butterflies currently residing in the pit of her stomach flapped double-time, but she rolled her shoulders and headed out of the storeroom. After locking the back door, she climbed into Fiona's Cadillac—the thing was long and black and reminded Skyler of a hearse, especially with Fiona Mistress of the Dark behind the wheel. That thought, of course, made her think of Jack and his motorcycle and how the dangerous-looking machine fit him just as perfectly.

What would he say when he saw her? More important, what would he *do?* She'd never deliberately seduced a man before and wasn't sure she could go through with it now.

"Maybe I should take my car, too," she said to Fiona as they pulled out of the parking lot.

"What for?"

"Just in case."

"In case what?"

"In case I chicken out."

"You're *not* going to chicken out," Fiona said as she whipped around a corner.

Skyler braced herself against the door. The girl certainly didn't drive like she was leading a funeral procession.

"Monica and I won't let you," Fiona continued. "Just remember what she said."

"'Smile and lick your lips a lot,'" she echoed dutifully. Man, could *that* woman be bossy sometimes. This taking chances business was more complicated than it looked. "What do I say to him? I'm not good at flirting."

Fiona sighed. "You don't have to *say* anything. He's going to take one look at you in those pants, grab hold of you with both hands and never let go."

Skyler had her doubts, but the butterfly wings flapped madly anyway.

The outfit is just a symbol, she remembered Monica saying sagely last night. *You feel powerful and sexy, don't you?* After a hard nudge by Fiona, Skyler had admitted she did. So instead of overanalyzing her feelings about Jack, she decided to start taking some chances, starting with walking into the Leather and Lace. Actually Monica had said *strut,* but Skyler wasn't sure how she could accomplish that feat in four-inch heels.

When they pulled into the parking lot, the asphalt was already jammed with cars. A teenager was directing customers into spaces in a field adjoining the bar. Jack's doing, no doubt. Having been around firefighters all her life, Skyler wasn't the least surprised by the heavy turnout or the organization. Firemen all knew how to motivate and coordinate in ways beyond the abilities of normal people.

Skyler swallowed the lump in her throat as she and Fiona approached the door. Regardless of her feelings, tonight was the debut of The Metal Heads, and no matter what happened she was going to cheer on the band and have a good time with her friends.

And her best one, thank God, was currently leaning against the wall beside the door, examining her nail polish, oblivious to the stream of panting men walking past her. When she spotted Skyler, though, she strutted—she definitely knew how to do so in four-inch heels—toward her.

"I was beginning to think you'd chickened out," she said, her gaze raking Skyler from head to toe.

Monica knew her well. "Of course not," Skyler said, as if offended.

Fiona rolled her eyes.

"Turn," Monica commanded.

Long past the point of arguing, Skyler turned.

When she faced her friend again, she smiled. "You look hot, girl."

"Told you," Fiona put in.

Skyler grabbed Monica's arm. "Let's go in. You two are making me self-conscious."

"Get used to it," Monica said as they moved toward the door. "Well, not being self-conscious yourself, but men being *un*conscious whenever you walk by." She tossed back her luxurious mane of red hair and laughed.

They entered the bar, and Skyler was thrilled to see a near-crushing crowd had gathered. The lighted stage was bare except for the band's equipment, and someone had hung a large banner announcing The Metal Heads' Premiere. She hoped the guys were ready. They had worked so hard with Jack over the past two weeks.

With a dash of amusement, she noted the presence of the other committee members—including the mayor and his wife. She knew they'd wrangled a promise from the band to play "American Trilogy" as a required audition song.

From behind the bar, Gus grinned like the Cheshire cat. She recognized Flash and her gang, as well as many of the patrons from the night of the brawl and food fight. She hoped they behaved, but worried only a moment, since she spotted Wes lounging against a booth on the far side of the room. Lounging next to a skimpily-dressed brunette.

Monica, unfortunately, noticed as well.

"That son of a—"

"Settle down, girl," Skyler said, grabbing her friend's arm in case she got the big idea to bolt in Wes's direction. "He's just talking to her."

Fiona snorted, then said in her deadpan voice, "If that's just talking, I'm Mother Teresa."

Monica's eyes lit like a strobe. "Wes has really been irritating you lately, right, Sky?"

Skyler winced as the brunette laid her hand on Wes's forearm. "Uh, a bit."

"And you've got two other brothers, right?"

"Yeah."

"Good—'cause I'm gonna kill this one." She yanked her arm from Skyler's hold and took two charging steps forward before Jack, bless him, suddenly appeared in her path.

"This party just got a lot better," he announced in a low, smoky drawl that set every nerve in Skyler's body fluttering. And though his muscular body stood in the way of Monica's deadly mission, his heated gaze was all for Skyler. She might have flushed at the frank appreciation in his eyes, but she was too busy checking out the trim fit of his worn Levi's and tight black T-shirt.

When his glittering gaze finally locked back on hers, he said, "You fit right in, *chère.*"

She shifted her stance, and the cool leather slid against her legs. The sensation caused the desire pooling in her belly to coast lower. She swallowed, wondering if it was really possible to have an org—

Fiona nudged her. "Tell the man thank you," she whispered.

"Thank you," she parroted, but while his appreciation of her outfit was stimulating, she couldn't help feeling a touch disappointed that he hadn't grabbed her and declared he'd never let her go, as Fiona had predicted.

"Can I get you ladies a drink?" he asked, then smiled in a way that left no doubt any woman in the vicinity would let him get anything he wanted.

Monica started around him. "Maybe later. I'll be thirsty after I commit murder."

Jack grabbed her hand, swinging her around. "I bet you're looking for Wes." He pulled a walkie-talkie off the waistband of his jeans. "I'll get him for you." He paused a moment, glancing at Skyler for support.

Hoping this little drama was the only one she'd have to go through during the night—she wanted to spend time with Jack, dammit—Skyler slid her arm around Monica's waist. "How about a martini? They always put you in a giggly mood. You can always kill Wes later."

"I don't know, Sky. The spirit's really moving me now."

Skyler squeezed her waist tighter as Jack spoke into

the walkie-talkie. "Lieutenant," he said, "your date is here."

"Yeah? I'll be there in a minute," Skyler heard Wes say in a bored tone. That boy was a complete idiot. He was going to lose Monica for sure.

Moments later, though, her brother strolled around Jack, then embraced Monica. "Hey, babe."

Her body stiff, Monica glared up at him. "We need to talk."

Wes shrugged. "Sure," he said, leading her away from the group.

Maybe her friend had decided Wes wasn't worth jail, but Skyler wasn't taking any chances. "Stay with them for a few minutes," she said in a low tone to Fiona. "I'll get us a table."

"Gotcha, boss." She slinked off like a shadow after the couple.

Disgusted, Skyler stared after them. Oh, Wes was guilty of something all right. He'd been so distracted he hadn't even noticed her outfit. How was she supposed to be a rebel if nobody even noticed the change?

Suddenly, she felt a large hand slide across her hip. Hot breath caressed her temple. "*Mon Dieu, 'tite ange,* those pants are incredible."

She glanced up at him, noting the smoldering heat in his eyes, like a decanter of whiskey backlit by fire. Her heart pounded against her ribs. Dizziness rushed over her, even as the tingling between her legs intensified. She was *absolutely not* going to faint. This moment was too precious.

Just before she answered him, she remembered to lick her lips. "I'm glad you approve."

His gaze flicked to her lips. Was he thinking about

kissing her? His palm slid down the curve of her hip, then back up, his fingers caressing the silver studs, so they pressed lightly into her bare skin. "I had no idea your wardrobe was so...varied."

She smiled, trying to draw more attention to the lips, currently painted Fire Engine Red. So appropriate. "Bud's Leather Palace," she said. "I have an account, remember?"

"More of your revolt against your brothers?" he asked quietly.

"Sort of." She didn't think she could admit the pants were chosen more for his seduction than her brothers' aggravation. Somehow, someday she'd have to make him understand he wasn't a pawn in her plan to break free and take chances; he was the catalyst.

"You know this bad girl side of yours turns me on," was his welcome response.

"It does?"

He pulled her against him, pressing her hip into the crotch of his jeans, so she had no doubt about the truth of his confession. Heavens, he smelled wonderful. Spicy and manly. Sexy and tempting. She wanted to lose herself in him, in the exhilarating feelings he triggered in her body.

"It's gonna be a long night," he said, mirroring her thoughts.

"Mmm," she said, closing her eyes briefly. His nearness, his cologne, his words had her head whirling as if she'd gone three rounds on a carousel at extreme fast forward.

"This may kill me, *chère,* but I gotta know." His fingers drifted across her backside. "What do you have on underneath those pants?"

Heat suffused her face. She'd tried to balk about

this, but Fiona insisted panty lines would ruin the fit of the leather. "Uh, well..." She cleared her throat and stared at his chest. "See, Fiona insisted...so, um, nothing."

His hand trembled. The hardness between his legs jumped. "Oh, man."

"Jack, Jack." The walkie-talkie on his belt practically vibrated with urgency.

Vibrated. Urgency. *You ain't whistling Dixie, pal.*

JACK STALKED into the band's dressing room. "This better be good," he said sharply to his would-be rock stars.

Masher, reclining in a chair with his feet propped on a table, paused with a plump, ripe grape halfway to his mouth. Golden Boy set down his glass of champagne. The drummer, K. C. Hammond, let one rhinestone-studded drumstick clatter to the floor. The lead guitar player—Bob Smith, if you can believe it—sat on the sofa, but he tore his attention away from the scantily clad twin bimbos on either side of him long enough to glance up.

These guys thought they were Bon Jovi, and they had yet to give a performance. Jack fumed.

"What brand of champagne did we ask for in our contract?" Golden Boy asked, slumping insolently against the wall.

Jack glared at the prima donna bassist. "Whatever Gus had on hand. And there's no contract—you guys are *auditioning* don't forget."

"Do you think colored rhinestones would have looked better?" K.C. asked, frowning at one glittering drumstick.

And he'd walked away from Skyler and her skintight leather pants for this. Jack shook his head. The moment this festival was over, he was firing himself as band manager.

He leaned over and picked up the other drumstick, handing it to K.C. "I think you'd better hang on to these." His gaze swept the room. Desire for Skyler had knotted his belly, and he wanted to spend the night—and not just at the bar—with her. There was little he could do for the band he hadn't already done, and he definitely didn't need their attitude. "Any other questions?"

No one responded. He turned to leave.

"We're nervous," Masher blurted out.

Jack faced them, crossing his arms over his chest. *Now we get to it.* "Has Roland been by yet?" Last week, he'd attended a couple of Roland's performances—his Diana Ross impression was his personal favorite—and learned he could sell a song like a pro. He'd drafted the pet store owner into giving the guys performance tips.

"Yeah, man," Masher said, rising from his chair to pace. "We got it—showmanship and connection with the audience."

"You guys are ready. You'll be great." He headed toward the door, then paused. "And don't forget the one country song."

"Aw, man, do we have to?" Bob whined.

Jack wrapped his hand around the doorknob, thinking of Skyler and wondering if she'd see how much the song he'd requested defined him. She'd claimed she wanted to be with him, that she wasn't just defying her family. If that was the truth, she needed to understand. Not everyone could be an angel like her. He doubted he'd ever feel completely worthy of her attention, but he could live with her acceptance. "Break a leg, guys."

As the door closed behind him, he heard Golden Boy curse. "We pissed him off, guys. Now he's gonna break our legs."

Jack smiled briefly, then dismissed the band from his thoughts and went in search of Skyler.

He found her and Fiona tucked in a booth near the stage—with four grinning males drooling all over the table. And, no doubt, all over Skyler and her leather pants.

The image of her walking into the smoke-lit bar would be a moment he'd always remember with fondness. With anticipation. With immediate, unrelenting, aching desire. A fondness that continued to impair his walking abilities. How he'd managed to resist yanking her into his arms and declaring his intention to never let her go, he'd never understand.

Male interloper number three leaned his hip against the booth, not-so-slyly inching closer to Skyler. She smiled up at the guy, though he noted her expression was a bit edgy. Jack fought the impulse to use his greater size and strength to yank the four amigos out of their shoes and toss them into the graveled parking lot.

Instead, he swallowed his jealousy, swung by the bar for a pitcher of beer, then headed toward the booth. "Have a refill. The show's gonna start any minute."

Something—relief, or maybe even excitement—lit Skyler's eyes. "Can you stay, Jack?"

He threw a triumphant glance toward amigos three and four as he slid into the booth next to Skyler. "Sure," he said, refreshing her and Fiona's mugs.

But he barely had time to register the warmth in Skyler's eyes, the brush of her shoulder against his, the length of her leather-clad thigh alongside his before the lights dimmed.

As Gus ambled onto the stage and into the lone spotlight, Jack glanced across the table, smiling at Fiona's forceful yank of amigo number two's blue polo shirt and his eventual flop into the booth. A decisive woman. A joy always.

"Thank y'all for comin'," Gus began, squinting and holding his beefy hand at a high angle to counteract the intense spotlight. "We got lotsa special guests tonight. The mayor and first lady." He paused as the spotlight swung and Mayor Collins and his wife rose to wave.

They were greeted by mild applause, and one heckler who hollered "The King!", causing Skyler to giggle. Jack couldn't resist a glance at her, and mesmerized by the sparkle in her eyes, he barely heard the introductions of the Fourth of July committee members until the light illuminated her face and she waved.

"And one last special man to thank," Gus continued. "He organized this whole party and discovered a great new band."

If those guys blew this, he'd personally end their days of singing bass.

"…Jack Tesson," Gus announced as the light hit Jack in the face.

He acknowledged the applause with a brief smile and wave, all the time wishing they could just get the hell on with the music so he could dance with Skyler.

Within moments, he got his wish. The band took the stage following Gus's enthusiastic introduction, then launched into a pitch-perfect rendition of "Jailhouse Rock." The mayor's smile could be seen clear across the room, and Jack relaxed.

He slid his arm across the back of the booth's vinyl seat, the tips of his fingers brushing Skyler's bare shoulder. The formfitting red halter top was nearly as provocative as those pants.

Time for more important matters...

WELL INTO the second set, and after a stimulating slow dance with Skyler, Jack decided if this firefighter thing didn't pan out, he could always go into music representation.

The Metal Heads covered Elvis through hits of the nineties with equal competence. They might not have much original songwriting ability, but they were terrific mimics. He had no doubts they would please young and old alike at the festival.

Heroic on his part? Maybe, maybe not. But he was proud. And since Monica and Wes had already left, and Skyler's other brothers had responded to a medical call, she was relaxed and flirtatious. All was right with the world.

The last raucous notes of "Smooth Criminal"— who knew four white guys could reproduce Michael Jackson with credibility?—rang out, and Masher leaned into the microphone, his sweaty fall of blond hair wrapping around the stand. "We promised to rock ya through the night," he began, "but we gotta slide in one country number. For our manager."

As the opening acoustic guitar licks glided through the bar, Jack instinctively sought Skyler's hand. She squeezed his in return, and he turned his head, focusing his gaze on her. A slight smile parted her full, pink lips. Even her jawline was beautiful, he realized. With his index finger, he traced the line from her chin to just below her ear. "Dance with me, *mon coeur.*"

Once the words were out of his mouth, he marveled at them, even as he wanted to call them back. *Mon coeur.* My heart. How revealing was that? He didn't even want to consider the idea. He wanted Skyler. He was crazy about her but his heart had no business focusing on one woman. He had plans, big plans, beyond Baxter for himself and his career.

Shaking the idea away, he drew her from the booth. Thankfully, she didn't ask about the translation of the phrase, and he led her onto the dance floor as the band launched into the chorus, singing about angels and saints and learning to fall. Holding Skyler in his arms felt like a plunge into both sin and redemption. Would she resent him someday for leading her down the wild path? Maybe she'd thank him.

As her delicate hands slid up his chest, the tips of her fingers gliding into his hair, he smiled, not much caring either way. Instead, he inhaled the womanly, flowery scent of her. He rested his hands at her waist, his fingers turned downward to brush the top of her trim backside, his thumbs pressing lightly against her hipbones.

"This song reminds me of you," she said, capturing his gaze with her direct, blue-eyed stare.

"You think?" he said, trying to pretend his heart wasn't pounding like K.C.'s taut set of drums.

"Maybe because you keep calling me little angel." She cocked her head as the song rolled along, then her eyes narrowed. "You think you're corrupting me."

He tried to laugh the idea off, but figured she wouldn't buy it.

Her eyes widened. "You do, don't you?"

He didn't see any point in pretending. "Aren't I?"

She shook her head. Then, unexpectedly, pressed her body against his. She had to feel his arousal, had to know how irresistible he found her, how helpless he felt in her presence. "Maybe *I'll* corrupt *you*," she said, her voice low and intimate.

The music, the heat in the bar closed in on him. He tried to maintain his cool. Not easy to do when one's body had turned into an inferno. He raised one eyebrow. "Try."

Never challenge a Kimball.

This warning might have held significance at a later date, but as Skyler leaned forward, her sweet breath caressing his neck, he couldn't remember his own name, much less pause to consider his impulses. "Come home with me."

His last coherent vision was of Fiona's thumbs-up as Skyler dragged him from the bar.

8

MAYBE I NEED to rethink this whole rebellion.

Skyler slid into the passenger's seat of Jack's Jeep, deciding her moment of pause had come too late. Once again, the impulsive Kimball genes had struck. Like a deranged animal, she'd dragged a grown man out of a crowded bar in front of her friends and half the town. She considered retreating now, but she wanted Jack with every breath in her body. Pressing herself against him, his erection rubbing against her belly, she had felt dizzy, but powerful. The heady rush still coursed through her veins like warmed molasses. Was this the same sensation her brothers experienced when they fought fires?

As Jack opened his door, a much welcome breeze preceded him. Then he dropped into his seat, and the spicy, woodsy scent of his cologne, the warmth of his body, set her senses vibrating. She inhaled slowly, then exhaled, laying her head back against the seat.

Then again, impulsiveness wasn't necessarily a fault.

"Tired?" Jack asked quietly, his deep voice breaking through the charged silence.

Skyler straightened, staring at him. "Hel—" She cleared her throat. "I mean no, of course not."

A sly grin parted his lips. "You're in a mood tonight."

She returned his smile, knowing she'd made the right decision. No matter what the future held, she'd have Jack to herself. Maybe not for long. But for now. "Want to know what kind of mood?" she asked as she leaned toward him and ran the tip of her finger along his thigh.

His eyes flashed bright for a moment before he grabbed her hand, bringing her finger to his mouth. "I bet I can guess." Never budging his gaze, he slid the tip of her finger into his mouth, his tongue gliding across the delicate pad.

Her heart doubled its beat. Her mouth went dry. Her leather pants suddenly seemed too tight, too warm. How could the man cause such amazing lightheadedness with so little effort?

Then he bit her.

Instinctively, she jerked her hand back, but, laughing, he wrapped his hand around her wrist and pulled her against his chest. "Gotcha."

With his heart hammering beneath her fingers and her own pulse thrumming, Skyler couldn't have been more pleased with her position. "You certainly do."

His gaze roved her face, settling on her lips. She held her breath for the moment his mouth would meet hers. "Sorry, *ange,*" he said huskily. "I can't resist anymore."

Though Jack had certainly never been timid in his touch, this kiss echoed with a note of barely suppressed hunger, maybe even desperation. As if he'd waited a lifetime to touch her and wanted to absorb every molecule of her into his pores. His mouth was open, demanding yet gentle. As his tongue tangled with hers, he thrust his arms around her waist, molding her against his broad chest. Her breasts were tight and heavy with desire, and she longed for the moment they would finally meet skin-to-skin.

Arching into him, she moaned, and he answered her need by sliding his hands beneath her halter top. His warm hands against her bare back sent heat shooting through her body. She leaned back to shift her position, wanting to straddle him, dying to assuage the lust vibrating through her. But her back encountered the steering wheel…and the horn.

Ehnnnn!

Skyler leapt back into her seat, her face flaming. Sheerly out of habit, she glanced out the window, but the sparsely lit parking lot was deserted. Save them. Making out in Jack's Jeep.

"We'll get arrested at this rate," she said, still trying to catch her breath.

Jack slid his hand underneath her chin, and she met his gaze, noting the fire in his eyes. She wondered if her face was as flushed, her expression as needy. "Maybe the posse is already in pursuit."

She doubted it. Wes hadn't really noticed her all night, and Ben and Steve had merely smiled indulgently as if wondering how long her leather pants phase would last.

"I doubt we're in any immediate danger," she said lightly to Jack.

"Mmm. Still we should go…find some privacy, *oui?*"

She grinned. *"Oui."*

He fired the ignition, and the Jeep's engine rumbled to life. "Where?"

"Your place."

After glancing briefly at her face, he pulled out of

the parking lot. "This choice wouldn't be because you live next door to Wes, would it?"

"How do you know where he lives?"

"I've studied the town. Having a firefighter who can drive through neighborhoods without getting lost is usually a good idea."

"Oh, right."

"And you still haven't answered my question."

She angled her body toward him, enjoying the way his hands gripped the steering wheel, the smooth movement of his arms as he executed a sharp turn. She frowned, though, at his persistence. "Did anybody ever tell you you're pushy?"

"Often."

Actually, she hadn't considered Wes's proximity. She wanted to see Jack's place. She kept having fantasies about the bed he slept in. It had to be big to hold a man his size. Did it have red flannel sheets? White cotton? Black satin? She nearly moaned aloud at the possibilities.

"I'm not worried about Wes," she said finally.

"My place is small. Just an apartment."

"You're planning a big party?"

He didn't smile like she thought he would. "No. It's just…not much."

She studied his profile highlighted by the dashboard lights—his strong jaw, the curve of his lips…the worry lines along his forehead. Jack *worried?* "You don't want me to see your place?"

His gaze darted to her, then away. "No, *chère.*"

"Good, 'cause I want to see it."

"Okay."

He was still worried, though about what she had no idea. It's not like she lived in a palace herself.

Maybe someday, when the shop was more established, and she had a husband and kids to fill a big house. Those plans always seemed so distant, but with Jack riding next to her, the darkness surrounding them, the big step they were about to take in their relationship—

"Damn! I don't have any condoms." Immediately after she blurted out the words, she covered her mouth with her hand.

Jack screeched to a stop, throwing her forward, then backward. "You what?"

She couldn't look at him, maybe not ever. "Oh, God. I can't believe I said that aloud."

Chuckling, he once again put the Jeep in motion. "But it's important. I don't have any either."

Her head whipped toward him. "You don't?" That cheered her for some ridiculous reason.

He lifted her hand to his mouth, brushing a kiss across her palm, then sliding his tongue between her index and middle fingers. "I've been saving myself for you, *chère.*"

Her heart actually went pitty-patter. "Oh, Jack."

"Mmm. I like the sound of that," he said as he whipped into a 7-Eleven parking lot. He gave her palm one final kiss. "I'll be right back," he said, flinging open the door, then waving to a cop leaning against the hood of his patrol car.

The pitty-pat shifted to a full-on nervous race. Wes *would* mind his own business, wouldn't he? Skyler slunk down in her seat—just in case. "I'm not going anywhere."

JACK WATCHED Skyler walk around his modest apartment. He knew she wouldn't judge a man by the meager possessions he owned, but he'd still been uneasy inviting her here. He'd suspected, and now he knew, he'd never be able to erase the sight of her touching the picture frames of his grandparents and parents, running her hand across the back of his well-worn, denim-colored sofa, or the impressions her high-heeled sandals-*really* high-heeled, so that had to be Monica's doing—formed in the pale gray carpeting.

An apartment meant temporary. Baxter was just a stopover along the way to his prestigious career. But memories were permanent. And he had some wonderful ones with Skyler.

There's more to come, buddy, his shoulder devil assured him. *Quit worrying about later. The time is now.*

He leaned his head to the side, appreciating the teasing inch of Skyler's skin exposed by her halter top and the spectacular view of her butt in those impossibly tight leather pants. His erection pulsed. She wore nothing beneath. Who knew women worrying about minor details like panty lines could be such a benefit for a guy? *She was naked.* Well, nearly. And in his apartment. His forehead broke out in a sweat.

The memory of this particular moment would, no doubt, smolder in his brain for a long time to come.

"Your parents?" she asked into the silence, holding up a wooden frame.

He closed the few feet that separated them, more to inhale the scent of her than to discuss his parents. "And their whale."

She glanced at the picture. "Their…whale?"

Normal people had their picture made with the endless Pacific Ocean and a sunset in the background.

His parents had a blue whale. "Kiki. They adopted him. You know, save the whales."

He watched her closely for the usual amusement his parents and their crusades produced, but she just smiled. "A worthy cause."

Yeah. He guessed it was.

His lust for the petite blond, leather-clad woman in his apartment was much more urgent, though. Desire had grabbed him by the throat. While she seemed content to putter around the room, he wanted to lick his way down her body. Was she just nervous, or was there something more?

Standing so close their hips brushed, he tried to push aside his insecurities and the knowledge that he was all wrong for her. He drew the frame from her hands, set the picture on the coffee table and slid his arm around her waist.

Her eyes widened, but she didn't say anything as he turned off the lights in the den. Making his way easily in the dark, he led her into the kitchen, lifted her onto the counter, then flipped on the dim light above the stove. "The light's better in here," he said as he urged her knees apart and stood between them. They were almost eye-level in this position. He cupped her cheek in his palm and stared directly into her eyes. She deserved a hero like her father, and he would find a way to be one. "It's okay if you've changed your mind."

Shock flickered through her eyes. "What?"

"About being here with me." His erection pulsed, his blood roared, his heart ached. But he swallowed, knowing he couldn't let her make love to him on a dare, or to piss off her family. He wanted more. Admitting that, even to himself, was the hardest thing he'd ever done. "I'll take you home if you want."

She shook her head, smiling slightly and slid her hand up his arm, gliding her fingers into the hair at his nape. *Mon Dieu,* that drove him crazy. "I want you."

He let his gaze drift to the lips that had uttered those words, wishing he could swallow them. Holy hell, she was beautiful. She wanted him. Why should anything else matter? But, dammit, it did. "Why?" he made himself ask.

"Jack, you're being difficult."

"I know. But it's important."

Her gaze held his for a long moment, her blue eyes tender, contemplative, as he tried—and failed—to put a finer point on his feelings. Did she feel the same confusion? Women always seemed much better equipped to deal with emotional issues, so maybe not. For the first time in a long, long time, he wished he had a closer relationship with his mother.

"Because of Casey," she said softly.

The fraternity pledge? Maybe the sight of her in leather had fried all his brain cells.

"I know you hid him here so my brothers wouldn't find him. He broke the record, you know."

"So he said."

"You're a true hero," she whispered then pulled his head down to her and kissed him.

She probed his lips with her tongue, pushing easily into his mouth as he tilted his head and slid his arms around her. She couldn't possibly know what her confidence in him meant. Nor did he understand why he needed it so badly. The idea that she was an angel he had no business touching was shoved far back into his mind. He didn't care about listening to his conscience at the moment. He wanted Skyler's curves, her warm, wet welcome into carnal ecstasy.

Laissez les bon temps rouler, the devil on his shoulder whispered seductively, confidently.

Following that advice, he slid her toward him, pressing the vee of her thighs against his hardness. He moaned into her mouth. Relief, yet more hunger. His heart hammered as his erection throbbed. He needed more.

He slid his hands along her stomach exposed by the red halter top. That tiny inch of skin had teased him all night, and now he wanted the whole shebang. Easing back a bit to give him room, he pulled the shirt up, and—what the hell—off.

She gasped and pulled away from the kiss then glanced down at her nude upper half.

"Oh, my," she said.

"You're not wearing a bra," he said at the same time.

Their gazes met, and her blue eyes laughed daringly into his. "The bra is sewn into the top—it's the new thing."

The top didn't interest him. Jack was too busy getting his fill of Skyler's pale breasts, contrasting with her summer tan, and the tightening of her nipples. What a picture! If he lived a hundred years, he'd never forget the sight of her sitting on his kitchen counter in nothing but high heels and leather pants.

"I'm all for progress," he muttered against the side of her neck.

As he cupped her breasts, he trailed kisses down her throat, working downward with deliberate slowness. He wanted to hurry. His body commanded that he strip off the leather, drop his zipper, and ease the torment coursing through him. But he wanted to enjoy her, to savor the taste of her skin.

At last, he reached the slope of her breast. Slowly, very slowly, he drew his tongue along the curve.

She moaned.

He laved the nipple and sucked it into his mouth.

She arched her neck and back, clenching her fingers into the muscles on top of his shoulders. "Jack," she gasped.

"*Ange,*" he muttered, intent on driving her past the point of reason—where he was.

"I want your shirt off."

Dazed, aroused beyond words, Jack raised his head long enough to yank his black T-shirt over his head. Then he tugged Skyler toward him, groaning as flesh met flesh. Her breasts rubbed against his chest hairs, her nipples hardening like small pebbles. The friction was incredible. Arousing. Frustrating.

He craved closer contact. He wanted to be inside her. He wanted her to purge this pulsing, inescapable hunger. Holding her tight against his chest, he lifted her from the counter. It was time to take this to his bed.

"Put me down," she said sharply.

He released her enough for her to slither down his body, contact that brought its own kind of acute torment. "What?"

Her lips pursed—in amusement or irritation, he couldn't tell. He was too far gone down the road to arousal. "You got to look at me. I want to look at you."

And Skyler looked her fill.

SHE'D ENVISIONED the breadth of his shoulders, the rippling muscles along his chest, the washboard abs, the sprinkling of black hair that arrowed toward his navel for so long she could hardly believe they were bare inches from her now. "Wow," was all she could manage as she blinked and prayed the gorgeous apparition wouldn't fade.

Grinning, he settled his hands at his waist. "Wow?"

Reaching out, she grabbed him by the belt loop on his jeans. "Big wow." Their chests brushed, and she inhaled sharply, her breath catching in her throat, her head spinning. The man had *such* an effect on her. "You can pick me up again."

He did so with a swiftness and ease that never ceased to take her breath away. He captured her lips immediately, his warm, hungry mouth coaxing her lips apart. She sighed deep in her heart. She knew she'd never before felt, and might never again feel, this kind of rightness, of completion with anyone else. He was all wrong for her, and yet he was so right at the same time.

She had little time for philosophy, though, as he led her into his bedroom, laying her gently onto the comforter. She also had little time to indulge her curiosity about the room, as he followed her onto the bed. His big body lay across hers, comforting, yet strong.

As she stared at his handsome face hovering over hers, the desire in his whiskey eyes so apparent, she wondered if she should say something. Something romantic? Something lighthearted? Something sexy?

But the words froze in her throat. He meant so much to her. Too much. She'd sworn from the moment she'd seen him she wouldn't get involved with a hero. Even worse, an ambitious hero. One who'd never let Baxter contain him.

She wanted to regret the steps she'd taken so far, and the big one she was about to take, but she couldn't. No matter what happened tomorrow she'd have him tonight.

Anticipation tingled through her limbs. She glided her hand across the top of his shoulder. Then she pulled him close for her kiss.

He teased her mouth, his tongue sliding across her lips. And his hands, *whoa baby,* his hands worked magic on her skin, gliding from her cheek down her throat, across her shoulder then following the slope of her breast. Her nipples budded in expectation. She craved his touch. She arched her back in a silent plea, and he nibbled her bottom lip, all the while his finger slowly circled toward the center of her breast, toward the center of her need.

He finally reached the bud, his finger skimming, barely, the tip. She nearly screamed in frustration.

A brief smile curved his lips. ''Slowly, *chère.* Seduction is key.''

''Yeah?'' Sheer frustration, and maybe a hint of the rebel she'd played, forced drastic action. She cupped his erection.

He went dead still.

She slid her fingers up and down, slowly, gently. With his jeans as a barrier, she couldn't tease him quite as well as he had her, but he had no problem getting the message.

''Then again, foreplay is highly overrated.''

It was her turn to grin.

In seconds, he'd stripped off her leather pants, tossing them at the foot of the bed. He stared down at her, his eyes fiery with passion. "You're beautiful."

She drew her finger down his chest. "You're not so bad yourself."

He slid off the bed suddenly, then stood and unbuttoned his jeans. He fumbled a moment with the zipper, muttering in French as he finally stripped them off.

When he faced the bed, she was able to appreciate the view south of his waist. He was certainly a man of even proportions. Large everywhere.

She tried not to giggle at the naughty thought. When he lay next to her, she rolled over to lie on top of him, her softness meeting his hardness, her mouth finding his. The hunger raced through her body, and the sense of rightness invaded her. His tongue caressed her mouth and his hands glided down the slope of her backside. She wanted to revel only in the physical sensations, but the emotions wouldn't cease. The laughter and secrets they'd shared, the conversations, even the arguments. They all tumbled together in a mix so powerful she knew escaping them might be impossible.

Rolling them to the side, she kissed him harder, more desperately, fighting against her feelings. She could drown herself in the passion of his body. She didn't have to face anything more. At least not now.

And with Jack's lips nibbling her throat on his way to her breasts, it wasn't a difficult task.

Burying her face in his hair, she inhaled his spicy, familiar scent. She gasped when his mouth closed around the burgeoning peak of one nipple. The pleasure shot down her body, centering between her legs.

Her belly trembled, and she rolled her hips against

him. Damp heat met solid muscle. She heard him rip open a package, then he grabbed her hips, lifting her on top of him, to the tip of his erection. A heartbeat later, he was inside her.

Tightening her thighs around him, she moaned at the fullness invading her body. The closeness was incredible. The connection overwhelming. She sat up straight, driving him deeper still.

He gasped, looking up at her, holding her in place by her hips. "I could come just looking at you, *chère*."

Desire pulsed through her. She lifted her hips, then lowered them in one smooth, sharp thrust. The pleasure was so intense, her head spun. She repeated the motion again and again, barely aware Jack met her thrusts with his own. The pleasure spiraled, coiling tighter and tighter. She drew shallow breaths, air flowing in and out in short puffs, as if she'd run three miles. Her climax was just beyond her reach, just beyond her fingertips. She strained for the pinnacle. "Jack," she said, her voice a mere gasp.

He seemed to understand her need. He slid his hand between their bodies, his fingers finding the center of her desire. Without a pause of his driving hips, he drew his fingertip over the crest. She felt him climax as she exploded.

Then she fainted.

SKYLER?...SKYLER?

As if through a long tunnel Skyler could hear Jack calling her name. He sounded urgent and worried. Mmm. She smiled. She kind of liked the idea of him fussing over her.

Stretching on the bed, she noted her heartbeat had

returned to its normal rhythm, probably explaining why she'd regained consciousness. She got dizzy when she *saw* the man, so it wasn't too surprising she'd fainted when he'd brought her to—

"Dammit, *chère,* if you don't open your eyes this second, I'm takin' you to the hospital."

Her eyes flew open. "I'm awake. I'm up." She tried to sit up, only to have a naked, angry Jack push her back down.

His face loomed over hers. "Did you eat today?"

"Yes."

"Do you feel dizzy or nauseous?"

"No."

"Are you—"

She pulled him toward her for a long, wet kiss. When they broke apart, a half smile graced his lips, and the anger in his eyes had been replaced by sensual heat. She could really get used to distracting him this way.

He drew her into his arms, then rolled onto his back, tucking her beside him. "I'm worried about you."

She lifted her head from his shoulder, looking at him directly. "I'm fine. Really."

"What did your cardiologist say about you fainting so much?"

"Uh, well…it only happens when I get too nervous or excited, so it's not a problem."

His eyes narrowed. "Did your doctor say it's not a problem?"

"Not exactly."

"Did you *see* your doctor?"

"Of course I've seen him."

"Recently?"

"Well…"

A stream of French—sounding mostly like curses—burst from his mouth. He leapt from the bed, then, naked, paced across the room. "Your heart is not something you mess around with."

"I'm not." She sat, drawing the comforter around her. The last thing she wanted to do was go into this discussion, but the fear in Jack's eyes and voice were troubling her. Jack wasn't afraid of anything—not fires, floods, tall buildings, ladders, brothers or motorcycles. But he was afraid for her.

Guilt made her eyes watery. She should have explained long before now.

"My dizzy spells really don't happen as often as you think. You're just always around when they occur."

"You're goin' to the doctor first thing in the morning if I have to drag you there myself."

"I get overexcited," she continued, undaunted by his dire warning. "Then dizzy, and sometimes I faint."

"What if you fainted while you were driving?" he went on, acting as though he hadn't heard a word she'd said. "*Mon Dieu,* I don't even want to think about being called to the scene of an accident…." He thrust his hand through his hair.

"Jack!" she said, a bit too sharply, but his imagination was racing out of control. He stopped and stared at her, and she couldn't help but admire the pure male vision within touching distance. From the porch lights peeking through a crack in the curtains she had an excellent view of his jet-black hair, tousled from her fingers; the wide expanse of his chest; his narrow waist and hips; his long, lean legs.

If she could just get through this discussion, she might have the chance to jump him again.

Fearing the desire stealing its way through her veins would distract her, she tore her gaze away from his body to focus on his eyes. "Sit down," she said. When he did, she asked, "Were you listening to me?"

"*Oui,*" he said, casting an irritated glance out of the corner of his eye, as if she were the one not paying attention to him. "Overexcited, dizzy, then fainting." He ticked the symptoms off on his fingers with an important, doctorish, know-it-all air. "All bad signs."

She leaned forward until she could feel his angry puffs of breath on her face. "All your fault." Shock widened his eyes, giving her a chance to go on before he could protest. "I get overexcited when *you're* around. Your size, those muscles, your voice, hell, all of you. *You* cause my dizzy spells."

"I—" He stopped, obviously trying to decide if he should take her seriously or not. Finally, the flattering aspect of her confession must have hit him. A slow smile bloomed on his lips. "I excite you."

She slid the back of her hand down his stubbled cheek. "All the time."

"I guess I really excited you tonight. You were out a good three minutes."

Skyler fought the urge to roll her eyes. Male vanity, good grief. "Yes, Mr. Modest, you're quite something in the lovemaking department."

She could have sworn his broad chest puffed out even farther. He slid his arms around her, placing a light kiss on her lips. "I have French ancestry, you know."

"You certainly do."

"This is kinda cool."

"If you're not the one doing the fainting."

"Of course, but what's the alternative?"

She frowned. "Staying away from you."

Easing the comforter off her shoulders, he guided her back onto the bed. "No way, *chère*. I've got you right where I want you."

Her body tingled in anticipation, and her heart hammered in her chest.

"I'll even catch you when you fall."

9

JACK PULLED his Jeep to a halt in Skyler's driveway. He nearly bounced out of the seat, remembering only as he stood on the front porch to play it cool. But, damn, he was happy.

Except for the abrupt phone call from Wes warning Jack about hurting his sister and making his life hell if he did, the last week had been the best he could remember. He and Skyler had spent every night he wasn't working together. In bed and out, she was a remarkable woman. And anytime he worried he wasn't equally remarkable enough for her in return, he reminded himself he was working on it. *You're a true hero,* she'd said.

After hearing her talk with such longing about her parents—the father she'd lost so young, and the mother she hardly saw—she reminded him of the precious gift of family. His parents might be a little over-involved and nutty, but they loved him, and he knew it was essential he accept them. He'd gotten in touch with them—in Brazil saving the rain forest—and they'd had a wonderful talk over the phone.

He owed that peace to Skyler, and he couldn't wait to tell her. Cradling a bottle of champagne in the crook of his arm, he rang the doorbell.

She answered the door wearing a see-through black

bra, matching panties, garter belt, hose and high-heeled shoes.

His jaw dropped, and the champagne nearly went with it.

Before he could utter a word, she grabbed his hand and pulled him inside, leading him into the den. The room was glowing with lit candles. Dozens of them flickered around the room.

But he couldn't seem to budge his gaze from the erotic vision before him. Her silky, tanned skin glowed through the transparent material. Every curve was exposed, yet teased. Her face was artfully made-up; her hair fluffed and curled.

Ever since he'd learned about the back room business of her shop, he'd had fantasies like this, but none of the cool remarks he'd imagined himself saying came to mind. Ridiculously, he said only "I guess you don't want to hear about the phone call I made to my mother."

Her red-tinged lips parted in a smile. "Later." She took the champagne from him, then tucked the bottle into the fridge. "We'll save this, too."

He followed her into the kitchen, hoping to catch another whiff of the sensual perfume drifting after her. The scent was different from her usual perfume—more musky, forbidden. "My *'tite ange* has turned into a devil."

She turned away from the fridge, settling her hands at her hips. "You think so?"

He grabbed her by the waist and nuzzled her neck. She smelled like heaven, or maybe hell—he wasn't sure. *"Oui."*

She slid her arms up his chest, causing every muscle in his body to tighten. "You approve?"

"Definitely," he said, his voice low, his erection pulsing against his jeans to give "his" added opinion. He trapped her between him and the refrigerator.

"Ooh, that's cold."

"Not for long."

He captured her mouth with his, pouring all his hunger into the kiss. Every time he touched her he wanted her more. Would he ever have enough? Would there ever be a time he didn't want her?

He had a hard time seeing that future moment. Which might have worried him—if she hadn't slid her hands around to squeeze his butt.

Groaning, he lifted her off the floor and ground his hardness against her. She wrapped her legs around his hips, cradling him between her legs, increasing the pressure behind his jeans. His blood caught fire. Roaring need pounded in his head. He continued his assault on her lips, demanding she feel the same all-consuming passion.

Through her thin bra he could feel the hard points of her nipples smashed against his chest, and she whimpered in the back of her throat as if she understood and returned his torment. "Jack," she gasped against his mouth, her breath escaping harsh and fast.

His own heart felt as thought it might jump from his chest any second, so he held tighter, hoping she wouldn't faint, and not sure if he might. He rocked his hips against the juncture of her thighs, knowing the soft, wet heat that would soon surround him, consume him. Anticipating the moment their bodies connected had almost become as addictive as the act itself.

Unable to reign in his need any longer, he cupped his hands underneath her backside and carried her to the kitchen counter. Without breaking the contact of their lips, he fumbled for the cookie jar containing the condoms.

Finding one, he lifted his head long enough to see as he ripped open the packet and she ripped open the fly of his jeans. "*Chère,* have I told you lately how efficient you are?"

"We always burn the cookies," she said as she lifted her hips to strip off her panties. "It seemed more prudent."

"We burn the cookies 'cause you're so insatiable."

She crossed her legs, her panties dangling off the toe of her high-heeled shoe, candlelight dancing across her long, bare legs. Her gaze flicked to his erection. "Me?"

He slid his hand around the back of her neck and pulled her to the counter's edge. "And maybe me."

Eyes wide in mock alarm, she leaned back. *"Maybe?"*

It occurred to him in that moment how contrasting their easy conversations and overwhelming sexual attraction were. His heart lurched at the realization of how perfect she was for him. But he fought back tender emotions and grinned.

Saying nothing, her bright blue gaze locked on his, she uncrossed her legs, her knee just barely brushing his hardness.

A bolt of electric heat started at the tip, slicing through his body. He yanked her against him, easing himself between her legs, nudging the entrance of her body. "You know I can't get enough of you," he said, almost angry at how addicted he was to her.

"Me either." She grabbed the hem of his shirt,

jerking it up and off his body, then she clutched him at the waist, bracing herself as he plunged inside her.

He arched his neck backward as her sweet heat surrounded him, drew him more completely under her spell. She crossed her ankles at his back and rocked her hips. Her fingernails dug into his skin. Sharp pleasure coursed through his veins, and he fought to slide out and in with controlled movements. As much as his climax chased him, he longed to stay buried in her welcoming warmth forever.

The silky material covering her breasts rubbed against his bare chest; the stockings she still wore glided along his sides, the friction and the slight barriers only heightening the fantasy of their lovemaking. He wished he could get control of himself long enough to study her. He settled for a brief glance at the arch line of her slim body, her tousled blond hair, her half-open mouth gasping for air.

I don't deserve her. Probably never will.

The criticism echoed through his mind just as it snuck into his dreams. He clutched her tighter, increased his pace, fighting to dismiss the insecure thoughts. *She needs me. She enjoys me.* He clung to these truths just as she moaned low in her throat, signaling her approaching orgasm. Sweat rolling down his face, he drove harder and faster into her, hanging by a bare thread to his own climax.

She gasped suddenly, just before her inner walls pulsed around his hardness, pushing him to the end. Shuddering ecstasy and relief pulsed through his body. He rode the waves, followed the crest down, leaving him drained, satisfied and ridiculously happy.

He leaned against her and the counter, praying she

wouldn't faint. He wasn't sure he could hold himself up, much less her, too. "Are you with me, *chère?*"

"Mmm," she mumbled against his shoulder, obviously conscious, but not too coherent.

Jack concentrated on drawing deep breaths, which he managed comfortably for a few minutes, then a new rumbling started in his stomach. "What's for dinner?"

Her head jerked up. "Jackson Phillipe Tesson, how can you think of food at a time like this?"

He scooped her up into his arms, feeling a new pulse of desire at her scolding tone. "I need to replenish my strength. How else am I gonna satisfy you?"

Laughing, she tossed back her head. "Oh, Jack, I—" She slammed to a halt, her eyes widening. "I'm hungry, too," she finally finished quickly, leaving him to wonder if she'd been about to say something else and had changed her mind.

His stomach grumbled again, distracting him. "Take-out or pantry surprise?"

"Take-out Chinese and champagne."

Jack shrugged and headed for the phone. He had no intention of arguing with a woman wearing a see-through black bra and no panties.

REPLETE WITH General Tso's chicken, pork lo mein and champagne, they were flopped on the sofa—her lying back between his legs, wearing his shirt and cuddled against his bare chest—and watching a sitcom on TV when the emergency scanner beeped, signaling an impending announcement.

Jack glared at the infernal thing. He understood Skyler's fears about her brothers and the need to know what calls they were answering, but between the three of them someone was *always* on duty. He hated seeing her worry.

"House One, this is dispatch. EMS anonymous 9-1-1 call for trapped individual residing at 445 Oakdale Road. No further details. Police notification impending."

Skyler's whole body went rigid even as Ben's voice crackled out of the scanner, notifying dispatch of their departure to the scene. But something about the call besides Ben's involvement had Jack frowning. Skyler lived at 443 Oakdale. They were sitting in the living room of 443 Oakdale. That meant the call was...

Next door.

"Wes!" Skyler yelled as she shoved herself off his lap.

Jack was a half step behind her as they flew down the hall and out the front door. It seemed every light in Wes's house blazed. His truck sat in the driveway along with his patrol car. An eerie sickness rolled through Jack's stomach. *Please let him be okay.*

Finding the door unlocked, they rushed into the house with Skyler calling Wes's name, and Jack's heart slapping against his rib cage. He'd made calls like this many times before, but the possibility that Wes might be his next patient had his mouth stone dry.

"Wes?" Skyler screamed into the seemingly empty house.

They rushed from room to room, finding no one, hearing nothing. As they darted up the stairs, Jack considered the shocking possibilities they could encounter. After so many years in paramedic work, even in small towns, he'd seen some sights he'd never want Skyler to witness. He wanted to pull her into his arms, shelter her from whatever they might find.

As they darted down the hall, Jack heard a muffled voice.

"Wes!" Skyler shouted back.

Charging toward the sound, Jack managed to reach the closed door at the end of the hall first. "Wes?" he called.

A very direct cussword was the response.

Skyler's gaze met his, her blue eyes stark with fear, then he turned the knob and flung open the door.

Words failed him. Medical responses froze. And, as a man, he winced in sympathy.

"Oh, my God," Skyler gasped, rushing to her brother's side—where he lay, spread-eagle on his bed, handcuffed to one bedpost, tied to the other three with rope, wearing red lipstick, bright blue eye shadow and a black merry widow.

Laughter tried to bubble up from Jack's throat, but he managed to cross his arms over his chest and swallow his amusement.

Especially since Wes's face was already beet-red with embarrassment. "Well, don't just stand there, get me out of this!"

"Which *this* would that be?" Jack couldn't help asking. "The handcuffs? Or maybe that…fetching undergarment?"

Wes simply glared at him.

"Where are your keys?" Skyler asked, her voice gentle and soothing, but her face pink and her eyes amused.

"Hell, I don't know!" Wes struggled uselessly

against his secure bonds. "Untie me first, and quick, before they get here."

They. The importance of the dispatch information finally reached Jack. Someone—certainly not Wes—had called 9-1-1, knowing the police and fire departments would rush to the scene. Somebody certainly had it in for the ornery lieutenant.

A woman was his bet. And as he studied the lingerie he realized he'd seen it before—on Monica O'Malley the day he'd barged into the back room of Skyler's shop.

Wes glared at him. "Dammit, Tesson, get over here and help her."

Smiling, Jack considered letting him reap the consequences of his actions but made a mental note to send Monica flowers. He sat on the bed and worked on the knot holding Wes's right wrist.

"What'd you do to her?" he asked without looking at the lieutenant—the laughter he was holding in his chest wouldn't stay contained much longer.

Wes stilled his struggles. *"Her?"*

"Monica," Jack continued casually as he slid the rope from Wes's wrist. "I'm guessin' she's pissed off." He glanced at Wes as the lieutenant sat up, glaring at Jack and shaking his wrist. "Unless you two got into a little S&M..."

Skyler shoved his shoulder. "Jack!"

Looking at her, Jack noted tears of laughter sparkling in her eyes, though she struggled to keep them at bay. She glanced away and worked on the ropes holding her brother's black stocking-clad feet.

"Crazy woman," Wes ground out between clenched teeth—as he tried to unhook the back of his corset one-handed.

"Allow me," Jack volunteered, reaching behind

Wes to untie the strings Monica had cleverly used to connect the two sides of the corset together, since Wes's chest was way too broad to use the delicate hooks sewn onto the garment. The lieutenant merely grunted, so Jack continued, "How did she manage to tie you up?"

"She had help."

Jack raised his eyebrows. "Help?"

"Mandy."

Skyler tossed the final rope onto the floor as she rose, crossing her arms over her chest. "Who's Mandy?"

"The woman I was in bed with when Monica showed up wearing this thing." He gestured at the lingerie he wore. "Neither one of them was happy."

Skyler narrowed her eyes. *"Really?"*

"I made a mistake, okay? Is that any reason to tie me up? Truss me into women's...understuff?" With his free hand, he shoved one stocking down his leg, ripping the delicate material in his struggles.

Skyler's expression showed no sympathy. She whirled, then crossed the room, disappearing into the bathroom.

"The woman has really gone over the edge," Wes went on. "When I get out of here, I'm sending a squad car to her house. She's gonna pay for this!"

"I wouldn't do that," Jack said as he slid the corset off Wes's body. With his wrist still handcuffed to the post, and the headboard preventing him from sliding the cuff up and off, he couldn't get the corset completely off. "Hey, Skyler," he shouted toward the bathroom, "see if you can find some scissors in there."

"Why the hell shouldn't I arrest her?" Wes asked, craning his neck around and glaring at Jack.

"An arrest makes all this public," Jack reminded him, now unable to hold back a smile. "An arrest means official statements, evidence gathering... photographs."

A muscle along Wes's jaw pulsed, but he said nothing.

Skyler returned with scissors and some towels. While Jack cut the corset's strap, leaving the lieutenant in a way-too-small G-string—which Jack wasn't touching—she dropped a towel in her brother's lap, then began wiping off the makeup with the other.

"Instead of worrying about how to punish Monica," she said as she wiped off his lipstick, "maybe you should consider the idea that the blame for this entire mess can be laid right at your own feet."

"Bull—"

"I wouldn't say another word that isn't an apology or a thank-you." She pursed her lips. "Unless you want Jack and I to leave you handcuffed to your bed with nothing but a towel to save your dignity."

Wes looked ready to argue, but wisely kept quiet. Skyler leaned over and kissed him on the forehead.

The moment of affection released some of the tension in the room, and gave Jack his own attack of the guilts. *He* had caused tension between the siblings. He wanted Skyler and refused to let anyone stand in his way, even though her family was permanent and his presence in her life temporary. Was that as selfish as Wes cheating on Monica?

"Where should I start looking for your keys?" Skyler asked Wes before Jack could consider his feelings further.

"Try the patrol car," Wes said, just as sirens rang in the distance. "Fast," he added.

When Skyler raced from the room, Jack gathered

the lingerie, stuffing the outfit and stockings in the bottom drawer of the bedside table. ''You can get rid of 'em later,'' he said to Wes.

''Yeah. Thanks, man.''

''How 'bout some clothes?'' he asked, noting the awkward way Wes held the spare towel around his waist. In light of the imminent arrival of his colleagues and questioning his actions in his own relationship, Jack found his humor gone.

''There are jeans in the bottom dresser drawer.''

Jack retrieved the jeans, then stood awkwardly next to the bed, glancing from Wes's handcuffed wrist to his lower body. He knew Wes still wore the G-string beneath the towel.

The bright lights of the fire truck flashed through the window. The sirens screamed. They had only seconds.

He rolled his shoulders. ''Oh, hell, let's just get this over with.''

Red-faced, Wes nodded. He wrangled his way out of the undies, keeping the towel over himself and without Jack having to help. After stuffing the panties between the mattress and box spring, he slid one leg at a time in the jeans Jack held out.

By the time they heard the pounding footsteps on the stairs, Jack was standing by the window, and Wes was wearing his jeans and sitting calmly on the bed.

''Don't stray too far from the truth,'' Jack warned him quietly.

''She got pissed and handcuffed me to the bed. The rest of it never happened.''

The words were barely out of his mouth when Ben charged into the room, followed by two other firefighters, a uniformed police officer and Skyler.

Ben glanced oddly at Jack before he addressed Wes. "You okay, little brother?"

Skyler handed Ben a small key then stood next to Jack. When she leaned against him, he slid his arm around her waist, hugging her to his side. He wanted to take her home.

"I'm fine," Wes said, his face flushed under the scrutiny of his brother and colleagues. "Just a fight with Monica."

Ben unlocked the handcuffs, dropping them on the bed. "A fight? So she handcuffed you to the bed and called 9-1-1?" he asked in disbelief.

Wes stood, rubbing his wrist. "Redheads are temperamental." He smiled wryly at the other guys. "But fun as hell."

The men snickered briefly—until Skyler cleared her throat. "I'm sure you gentlemen have better things to do. The emergency is over."

With mumbled apologies to the lady present, they all headed out of the room, but Ben stopped Jack and Skyler at the door. "You two got here awfully fast," he said, his gaze raking them from head to toe.

For the first time since they'd heard the call on the scanner, Jack realized what he and Skyler were wearing. He had on only his jeans. She wore his T-shirt.

"We were watching TV at my house," Skyler said slowly, cautiously.

Ben's hard gaze met Jack's. "What exactly are you doing with my sister, Tesson?"

Stiffening, Jack fought to hold on to his temper, telling himself Ben was just being protective. He'd object to any man sleeping with his sister.

Skyler jumped between them before Jack could respond. "Nothing." Her smiled was forced and fake. "Relax, Ben, it's nothing serious."

Jack's heart lurched. He stared at her, shattered by the desperate look in her eyes.

"We had some committee business to go over," she went on, either not aware or not caring about the stabbing pain each word she uttered caused him.

She was denying him. She didn't want him. He wasn't good enough for her.

Ben stared at her. "How did you manage to wind up wearing his shirt?"

"Uh…" Her panicked gaze flew to Jack as if she wanted his help in the cover-up. He couldn't have uttered a word if he tried. "It's, uh, not his. It's one of Steve's old ones."

Everything inside Jack froze. The pleasure he'd found in seeing her wear his shirt turned to pain. Everything they'd shared, every word and gesture of affection she'd given him suddenly seemed like a lie.

He vaguely realized Ben was shaking his head, as if he didn't believe a word of her story. "Try again, Sky."

He started to turn away, but Skyler grabbed his arm. "Don't fire him."

Several beats of silence passed, then understanding lit Ben's eyes. "You think I'd fire him for getting involved with my sister? I couldn't even if I wanted to, which I don't. I can't believe you'd think I'd do something like that."

Jack watched Skyler's face as she realized his job wasn't at risk. She'd denied their relationship for nothing.

But then, he thought angrily, her family had always just been an excuse anyway. She'd never intended him to be anything more than a walk on the wild side. A temporary walk. And that was just fine by him. He had bigger plans for his future than Baxter. She'd done him a favor really. Now he wouldn't have to worry about hurting her in a few months when the newness of their relationship wore off, and he needed his space.

And that was the biggest bunch of crap he'd ever tried to sell anyone. Even the devil on his shoulder jabbed his pitchfork at him.

He'd been falling in love with her since the first moment he'd set eyes on her.

"Well, it's not serious, anyway," she said again, turning the knife in Jack's chest.

Ben raised his eyebrows, and it finally registered with Jack that his captain wasn't mad anymore, he was amused. "Looks serious to me. A firefighter, Sky? Not your usual cup of tea."

Skyler glanced from her brother to Jack. She must have finally seen the pain he knew he was doing a lousy job of hiding. "No, I guess not."

Ben clapped Jack on the shoulder. "Though Jack's a great guy."

The spark of pleasure Jack got from Ben's compliment had about as much effect as throwing a teaspoon of water on a three-alarm fire. He stood stiff, debating the possibility of escape. He didn't want to be near her, smell her, feel her. Not when he knew how little he meant to her.

"I'm heading back to the station," Ben said, turning away. "Thanks for dealing with the situation here."

"No problem," Jack managed to say, walking beside his captain and away from Skyler. "Are you covered this week? I could work extra shifts." He had a feeling a lot of brooding lay in his future, and he'd rather work.

"Jack?" Skyler's soft voice called after him.

He stopped in the hall, drew a bracing breath, then glanced over his shoulder. She stood in the bedroom doorway, his T-shirt brushing the tops of her knees, her eyes liquid with regret.

"Can we talk?"

He forced his heart to harden at her plea. "Our business is finished, *oui, chère?*"

But even as he turned away, her voice followed him. "I'm sorry I tried to cover up our relationship. I should have known Ben was too honorable to fire you over me."

Her words did little to ease the ache in Jack's heart. In fact, the sound of her voice intensified the pain. He said nothing.

"But I didn't lie about our relationship not being serious. I mean, it's not, is it?"

He stared at her over his shoulder. Now, rather than looking regretful, she looked angry. "If you say so."

"No. *You* said so. You're not looking to settle here permanently. You want bigger and better things than Baxter. Than me."

He couldn't deny the truth of her words. He wanted bigger and better things. He wanted to succeed at his job. But did he want to lose her in the process?

She won't stay with you anyway. You're not good enough for her.

"You're leaving," she prompted.

He sighed. "Yeah. I guess I am."

He turned and walked away, wondering if he was making the biggest mistake of his life.

10

SKYLER PACED the kitchen floor.

The man is leaving, Sky. You threw yourself at him once already. Why in the world are you considering doing it again?

As she huffed her way back and forth in front of the sink, all she could think about was the way she'd wrapped her legs around his hips and invited him into her body, into her heart. About the laughter and fun and tender moments they'd shared. Why couldn't she forget all that? Why did that horrible scene in Wes's bedroom three days ago have to happen? Why did she constantly relive the moment she'd reminded him he was leaving, and he'd stared at her with pain in his eyes?

Maybe she'd fallen in—

No. No way she was using the *L* word. She just liked Jack. That was it. She really, really *liked* him.

Damn. That was an *L* word, too.

Biting her lip, she leaned against the counter and contemplated the patriotic outfit she wore. At the festival today she was going to do something about all these icky, turbulent feelings rolling around in her stomach. She was going to confront Jack about their relationship. She was going to question that pain in his eyes.

Maybe he did want her. And Baxter. Maybe he was

just too stubborn or prideful to admit it. Maybe she was more important than fires, flood and disease.

After brooding and sulking and regretting for three long days, she'd also decided it was damn time she came clean to him—and herself—about her family. She'd let her brothers threaten her dates and scowl at any potential man's interest in her just to cushion her against hurt or to get her out of a relationship with a loser. Hadn't their protection always just been a convenient excuse to ward off chances? Chances to risk her martyrdom. Chances to risk her heart.

But today was Independence Day after all, and she was asserting hers.

No more Ms. Wishy-Washy—pretending to be a rebel one minute, scrambling for excuses to cover up the lingerie business the next. She'd come to the realization, odd as it might be, that Jack had a lot in common with her secret storeroom. They were parts of her life she wanted, but was afraid to fight for. She'd tried selling her lingerie legitimately, but when told no, she'd quietly accepted the decision. She'd tried to take a chance on Jack, but when things got sticky—Ben's confrontation—she'd darted back to safety.

Not anymore.

And when Jack's job called him to risk everything, *if* he eventually left her and Baxter behind, she wouldn't be able to hold back her worry and grief, but she'd stay strong. And survive.

She snagged her keys from the hook by the door. She was standing up to her family, to Jack, and to the town council.

As she locked the door behind her, she decided she might as well present the council with her proposal to sell lingerie in her shop. Searching through her purse, she pulled out the completed forms and shoved them in her back pocket.

Look out Baxter. Skyler Kimball, Rebel In Training, is on the loose!

JACK LEANED against the ladder truck, staring out across the packed fairgrounds but seeing none of the Fourth of July revelry.

He saw the guilt and anger in Skyler's azure eyes.

It's not serious, anyway. He heard the words over and over in his mind.

A swamp rat from St. Francis, Louisiana, wasn't much, he knew, but he'd come so far since his bouncer days. He'd saved buildings and lives. He'd earned the respect of his captain. He'd been accepted by the town council.

Why wasn't that enough for her?

"Come on, Jack," Steve Kimball said, punching him lightly in the stomach. "It'll be a blast."

He glanced at Skyler's brother, then looked away. Their eyes were too alike. "No, thanks. I worked a double shift. I'm goin' to bed after the fireworks."

"Ah, man. You're gonna miss a great party."

Jack worked up a half smile. "There'll be others." Though he couldn't imagine a time when he'd feel like celebrating. If Skyler didn't want him, if she was *embarrassed* by him, he just wanted out. He didn't want to care about her. He didn't want to be distracted by her.

But, dammit, she had a point. He'd never pretended to want forever. He wanted big city fires and big city excitement. He didn't want things to get serious between him and Skyler. But they had.

And he had no idea what to do about *what* he'd always wanted. And *who* he desired.

"How's it going?" Wes said as he walked through the emergency services tent where Jack and Steve were stationed to treat minor injuries and ailments for the festival. So far, their skills had been tested only by three kids with nausea from eating too much cotton candy and four cases of heat exhaustion. But lack of business was a good thing in their line of work.

"We've got three hundred signatures for our petition to redecorate the firehouse," Steve said, motioning toward the clipboard they had set up on a folding table.

Stopping beside the truck, Wes hooked his thumbs around his gun belt. "That ought to get the mayor's attention. That place looks like it hasn't been updated in ten years."

"It's closer to twenty. Have you sat in that Naugahyde recliner in the den?" Steve handed his brother the pen. "Sign."

After Wes had added his signature, he looked up at Jack. "Can I talk to you a minute?"

Jack hadn't spoken to the lieutenant since the night of his emergency, but he'd suspected that silence wouldn't last. No doubt Ben had told him about his relationship with Skyler, and Wes probably had no intention of accepting the truth gracefully. "Sure," he said. In his present mood, a fight would probably do him good.

As if sensing the need for privacy—or maybe it was the willowy brunette strolling toward the truck—Steve tucked the clipboard under his arm and headed in her direction.

Wes rubbed his jaw and contemplated Jack out of his Kimball blue eyes. "I just wanted to say thanks."

In the process of tensing for another round with the lawman, Jack angled his head in confusion. "You what?"

"For the other night. If you and Skyler hadn't found me first..." He trailed off, and Jack had no trouble picturing the snickers Wes would have endured, probably forever, from friends and strangers alike. "It was decent of you. Especially since we haven't exactly gotten along."

"You're welcome," Jack said simply, wondering if he and Wes might actually form a permanent truce—especially since they wouldn't be butting heads over Skyler anymore.

"And I wanted to give you my blessing to see Skyler."

His flabber was definitely gasted. "You're kidding."

"No." Wes paced in front of him. "Look, I know I was a jerk about you two, but, well, I've been protecting her so long, I don't know how not to. I love my sister, Jack, and I didn't want to see her hurt. She freaks out all the time about my job, about Steve and Ben making calls, and I didn't think a fireman was the best choice for her."

Jack crossed his arms over his chest. "She's a grown woman. I doubt she needs you to make her choices."

"Maybe so." He sighed. "Like I should be giving advice. I've got *two* women pissed off at me."

Jack was amused to see that he seemed completely baffled at how he'd wound up in that position. "Have you talked to Monica?"

Wes shrugged. "I apologized to her answering machine." Not the best route to make amends, but who was he to criticize? What had he done to fix things with Skyler? Nothing but be miserable. "Thanks for the encouragement with Skyler, but we broke up."

Wes halted in his tracks. "When?"

"That same night."

"Because of me?"

"In a way." *You're leaving,* she'd said. No, she'd *accused.* "But not really."

Wes tunneled his hand through his hair. "Ah, man, I'm sorry."

Jack waved away the apology. "I'm not blaming you. It's nobody's fault. It just wasn't meant to be."

"What happened?"

Though Jack didn't really feel like rehashing the whole thing, he did, hoping to purge the moment from his mind. He recounted the conversation between Ben and Skyler, then him and Skyler.

"That's it?" Wes asked when he finished. He shook his head. "You guys have nothing on mine and Monica's drama."

"And that's a *bad* thing?"

Wes shrugged. "Probably not. That makeup gave me a rash."

Jack waved to a couple of kids who were running their hands along the side of the truck in fascination. "It doesn't matter anyway," he said to Wes. "I don't belong with her."

Wes's eyes narrowed. "What's wrong with her?"

"Not with her. With me. You investigated my background. You know where I come from. I'm 'Wild Jack.' She's a fallen hero's angelic daughter."

To his surprise, Wes burst out laughing. "When she's not wild as a buck."

Of course Skyler had a wild side. The lingerie, her friends. Her...taking a chance on him, he realized. When her family clearly hadn't understood her risk on a firefighter. On a backwater bouncer. On a man who hadn't thought he deserved someone like her.

You're a true hero.

And he suddenly knew those words were true. He didn't need to find his self-worth in his job, in Atlanta, or anywhere else. He had it in Skyler.

Wes rocked back on his heels, looking just as determined as the first time he'd confronted Jack about his sister. "You need to talk to her. She doesn't care anything about your past, or where you come from. She's crazy about you."

Jack absorbed this with a grunt. His shoulder devil smiled.

The truth was pounding against him, demanding recognition. He'd let his insecurities rule his actions. The stabbing pain of her denying their relationship to Ben had clouded his judgment.

"I think she's really fallen for you, man," Wes put in. "When Ben and the others burst into the room and she leaned against you..." He cleared his throat and looked away as if uncomfortable. "Well, you should have seen the look on her face. I've never seen her look at anyone like that."

The moments he'd shared with Skyler slid through his mind like a projector on fast forward. Her watching him during the band meetings, her sliding into his arms in his Jeep, her pink cheeks as she'd admitted *he* caused her fainting, her in those leather pants.

You're a true hero. If she could believe it, so could he.

"A man's pride can be a dangerous thing," he said slowly.

Wes held up his hands. "Hey, man, you're preachin' to the choir."

Grinning, Jack stuck out his hand, and Wes shook it. "I'm not giving up your sister."

"Glad to hear it."

"I work till four, then I have to help the band set up."

"I'll buy the beer."

"HEY, I TOOK A CHANCE on a man, and look where it got me."

Skyler eyed her best friend from across the table in the wine tasting tent. "You're a bad example. You and Wes are all wrong for each other."

"No kidding. I'm through with cops." Monica gestured with her wineglass. "How are firemen?"

"What do you mean 'how are firemen'? How are they at what?"

Monica rolled her eyes. "At bowling. What do you think I mean?"

Of course she meant sex. But the lingering sadness in her friend's eyes kept her from making a sharp retort. "They're loyal." *And they follow through.* She'd learned Wes and Monica hadn't exactly gotten around to the intimate stuff.

"There's a plus."

Skyler bit her lip, wondering how to help her friend. Monica was the reason she had yet to talk to Jack. After running errands for the festival committee, she'd rushed to the fairgrounds, only to spot Monica staring at the children riding the merry-go-round. They'd shopped, chatted with friends, eaten candied apples, ridden two roller coasters and the Ferris wheel before ending up here. And she still didn't really know what was bothering her. It wasn't the breakup with Wes. There was more.

"Did you really love him?" she asked.

Monica blinked. "Who?"

"Wes."

"God, no. I *way* overreacted the other night. I mean, we weren't even exclusive."

"Then what's up?"

Monica stared into the distance for several minutes. "I don't think I'm cut out for a long-term relationship."

Skyler laid her hand over her friend's. "Of course you are. You'll find someone."

"And live happily ever after?" Monica laughed harshly. "I don't think so."

Skyler knew Monica's parents had divorced when she was a child, and the aftermath hadn't been pretty. She prayed that experience hadn't colored her belief in true love. Of course, she didn't have much experience herself. The man she lo—really, really *liked* didn't want her. At least not enough.

"Hey, gals."

Skyler looked up to see Fiona approaching the table. "Hey, yourself. Join us."

Fiona set down her glass of dark red wine, which coordinated nicely with her burgundy-black lipstick and long black sheath dress, and slid into a chair.

Her appearance gave Skyler a pang of guilt. The application for adding the lingerie to her inventory lay in her purse, awaiting the moment she saw the mayor. She hoped he wouldn't blow a gasket and demand she forget such a controversial idea, leaving her and Fiona unemployed. But she'd gotten to know her assistant pretty well in the last month, and she suspected Fiona would support her decision.

They all chatted a while, agreeing that Skyler's cheating brother was no good for Monica, and all vowing to find the perfect man for the flamboyant, volatile redhead.

They were laughing over the list of potential suitors when Skyler heard the mayor's voice booming from the direction of the stage. She turned her head to see Mayor Collins decked out in full Elvis Vegas-style regalia. Plucking at her red tank top with sparkly stars scattered across the front, she wondered how the man survived polyester and a cape in this heat.

"We'll be starting our entertainment momentarily with an opening song by Baxter's own music sensation…The Metal Heads."

Cheers, whistles and girly squeals followed this announcement.

The Metal Heads had *fans?* Good grief, when did that happen? Had their debut at the bar been that big of a hit?

Leaning back, she sipped her wine. What a wonder Jack was.

Jack!

She straightened so quickly she sloshed wine over the rim of her glass. He'd be with the band. She squinted in the distance, across the main walkway, straining for a glimpse of him. He'd probably be wearing his uniform—the red polo with black pants. God, he looked good in clothes. He looked even better out of them.

Then she spotted him. He stood at the back of the stage, lifting a huge speaker. What muscles. What strength. What a man. She fanned her face. Her pulse fluttered. Half a glass of wine had already gone to her head. Or maybe it was Jack who'd gone to her head…and her heart.

Monica nudged her with her foot. "What's with you? You got all dreamy-looking suddenly."

"I, uh, just—"

"Cajun firefighter at ten o'clock," Fiona broke in. "He's wearing the red polo. Somebody catch her if she faints."

Skyler straightened her shoulders. "I'm absolutely *not* going to faint."

Fiona and Monica exchanged a look. "Right," they said together.

Skyler rose. "I have something I have to do. I'll see you guys later."

"I saw his motorcycle parked at the gate," Monica said with a devilish look in her eyes. "No back seat, you know. The ladder truck's got more room."

Her face burning like the July sun, Skyler leaned close to her friend. "We're not going to have sex. We're going to talk." She straightened and stared wistfully at the side of the stage, where Jack was talking to Masher. "If he'll speak to me."

"If he'll speak to you?" Fiona repeated, her voice rising with alarm. "Why wouldn't he? What's going on? I *knew* you were acting weird yesterday."

Skyler forced herself to smile. She hadn't shared her and Jack's breakup with anybody. Monica had her own relationship to deal with, and voicing the awful moment when Jack had turned away from her the night of "That Incident" would have made everything too real. She still clung ridiculously to the hope that she could make him want her again. Was that happily ever after in her future?

"We just had a misunderstanding," she said to Fiona and Monica, who stared back at her suspiciously. "I'll see y'all later."

She started toward the stage, working her way through the crowds of festival attendees, knowing Monica was safe in Fiona's hands. She nervously smoothed the folds in her denim miniskirt. Jack had looked at her with such hunger in his eyes the night she'd worn it to The Corner Pub. Maybe he'd remember that night. Maybe he'd remember the rebel she'd started to become.

Closing her eyes, she could almost smell him, nearly feel the sensation of running her hand down his muscled chest. She had to find a way to make him understand how much she lo—

Liked him. How much she really, really liked him.

As she stepped over a tangle of electrical cords and past a guitar leaning against the stage, she heard his voice.

"Nothing's wrong, Masher. I just worked a double shift. I'm tired."

"You look sad," Masher said, sounding insistent, his head angled as he faced Jack, whose back was turned to Skyler.

"Pas du tout," Jack returned.

Masher looked even more confused, but Skyler had spent the last few days with a Cajun-French dictionary, and she knew how the common expression translated. It seemed as good an opportunity as any to intrude.

"He means *not at all*," she said quietly, stepping forward, bracing herself.

Jack whirled. For a moment, pleasure and hope lit his eyes as if he saw something he wanted desperately, but wasn't sure he could have. Did he want her? Or was she just projecting her own need?

Since he said nothing, she swallowed the fear bubbling its way up her throat and addressed Masher. "Everybody's thrilled about your performance." She grinned. "You even have some groupies out there."

Masher glanced from her to Jack then back. "We owe it all to Jack."

Skyler shifted her gaze to Jack. Her stomach fluttered and sweat rolled down her back, but she met his gaze boldly. "Yes, I'm sure you do."

"I gotta tune my guitar," Masher said, backing away. He couldn't possibly miss the tension shooting through the humid air. "I'll see you guys later." Grabbing his instrument, he rushed off.

Skyler was left alone with Jack—well, as alone as anyone could be in the middle of a festival attended by most of the town. They stood barely five feet apart, but the distance felt like a mile. His gaze never budged from hers. She started trembling from deep inside and couldn't seem to stop. She wanted so desperately to touch him, to have him hold her. But she suddenly didn't know where to begin. How did she reach him?

"Come here," he said quietly.

She took two steps, then she was in his arms.

She inhaled the spicy scent of him, the familiar warmth and hardness of his chest, and she finally breathed a sigh of relief. She hadn't been entirely sure she'd ever feel this acceptance, this sense of completion again. "I'm so sorry," she said against his throat. "I didn't mean to hurt you. I was just so confused and scared—"

"Me, too." He pulled her tight against him. "Thank you for trying to protect me."

She shook her head. "I was protecting myself. Your job, your motorcycle…your kiss—they were all too dangerous for me. I was so afraid of caring too much about you." She smiled ruefully. "In case you haven't noticed, I'm a worrier."

He raised one eyebrow sarcastically. "Really?"

"But I'm not going to be afraid anymore." She paused, realizing that wasn't a possibility. She would never forget the loss of her father, but she couldn't let tragedy keep her from living. "That's not really true. I'll worry. But I won't let my fears keep me from you." She stared directly into his whiskey-colored eyes. "I won't push you away again."

He leaned close and kissed her, his lips moving over hers in slow deliberation, as if he wanted to absorb the taste of her deep inside and hold her there forever. When he lifted his head, his eyes reflected tenderness and hunger. Her heartbeat doubled its speed. Three whole days had passed since he'd touched her, since she'd felt the heat of his body, the racing of her blood.

"As soon as I finished setting up, I was coming to find you."

A warm rush of pleasure flooded her. "You were?"

He nodded, his expression suddenly serious. "I realized something important today, too." He drew a deep breath, looked away, then back. "I deserve you."

Skyler angled her head. *He what?* "Of course you do. Why in the world—"

He laid his finger over her lips. "From the first moment I saw you, you reminded me of an angel. A pure angel with golden hair, big blue eyes and innocence radiating all around."

"Oh, please," she said automatically, but then she remembered the night of The Metal Heads' debut, when she'd heard that song about angels and questioned him about corrupting her. She didn't realize at the time the meaning went deeper. He'd cast her in the role of angel, while he was Wild Jack.

Even heroes had insecurities.

"You're the daughter of a town hero. Your brothers are revered in the community. You own a shop that sells frilly dresses."

And naughty lingerie she wanted to add, but she could tell this confession was hard for him, and she didn't want to interrupt.

"You were pampered and protected by your family all your life. My upbringing was a bit more colorful, on the dark side even. I was raised in a bar. I broke up fights for a living until I trained as a fireman. My parents barely acknowledged me."

Skyler couldn't stand to see that lost look in his eyes, and they'd talked a lot about his parents this week, so she couldn't let that point pass without comment. "They're committed to their causes." Though she'd like to give them a swift kick for not noticing their son was the best cause in the world. "That doesn't mean they don't love you."

He smiled, and all the lingering sadness was gone. "I know that now. Thanks to you. I've worked a long time to put my past behind me. I worried I'd never be the kind of man who was good enough for someone like you."

Her heart swelled, and tears flooded her eyes. "But you are."

"Yes, I am."

"Hey, Jack, where does this plug in?" K.C. held up a thick orange extension cord.

"Damn." Jack tightened his hold on her. "I gotta set this up."

"I'm not going anywhere." She prayed *he* wouldn't, but didn't want to bring up the subject of his leaving again. The possibility would loom in their relationship, but she wouldn't let it rule her life.

She helped with the setup, all the while desire coiled tighter and tighter in her belly. Sweat trickled down Jack's face from the afternoon heat. His forearms bulged as he lifted speakers, microphones and drum kits. She had to sit down four times from dizziness. Of course, Jack raced to her side to check on her, smiling secretly when he learned she was lightheaded.

The concert went off without a hitch. Children and adults danced, some sang along, some spread blankets in the shade and ate barbecue. The Metal Heads were a hit, and would no doubt get the key to the city after their touching patriotic rendition of "God Bless America."

As the sun set and the band launched into a ballad, Skyler lay on a blanket Jack borrowed from the fire truck, her head resting on his lap.

"This song would be a lot more romantic, *chère,* if you'd move your head three inches to the right."

Skyler laughed and did so, feeling a hard ridge of male flesh beneath her head. Her own body quivered with sexual awareness. As much as his uniform turned her on, she couldn't wait to strip it off him. "Why are we still here?"

"The fireworks. I gotta supervise."

She groaned and slid her hand up his chest, curling her fingertips against the back of his neck, pulling him close. "How much longer?"

He pressed his lips to hers briefly, then, with regret in his eyes, straightened. "An hour or so."

She sat up, sliding her bottom into his lap. "Where'd you go?"

He stroked her cheek. "If I start kissing you now, I won't stop. You make me want to forget responsibility."

"Break it up, you two." Ben knelt next to them. "Jack is working here."

Skyler giggled. Jack moaned.

But they rose and headed with Ben to the area where the fireworks would be shot off. They chatted easily as they walked, and Skyler smiled at the amicability. Jack was accepted by her family in a way no other man ever had. Because they understood how much he meant to her.

How much she lo—

She shook the thought away, but the emotion refused to budge.

Someone had moved the ladder truck to the fireworks area, so she leaned against it as Jack and the others made preparations for the finale to the festival. They'd set up the big pyrotechnic cannons to shoot high over the park across the street from her shop, the same park where she and Jack had first met. She hoped Roland had Fluffy locked up tight.

As the first shower of colors lit the darkened sky,

Jack slid behind her, wrapping his arms around her waist. "Does Fiona have a key to the shop?" he whispered in her ear.

"Yes, why?"

"'Cause she'll have to run things tomorrow." He bit her ear, sending shivers of desire down her spine. "I'm not letting you out of bed."

"Mmm. Sounds great."

"How's the cookie jar?"

"Hey, man! I wanna shoot one of those things!"

Skyler glared in the direction of the obnoxious voice—and saw some drunken idiot trying to drive his pickup truck over the curb. Waving his hand and leaning out the window, he couldn't possibly see where he was going.

Jack took two steps toward the commotion. "I'll be right back."

As he moved, though, Wes appeared next to the truck, shouting for the driver to cut the engine. The fool gunned the gas instead. The truck surged over the curb, and Skyler's heart jumped into her throat just as Wes leapt out of the way. The pickup slammed into the truck holding one of the fireworks cannons, rocking it dangerously from side to side.

Jack, Skyler and several others raced toward the truck, but an explosive shot from the cannon before anyone had moved more than a few feet. People screamed. The missile shot low across the field, barely missing the carousel, heading toward the park, leaving a red trail of fire in its wake.

The entire town seemed to collectively hold its breath for a split second. Then glass shattered. A loud explosion reverberated through the air. Smoke billowed toward the sky.

"It hit a building across the street!" she heard Ben yell.

My shop.

She bolted in that direction, only to be grabbed from behind.

"Stay here, Skyler," Jack said, spinning her to face him.

"My shop!"

"I know, but you have to let us handle it."

"Jack, let's go!" Ben shouted as the ladder truck's engine and sirens sprang to life.

Skyler stared at Jack. He was leaving to fight the blaze. He was racing headfirst into danger. She knew his job required it, but to see him leaving…she shuddered. Her worst nightmare was coming true. Ben and Steve and probably Wes were going, too. The heat and smoke would surround them…engulf them. And she knew she couldn't let him go without admitting the truth—to him, to herself.

"Don't go, Jack. Please."

He placed a quick kiss on her lips. "Don't worry, *chère.* I'll be careful."

When he turned away, she clung to his hand. "No, please. I—" A maelstrom of emotions assaulted her. Fear, regret, even hope. She tried to blink back the tears in her eyes, but one fell anyway. As the warm liquid rolled down her cheek, she squeezed his hand. "I love you."

She hardly had time to acknowledge the stunned expression that crossed his face before Wes grabbed his arm and pulled him into the truck.

11

SHE LOVES ME.

Skyler's confession echoed through Jack's head even as he threw on his gear within the confines of the truck crammed with firefighters and equipment. He knew he should concentrate on his job, but he couldn't help reveling in the thrill pulsing through his veins. Shouldn't he feel panicked? Shouldn't he be worried about how this was going to affect his future? Shouldn't he examine how he felt about her?

"Those shops share walls, guys," Ben said from the front passenger's seat, drawing Jack's attention to the more immediate problem. "We need to set up some preventative efforts to keep from losing the whole block."

The driver ran the light at Main Street, and they braced themselves for the turn.

"I got crowd control," Wes said, yanking a walkie-talkie off his belt.

As he muttered communications to his men, Jack dropped his helmet on his head, running the scene protocol through his mind. While it was unlikely anybody would be in the stores this time of night—

"The animals," he said softly.

"What's that, Jack?" Ben asked, craning his neck to look at him.

"The pet store is right there. Aren't they kept in cages at night?"

The men around him grew still and silent. They exchanged glances, each one understanding the possibility that this could get much worse, very quickly.

"Steve," Ben ordered, "I want you in charge of civilian assistance. Most of the volunteers are probably around. Find them."

"Yes, sir."

"Paul and Jim, I want you at the hoses. Jack, you're with me."

Jack had barely registered the order before the truck screeched to a stop, and they flung open the doors.

Smoke billowed from the front window of the pet shop.

Ben charged forward, with Jack just behind him. They pulled their masks over their faces and engaged the oxygen. Too many precious seconds seemed to tick by as the hose was hooked to the fire hydrant. The sound of barking dogs filled the air.

Better than silence.

As a stream of water shot through the window, Jack slammed his ax into the front door. With his shoulder, he forced the door open. Smoke filled the air, but as he moved toward the heat, he could see the flaming path the wild firework had made. A blackened streak marred the countertop, and a flame-tipped hole burned in the wall separating the pet store from Skyler's shop.

"Shift that hose to the left," he said into his communicator, his heart pounding as he strained to see the damage to Skyler's shop. "And get a team into the shop next door."

He and Ben trudged forward over broken glass and smoldering wood as the ceiling sprinkler system spat water on them, and the fire hose fought to douse the flames through the window. Their quick response had no doubt saved the buildings from extreme damage.

At the moment, though, the animals' lives were their biggest concern.

"The cages are toward the back," he said to Ben.

Now Jack could hear kittens crying and birds squawking. He squinted through the smoke and saw steel cages lining the walls. Dropping the ax, he flipped the latches of as many as he could reach. In seconds, tiny claws had attached themselves to his thick gloves. One particularly nimble kitten raced up his arm, perching on his shoulder. Two clung to his pant legs.

He glanced at Ben and saw his captain grab an armful of golden retriever puppies. They yipped and shook. "I'm heading out," Ben said. He stopped suddenly, shaking his head. "Hell, I think somebody peed."

Jack smiled as a deep *woof* resounded from the back wall. Jack headed toward the sound. A giant St. Bernard with soulful eyes determinedly pawed his wire cage. When Jack flipped open the latch, the dog lumbered out, gazing up at Jack as if bored and wondering what all the commotion was about. Jack shooed him toward the back door, where Skyler and Roland were gathering puppies from Ben. "Go on, boy."

The dog broke into an easy trot, but then, just as Ben turned to head back into the shop, the two collided.

Ben flopped headfirst over the enormous dog, his helmet sailing off, his head striking the concrete.

As Jack charged toward them, Skyler dropped to her knees beside her brother. "Ben!" she shouted into his face.

The dog licked his cheeks.

His pulse racing, Jack threw off his helmet and mask, but when he reached out to check Ben's head for injuries, his eyes flew open.

Pupils round as saucers, he stared at the panting, drooling face inches from his face. "What the hell?"

Wedging his body between the dog and Ben, Jack completed his examination of the captain's head, finding it damp, but not with blood. With dog drool.

His heart finally settled into a normal rhythm. "Can you sit up?" he asked Ben.

"As long as that monster backs up."

Jack and Skyler exchanged a smile, and Skyler plucked the clinging kittens from his body. She loves me, he thought in wonder, wishing this nightmare would end so he could concentrate on the dream wavering before his eyes.

But Roland and Steve rushed forward. The pet store owner took charge of the dog, while Steve and Jack helped Ben to his feet.

He sagged against them. "I don't feel so hot."

"Probably a concussion," Jack said.

"Gonna have a hell of a headache," Steve added.

"Let's get him to the ambulance," Jack said as he and Steve half guided, half carried Ben from the shop.

"Not going to the hospital," Ben said, glaring at Jack, then frowning. "Why are there three of you, Tesson?"

When they reached the street, a pair of firefighters

rushed forward with a stretcher. As they lifted Ben, the captain's eyes suddenly cleared. He exchanged a look with his brother, then met Jack's gaze. "This is your scene, Jack."

"My—"

He stared at Ben, then glanced at Steve, who was smiling at him. Acceptance in his eyes.

Steve was higher ranked. He should take over. But Ben wanted Jack. They both did.

Emotions crowded his heart that he couldn't possibly give voice to, so he simply nodded. "Yes, sir."

As the techs rolled the stretcher carrying Ben away, Jack took in the scene.

The hose team began to retreat from the building, so thankfully the fire appeared out, but smoke inhalation was still a grave danger. Crowds had gathered along the sidewalk. Wes and his men were directing the sparse traffic and setting up barricades around the block. Several volunteers stood next to Jack, waiting for orders. Steve stood to the side, talking intensely with one of the guys. As a tepid breeze slid across his face, he approached the culmination of years of determination and hard work with pride.

"Let's get the rest of the animals," Jack said, his voice firm and commanding.

As the men started off, Steve and his distinguished-looking companion strode forward. The man shook Jack's hand. "Chris Martin, Atlanta Fire Department. I've been visiting my sister here in Baxter. I'd like to help."

"Jack Tesson. We appreciate it," he said, spinning away to enter the shop. The ceiling at the back left had collapsed, the floor between the shops was singed and blackened from the impact of the firework, but the fire was down to a smolder, and the damage—other than the wall—seemed to be contained to the pet shop.

Working quickly, the men opened cages, carrying armloads of dogs and cats to the triage area across the street. Roland volunteered the St. Bernard—Bernie—as help, and the dog turned out to have quite an impact, sniffing out a family of kittens sleeping in a crate. He even personally carried the mother cat out by the scruff of her neck.

They unplugged the fish tanks and carried them out in two-man teams to the pump truck, where Jack had ordered huge commercial extension cords attached to the generator. Only once did he experience a moment of full-on panic. When he heard a voice crying from the storeroom.

Bursting inside, he and Steve discovered not a person, but a blue and yellow macaw on a perch who was none too pleased at the idea of having his feathers roasted. He bit and pecked everyone who came near him, though, and wound up waddling out the door on his little bird legs, squawking cusswords the whole way.

Jack grabbed a pair of basset hounds and followed Chris and the boa constrictor he was carrying out of the shop. That was everything. He stepped outside to hand off the dogs. The smiling elderly woman he passed them to told him they'd just announced Ben Kimball had been reluctantly released from the hospital with a mild concussion, and he was on his way back to the scene.

Pulling off his mask, Jack marveled at Ben's stubbornness. "Runs in the family," he muttered his gaze locking on Skyler, who sat on the curb, the family of

cats Bernie had saved sleeping in her lap. He wanted
to go to her, to hold her, to share the relief with her,
but his brain buzzed with adrenaline and confusion.
What would he say? What did he feel? He couldn't
let her confession of love pass without comment. He
wanted the moment to be right. He wanted to give
her the emotion she deserved.

Everything he'd thought he wanted had changed
since meeting Skyler. He'd come to Baxter to use the
experience as a stepping-stone to bigger things. He'd
wanted to earn and deserve the respect of his captain
and his colleagues. But he'd realized today he only
needed respect for himself. To accept himself. He
didn't really care what anybody else thought. He
knew what *he* thought. And he knew what Skyler
thought. And he knew he was crazy about this crazy
town.

Smiling—either from relief or the utter ridiculous-
ness of the scene—he looked up and down the street.
Residents, police, fire and city officials alike were
holding, stroking and soothing animals. Roland held
Fluffy in his arms, trying to fit an oxygen mask over
her furry face. The mayor, surrounded by his wife and
members of the city council, shook Bernie's paw, his
face serious as anyone could be wearing rhinestone-
studded polyester, the dog looking resigned. The
Metal Heads had obviously adopted the macaw, who
was perched on K.C.'s drumstick, whistling "Hard
Day's Night."

Deciding everything was under control for the moment and giving in to the urge to save Bernie, he
headed toward Mayor Collins. "Good evening, sir.
I'd like to borrow Bernie for a moment, if you don't
mind. We need to make a final pass."

The mayor puffed out his chest. "Of course. Good job here, Jack."

"Thank you, sir." Jack snapped his fingers, and the dog trotted to his side, looking up at Jack with his solemn brown eyes. Despite his collision with Ben, he really liked the dog. He wondered if the animal was part of Roland's personal collection, or if he was for sale. Every firehouse needed a dog.

As he walked away, Bernie lumbering at his side, the mayor, his wife and the council members followed them. "We should probably assess the damage personally," the mayor said. "City property and all."

Jack noticed the festival photographer hovering behind the city's leader, and decided they could both come in handy for testimony when the city sued that idiot truck driver blind. "Stay to the right. The damage is mostly on the back left side."

They entered the still-smoldering shop with shuffling steps, as if they were nervous about disturbing the eeriness of the scene. Poor Roland. He would have so much rebuilding to do.

"Need any help?"

Jack whirled at the sound of Skyler's soft voice. His heart pounded at the sight of her, her proximity to his body. He wanted so much to touch her, breathe her in. He probably smelled like smoke and dogs and sweat, and looked even worse, but she smiled at him, her eyes soft with relief.

And he knew he loved her.

It was the oddest thing. One moment his heart was confused and troubled; the next everything was clear. If he was completely honest with himself, he had to admit he'd fallen in love with her the first moment he'd seen her in that tree in the park, trying to save

Fluffy. Or maybe it was two minutes ago, when he'd watched her sitting on the curb with the cat family. Then again, maybe it was the moment he'd spotted her purple lace panties....

Stripping off his gloves, he held out his hand. In an instant, she was beside him, touching him. "Still want to raid that cookie jar later?" he said against her ear, wishing they were alone and he could say more.

She slid her arm around his waist and hugged him. "Absolutely."

"The damage looks extensive," Mayor Collins remarked, completely oblivious to the sparks between Jack and Skyler. "The wall between the shops will have to be rebuilt."

"It's a miracle the fire didn't spread to Skyler's shop," Deacon Jones, one of the council members, said.

Since he was busy staring at Skyler, Jack barely heard the exchange. But the words *Skyler's shop* finally penetrated his brain. Still holding tight to her waist, he glanced in the direction the mayor and the others were staring. The charred hole where the firework had impacted measured approximately five feet by eight feet. Through the damaged wall, Jack could just make out sopping wet boxes on the floor, the mirrored back wall and curtained dressing rooms.

"We'll fix everything," he said, looking back at Skyler.

Her gaze was fixed on the hole.

Bernie woofed, straining against his collar. Jack let the dog go, concerned by the expression on Skyler's face. She was pale, in shock.

"Ben's okay," he said, suddenly wondering if

someone had bothered to tell her about her brother's
condition.

She didn't move or acknowledge him.

"I'm okay."

She nodded once.

"The animals are okay."

"I know."

"I love you."

That got a response. Her head whipped toward him.
"You do?"

He smiled. *"Oui."*

"Say it again."

"I love you."

She threw herself into his arms, clinging to him as
if she never planned to let him go. Even through his
fireproof jacket, he could feel the quick beat of her
heart against his chest. He inhaled her smoky, flowery
fragrance, knowing he'd never tire of the smell of her,
the taste of her, the sound of her.

"Uh, hate to break this up," the mayor began, forcing them to look at him. "But what the hell is this?"

He laid a black satin thong in Jack's hand. A *wet*
black satin thong.

Jack glanced from the panties to the mayor, to the
mayor's wife, to the semicircle of council members,
then finally to Skyler.

"Uh-oh," she said.

SKYLER HELD Jack's gaze, realizing where the dog
had unearthed the thong. The hole burned through by
the fire had exposed her secret storage room.

Her heart pounded and, for one really scary moment, she considered stumbling out a ridiculous explanation. "Well, golly, I'd wondered what happened

to those," she blurted out, stumbling and ridiculous as she grabbed the panties from Jack.

At the same moment the mayor's wife reached for them.

They engaged in a brief tug-of-war, which stretched the panties right before the mayor and the various city council member's eyes, revealing every satiny, risqué detail, including the red rhinestone heart at the top of the thin strap in the back.

Then a familiar voice asked, "How's the damage?"

At Ben's voice, Skyler let go of the panties, which snapped back and slapped the First Lady across the face.

Mrs. Markenson and the deacon gasped, and, wincing, Skyler turned to see Roland stroll into the room. Behind him, Wes and Steve carried Ben each holding one of his arms.

In addition to being impulsive, the Kimballs also had lousy timing.

Though she was thrilled to see Ben vertical, Skyler hadn't planned on quite this explosive of an entry into the world of retail lingerie. But as she was fighting to swallow her fear, Jack squeezed her hand.

She met his gaze and saw the love and support she needed.

Reaching into the back pocket of her skirt, she handed the mayor the folded slip of paper. "I guess now's as good a time as any to give you this."

"What's this?"

"An application to add lingerie to my shop's inventory."

The mayor pursed his lips. "I seem to recall us discussing this two years ago, Ms. Kimball. A shop of this nature, in the middle of Main Street, is not the kind of image—"

"Oh, Franklin, wouldn't this just look ravishing on me?"

Everyone turned to stare at Mrs. Collins, who'd obviously discarded the panties and rummaged through the boxes in Skyler's shop. She held a hot pink see-through teddy next to her voluptuous body.

The mayor's eyes nearly bugged out of his head. "*Then again,* a public servant should always be fluid and ready for change in meeting the demands of his citizens. What do you say, fellow council members?"

The men nodded enthusiastically.

The deacon muttered, "Amen, sister."

Only Mrs. Markenson scowled.

The rest of the room's occupants broke into applause.

"When did you decide this?" Jack whispered in her ear.

"This week. I just haven't had time to give the mayor the application. I had to get you back first."

He pulled her into his arms. "Well, you have me back—forever."

Ridiculously hopeful, her heart fluttered. "I do?"

"I hope I'm not interrupting anything."

Skyler turned to see a tall, distinguished-looking man enter the shop.

"Great job, Jack," he said stepping forward to shake Jack's hand. "Evening, everyone," he added, nodding to the crowd.

"Chris Martin is with the Atlanta F.D.," Jack said. "He was a big help tonight."

Chris handed Jack a business card. "I'm a battalion chief in Atlanta."

Surprise flickered across Jack's face. Clearly, he hadn't realized his volunteer was so highly ranked.

"I'd like to talk to you about a job," Chris went on.

Skyler was pretty sure she wasn't breathing. Everything Jack had worked for was suddenly being handed to him. The men in the room stared at him with new respect, the visiting commander wanted him…in Atlanta.

"Call me," Chris said, then turned and waved as he left.

Jack stuck the card in his pocket and received the congratulations and pats on the back from his colleagues with a wan smile. In the confusion, he and Skyler were separated, and she took the opportunity to slip outside.

Her chest hurt. Her throat hurt. She had the feeling she was going to bawl her eyes out at any minute. She sat on the curb, clenching her hands, as if she could hold on to her happiness with that useless gesture.

"Why'd you disappear, *chère?*"

She forced herself to look at Jack as he joined her on the curb. "Congratulations," she said, amazed to find her voice mostly steady. "You've finally got everything you wanted, and deserved."

He captured her hand in his. "I hope so." Leaning toward her, he kissed her gently on the lips. "Marry me."

Her eyes widened. "Do *what?*" She shook her head. "What about Atlanta? The big city job? The excitement? Your career?"

He stroked her hair back from her face, his gaze locked on hers. "You're all the excitement I'll ever need. Baxter is all the city I'll ever need. Everything I want is right here.''

His soot-stained face was never more precious and gorgeous. She saw her future in his eyes. A beautiful, forever kind of future, full of risk and safety.

''Marry me,'' he said again.

She grinned, sliding her hand around his neck. *''Oui.''*

Wendy
Etherington

Hunka Hunka
Burnin' Love

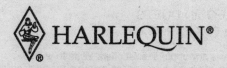

HARLEQUIN®

TORONTO • NEW YORK • LONDON
AMSTERDAM • PARIS • SYDNEY • HAMBURG
STOCKHOLM • ATHENS • TOKYO • MILAN • MADRID
PRAGUE • WARSAW • BUDAPEST • AUCKLAND

Dear Reader,

The inspiration for Monica came as I was writing *Can't Help Falling in Love.* She was one of those secondary characters who just wouldn't stay in the background. No, sirree, Monica is a front-and-center kind of gal. She's the one who always has the perfect comeback to an insult, the wardrobe you covet, and could probably give Mae West a run for her money in the flirting department. But she needed a deep, serious guy to bring out her vulnerabilities and to balance her. And Skyler's overachieving brother Ben was perfect.

I hope you enjoy Monica and Ben's journey to happily-ever-after!

Wendy Etherington

P.S. Don't forget to visit me at www.wendyetherington.com or drop me a line at P.O. Box 211663 Columbia, SC, 29221-1663 and let me know how you liked the book!

Books by Wendy Etherington

HARLEQUIN DUETS
76—MY PLACE OR YOURS?

Don't miss any of our special offers. Write to us at the following address for information on our newest releases.

Harlequin Reader Service
U.S.: 3010 Walden Ave., P.O. Box 1325, Buffalo, NY 14269
Canadian: P.O. Box 609, Fort Erie, Ont. L2A 5X3

To my husband, Keith, a hero every day of the week

1

MONICA O'MALLEY hitched her laptop case on her shoulder as she strode toward the front door of the firehouse. She smoothed the creases from her favorite red power suit and checked for smudges on her leopard-print shoes. "With Dolce and Gabbana accessories, coordinating lipstick and a smile…a girl can accomplish anything."

She considered the importance of the meeting about to take place. The firehouse contract was essential to the bottom line of Designs by Monica. She'd been saving for a house on the lake for years, and now that she'd finally bought property and hired a builder, the pressure was on to keep income incoming, rather than outgoing. Even her shoe budget—the ultimate sacrifice—would have to be cut to make her dream house a reality, but she was determined to put down some roots. Everything in her life seemed temporary—apartments, cars, favorite lipstick shades, even men. Especially men.

Thinking of men naturally led back to her meeting. According to the town council, the contract to redesign the firehouse depended solely on Chief Benjamin Kimball's decision.

Her brows suddenly knit in concern. Maybe she shouldn't have handcuffed his brother to his bedpost, dressed him in lingerie and called the fire department last summer.

Shrugging, she pulled open the front door. Wes had deserved it. The cheating bas—

"Good afternoon," she said, walking into the den where several firefighters lounged on beat-up sofas and recliners. Good grief, was that sofa *Naugahyde?* Yick! These guys *really* needed her help.

The men leapt to their feet, and she recognized a few faces from around town. Their gazes flitted over her face, then zeroed in on her body. Specifically, her legs. They were her best feature, and moments like these kept her in kickboxing class three days a week when she'd rather say the hell with exercise and tuna fish.

"Ma'am," they said, nodding and speaking in unison.

Southern men are just so darn cute! Born and raised in California, she'd never quite gotten used to their innate charm and politeness. When they weren't eating or drinking her bankrupt, wrecking her car or screwing twenty-year-old cocktail waitresses, that is.

That was behind her, though. All men weren't lazy, or wild, or cheats. And if she had to search the whole state of Georgia, she'd damn well prove that theory. What she needed was a nice man, a respectable man. One who oozed sex appeal, one she could knock off his feet the moment they met, and *bam,* she'd get her confidence back.

"I'm Monica O'Malley. I have an appointment with Chief Kimball," she said, then smiled. When she got the contract, she'd be working day to day with these men, so she wanted to establish friendly professionalism from the outset.

"Yes, ma'am, Ms. O'Malley," a beefy, fair-headed guy in the middle said. "This way."

As they walked out of the den, Monica noted the long, Formica-topped bar separating the den from the kitchen was chipped and stained. The kitchen cabinets were dark faux-wood that looked like they were actually made of Formica. The appliances looked rickety and out-of-date. The place looked like it hadn't seen the decent side of fashion since 1972. She resisted the urge to rub her hands together in glee.

Instead, she glanced at the name stitched over the breast pocket of her guide's shirt. "How long have you been a firefighter, Ted?" she asked as they walked down the hall on threadbare gray carpet.

"Three years, ma'am."

"And how do you feel about the idea of redesigning the firehouse?"

He stopped in front of a closed door with a smoky glass panel, his hand gripping the worn, brass knob. Almost shyly, his gaze met hers. "Well, ma'am, the guys and me...we were hopin' for a new PlayStation."

Monica angled her head. "Like video games?"

Ted glanced up and down the hall, then lowered his voice. "Yes, ma'am. It gets kinda boring around here sometimes. The chief usually has us cleanin' everything, but even then we run out of stuff to do."

Monica's gaze darted to the closed door, then back to Ted's face. "And how does the chief feel about your idea?"

Ted winced. "He's not too enthused. You ever met the chief?"

She had, actually. Her best friend Skyler was his sister, so they'd occasionally found themselves at the same social event. But she'd never really gotten to know him, as he always seemed to stand off from the group. She had a vague impression of the strong, silent type. "Briefly," she said to Ted.

"He's very...serious."

That certainly jibed with what Skyler had told her. In preparing for this interview, she'd probed her friend for information about the chief, hoping to gain some insight into ways of impressing him. Skyler had told her that the loss of their father had forced Ben into the role of father figure and family patriarch, even though he'd only been fifteen. And he, like her other two brothers—Wes and Steve—had always felt compelled to live up to the image of their heroic father. Ben probably more than the others.

He'd worked his butt off to get the promotion to chief. Respect and his professional reputation meant everything to him.

Monica focused her attention on Ted. "But if an outsider suggested all work and no play makes for cranky firefighters..."

Relief washed over his face. "A taxpayer, ma'am. Remember you're a taxpayer."

She smiled, knowing this info-gathering conversation had just given her an edge. "I'll do my best."

Ted knocked once on the door, then turned the knob after a brisk "Come in" echoed from inside. "Chief, Ms. O'Malley's here," he said as they walked in the office.

Fire Chief Benjamin Kimball, sitting behind a large wooden desk, looked up.

Monica's heart flipped over in her chest.

She clutched the strap of her laptop case as she stared at him. Of course he looked familiar, yet she had the oddest feeling she was seeing him for the first time.

Why had she never noticed his hair was darker than Wes's? And that the inky black locks waved slightly in the front, as if he had a natural curl he'd tried to tame? Had his eyes always been that remarkable shade of bright blue? And while she recalled having noted the serious assurance of his face before, why had she never noticed his strong jaw and the breadth of his shoulders?

Confidence shimmered all around him. This is why the man ran the fire department, she supposed, but his composure also spoke to her as a woman. Actually, he turned her insides to absolute mush. And she'd never considered herself mush potential.

He's nice, her conscience reminded her. And highly respected. And while he didn't *ooze* sex appeal, he had intensity in spades. *You're on the job,* she tried to remind her libido, but it wasn't listening. She licked her lips as her professional intentions buckled under her womanly needs.

Approaching the desk, she held out her hand as he stood. "Chief Kimball."

He leaned over his desk, then fell on top of it.

Good grief, she hadn't meant to *literally* knock the man off his feet.

"Dammit, Edwin!" The chief pushed himself up and regained his footing as a small man, his glasses knocked askew and his face flushed, appeared from behind the desk.

"Sorry, Chief," he said.

The chief sighed. "Why don't you fix the drawer later?"

Edwin shrugged, then scooped a large metal toolbox off the floor. Monica was tempted to help him, as he didn't look strong enough to carry his own weight, much less the toolbox, but he shifted its weight to rest on his forearms as if he'd done so many times. "Ma'am," he said politely as he shuffled by her.

When she smiled at him, he ground to a halt, staring openmouthed at her.

"Edwin…" the chief began in a warning tone.

Edwin scooted to the door. "I'm going, sir."

Smiling, she turned back to the chief and held out her hand. "Shall we try this again?"

He didn't return her smile, but his gaze met hers directly as they touched. Heat shot through her body, and she watched his eyes widen, just for a moment, as if he felt the same electricity as her. "Ms. O'Malley. Sorry for the interruption. Please have a seat."

She lowered herself into the lone wooden chair in front of his desk and set her case on the floor. Distantly, she heard the door close behind her, and she shivered deliciously at the thought of her and Ben Kimball left alone together.

She shouldn't have been surprised by her attraction to him. Ever since "That Incident" with Wes, she'd avoided close contact with men, as she'd nursed her bruised pride and sensitivity. She couldn't remember the last time she'd flirted with a man, much less touched one in an intimate way.

Shifting uneasily in her chair, she fought for professionalism and distance when what she really wanted to do was plop down on Ben's desk, yank him on top of her by his stark black tie and tear open his perfectly pressed white shirt.

Was it the March blush of spring that stirred her libido? Or just a man in uniform?

The chief tapped a stack of paper straight. "So, Ms. O'Malley, I understand you're interested in the design contract."

Monica resisted the urge to salute and say "Yes, sir"—the man had that kind of effect on a person. "I am."

"Qualifications?"

A knock on the door interrupted her reply. A firefighter walked in, handing a file folder to the chief, while managing to simultaneously stare at Monica. "You said you wanted these time sheets right away," the man said, his gaze still fixed on Monica.

The chief waved the folder. "I'm over here, Andy."

Andy swung to face his boss. "Sir. Yes, sir."

"The time sheets could have waited until after my meeting," the chief said, dropping them on his desk.

Andy cast a glance over his shoulder at Monica. "Yes, sir."

"Dismissed!"

Andy spun on his heel, then darted from the room. Chief Kimball stared after him in disgust, and Monica held back a smile. Apparently, a woman was a rare commodity in the firehouse.

"You were explaining your qualifications," the chief said, leaning back in his chair.

She took a deep breath. "I have both an undergraduate and masters degree from UCLA. I worked for six years at an international design firm in Atlanta, then I branched out on my own three years ago."

"And moved to Baxter."

The confusion in his voice was nothing new. Why

leave the big city and a thriving firm for the sleepy back roads of Baxter? She'd questioned her decision many times herself—especially when she had to make the hour-long commute to Atlanta so often to keep her business afloat—but the moment she'd set foot in Baxter she'd known she was home. The closeness of the community, the slow pace and the history had worked their magic on her tradition-starved senses. She wanted it all—a successful business, access to a big city and a quiet lake house to build permanence on. And she was really close to achieving that dream.

"Even though I do a great deal of business in Atlanta, Baxter is home. When I heard about the planned renovations for the firehouse, naturally I wanted to apply my services."

"You have experience? With firehouses specifically?"

Another knock interrupted her reply as another firefighter entered. This one ambled into the room, glancing at Monica with every other step, before stopping beside the chief's desk. "Just about to start lunch." His round cheeks turning red, he smiled at Monica. "Are we havin' any company?"

"No, Phil, we aren't," the chief said, his face stony. "Go away."

"Are you sure we—"

"Goodbye, Phil. And tell those clowns out there that the next guy who interrupts me washes the windows."

Phil raced out.

"You seem to have attracted quite a bit of attention," the chief said, looking annoyed about it.

From the wrong man, though. She frowned at the chief. She liked attention, had fun attracting attention.

She'd never had trouble engaging a man's interest before. His men noticed her, but Ben looked aggravated, not attracted. *What's wrong with me?*

"They're probably just anxious about the renovations," she said diplomatically, dragging her gaze from his—not an easy task with those sigh-inducing blue eyes. "I do happen to have experience with firehouses." She handed him the recommendation letters from her briefcase.

The first assignment she'd ever completed as a designer had been a firehouse in Palm Beach, California. The fire chief there had given her glowing reviews, and she'd had similar luck with firehouses in Atlanta. She had the degrees and work experience, she thought with a sigh, but what she didn't have was a solution for dealing with a glitch in her plan to find a respectable man. Ben Kimball was perfect, yet he was a potential client, and he hadn't shown an iota of interest in her. *What's wrong with me?*

As he perused the letters in silence, she fidgeted. She swallowed. She noticed a chip in her nail polish.

"Problem, Ms. O'Malley?"

Monica jerked her head up. The chief still had his head bowed over the papers in his hands. Nice, long-fingered, strong-looking hands. "Uh, no."

"You're fidgeting."

His voice was deep, she noted. Slow and measured, with a dreamy Southern drawl. Wow, what a package.

Then his words sank in. He'd noticed her fidgeting. He'd noticed *her.*

That's one iota. Should we try for two?

Anticipation rolled through her as she leaned forward, hopefully close enough for him to catch a whiff of her perfume. "Just a touch uncomfortable. These chairs are…'' She uncrossed, then recrossed her legs, with his gaze glued to the movement. ''A little hard.'' Pausing, she waited for his gaze to meet hers. ''We can work together to change that. A man in your position should have the best.''

''And you're the best,'' he asked slowly.

She smiled. ''Oh, absolutely.''

''Hmm.'' The chief stood, walked around the desk, then leaned back against it. His proximity increased her suspicion that he felt the attraction between them, but he wasn't smiling about it. ''Well, about that— your qualifications, I mean—were those fire departments more interested in your degrees, or your legs?''

Why didn't that sound like a compliment? And why did she have the awful feeling he was implying she'd slept her way through her client list?

The burn of desire turned to anger. She rose, and in her four-inch heels they were nearly eye-to-eye. ''I can assure you, Chief Kimball, none of my clients have ever been intimidated by either.'' She paused, cocking one eyebrow. ''Are you?''

Heat flashed across his eyes. ''This is a firehouse, not a dating pool.

''How dare you suggest such a thing. You don't even know me.''

He glared at her. ''I know who you are.''

Aha. Now we get to it. The Incident. Just how much did he know? Since Skyler had arrived in time to rescue her brother before the fire department could, very few people knew exactly what had happened that night. The rumor mill had snaked around town that she'd handcuffed Wes to the bed and called 9-1-1, but the ''dressed in a merry widow and makeup'' part had been left out.

"This is about Wes," she said finally.

"That incident last summer wasn't your finest moment."

"Trust me, sweetie, it wasn't your brother's either."

They stood almost nose-to-nose, her hands propped on her hips, his crossed over his chest. His really broad chest. And what was that cologne? He smelled crisp and spicy. What layers hid beneath that starched personality? Dammit, she wanted to know.

His gaze fell to her lips, and she nearly groaned. Her stomach trembled; her knees weakened. She seemed to remember being furious at him just a few seconds ago. Where was her anger now? Her righteous indignation?

She drew a deep breath, then let the air escape slowly, hoping to calm her racing heart, but his gaze dropped briefly to her chest. Awareness sizzled in the air. Monica needed desperately to back up, to escape the heat rolling off him, but she had no intention of being the first one to break.

Fortunately, she didn't have to.

The door opened again. But before the chief could launch into a tirade, Monica saw the intruder.

A St. Bernard. A big one. A really big one.

He lumbered toward her, then sat, gazing up at her with adoring brown eyes, drool dripping onto her shoes. She patted his enormous head, hoping the slobber wouldn't stain the leather.

"Good grief," the chief said.

"He's adorable." She smiled at the chief, relieved to have the tension broken. "Yours?"

"Hell, no."

"*Woof!*"

Monica jumped. She braced her hand against the desk, certain the room was vibrating.

"Well, sort of," the chief amended, taking a step back from the dog. "Bernie belongs to the fire department."

"The dog from the festival fire." Monica reached for his collar, running her finger along the gold medal the dog had been given by the mayor for saving several animals in a fire back in July. "What a good boy you are," she said, scratching his side. As Bernie licked her arm, she remembered something else about him, something that explained the chief's lack of enthusiasm. "The one who knocked you out."

The chief rubbed the top of his head, obviously remembering his injury. "He didn't mean to."

Monica glanced at him, wondering if he was trying to convince her, Bernie or himself.

The chief pointed at the door. "Go on, Bernie."

The dog cocked his head, but didn't move.

Stepping back, Monica crossed her arms over her chest. She wanted to see Almighty Chief Kimball move a 150-pound dog single-handedly.

"Go, Bernie!"

The dog lay on the floor, looking up at them out of his solemn brown eyes.

Monica waved Bernie aside. "Let's get back to our meeting." She met the chief's gaze directly, refusing to yield to the anger lingering in the bright blue depths, and wondering how she could be so aware of him, while he simply looked at her as just another irritation to master. "I don't appreciate your insinuations about my personal life."

He was silent a moment, then he nodded. "Understood. I was out of line."

"Can I continue with my proposal?"

He sat on the desk. "Let's hear it."

His tone implied nothing she said would get her the contract, and she wondered whether it was her past relationship with his brother or just *her* that bothered him so much, but she reached for her briefcase anyway. "I have a computer program that gives three-dimensional images of the room to be designed," she explained as she unpacked her laptop, using the edge of his desk as a workstation. "You can program the measurements of the room, and see a blank canvas to begin with. Then, I can scan in wallpaper, paint colors, floor coverings, even accessories."

"Virtual decorating," he said, turning toward her, and she could tell she finally had his attention. Not with her, of course. With the program. Great.

"Sort of." She started the program, then pulled up the initial work she'd done on the firehouse's den. Okay, so it helped to have inside sources. She'd asked Skyler's firefighter husband, Jack, to take rough measurements of the room for her presentation. "It's a wonderful tool for allowing clients to visualize the finished product."

She watched the chief's eyes widen as the room, including the expanded square footage the contractors had recently added, appeared on the laptop screen. She'd transformed it—now that she'd seen the *Brady Bunch* disaster for herself, she knew it truly was a major transformation—into a twenty-first century media room: leather recliners, sofas with drop-down tables and cup holders, surround-sound stereo, TV and DVD player, track lighting and steel-colored carpet.

The chief leaned closer. "It's amazing." Then he shook his head. "We could never afford it."

"While this is only an example, I'll work within your budget, and many of these additions will be possible."

"The guys work hard," he said, as if considering the idea. "They're away from their families a lot. They live here, sleep here, eat here. They deserve a nice place."

She hit another button on the laptop, giving him a bird's-eye view of the room. "Even a PlayStation?"

He turned his head, surprise evident in his eyes. "You've been talking to them."

"A bit. It's their firehouse." She hoped he didn't miss her implication that if his men liked her, if they could work with her, then what was *his* problem?

"There's too much work to justify video games."

"They get breaks, don't they?" she argued. "They watch TV."

"Of course. But they're always setting up tournaments with those ridiculous games. They get so involved I worry I'll have to drag them away to a fire."

"Maybe the games will improve their reflexes."

"I don't see how."

She grinned. "You're lousy at them, aren't you?"

His eyes lit with surprise and frustration just long enough that she realized she'd hit the mark, but he quickly resumed his sober expression. "They're too involved."

Monica shrugged. He was in charge, after all, but she had no intention of giving up. Did he have a problem with *fun?* Nice, respectable men had fun, didn't they? Her past relationships might have ended badly, but at least they'd never been boring. Skyler had said her brother took on too many responsibilities, which made Monica wonder how often he let go and relaxed. The challenge of tempting Ben Kimball made her mouth water.

"Your presentation is certainly impressive," he said, jolting her from her thoughts.

"Thank you."

"But I'm not sure how comfortable I'd be with you working around here."

"Because of your brother," she said, determined to keep the disappointment from her voice. Damn you, Wesley. Either stupidly or wisely, she'd always plunged ahead in life. She cared little what others thought of her, except for the friends and professional colleagues whose respect she'd garnered. But ever since That Incident she'd not only had to endure chuckles and whispers, she'd been plagued by self-doubt. What was it about her that Wes found lacking? Why had he slept with someone else, when he could have had her? *What was wrong with her?*

Ben raised his eyebrows. "We agreed to keep personal lives out of this, remember?"

Relieved, she nodded. If he could keep from frowning or acting like the dry cleaners had overstarched his boxers, Ben Kimball might actually be charming.

"It's the men. They get distracted easily. They'll never get any work done with you around."

Warmth flooded her veins. Her fingers and toes tingled. Desire captured her. Truth be told, *he* had captured her. Her fascination. Her fondness for challenges. Her libido. "And what about you, Chief Kimball? Can you…work around me?"

"I can work around anything." Then his face flushed. "How do you feel about wearing pants?"

As BEN WALKED DOWN the hallway toward Mayor Collins's office at City Hall, an image of That Woman rose, unbidden, before him.

That Woman who'd bewitched his men. That Woman whose exotic scent still lingered in his office. That Woman and her luscious legs.

How he'd survive the next few weeks with her, he had no idea. But out of the three candidates, That Woman, damn her, had come in with the lowest bid, her presentation was the most organized, and she was the only one who'd thought to consult the firefighters, not just him. All of this was in her favor, yet he didn't want her there. She was a loose cannon, obviously temperamental, and then there was that driving-his-men-insane-with-distraction business. Every male in the house—even the dog—was moony-eyed over her. Except him, of course. He wasn't tempted by her *in the least*. Thank God.

She was just a woman, for heaven's sake. A rarity in their firehouse to be sure, but just a distraction from the work to be accomplished.

And she used to date his brother. His dark, brooding, dangerous brother. Even if Ben cared about her beauty, mischievousness and intelligence, she couldn't possibly be interested in him. Not really. She flirted, but obviously not seriously. Not unless she thought he was like Wes. Which he wasn't—in the least.

And because of her, he suddenly regretted moving his office into the firehouse. As chief, he was entitled to a spacious office here at city hall. After the former chief had retired three months ago, Ben thought moving into the firehouse and being a hands-on leader would improve morale. While the volunteers loved their occasional dip into firefighting, the regular employees were bored and unmotivated. He had a lot of young guys, and Atlanta was temptingly close to bigger and better action. He'd lost two guys this year in big city moves, and would have lost Jack, one of his best men and now his brother-in-law, if love hadn't intervened at the right time.

He couldn't very well complain about the lack of business. After all, that was a *good* thing in their line of work. But the fireworks disaster last July had been the biggest event in years. He tried to occupy his men's time with training, drills and charity work, but he could tell their interest was waning. He wanted a crackerjack department. Top-notch. Even better than the legendary team of '83. The team who'd fought the factory fire. The team who'd mourned the loss of their captain. His father.

As he approached the mayor's secretary, he shook aside the past. He'd never get anywhere dwelling on things he couldn't possibly change and legends he'd never live up to.

"He's expecting you, Chief," she said, glancing up briefly. "Go on in."

He opened the door and stood frozen, stunned to find the mayor having a cozy little coffee-and-croissants chat with Monica O'Malley.

They both looked toward the door, and when she smiled, Ben could swear her catlike green eyes glittered with triumph.

He resolutely ignored the tightening of his gut. He was *absolutely not* moved by that sexy smile. Or her sexy scent, so powerful he imagined he could smell her clear across the room. Or her incredible, mile-long, sexy legs. Hell, everything about her screamed sex. Not that he cared. Or noticed. He was the chief.

And acting like a greenhorn high-schooler was not his idea of professionalism. In fact, he couldn't recall acting like a high-schooler when he was in high school.

"Chief. Glad you could make it," the mayor said, rising and indicating the chair next to Monica. "Have a seat."

The mayor's fanaticism with Elvis has finally gone over the edge, was Ben's first thought as he took in his boss's latest getup. Previously fascinated with The King's Vegas style, he'd obviously felt the need for a change of pace. His new dress code resembled Elvis—the early years. Since the mayor was very short and very round, his black leather jacket, black leather pants, greased hair and stick-on black sideburns made him look like a reject from *Grease.*

Ben didn't comment on the fashion faux pas—what gracious comment could he make?—instead he merely nodded, crossed the blue suede carpet, then lowered himself into the chair. "Afternoon, Mayor. Ms. O'Malley," he added with a cool stare in her direction.

"Coffee?" the mayor asked.

"No, thank you. I don't have a lot of time. I thought you wanted to discuss the candidates for the firehouse's design project."

"Oh, of course." The mayor folded his pudgy hands on the desk and gave Monica a fond look. He was known to have a weakness for flashy ladies with bods extraordinaire. He was married to one, in fact.

"Ms. O'Malley and I were just getting to that. I'm sure we can all come to some agreement. Don't you think so, Chief?" Ben didn't have time to comment as the mayor rolled on importantly. "The other candidates weren't up to snuff. The one other gal has just started her business and has no real experience. She was sweet but—'' he smiled conspiratorially at Monica and lowered his voice ''—she was basically clueless. And that guy.'' The mayor rolled his eyes. ''As I recall, he had visions of purple walls and fabrics that cost a hundred dollars a yard.''

Gee, Mayor, why don't we just skip that annoying step in the city council bylaws that states the fire chief has an equal vote in determining vendors affecting his department?

''I assumed we'd make the decision in private, Mayor Collins,'' Ben said, proud he'd kept from grinding his teeth as he spoke. Knowing That Woman was the best choice for the job was entirely different from being told she was.

''Oh, of course. Just let me know who to congratulate, Chief. Remember, it's your decision.''

Monica's gaze bounced between him and the mayor. An odd expression, maybe regret, crossed her face before she rose from her chair. ''I appreciate your confidence in me, Mayor Collins, and your advice has been invaluable. But I'm sure the chief will do what's best for his department. I should let you two get on with your meeting.''

Ben hoped he hid his shock as he watched her walk to the door. Monica O'Malley had an honorable streak beneath her flamboyance?

She's not your type, he reminded himself, firmly reestablishing the miles between them. So it hardly mattered how she acted, what she did, or what she wore. If he awarded her the contract, he'd insist on the ''pants only'' rule for his men's sake, but his day-to-day routine wouldn't be affected. No siree. He wanted the best for the firehouse. If he decided Ms. O'Malley could provide that, she'd win the contract. If not, she'd be out on her curvy—

Wait just a damn second. She'd been cozying up to the mayor when he came in—about the contract surely. Had she suddenly developed a conscience, or had she just been caught?

"I'll be right back, Mayor," Ben said, darting from the room after her.

He caught up with her in the hall. "Just what do you think you were up to in there?" he demanded.

As she turned, her exotic perfume drifted to his nose, bringing to mind warm, tropical breezes and cool satin sheets. "Having coffee," she replied coolly.

"That's not what it looked like to me."

"I ate a croissant, too." She stepped closer. Her laptop case brushed his side. Ben breathed through his mouth. If he inhaled any more of that perfume, he was going to lose his mind. "Is that relevant...*sir?*"

Was she mocking him? He narrowed his eyes. "It looked to me like you were getting cozy with the mayor so you could get the contract."

"I thought the decision was yours."

Now she thought she could confuse him with logic?

Since he couldn't think of a single comeback to that bit of truth, he was relieved when she continued. "Actually, I'm redecorating the mayor's rec room. We were finalizing the color selection."

"Oh." Feeling ridiculous by his burst of righteous anger, he nevertheless glared down at her. "Fine. You'll hear my decision by morning." He turned to leave.

"Are you really willing to work with me?" she asked, forcing him to look back at her.

Even as sweat trickled down his back, he raised his eyebrows, desperate to appear cool and unaffected by her. "I don't have any problems. You?"

"You're not bothered by my relationship with your brother?"

"No," he lied. "And that's past anyway, isn't it?" He could have kicked himself for adding that question.

She smiled. "Yes."

He was absolutely not tempted by that smile. Not tempted to say the hell with ethics and goals and rules. His fingers didn't itch to touch her. He turned away and called over his shoulder, "You'll hear from me about the contract by tomorrow morning."

2

MONICA STIRRED her martini with a toothpick-speared olive and pouted. "What's wrong with me, Sky?"

Her best friend, Skyler Kimball Tesson, frowned. "Nothing's wrong with you. What in the world gave you that idea?"

"Your brother. Actually, bro*thers.*"

"Wes's cheating on you wasn't your problem, it was his. And you just told me you got the firehouse contract. Ben must be impressed with you."

"My presentation, yes. Me, no." The embarrassment of yesterday washed over her again. She'd done her best subtle flirting, and he'd taken off like a priest at a *Playboy* convention.

Skyler waved this assessment away. "Of course he was impressed with you. Every man is."

Monica ate an olive, then gestured with her toothpick. "Bull."

"Please, girl. You should follow yourself around every once in a while. Take tonight, for instance. I got here fifteen minutes before you did, ordered my wine and spent my time revamping my 'to do' list. Then you walked in." She swept her hand out, indicating the more than half-dozen still-full martinis decorating the table. "And four-for-one happy hour started."

From one of the glasses, Monica snagged a toothpick laden with olives. "It's the S&M crowd."

Skyler angled her head. "Come again?"

"Ever since That Incident with Wes, I keep getting propositioned by guys who're into handcuffs."

"Ewww."

"Exactly." She supposed she attracted attention from time to time, but all the wrong men went for her, and she was beginning to seriously think it wasn't their problem, but hers. "Now, you wanna know who's impressed by me? I'll tell you." She ticked off her last three boyfriends on her fingers. "One quit his job to write the Great American Novel, and wound up eating and drinking me into major Visa debt."

Skyler bit her lip. "He was sweet, though, in a poetic way."

"Poetry doesn't pay the bills, honey. The next one stole, then wrecked the car my grandmother left me in her will."

"That Corvette was way too dangerous anyway."

"I was on the verge of selling it to a collector for forty thousand dollars," Monica informed her friend. "Last but not least is Wes and his fidelity issues."

"You don't have to tell me about bad dating decisions. Before I met Jack, I didn't have a stellar track record myself."

"But you did meet Jack."

Skyler's blue eyes turned dreamy. "And he's wonderful. He's so supportive of me and my career. The shop's doing better than ever, thanks to the lingerie becoming a more visible presence." She smiled secretly. "And he's a great test market for new products."

Monica said nothing for a few moments, watching

her friend bask in the blush of love. "You know, I've come to a decision."

"Yeah?"

"Having a best friend who's a blissful newlywed sucks."

Skyler rolled her shoulders. "Sorry." She waggled her finger at Monica. "But remember Fiona and I tried to set you up this summer. You just refused to go."

She knew. Oh, boy, did she know. She'd brooded all summer. She'd worked and brooded. Her professional dedication had led her to the threshold of home ownership, but her personal confidence still hadn't recovered.

In that moment, she remembered her mother's words from so many years ago. *There are two kinds of men in the world, Monica, honey. Ones that want your body and ones that want your bank account. Just be sure you know where you stand.*

She had no idea where she stood.

But Ben seemed like a beacon of hope. He was stable, professional, respected, gorgeous, sensuous— in an understated way—and…not interested. There were a couple of moments yesterday when she'd wondered if he felt the same fiery attraction she did, but those moments had been all too brief.

What's wrong with me? she wondered for the hundredth time.

"He sure is sexy," she said moments later, thinking of Ben's broad shoulders, the layers of emotions in his hot blue eyes.

Skyler's eyes widened. "Ben? My brother Ben?"

"Mmm." She got tingly just thinking about him in

that starched uniform. "He's so forceful, commanding."

"You're kidding."

"No, I'm not kidding. Are you trying to tell me Jack in uniform doesn't turn you on?"

"Of course his uniform turns me on, but he turns me on all the—"

"Remember what I said about annoying newlyweds?"

"Sorry." Skyler tapped her fingers against the table. "Maybe you and Ben..."

Now this was a topic she could get into. "Maybe me and Ben...what?"

"Well... Maybe you two as a couple isn't as far-fetched as it would seem. It's true you're opposites on the surface, but you're both products of broken homes. For different reasons, but still broken. And you both carry a kind of undercurrent of loneliness." She paused a moment, and Monica wanted to tell her friend she wasn't lonely, that her life was full and exciting, but she couldn't lie to Skyler, or herself.

"We are going to be working together, though," Monica said, voicing the main objection that had rolled through her mind since meeting Ben. She couldn't afford to lose this contract.

Skyler waved her hand. "You can keep that separate. It's not as if you're going to wind up having sex on his desk."

Monica felt her face redden. She'd had that very thought yesterday.

Skyler obviously realized her mistake. "Ah, well, just make sure you lock the door." She smiled. "This is exciting. You and Ben. I might get you for a sister-in-law after all. When you and Wes broke up, I—"

"Hold it, sister. I'm interested in Ben, but I'm not looking to marry the man."

"Why the devil not?"

Monica didn't really want to rehash her past, the lousy example her parents had set with their marriage, her own lack of commitment to her relationships. She just wasn't cut out for a long-term relationship, and she couldn't picture Ben taking a flamboyant woman like her seriously.

"It'll be fun—for a while," she said lightly. "To get my mojo back."

Skyler pursed her lips, looking as though she might argue.

"There is one thing about me I think your brother's interested in," Monica said. "He insists I wear pants."

"Pants? Why would he—" She stopped, nodded knowingly. "You do have some short skirts."

It was so nice to have a friend to be in tune with. And as she considered the sexy chief, dozens of attention-getting ideas danced in her head. She just knew the man was her ticket back on the road to self-confidence. Besides, it was way past time to stop brooding over past mistakes. "I'm thinking he's at least noticed I *have* legs."

"He had to."

"Maybe I was just too subtle."

"*You* were subtle?"

"I can be—when absolutely necessary." Monica tapped her fingernails against the table. "Men are so thickheaded sometimes."

"Ben more than most." Skyler angled her head, considering. "Still, Ben is quick, so if you're too obvious, he'll catch on to it right away. The work thing will help, though.''

"But I won't really have much need to work directly with him.''

"So invent something. He's the boss, right?'' When Monica nodded, she smiled. "So consult him.'' She giggled. "While wearing really tight pants.''

"I do have to measure his office, and he has to decide on color schemes and things. I actually thought I'd come up with several themes for the den and kitchen, and ask him to let the firefighters vote on the one they like best.''

"Have him approve them first.''

"I could do that.''

"Ooh, ooh! I know.'' Skyler bounced on her seat, really getting into the spirit of the idea. "Pick out a couple of paint colors, ask him to decide, then leave. Then, you come back two minutes later with another color you like better, then another, and another…it'll drive him nuts!''

Monica sat back, satisfied. "That brother of yours won't know what hit him.''

BEN STARED OUT his office window, watching raindrops roll down the glass. "What's wrong with me, Jack?''

"Come on, *mon ami.* Don't do this to yourself.''

Ben turned as his brother-in-law sank into the chair in front of his desk. "She was inches away from me, smelling like some kind of damn tropical flower, those incredible legs within touching distance. She *wanted* me, and I ran in the other direction. I've lost my mind.''

"I could see Monica overwhelming a guy," Jack said neutrally.

"You?"

"Well, no, but—"

"Do you think she's attractive?"

"Yes, but I ain't sayin' more than that. Skyler and I have an exclusive thing goin'."

Ben crossed his arms over his chest and sank onto the window sill. "I hope so."

Jack propped his feet on his desk—a move Ben would have normally frowned over. But tonight nothing was normal. "You want my advice?

"That's why I called you in here."

"Sleep with her."

"I think sleeping with her would be a really bad idea." He couldn't go around having sex with every attractive woman he ran across. He wasn't some alley cat. He wasn't Steve.

And thinking of one brother made him think of his other brother and another sticking point in this…*thing* with That Woman. He wasn't *Wes*. Did she expect him to be? *Want* him to be?

"It worked with Skyler," Jack said.

"Don't give me details of yours and my sister's sex life. It makes me want to punch you."

"I wasn't gonna give you a play-by-play. And I did marry her, remember?"

Ben was glad his sister was happy. In fact, he and his brothers found themselves overjoyed they didn't have to spend so much time watching out for every jerk in town who wanted to make a move on Skyler. And he loved the irony of her marrying Jack. After all the times she'd complained about their heavy-handed techniques, her tall, two-hundred-and-ten-pound husband had every male in the county terrified to so much as look at her. Not that she cared.

That Woman, on the other hand, with her short red skirts and flashy stilts masquerading as shoes, probably loved having every man in town panting after her. "What am I going to do?" he asked Jack, hating the whine in his voice. "She'll be here in two days."

Jack shrugged.

Ben fought an odd sense of envy for his brother-in-law. He could never match his innate coolness, his what-the-hell philosophy. But then Jack didn't feel helplessly attracted to a woman like Monica O'Malley. He sighed in disgust. The woman was completely outrageous. What did he see in her? Besides those eye-popping legs. "You should see the clothes she wears," he said, half to himself.

"You should see what's beneath the clothes."

Ben ground his teeth. "I'm feeling that urge to punch again, Jack."

"She spends a lot of money in Skyler's shop," Jack explained quickly. When Ben continued to stare at him, he sighed. "I see the sales receipts."

"Oh." Relieved to know Jack wasn't spending his time peeking beneath Monica's clothes, Ben's imagination supplied the picture of her in one of those lacy, see-through thingys he'd seen in his sister's shop. Having Skyler as the chief supplier of scandalous merchandise in town suddenly seemed a lot more positive.

"Though there was that one time…"

Ben's gaze shot to Jack. "What time?"

Jack looked uncomfortable. "Well…I walked in on Monica and Skyler once. And she had on one of those black bustier things."

"Which she?"

"Monica."

The jealousy that roared through Ben surprised the hell out of him. Why should he care who had seen That Woman in her underwear?

Jack stood, spearing his hand through his hair. "Hell, Ben, it sounds a lot worse than it was."

"I hope so."

"How did we even wind up talking about Monica's merry widow?"

"She has a merry widow?" Actually, Ben wasn't exactly sure what qualified a garment as a merry widow precisely—maybe he should have a better look at Skyler's merchandise—but he didn't have any trouble picturing Monica in a scandalously brief bra and panty arrangement. "You brought it up."

Jack shook his head ruefully. "I can't imagine why."

"Me either." He was trying to get the woman *out* of his mind, not spend the night dreaming about her in provocative lingerie.

"My point is—at least I think I had a point—a confident woman is a good thing. No offense, but I think that quiet little gal you brought to Christmas dinner was scared to death of us. She kept lookin' at me like I was an ax murderer or somethin'."

"She gets paid to be quiet. She's a librarian."

"No surprise there."

"No offense to you either, Jack, but you haven't helped me a damn bit."

"What was I supposed to do?"

"Remind me why I have no business with That Woman."

Jack grinned. "Actually, I've always thought you

could stand to loosen up a bit, and Monica could help—''

''Out.'' Ben pointed to his office door.

Jack backed away, holding up his hands. ''I'm goin'. If you're really determined to stay away from her, then stay away from her. Park yourself in your office when she's here.''

For the first time in two days, Ben smiled. ''That's good! Simple. Direct.''

Jack bowed. ''Thank you.'' He turned toward the office door. ''I'm gonna call my wife. All this lingerie talk has me…thinking of her.''

Ben moved behind his desk. ''No illicit conversations, Tesson. That phone's city property.''

ON THURSDAY MORNING, the first thing Monica did was consult Ben about color schemes.

She poked her wavy, red-topped head around his door. ''Chief, how do you feel about green?''

''Plants seem to like it.''

She smiled. ''Right.'' She waved. ''Thanks. Bye.''

He let out the breath he'd been holding.

Less than three minutes later, she was back. This time she came far enough into his office that he could see what she wore.

Oh, she'd followed his rule all right. She'd covered those spectacular legs with pants—fitted black pants that clung to her every curve and accentuated her height. The four-inch snakeskin heels might have had something to do with that as well.

What had he ever done to deserve this torture?

''Would you mind terribly looking at a few of these color schemes?'' she asked as she walked toward him.

"I'm having a terrible time deciding between Icy Green and Sea Foam Green."

He did his best to look put out. "Sure."

She plopped her curvy behind on the edge of his desk, laying strips of paint samples in front of him. Her perfume drifted toward him.

Wasn't there some Lysol around here somewhere?

She pointed one long, red fingernail at a pale shade of green he had to blink three times to bring into focus. Did perfume fumes cause blurred vision? He needed to check his medical textbooks.

"Which do you like better?" she asked, and he could have sworn she inched closer to him as she spoke.

"Uh..." They looked so close to identical he didn't see how it could possibly matter, but he knew if he didn't give her a satisfactory answer she'd never go away. He cleared his throat. "The ice green, definitely."

"Yeah?" She pursed her shiny, red lips. "It is a little more subtle." Then she smiled down at him as if she knew some secret she was just dying to share.

Like an idiot, he found himself returning that smile—for about ten seconds. Then he remembered why he shouldn't. They were working, not dating. She was outrageous. She was flashy. He didn't want anything to do with her. He didn't know what her game was, but he had no plans to participate.

"Is that all?" he asked, glaring up at her.

She looked startled for a moment, then slid off his desk, bracing her hand on his shoulder until her feet hit the floor.

He fought his heated reaction to her touch, and, thankfully, she moved her hand quickly.

She strutted across his office, her curvaceous back-side rocking hypnotically back and forth. "Thanks, Chief," she said, then waved and slipped out of the room.

He laid his head on his desk and prayed for strength.

IN THE HALL outside Ben's office, Monica stamped her foot. Too subtle again?

Impossible.

She'd batted her lashes, she'd swayed, she'd cooed. She'd sat on his desk, practically drooling on his head! Did he look deeply into her eyes and say *I must have you now?* Did he say, *Don't you look nice to-day?*

Noooo. He'd said, *Is that all?*

Flipping her hair over her shoulder, she spun on her heel.

No, Chief Kimball. That's far from being all.

ON FRIDAY MORNING, she came at him again about color schemes. This time it was shades of brown. Her pants were white today. The shoes, red with blue and white stars.

Ben somehow resisted the temptation to stand up and hum "God Bless America."

"So you really like Milk Chocolate over Brownie?" she asked, leaning over his shoulder, her long, silky hair brushing the side of his face.

He stared down at the paint swatches and tried des-perately to concentrate. He had visions of a wedge of brownie, chocolate syrup pooling on top, dripping over the sides...onto Monica's tawny skin. He envisioned his tongue dragging over her body, lapping up every succulent, sweet morsel.

He wanted to know if her skin felt as soft as it looked. He wanted to see those wicked green eyes of hers smoky with passion. He wanted to bury his hands in her mass of wavy red hair. *He wanted her.*

Oh, hell. His heart pounded against his ribs. His palms dampened. He had to get her out of here—fast. Before he said something or did something he'd regret. He had no business thinking erotic thoughts about her. She was a distant acquaintance at best. She was dangerous. She used to date Wes. She was too overwhelming. The whole situation was impossible. Him and her? Ridiculous.

"I, uh, like—" *You, in my lap.* He shook his head. "The chocolate—definitely."

She sighed, and her breath tickled his ear.

He gripped the arms of his chair.

"Are you okay, Chief? You look a little…tense."

No way, no way in hell was he turning his head. He knew she was looking at him, her face, her lips inches away. A bead of sweat rolled down his face. "I'm fine."

Her finger swiped away the bead. "You seem hot."

His body went instantly hard.

"Should I adjust the air conditioner?" she asked sweetly.

He managed a nod. Swallowed. Good idea. The control for the air conditioner was in the supply closet. Out of this office. Down the hall. *Out of this office…*

Jumping up, he shoved his chair back. "Thanks a lot. The control's in the supply closet." Making sure he arranged his face into a suitably serious expression, he crossed the room, then opened his office door. "Ask Phil or Jack if you have any trouble. Thanks," he added idiotically—again.

Smiling as if she knew he was scrambling for an excuse to get rid of her, she walked toward him. "Maybe it's just too much—" she stopped in front of him, gazing up at him, her eyes gleaming "—body heat."

Ben practically shoved her through the door.

Then he leaned against it.

Then he locked it.

"SKYLER, YOUR BROTHER is the single-most frustrating, uncooperative, stubborn man I've ever known!" Monica paced her bedroom and shouted into the phone.

"I can't believe he hasn't responded at all."

Monica recalled Friday's tense sweatiness. "Well, I wouldn't say *that*."

"Keep pushing. Don't let up. Sooner or later, he'll crack."

Monica was fast loosing confidence, but she figured Ben was worth the effort. As long as she didn't get caught in her own sensual trap, of course. Being next to him, breathing him in was quickly becoming addictive. She found herself making excuses to see him not just so he could be tempted by her, but just so she could be near him.

"I don't know how much more obvious I can be."

Since she'd given Skyler nightly updates, her friend knew every nuance of her time with Ben. "You've tempted him with your body, now use your brain. Talk to him."

"Talk?" She could barely keep her body concentrated on systematically seducing him, using her intellect seemed out of the question.

"You can do it. Mind over matter."

"My matter's pretty shaky and squishy at the moment, plus I'm way behind in my work on top of everything else." The big problem was, she'd spent so much time consulting Ben every five minutes, she'd been forced to play catch-up and frantically work on her theme presentation over the weekend. She had convinced Ben to allow the firefighters to vote on the kitchen and den designs based on three themes she was to come up with. The painters, plumbers and other contractors had already begun work on the bunk hall and bathrooms, leaving the main room for last, until the theme was decided.

And she still had more measuring to do and product catalogs to pour over before she could call for a vote.

She sighed. "I guess we could talk. Hell, I've tried everything else."

3

MONICA SPENT all day Monday and Tuesday measuring Ben's office. By Wednesday afternoon, Ben was clutching his pen and grinding his teeth in frustration as he watched her lean over and measure the windowsill. For the third time.

She made a notation in a small notebook, then cocked her hip, and, like a magnet to steel, his gaze dropped to her butt.

Today the fitted pants were orange and stopped at midcalf. The shoes were strappy, sandal-type high heels with a big sunflower covering the top of her foot. The tight fit of the pants and lack of lines had him wondering lately about her underthings. Did she have on one of those merry widows beneath her clothes? He squinted, wishing the light was better.

"Chief?" She whirled, and he forced his gaze to hers. That view wasn't any less enticing. Her green eyes reminded him of a cat's—sleek and mysterious. "Any plans to expand your office?"

"No." He had to look away from her, so he stared at the stack of supply order forms in front of him. He doubled the order of Lysol. Why did she always smell so damn good?

"You don't want bigger windows?"

Windows. More light. Tearing down the wall

seemed a little too drastic, though. "How about track lighting?"

"Excellent idea." She paused, then she slid one silver-tipped finger across the front of his desk. Hell, even her hands were sexy. He could envision those long nails digging into his back as he plunged—

Stop. He wiped a bead of sweat from his brow.

"This desk goes, as well, right?"

He tried to blink the supply form back into focus. Those perfume vapors of hers were making everything fuzzy again. "Uh, yeah."

"Do you have any other…needs?"

He dropped the pen. He was so hard, if he stood, Miss Suggestive Decorator would get a real idea of what he needed. And he was damn tired of feeling this way. She'd only whirled into his life a week and a half ago, and he hadn't spent a peaceful moment since. The firefighters talked incessantly about her, and, being men, their discussions leaned on the lustful side. Jack advised sleeping with her. Even Skyler had called him yesterday to list her friend's many assets.

Well, they weren't getting away with it. He needed to work. He needed to get organized. He didn't want or have time for any grand love affair. And if he did, it certainly wouldn't be with That Woman.

Sufficiently worked into indignation, he glanced up. "I suggest you measure somewhere else."

Her eyebrows arched. "Am I disturbing you, Chief?"

"Not at all." He was proud of the controlled timbre of his voice. "But this room isn't top priority. I just need a new desk and some chairs."

She smiled, and he wanted to lean toward her, bask in that glow. "And track lighting."

He cleared his throat. "Right."

"What about a plant or two?"

The bare corners of the room seemed to glare back at him. Not even a spiderweb graced them. His firehouse was spotless. He could live with a plant. "Fine."

She marked in her notebook. "Paint on the walls?"

"What's wrong with beige?"

"Not a thing." She wrote again. "If you're into plain."

"I like plain."

"So I hear."

Finally, her detached tone brought him to his feet. "From who?"

She had the nerve to grin at him. "It's *whom.* And from everyone."

"Really?" He crossed his arms over his chest. "I hear you're flamboyant."

"That's pretty accurate."

"I'm not plain," he repeated, flustered by her blunt agreement.

"I'll make a note." She scribbled in her notebook. *Why do you have to be so damn beautiful? So exciting? Tempting?* "Damn."

She cupped her hand behind her ear. "Speak up, Chief."

"I have work to do. And I can't do it with you here."

"I'm sorry." Her eyes darkened. "I could go."

As she started to turn away, the very thing he wanted, he found himself already mourning her loss. "No. Don't." Bowing his head, he laid his hands on his desk, leaning forward. She was just too much for him. She could never belong to him. They were too different.

"I'll go," he said, striding across the room. "I have training drills to run." He'd opened the door, pleased with himself for his control, even if success involved a temporary retreat—at least he hadn't dragged her on top of him on his desk—when he remembered her pants. *Big* miscalculation there. He could resist her legs, but that backside...whew. He turned back. "By the way, wear whatever you like. I have no business telling you what clothes you should wear. My apologies."

He backed out of the room on her puzzled frown.

WELL, HELL. He'd never have changed the dress code if he'd known about the mole.

On Thursday, Ben buried his hand in his hair as he stared at fire inspection schedules and tried desperately to purge the sight of Monica's mole. On the back of her thigh. *High* on her thigh. Just where her leg curved inward.

Before she'd climbed on the chair to measure for window treatments—dressed in a short, black skirt, hence the spotting of the mole—he'd decided his behavior yesterday had been ridiculous. Running from his office. How absurd. He was the chief. He was in charge. In control.

A woman wasn't going to affect him like this. Her legs and backside were just body parts. He'd seen many before. He was an experienced medic for heaven's sake.

That was all before he'd seen the mole, of course.

How could her legs be so flawless? Why did that one mark intrigue him so much?

"Don't you have any sweatpants and an old, ratty T-shirt?"

She glanced at him over her shoulder. "What?"

He waved his hand. "Nothing." Swiveling, he faced her, clenching the chair's arms. "How long are you going to be in here today?"

"Just a few minutes more," she said, turning back to face the window. "I'm sorry for—"

She wobbled.

He leapt from the chair, grabbing her by her waist to steady her. And found his face inches from her breasts. Those body parts were equally impressive, he decided, his heart thundering in his chest. Was there any part of her that wasn't? If he ever got her naked, he was looking for flaws first thing.

Oh, yeah. *Sure* he was. Delusional that's what he was. Her perfume had made him delusional.

Her hands gripped his shoulders. "Thanks for saving me. I don't know what happened. I normally have very good balance."

"You'd have to, wearing those impossibly high heels."

"They make my legs look longer."

He looked up at her face. "Baby, your legs don't need any help."

She smiled. "They make me feel feminine and— Did you just call me *baby?*"

"I'm not sure." He suddenly realized he was still holding her. His hands rested on her waist, the blue silk shirt she wore teasing his palms with softness. One auburn-colored curl nearly brushed his nose. He could feel her labored breathing. If he leaned forward, he could bury his face between her breasts. The temptation to do so clawed at him. His fingers twitched.

"I think you can let me go now," she said, though she didn't move her hands from his shoulders.

He released her as if she'd caught fire, then purposely wiped his face of expression. Even as sweat rolled down his back. "You should wear flat shoes if you're going to climb on the furniture."

She frowned. Because of the advice or the emotionless tone he'd delivered it in, he wasn't sure.

He calmly walked back to his desk, proud of his control. He could resist her. He *had* resisted her. Jack would have kissed her. Steve would have kissed her. Wes would have—

Wes *had* kissed her. He might have done a great deal more as well.

He suspected Wes had a healthy sex life, though they hadn't discussed a woman in detail in years. They had only dated a short time, but just how far had he and Monica...gone? In despair, he realized the comparisons she might make between him and his brother bothered the hell out of him. Is that why she was flirting with him? To get back at his brother for cheating on her? Because he reminded her of his brother?

"What about wallpaper?" she asked from behind him.

He turned around, shoving aside the problem of Wes. He had to apply all his efforts to having a work-related discussion without wanting to rip her clothes off. "I thought you wanted to paint," he said.

"Well, Mayor Collins called yesterday. He suggested wallpaper." She paused. "Blue suede wallpaper."

Naturally. "He can forget it."

Monica smiled. "I figured. He also mentioned his nephew."

Ben rolled his eyes. "Edwin."

"The little guy with the glasses who was fixing the drawer."

"That's the one."

"The mayor thought he'd be a good assistant for me. I hedged."

Ben sat on the edge of his desk, wondering how to delicately describe Edwin Collins and wondering if the kid would do more or less damage working with Monica. There were some advantages to keeping them both occupied and away from him. But would his newly renovated firehouse survive?

"Actually, Edwin would probably make you a great secretary. Just keep him away from stairwells, ladders, motor vehicles, large bodies of water and any delicate equipment—your laptop comes to mind."

Her jaw dropped. "But he's a firefighter."

"A volunteer," he corrected.

"But even the volunteers have to meet certain physical qualifications, don't they?"

"Yes, and he can pass all the written tests. He knows *what* to do, he just can't *do* it. On the scene we usually have him guard the truck."

Monica bit her lip, and he had to look away to keep from wanting to do the same. "I guess he is a bit small."

"It's not his size really." He snapped his fingers. "Which reminds me. He's not allowed in the weight room. We just repaired the wall from the last time he tried to play Arnold Schwarzenegger."

Crossing her arms over her chest, she narrowed her

eyes. "Why do I have the feeling you're trying to dump the troublesome Edwin on me?"

"You can handle him." He paused, deciding Monica probably relished a challenge. "Can't you?"

She tossed back her head, her wavy red hair swinging. "Of course I can. Why should I?"

"The mayor asked you—"

"I can say no to the mayor. I want to know if I'm doing *you* a favor."

He gleefully pictured Edwin with a pen and clipboard, taking down measurements at Monica's direction. Harmless, for once. But he hesitated to admit to her how much Edwin's occupation would please him. Being in Monica O'Malley's debt seemed like a bad idea. "You could just as easily say no to me."

"I'm not so sure."

He hoped he hid his amazement. *She* wasn't sure?

He certainly wasn't sure what she saw in him, and he definitely wasn't sure he could fight his attraction for her much longer, but he couldn't imagine her uncertain about anything.

Was it possible the self-assurance was an act, and she just hid her emotions well? He knew one thing— these glimpses of layers beneath her flamboyance were unnerving.

"Are you saying you're not certain you could say no to me if I asked a favor of you?" he asked finally.

"That's what I'm saying."

It was impossible not to be flattered by that revelation.

"So about Edwin..." she began.

He winced. He wanted to dismiss Edwin. He wanted to get back to the reasons she found him irresistible. That was what she meant, right?

"…would you like me to occupy him?"

"If you don't mind." He hoped she'd agree just with that, but he couldn't help doubting, so he added, "He's actually very good with numbers. And he can breeze through organizational work like filing. Working with you will suit him better than firefighting drills."

"Fine." She waggled her finger at him. "But the fire department is taking the hit if he ruins my clothes, laptop or car."

"Which one of those things is the most expensive?" he couldn't resist asking, then grinned.

A slow, sexy smile spread across her lips. She walked toward him, stopping when they were only inches apart. Her sensuous scent washed over him, and his mouth went dry. Trailing one long fingernail down the front of his shirt, she said, "You, Chief Kimball, are adorable."

He captured her finger in his hand. "*You* are a tease."

"Maybe so." She angled her head, her gaze never budging from his. "I guess that depends on whether I back up my flirting with action."

He swallowed hard. "I guess so."

She pressed her lips to her fingertip, leaving a dark red smudge, then pressed her finger to his lips. "I'll let you know when I decide."

He stood rigid. Shock, desire and intrigue all danced through his veins as she turned, her backside swaying as she walked across his office. At the door, she flipped her hair and stared at him over her shoulder. "By the way, you didn't need to list Edwin's strengths. I would have baby-sat him, or done pretty much anything else you asked.'' She blew him a kiss across the room, then left.

As the door closed behind her, he slumped. That Woman would be the end of him. But he was becoming less sure he cared.

''MAY MY CHANEL SUIT get a snag, if he isn't the most stubborn man on earth.''

Monica leaned her head against the steering wheel of her Mustang and moaned with suppressed longing. She'd definitely lost it. Whatever ability she'd ever possessed to attract a man—and she figured those abilities worked on a downward sliding scale once a woman hit thirty—had hit bottom.

She'd been absolutely shameless all week. She'd measured his office so many times she could recite the dimensions by heart. She'd worn short skirts, tight pants, her best perfume. She'd flirted. She'd talked. She'd consulted. She'd been subtle. She'd been obvious. *She'd taken on Edwin as an assistant.*

Still, Ben gave her that wary, blue-eyed stare whenever she was near him. As if she was some odd species he'd never encountered and wasn't sure he wanted to investigate.

He didn't want her. And she was absolutely ready to scream in frustration. What was she doing wrong? It wasn't as if she expected a commitment, or undying words of love and devotion. She just wanted to be with a good guy for once. Even conservative guys liked to walk on the wild side occasionally, didn't they?

Hell. She didn't know anything anymore. It was definitely time for a new plan.

On top of her personal aggravations, her work was

suffering. She'd spent *way* too much time in his office. Though she'd managed to develop three den and kitchen decorating themes for the firefighters to vote on, she still had measurements to complete for Monday's big presentation. As a result, she was back at the firehouse at ten o'clock on a Friday night. A time she'd been told would be chief-free.

According to Phil and Ted, he rarely spent weekend nights at the firehouse. So, during the guys' video game tournament—played with an old system they hoped to update with the renovation—she could get her work done.

She entered the code to open the front door, then shoved up the sleeves of her sweatshirt as she stalked down the hall. Time to get serious.

As she neared the den, she knew something was wrong. No sounds of joking rivalry, no shouts of triumph. All was quiet and dark. She walked into the deserted den, with only the light above the stove and the emergency lights above the exits to light her way. Maybe they'd responded to a call. In that case, though, she'd have expected abandoned game controllers, popcorn and soda littering the floors and tables. But the room was neat and tidy.

Resisting the urge to tiptoe, she set her laptop on the bar, then hit the power button. She had just a few measurements to take. She'd be out before anyone knew she was here. She rolled her shoulders as she called up her file of room dimensions. The stillness was eerie. She'd never been in a firehouse that wasn't buzzing with activity, so the whole scene made her feel illicit—which, naturally, made her think of Ben.

Heavens, those eyes of his were awesome. Blue and fiery and piercing. She wondered if he knew the effect they had on her, or if his gaze was just naturally that penetrating. She propped her chin on her fist, deciding she didn't care either way, as long as they occasionally lightened with humor. He could be awfully serious sometimes. Most of the time, really.

"Hello."

Monica nearly jumped out of her shoes as Edwin's face popped up on the other side of the bar. She laid her hand against her racing heart. "Dammit, Edwin. Announce yourself next time."

He looked confused. "I just did."

"I mean before—" She drew a deep breath, trying to calm her panic. "When someone, especially a woman, walks into a darkened room where you're—" she resisted the urge to say *lurking* "—standing, you should call out, so she knows you're present."

He smiled sweetly. "Okay."

This was the reason she couldn't possibly get too aggravated with Edwin, and the reason she understood Chief Kimball's frustration. He tried. He tried so hard. "Where is everybody?" she asked.

"Asleep."

She knew she'd brooded for a few minutes in the car, but she couldn't imagine she'd let hours go by. She glanced at her watch. Ten-fifteen. "At this hour? Did they have a call earlier?"

"No."

"What happened to the tournament?"

"Canceled."

Monica resisted the urge to sigh. Getting information out of Edwin was like prying pearls from oysters. "Why?"

"Chief decided to stay for the night."

"He's *here?*" Everything inside her tightened at

the thought. Her stomach fluttered. ''Sleeping back there?'' She glanced down the darkened hall, wondering what he slept—or didn't sleep—in.

''Last time I saw him he was in his office.''

Her heart jumped. ''He's awake?''

Edwin shrugged, pushing his glasses higher on his nose. ''You're sure full of questions tonight.''

''Sorry.'' She fought to calm the excitement racing through her veins. *He's here.* Either in his office, or back there in one of the bunks. The quiet, darkened firehouse, full of sleeping firemen suddenly lent a forbidden aspect to her visit.

You're here to measure. Work. Bills to pay. Remember all that?

She did. But only vaguely.

''What are you still doing up?'' she asked Edwin. If she got rid of him, made some noise outside Ben's office…who knew what could happen?

''Measuring the openings for the appliances. This building has been here since the sixties. When we order new ones we need to make sure the openings in the cabinets still match.''

In the interest of conservation, they'd decided to get bids on resurfacing the cabinets and countertops, as opposed to replacing them. But all the old appliances needed to be replaced. Edwin's idea was sound, even proactive.

She walked around the bar. ''That's a great idea, Edwin.''

He ducked his head. ''You would have thought of it.''

''Later maybe.'' She paused. ''You ought to measure in the hall bathroom next. I'm thinking we'll replace those orange countertops in there.'' And that was one of the rooms on her to do list.

Edwin snagged a tape measure off the counter, then saluted. "I'm off, Chief."

"Don't call me chief, please. It's Monica."

"How about Chiefette?"

Monica was pretty sure that was sexist, but didn't think Edwin would grasp the concept. She nudged him in the back. "Why don't you get started? It's getting late."

Edwin ambled from the kitchen. He'd nearly cleared the room when the edge of the countertop got him. His shirt snagged on the rough edge, and he tumbled head over heels, landing with a plop on his backside. The heavy metal tape measure sailed across the room, slamming into and shattering the lit exit sign above the back door.

Wincing at the noise, Monica knelt to check on Edwin. "Are you—"

Chief Kimball stormed out of the darkened hall toward them. "What the hell was that?"

Monica glanced up. "Edwin—" *Whoa, baby.* The chief loomed over them, breathing hard, eyes lit like blue flames. Wearing an unbuttoned, untucked shirt. Tanned, rock-hard abs peeked from the opening of his white uniform shirt. Black hair dusted the top of his chest.

Drool collected at the corners of Monica's mouth.

His hot gaze shifted to her. "What are *you* doing here?"

Chief Hot Bod was really starting to tick her off. What did he think he was doing, brushing her off during the day while he ran around here half-naked at night? Why hadn't she thought to stay after hours before?

Disgusted at him and herself, she helped Edwin to his feet, then straightened his glasses, obviously knocked askew from his fall. "Are you all right?" she asked him.

He rubbed his backside. "I think so." His gaze shifted uneasily to the busted light. "Sorry, Chief. You can take the damages out of my paycheck."

The chief sighed. "You're a volunteer, Edwin. You don't get paid."

"Oh, right." Looking relieved, he inched toward the hall. "I've got work, Chief. See ya." He darted off.

Well, she'd gotten rid of Edwin. But having Ben mad and breathing fire wasn't the way she'd anticipated interrupting his evening. She really wished she could quietly slink out. In addition to frustrating, her idea of regaining her confidence with the chief was looking really lame. And hopeless. Maybe there was a tub of Ben & Jerry's in the fridge.

You're not giving up yet. Be bold, girl.

Her gaze slid down his body. "You certainly dress down after hours."

He glanced down. "Oh."

As he buttoned his shirt, Monica silently cursed. *What'd ya have to go and call his attention to it for? You had a perfectly lovely, lustful view, and you blew it.*

"You do, too," he said, his eyes surveying her briefly.

She glanced down at her ratty sweatshirt and jeans. Where her best attention-getting outfits had failed, this coordinated ensemble was sure to turn him on. *Right.*

"And you're shorter," he added.

Without her heels, her head was about level with his chin. The difference made her feel oddly vulnerable. In the darkened room, he seemed large and intimidating, even…dangerous. The very idea shot a thrill through her body. She shivered.

"Cold?"

She met his gaze. The anger there had dimmed, leaving a different kind of heat. Could it be sensual? "No. I'm pretty warm." The understatement of the year. She was burning up.

He dragged his hand through his hair. "Edwin was probably messing with the heat again."

She shook her head. "That's not what I—" She stopped. Even she couldn't imagine saying *I'm hot for you.* He had her too flustered and uncertain. She was deathly afraid he'd laugh. "I mean it's pretty warm outside, so…"

He laughed.

She considered crawling under the table. *I wonder if Edwin needs any help…*

"Monica O'Malley reduced to talking about the weather?" he asked in amusement. "Come on, what's up? Are we over budget? Did Edwin break something besides the light?"

"No." This was ridiculous. *She* was ridiculous. She'd been obvious. She'd been subtle—well, maybe briefly. She'd advanced. She'd retreated. And nothing. He wasn't interested. Whereas she fell more under his spell every day. She'd just wanted her confidence back. She didn't think it mattered who helped her get it. But it did matter. Very much.

Maybe too much.

Obviously, she'd kidded herself about Ben. He was the highly respected fire chief. She was that wild and crazy redhead. "I've got to finish measuring," she said, spinning away, then grabbing her laptop as she walked by the bar.

To her surprise, he followed her. "You've spent four days measuring. Aren't you finished yet?"

No, thanks to you. But she couldn't be ticked at him. She had only herself to blame for being behind schedule.

What's wrong with me?

"Helloo, Monica? Are you still with me?"

She stopped, her head whipping toward him. "You called me by my first name." And it had sounded wonderfully arousing. She wanted him to say it again, lower, in a whisper.

"So?"

"It was nice," she said simply, wishing she hadn't called attention to the moment. He was giving her that strange species look again. She headed toward the weight room. From the looks of those abs, Ben must spend a lot of time in here, and the image of him half-naked and sweaty had her silently moaning. It didn't help her fragile control that the object of her fantasies followed her into the room. She needed to get these measurements done before she did something drastic to embarrass them both.

"You never call me by my first name, either," he said as she hooked her tape measure on the open doorway.

She supposed she didn't. He was "the chief" to her, which sounded awfully distant now that she thought about it. Though she doubted he'd have the same reaction she did, she said, "Okay, *Ben,* since you're here, would you hold the end of the tape measure, please?"

He didn't bat an eye. He didn't look aroused in the least. "Sure." With the tip of his finger, he held the end, and she pulled. Working together, she had the dimensions recorded in a matter of minutes.

"Why in the world did my office take so long?" he asked as she strode briskly from the room.

The night was going from bad to worse by the minute. She really had the urge to bang her head against the wall. She didn't dare turn around to look at him. "Windows," she lied. "Windows complicate the measurements." She headed toward the front hall.

Again, they worked together to record the results. She hooked the tape measure to the waistband of her jeans, then checked her list. Just the bathroom, which Edwin was handling, and she was done.

Suddenly, Ben lifted the laptop from her hands, setting the computer on the hall table. "Can I ask you a question?"

The strange expression in his eyes and the quiet timbre of his voice had her emotions clanging with nerves. She flattened her back against the wall. "Sure."

He laid one hand on the wall beside her head, effectively trapping her. She swallowed as his gaze searched her face. "For nearly two weeks, you've been there every time I turned around. Now, you're constantly walking away from me. You're confusing the hell out of me."

She blinked in astonishment. "*I'm* confusing *you?* Ha! You bark orders at me, accuse me of using this job to get dates with your staff, glare at me when I laugh. Hell, you glare at me when I breathe. You *ignore* me." And that was the worst offense.

"At least I don't prance around here dressed to tease every man within five miles and soaked in two gallons of perfume."

Monica was certain her blood was actually boiling. "For your information, I'm not interested in teasing every man—just you." She registered the surprise in his eyes, but was too ticked off to stop now. "I've been trying to get you to notice me." She tossed up her hands, then planted them on her hips. "And, by the way, there's absolutely nothing wrong with the way I dress. If you'd quit inhaling so much of that damned starch in your shirts, you'd realize that."

He leaned so close she could see flecks of icy blue in his eyes. "If you'd take a good look in the mirror every once in a while, you'd see you don't need all those fancy clothes. You look sexy as hell right this minute in that sloppy sweatshirt."

Before she managed to do more than absorb the compliment, he went on. "In fact, you're irresistible."

Then his mouth claimed hers. His lips were fierce and hard. He pushed his tongue inside with an insistent thrust, and after a shocked pause, she angled her head to fuse their mouths together.

Finally was all she could think, wrapping her hand around the back of his neck and plunging her fingers into the hair at his nape. In the low light, the strong slope of his jaw beckoned her fingers. She lifted her other hand to cup his face. His pulse, pounding beneath her fingertips, seemed to echo the drumming of her own heart.

He tangled his tongue with hers, stoking her hunger

for him higher, even as his body pressed her firmly against the wall. His chest was a wall of muscle against her breasts. The metal buckle on his pants dug into her stomach, and desire rippled between her legs.

She'd suspected he was a commanding guy, and now she knew that trait would make him a powerful lover. The discovery was thrilling, enticing... irresistible.

He tangled his hand in her hair, while he left her lips, trailing kisses beneath her jaw. "Damn, you smell even better up close."

She clutched him to her as his teeth scraped her earlobe. "Ben..." she gasped.

His breath hushed out over her skin. "*That's* how I want to hear my name."

Her stomach vibrating with need, she clutched his shirt, feeling a certain amount of power in crumpling the starched fabric. "Kiss me again, or I may have to hurt you, *Ben*."

His smile flashed briefly before he complied, his mouth moving across hers in need, but also exploration, as if he was memorizing and relishing the taste of her. The whole experience was just so amazingly intense that she actually heard bells. Monica was certain she'd never felt so powerful and helpless at the same time. And this was just one kiss. How much better could it get? She leaned in again to try for kiss number three when Ben pulled away abruptly. *What the...?* Monica opened her eyes as the sound of bells was replaced by shouting and heavy footsteps. *Those weren't bells,* she thought dejectedly, *it was the blasted fire alarm!*

4

FOR A SECOND, just a second, Ben considered not letting go.

The shock of that brief temptation—and the alarm reverberating in the air—forced him to step back. Monica stood against the wall, her face flushed, her expression dazed and aroused. Her hair was tangled as it spilled over her shoulders.

I did that to her.

The thrill of power raced through his veins, even as he felt ashamed at the way he'd accomplished the feat. He'd *shoved* her against the wall, he'd smashed his body against hers...and enjoyed every second of it.

Enjoyed? Hell, he'd reveled in losing control.

As the sound of feet tramping down the bunk hall reached his ears, the responsibilities of the fire chief finally kicked in. And he realized the alarm wasn't a warning from dispatch. It was the internal alarm.

The firehouse was on fire.

He shoved open the front door. ''Out!'' he ordered Monica.

''Look, Ben, I know things got out of control there, but—''

He grabbed her by the arm and pulled her through the opening. ''The fire's in *this* building.'' He didn't even want to consider the idea that his first thought had been to get Monica to a safe place. She's the only civilian, he rationalized.

"But this is the firehouse," she said.

"Don't move till I come for you." He propped open the door, then spun away and ran down the hall.

Since his men had ninety seconds to get from their beds to the trucks, and he'd wasted at least that long with Monica, he found them in the garage raising the door. He raced to the ladder truck, yanking open the passenger door. "The fire's inside." He glanced around the truck, making sure everyone was accounted for. His heart jumped as he realized someone was missing. "Where's Edwin?"

Even as he voiced the question, they all leapt from the truck, racing across the garage, nearly plowing into Monica as she jogged toward the den. Ben snagged her by her waist, lifting her off the ground. "You're supposed to be outside."

She struggled against him, trying to pry his arms off her. "Dammit, Ben, let me go. There's smoke coming from the bathroom window."

Ben nodded down the bunk hall. "Steve, Ted, check it out. I'm right behind you."

As they took off, barking echoed down the hall.

"Bernie," Monica gasped. She managed to kick Ben in the shin, and he dropped her.

Wincing and furious, he rubbed his leg. "Are you crazy?" But he was talking to air. Monica was running down the hall, presumably in search of the dog.

That Woman is going to be the death of me, he decided—again—as he charged after her.

He skidded to a stop at the doorway leading from the hall to the commercial-style, two-stall bathroom that was due for retiling next week. Blinking, he tried to absorb the ridiculous scene in the smoke-filled room.

Steve and Ted each held one of Edwin's legs. At least he thought the small man kicking and screaming was Edwin. He could only see the back half of him, since the other half was hanging out the open window.

Monica was braced, legs apart, as she fought to hold Bernie's collar while the dog barked frantically at something smoking in the corner.

Leaning sideways, Ben noted the smoking object was a small, metal trash can on fire. *That* he could deal with. The rest of this mess was too humiliating to even consider.

He walked to the sink, stripped a paper Dixie cup from the dispenser, filled the cup with water, then poured the liquid on the smoldering fire.

The dog stopped barking. Both the animal and Monica angled their heads as they stared at Ben. "That was efficient," she said.

He shrugged, then turned to Edwin just as the guys managed to free him from the window. Without the dog's barking and Edwin's screaming, the room fell uncomfortably silent.

Ben slid his hands in his pockets as he examined Edwin's flushed face for injuries. Other than his fogged-up glasses and a soot stain marking his cheek, he seemed fine. "Are you having any trouble breathing?" he asked Edwin.

Edwin coughed and stared at the floor. "No, sir."

"Steve, why don't you take the trash can outside? And, Ted, go get an oxygen tank. Just in case."

As the men left, Ben wondered how long it would be before this public relations nightmare wound up in the papers. Black stains marred the tile floor and wall where the trash can had sat. He'd have to file a report with the mayor. He shook his head as he envisioned the future humiliations. At least no one had been hurt.

With a sigh, he focused on Edwin. "What happened?"

"Well, sir, I was changing the lightbulb…"

From behind Ben, Monica giggled. He glared at her over his shoulder, and she promptly cupped her hand over her mouth. "Sorry," she mumbled, though her green eyes were still bright with laughter.

She looked so adorable, Ben had to fight to keep from smiling at her.

Adorable? Monica O'Malley? Man, he had to get a hold of himself.

Charming, maybe. Irresistible, definitely. But not adorable. Adorable described puppies and babies in bonnets. With Monica, he could still smell her enticing, sexually charged scent in the air. Her eyes promised wildness and pleasure. Her body tempted men to rashness.

"…well, anyway," Edwin was saying, "I turned the bulb too tight, so it broke in my hand and cut my finger."

Ben faced Edwin in time to see him holding up his hand as evidence. "Is there a point somewhere in this opus?"

"So, I wrapped a piece of toilet paper around my finger, got another lightbulb, and started to screw it in. But a spark flew out from the light and caught the toilet paper on fire." His eyes widened behind his thick glasses. "I thought my hand was going to catch on fire. So, I flung off the paper, and it landed in the trash can, and the whole thing went up in flames like that." He snapped his fingers. "Smoke filled the room, and I...I guess I panicked. I shoved open the window and hoisted myself up."

Ben wanted to ask him if he'd paid attention—or was even conscious—during training sessions. He wanted to ask if Edwin's common sense had taken a vacation. He wanted to rail at the mayor for saddling him with this walking disaster area. But the poor guy had obviously been through a lot. "Why don't you get some antiseptic for your cut, then get some sleep? We'll deal with this mess in the morning."

Edwin smiled brightly. "Yes, sir, Chief." He scooted around Ben, then darted out the door.

"Woof!" roared Bernie.

"I couldn't have said it better myself," Monica added, walking toward him. "You were very kind to him."

"It's late. He won't get off so easily in the morning."

She smiled. "Right."

He could tell she wasn't buying his threat. *He* didn't even buy it. As the chief, he knew he had to be tough at times, but he just couldn't find his ruthlessness with Edwin. The poor guy tried. He tried so hard.

"You can't help but have a soft spot for him," Monica said.

Glancing at her, he could see she understood. She'd worked with him, too, he remembered. Then the importance of her words hit him. *She* obviously had a soft spot for Edwin. Why did she have to continually surprise him? She should be irritated by Edwin, she should have complained bitterly when he'd sloshed coffee on her expensive suit yesterday. Why couldn't she be self-absorbed and hard? Maybe he couldn't help being attracted to her, but he sure as hell didn't want to *like* her.

But he did.

It was long past time he faced his attraction to her. She certainly had. *I've been trying to get you to notice me.*

He'd noticed plenty. But he hadn't acted. Except like an idiot.

Ordering Lysol when he craved her scent and her touch more with every passing hour. He liked her sense of humor, admired her intelligence and strength, valued her opinion.

But what did she see in him? He led a really ordinary life. Boring, in truth. He'd never considered himself Mr. Excitement. He'd never match her flirtatiousness and vibrancy and boldness. He'd probably bore her after one date.

He needed advice. And a clear head. That kiss had blown his mind. For once, he'd wanted to give in to his own needs more than he wanted responsibility and duty. The impulse scared him, excited him.

"I'm sorry about tonight. We made—" He stopped, recalling the way he'd pinned her to the wall. "I was way too forward—"

The shocked expression on her face stopped him. "You're *apologizing* for kissing me?"

"Well, sort of."

"Didn't you like it?"

Like was way too mild a word to describe their lip-locked foreplay. He tunneled his hand through his hair. "Of course I liked it, but…"

Her eyes narrowed. "But?"

But I can't measure up to the other men in your life. Even my own brother. Especially my brother.

"Don't you think we're too different to…get involved? I mean you're colorful and flamboyant, and I…like beige."

"We're very different."

"But it doesn't bother you?"

"No. Should it?"

Damn. He didn't know.

"Obviously our differences bother you." She sighed, looking annoyed. "I should have known this wouldn't work. Look, it's late. I'm going home." She stalked by him, then turned to glare back. "See ya around, Chief."

He wanted to call her back. He even opened his mouth.

Instead, he crammed his hands into his pockets and turned away.

MONICA FLUNG OPEN Wes Kimball's office door and stormed inside. "What's wrong with me?" she shouted at the man behind the desk.

Wes stood so quickly his wheeled chair shot backward, bouncing off the wall behind him. His Adam's apple bobbed as he swallowed. "Monica."

Monica noted his fear with a huff of frustration. *Hell, handcuff a man once…*

"Maybe we should have had this discussion a long time ago," she began, "but, well, I couldn't look at you without wanting to shoot you." She didn't really want to talk to him now, but her insecurities had pushed her past anger to desperation. "Anyway—" she paused, glancing at the chair in front of his desk "—can I sit?"

He extended his hand—slowly. "Sure."

She dropped onto the edge of the chair and crossed her legs, noting Wes's gaze dropped briefly to them as he returned to his own seat. She wished his interest could cheer her, but today nothing was swaying her from her path. She had to find out why Wes had found her so lacking, since apparently the disease was contagious—at least among the Kimball brothers. "Anyway, I need to know why you felt it necessary to sleep with that blond chick."

Wes stroked his jaw. "Well…"

"Oh, come on, Wes. We'd been going out for weeks. We were attracted to each other. I thought we were headed toward something more…intimate. I even bought a sexy outfit." She narrowed her eyes. "It cost eighty bucks, by the way."

"I guess I should have reimbursed—"

She waved that away. "Never mind. The point is I had my hair done, my nails done. I wore silk stockings. I *waxed*. Then, I walk in your bedroom, and you and *her* are naked and horizontal." She ground her back teeth as the moment washed over her again. "I was put out."

"I'm sure." Wes rose, leaning across his desk. His eyes, normally dark and shaded from his emotions, were actually shadowed with regret. "Look, I'm sorry. I didn't plan it. I mean I wasn't seeing her behind your back or anything. You're wonderful. Beautiful, exciting, fun." He smiled. "Really fun."

She crossed her arms over her chest. "Just because I prefer *Cosmopolitan* to *Time* doesn't mean I'm an idiot, Wes."

"Of course not."

"Then why are you trying to sell me this load of

bull? Empty compliments? Sincere expression? Please.'' She rolled her eyes. She wasn't any of those things—obviously. Wes didn't want her. Ben didn't want her. Maybe she ought to give up men entirely. She had a great career, after all. And depending on a man for entertainment and compliments and self-esteem was completely pitiful.

Oh, God. I'm not turning into my mother, am I?

"I'm being honest," Wes said as walked around his desk, wearing that same uncomfortably sincere expression that made her want to grind her teeth. He stopped just a few feet from her. "My reasons for being with Mandy are complicated."

"You're still seeing her?" Somehow, during and after the drama she hadn't even considered this idea.

"Yes, I'm seeing her. I was seeing her before you and I got together." He looked away, then back. "She wanted to cool things off between us. I didn't. But I was determined not to let her know how much her decision bothered me. When I met you, I thought you were the perfect woman to make her jealous."

She arched her eyebrows. "You did?"

His face reddened as he continued. "At first. But then I got to know you, and I was torn. You're so vibrant. So, I didn't know who or what I wanted, then Mandy showed up at my house that night. We got to talking, and she told me what a big mistake she'd made and how much she wanted me back…"

The realization of his explanation hit her. "What?" She jumped to her feet, poking him in the chest. "And you just—" she rolled her shoulders, trying to gain control of her anger "—you just took her back? Don't bother with any explanation to Monica. She isn't important."

"It wasn't like that. I didn't mean to hurt you."

Monica stared at him. And realized he hadn't helped at all. This big explanation of his made her feel worse. She felt even more insignificant and lacking than before. She'd assumed his being with that woman was just a spur-of-the-moment fling. Instead, he'd actually *chosen* someone else over her.

Why didn't anyone want her? Something was definitely wrong with her. How was she going to find out what?

She glared at Wes. She *certainly* had nothing to say to *him*. He'd started this whole demeaning mess.

She punched him in the stomach.

"Damn, that woman has a violent streak," he gasped as she stalked out the door.

BEN PUSHED OPEN Wes's office door. His brother sat behind his desk, file folders scattered around him.

"Go away," Wes said without looking up.

Ben stalked toward the desk. "What's wrong with me?"

Wes glared at him. "It's like a damn revolving door around here."

Ignoring his brother's hostility, Ben sank into the chair in front of the desk. "I used to be too busy to worry about stuff like this. The firehouse has to be my top priority. We have training to complete. We need to run more drills. Somebody has to take inventory of the supply closet. And I've *got* to figure out what to do with Edwin."

"Do you have a point?"

Ben glanced up at his brother, who scowled and tapped his pen against a stack of paper. "I've been making it for the last three minutes."

"I must have fallen asleep."

"I'm trying to figure out what's wrong with me."

Wes leaned back in his chair, propping his feet on the desk. "You want a list?"

Ben just glared at him.

Wes dropped his head back to stare at the ceiling, folding his hands across his stomach. "Tell me, Mr. Kimball, when did these feelings of inadequacy begin?"

"You're not funny."

"I thought I was hilarious."

Ben began to seriously reconsider the wisdom of coming to Wes. But in addition to trying to figure out what to do about his attraction to Monica, and why he couldn't make himself act on said attraction, he also needed to know just where his brother and her stood. Did Wes still have feelings for her? Did he want her back? And just how cozy had the two of them gotten last summer? He had to clear this mess up before he could consider what to do about Monica.

It's that kiss. That damn incredible, fiery, overwhelming, lustful kiss. He couldn't get her mouth off his mind—or body. He hardly cared anymore about her flamboyance clashing with his conservatism. Or her excitement versus his boredom. He'd overcome that. Though how, he had no idea.

He shook his head. "That Woman has me so messed up."

"What woman?"

"Monica O'Malley."

Wes suddenly went still. "What does she have to do with this?"

He really had been asleep. "Everything."

"I wasn't aware you even knew her."

"She's redecorating the firehouse."

"Oh." Then his eyes lit, and he smiled. *"Oh."*

"What's that supposed to mean?"

"She was just here, asking lots of questions, babbling just like you. She even punched me."

Confused, Ben shook his head. "Who?"

"Monica."

Ben swallowed. The image of Wes and Monica in a heated embrace flashed through his mind. "Monica was here? She came to see *you?*"

"Yeah." Wes chuckled. "At least now I know what that was all about." He swung his legs off the desk, then leaned forward. "You two have the hots for each other."

Ben jumped to his feet. "We do not."

Wes laughed. "Oh, yes you do."

Though this whole conversation made Ben more uncomfortable than he wanted to admit, the time for reservations was long past. "The point here is—do you?"

Wes laughed harder. "No way." Then he sobered abruptly. "I mean she's a wonderful woman and all, and there was a time…but there's another—"

"You don't want her back?"

"No."

"You don't have any regrets about ending your relationship?"

"I could have done without the handcuffs."

The tightness in Ben's chest eased a bit. But he still had questions. "About that night…" He cleared his throat, feeling ridiculous for feeling awkward. "Monica, um, caught you in bed with that other woman, right?"

Wes's gaze was wary. "Yeah."

"So, were you two-timing Monica in the most *basic* sense?"

"Mandy and I weren't discussing world peace."

Ben braced himself for the answer to his next question. Of course his brother had slept with Monica. He had that aura of danger and adventure that women found irresistible—something Ben had never been able to find in himself. She was sexy and beautiful. *Any* man would want to sleep with her.

"But then Monica and I hadn't slept together, so I guess it wasn't as bad as it could have been. Actually, I think her pride was hurt more than her heart."

Monica and I hadn't slept together. Ben blinked. "You're sure?" he asked like an idiot.

"I know Steve has to alphabetize his lovers by hair color and breast size, but I've got a pretty good memory on my own."

Though Wes had plenty of women to choose from. That had never bothered Ben before. He'd always been happy as the serious, responsible brother. Women had looked to him to hold their hand after they'd been tossed aside by Wes or Steve.

So what did Monica see in him?

I've been trying to get you to notice me. She'd actually said that to him last night. In the heat of anger, sure. But he had to assume it was true. What did she want from him? Did she regret losing Wes so much that any Kimball would do? Wes said her pride was wounded more than her heart. Maybe she just needed him to get her pride back. Prove to Wes she'd moved on. That actually made a lot of sense. More sense than Monica being irresistibly drawn to him.

Was he willing to be used that way? They could

have a cheap affair. He'd never had one, so maybe he should have the experience once.

But he waved away that idea immediately. Both he and Monica deserved better.

The big problem, as he saw things, was he could never hope to hold her interest for long. He couldn't be Wes, full of brooding danger. Or like Jack, with his smooth, Cajun charm. She'd be bored by him after half a date.

But, then...

What if he *wasn't* boring, serious and predictable? What if he could be the one overwhelming her senses instead of just holding her hand?

"Are you planning to mull in here indefinitely?" his brother asked. "I've got work to do."

"I'm not mulling."

"Yes, you are. You mull over everything. I should have warned Monica about that. By the time you get around to asking her out, we'll all be in the nursing home."

Ben braced his hands on the desk. "I doubt she was worried about that after I kissed her last night."

"You kissed her, huh?"

"Thoroughly."

Wes smiled. "She dared you to, didn't she?"

"Pretty much."

Wes tossed back his head in laughter. "This is so great! Finally, a woman to confound Mighty Chief Kimball."

"I don't find a single funny thing about any of this. Do you have any idea how long I've been torturing myself with visions of the two of you together?"

Wes held his stomach. "Jealousy, too. Stop, it's too much!"

"I'm suddenly seeing dozens of reasons for her punching you. Why did she, by the way?"

Still laughing, Wes shrugged. "I don't have the faintest idea."

Ben sank onto the edge of the desk. "She's a damn confusing woman."

"They all are, big brother."

Wes understood women? "She's a little wild for me, don't you think?" he asked, voicing his worst fear.

"Mmm. She's…been around." He paused, shrugging again. "Or so I hear."

Ben balled his hand into a fist. He'd meant wild in the unpredictable, flashy sense, but he realized Wes meant something much less innocent. "So you hear," he echoed in a cold tone.

Wes's gaze met his. "You really have it bad for her."

"So you hear," Ben said again, his stomach knotting at the thought of someone making sexual comments about Monica.

"Just guys making cracks. Obnoxious stuff."

"Unsubstantiated, I'll bet."

Silent for several long moments, Wes cocked his head. "Yeah, now that you mention it."

Ben leaned close to his younger brother. Of the four siblings, Wes had always been considered the most intimidating, standoffish and dangerous—with the exception of Skyler's preteen years—and Ben rarely exerted his strength as the family patriarch, but he would not have Wes, his cronies or anybody else making comments about Monica. The surge of protection he felt should have worried him. Maybe he'd fallen too hard, too fast, but there was no stopping the instinct.

"Do me a favor," Ben began, his gaze spearing his brother's. "Tell your rumor-mongering buddies, and anybody else who plans to walk upright for the next twenty years, that any man who makes a comment about Monica O'Malley will find himself on the wrong side of my normally amenable temper." He bared his teeth. "Got it?"

Wes leaned back. "I got it. Hell, man, I didn't say I'd repeated anything. That's just what's being said."

"Not anymore."

"Yeah, sure."

Having settled that issue, Ben rose, sliding his hands into his pants pockets. "Back to my original problem." Maybe he couldn't *be* Wes, but he could *act* like Wes. *If you'd quit inhaling so much of that damned starch in your shirts,* she'd said. "How do I act dangerous?"

"That threat twenty seconds ago worked for me."

"I want her to want me, not fear me. Come on. How do you do it?"

"What do you mean—how do I do it? You ask her out. You date. Buy condoms and flowers. Have fun."

"I'm not sure I know how anymore."

"Like riding a bike."

"I haven't done that in a long time either." Ben felt his face heat. "How do you have fun?"

Staring at him, Wes rubbed his chin. "Hmm. I doubt Monica will be charmed by fire drills and filing."

"I think I can manage something better than that."

"You can?"

Ben stalked toward the door. "You're really a jerk

sometimes. I come in here for a little advice and sympathy, and all I get are insults.''

"Hey, man, I was just kidding, don't—"

The door slammed on his apology.

Wes stared at the closed door for a second or two, then he pawed through his top drawer. When he found a black marker, he ripped out a blank sheet of paper from a notebook. In thick six-inch-high letters he wrote KEEP OUT.

With determined strides, he headed toward the door. Those two deserved each other.

5

BEN'S GAZE swept the smoky, crowded bar. He watched the couples specifically. If he wanted to be exciting and unpredictable, thereby holding Monica's attention, he had a lot of work to do.

Wes's advice hadn't helped a bit. Flowers and condoms. Ridiculous. Unoriginal. How many times had Monica been approached with that cheap, worn-out bit? He could be dangerous and exciting without his brother's help.

He had other siblings. So, he'd gone to Steve for advice. Steve had said it was all about the look and encouraged him to buy leather. Ben had felt like an idiot. So, he'd found another instructor.

"So when do my lessons on being bad start?" he asked his new teacher.

Jack choked on his beer. "Lessons on what?"

"Being bad. Like you."

"*Mon Dieu.*" He shook his head. "You said you wanted advice on how to get Monica."

"I do. I have to be bad to get Monica."

"You wanna talk bad? Those leather pants you had on earlier were bad. And not in the way I'm assuming you wanted."

Ben frowned. "Steve said they worked for him."

"And probably laughed his ass off the moment you

left. You can't take anything that joker says seriously."

So much for family loyalty. "He's getting kitchen duty the rest of the month."

"That'll teach him." Jack leaned back in the booth. "Leather pants are sexy on women. Leather pants on a man are for bikers and Village People. Not fire chiefs. Trust me, *mon ami*. I saved you. Take the mayor and his latest wardrobe disaster."

Ben winced at the mention of his boss's early-years Elvis fascination. He had a point there. And since Jack had refused to come out with him until he changed, Ben supposed he hadn't had a choice. He glanced down at himself. "So, do you think the black jeans and T-shirt work? Skyler once told me she faints whenever you wear all black."

"Hell, man, I don't—" Jack's dark eyes turned speculative. "She said that, did she?" After a moment of consideration, he waved his hand. "I think you should wear what's comfortable for you. Don't put on an act for her."

It wasn't an act, exactly. He was just tapping into his impulsive side. Skyler always said the Kimballs had impulsive genes in spades. And throwing himself into his attraction for vibrant, exciting Monica was an excuse to find them and prove to everyone he didn't get his kicks with fire drills and filing. "I'm not."

Obviously skeptical, Jack raised his eyebrows.

"I'm willing to do just about anything to get those long legs of hers wrapped around me," Ben admitted.

Jack smiled. "I've been there with Skyler." He looked at Ben over the rim of his frosted mug. "You could stand to loosen up a bit, I guess."

Ben sighed. "You really think so?"

"As long as we're talkin' man to man, instead of firefighter to fire chief."

"We are."

"Then the first step for you is unpredictability. Whatever you've been doing, do the opposite."

Ben stared into his tumbler of whiskey. "I've been scrambling and confused. And professional."

"Professional?"

"We work together."

Jack shook his head. "Whatever you do, don't talk about work. Be confident and bold. You're the chief. Women like that whole power thing."

"Right."

"And look at her a lot."

"All I've done for two weeks is stand around and look at her. Drooling."

"But now you need to look at her like you intend to do something with her."

"Something like what?"

Jack grinned. "Naughty."

That was good advice. Of course Jack had also been the one who'd told him to just retreat to his office to keep his distance from Monica. Like *that* had worked.

Jack leaned back into the booth. "Really, man, just relax. Buy her a drink. Smile at her. Compliment her."

Ben had a hard time picturing him and Monica engaged in witty banter. "I'm not very good at small talk."

"Let her talk. Women love to talk about themselves. And when she says something you don't know how to respond to, just smile, or sip your drink until you think of something."

For the first time all night, Ben relaxed a bit. More good advice. Simple, with manageable execution and a low looking-like-an-idiot quotient. He picked up his glass, clanging it against Jack's. "Thanks, buddy. I might survive this after all."

BETWEEN THEIR PARKED CARS, Monica twirled for Skyler's inspection. "How do I look?"

Skyler frowned. "Abnormal."

"I look normal."

"I know. For you that's abnormal." She laid her hand on Monica's arm. "Don't do this. Be yourself."

"I am. Just my conservative self."

"You don't have a conservative self."

Monica ignored that comment and strode down the sidewalk toward the front door of the bar. The bar where all the firefighters hung out, and where Skyler had arranged for Jack to bring Ben. It was time to put the new plan into action. After her disastrous talk with Wes earlier in the day, and realizing she didn't meet *his* standards, she'd decided she had to find a way to meet Ben's. She could be average. Even reserved. "Come on. I can't wait to see his reaction."

Skyler grabbed Monica's hand, pulling her to a stop. She tugged Monica's white silk blouse. "Let's untuck this, unbutton it a little, then tie the ends—"

Monica stepped out of her reach, smoothing her blouse back into place. "No." She glanced over the rest of her ensemble—the pleated-front navy slacks, the brass-accented belt, then the—

Skyler jerked up the hem of her pants. "At least you're wearing heels." She wrinkled her nose. "Even though they are navy. Solid navy. This whole deal would look much better with those patriotic shoes of yours with the stars.''

Monica shook her head, and her straightened, tucked-behind-her-ears hair barely swung. ''These are fine.''

Skyler stamped her foot. ''What are you going to do on your wedding day when you want to wear a skintight red tube dress and Ben is expecting a snow-white hoop skirt and lace?''

Monica hadn't thought that far ahead. Of course, there wouldn't be a wedding. Even if she managed to pull off this conservative bit, Ben wouldn't want to marry her. Deep down, she was all wrong for him. He was admired and respected by everyone in the community. With her wild reputation—and with That Incident last summer still fresh in everyone's mind— taking a relationship with her seriously wouldn't ex- actly be a great PR move for him. ''I guess I'll shock the hell out of the reverend, won't I?''

Skyler opened her mouth—no doubt to protest again—so Monica cut her off. ''When I called you earlier, didn't you agree that some men like the chase in a relationship?''

''Well...''

''And you were right. It's time I let *him* chase *me*. I just need to be the kind of woman he'd like to chase.''

''He likes you already.''

Monica merely stared at her.

''He kissed you.''

That kiss. If she could get that mind-blowing kiss out of her mind maybe she could remember why try- ing to be someone she wasn't might be a bad idea.

''He kissed me while I was wearing a baggy sweatshirt and old jeans. Do you see a pattern forming here?''

''Yes.'' Skyler stubbornly crossed her arms over her chest. ''He doesn't care what you look like.''

''Maybe, but he's bothered by our differences. So maybe we're not so different.'' Smiling, she held out her arms. ''I'm a walking visual aid of our similarities.''

''But—''

Monica cut her off this time by turning to tug open the door. Just inside the bar, she halted, staring in disbelief at a booth on the far right side. She blinked but Ben was still there, dressed in black jeans and a black T-shirt, having a drink with Jack. He looked good. Really good. Manly and dangerous and tempting.

Her mouth went dry. And she realized she'd never seen him in anything but his fire chief's uniform. Is this how he looked away from the office? Looking like…she let her gaze drift down his body…looking *nothing* like the fire chief.

''Oh, my.''

''What?'' Skyler's gaze finally found the men. ''Great. They're here.''

When Skyler waved, Monica batted at her arm. ''Don't. Let's not be obvious.''

Skyler blinked. *''You?''*

''Since when did you become such a smart aleck?''

''Since you decided to start looking like Deacon Jones's wife.''

Monica planted her hands on her hips. ''I do *not*.''

Skyler raised her eyebrows.

''I think I'll go put on some lipstick. You swing

by their table and let it subtly drop that I'm at the bar.''

Monica pivoted, then started to head off as Skyler whispered urgently from behind her, ''Make sure it's red, or he won't recognize you.''

That girl had gotten *so* bossy. She waggled her hand at her friend as she walked away, then reached into her purse for her lipstick compact. After applying a coat of Rascal Red and pursing her lips, she approached an empty stool at the bar, noting the one next to hers was occupied by someone she knew.

Edwin.

Poor guy. No doubt word of his pyromania had made the gossip rounds through town. She was surprised he had the guts to show his face in public. As one who'd survived scandal herself, she silently cheered his nerve. ''Hi, Edwin,'' she said, sliding onto the stool.

''Chiefette.'' When she glared at him, his face flushed and he amended, ''I mean Monica.''

''How are you?''

''My finger throbs a little, but I'm okay. I put on triple-antibiotic ointment and a Band-Aid.'' He held up his bandaged finger as proof. The Band-Aid had little yellow smiley faces all over it. ''The chief said to reapply the ointment several times a day to help with the pain and guard against infection and scarring. My prognosis is excellent.''

''I'm so glad to hear it,'' she said, trying to hide her smile.

''What can I get you?'' the bartender asked.

Monica turned to answer, noting the bartender was a tough-looking blonde with four piercings in her left ear, man-size biceps, inch-long sapphire fingernails and a tattoo of a butterfly on her forearm. *Dana* was embroidered on the red vest of her uniform. "I'll have a vodka martini with three olives." She glanced at Edwin's drink. His *pink* drink. "And bring Edwin another…whatever."

Smiling, Dana tapped the bar. "Got it. Martini and another Shirley Temple for Edwin."

A Shirley Temple? Good grief. But somehow the drink fit Edwin. "She must be new," she said casually to him, "or maybe it's just been a while since I was in here."

Edwin's mouth hung open.

Monica nudged him. "Are you okay?

"She—" He patted his forehead with a cocktail napkin. "She knows my name."

"Who?"

Edwin emitted a long, dramatic sigh. *"Dana."*

The man was absolutely glassy-eyed. Now why couldn't she get that kind of reaction from Ben? It was nice to know *somebody* was succeeding in the romance department, though. "You and Dana got a thing going?"

Edwin flushed again and stirred his drink. "No."

"But you like her."

He nodded frantically.

"Have you asked her out?"

He shook his head frantically.

Half the time you couldn't shut the guy up, but when there was something important to discuss he turned into an obstinate clam. "Do you want to ask her out?"

Another nod. Then a shake.

Oh, yeah, Edwin was in deep. Abject confusion— the first symptom of a crush. Since she'd worked out her own love life plan, butting into Edwin's seemed like great fun.

Dana returned moments later. "Here you go," she said, smiling as she set their drinks on the bar.

"Thanks," Monica said, then sipped from hers, finding the drink balanced perfectly. "You build a great martini." She elbowed the man next to her. "How's your drink, Edwin?"

He rubbed his arm. "Ow."

"Do you like butterflies, Dana?" Monica asked, realizing quickly she was going to have to be more obvious. "Edwin likes butterflies, don't you, Edwin?"

"Not really. Crickets are much more interesting."

Grinding her teeth, Monica kicked him, then ignored his glare. "But you like Dana's butterfly tattoo, don't you?"

"I, uh—" He glanced at Dana. "Sure," he mumbled, staring at the floor.

Just as Monica was regretting her impulse to help, Dana said, "I like crickets, too." She leaned over the bar and pulled her vest aside to proudly display a cricket tattooed above her collarbone.

Edwin's eyes nearly popped out onto the floor.

Monica grinned as the pair launched into a discussion of cricket songs and moods, deciding she'd have to think twice about whacking the loud little suckers the next time she found one hopping around her apartment.

"Hi, Monica."

Her hand jerked at the sound of the deep, familiar voice, knocking into her martini glass and sloshing liquid over the sides. *Stay calm, girl. Think demure.*

A demure martini-drinking woman wearing Rascal Red lipstick? Her conservative act definitely needed work.

"Chief," she said sweetly, blinking and staring over her shoulder at Ben.

Heavens, he looks good, she thought as she stared into his breathtaking blue eyes, which stood out even more dramatically than usual against his black T-shirt—which his broad shoulders filled out quite nicely. In the dimly-lit bar his inky hair glistened while his jawline remained partially in shadow. He looked big and strong and...dangerous. She remembered how that word had come to mind when she'd first spotted him from across the room. Not a description she'd normally apply to Ben.

But she shivered in delight at the idea of just how dangerous he might be.

"Can I join you?"

Even his voice sounded deeper. Her heart raced as she swallowed. "I'm sure we can squeeze you in."

Edwin looked up in time to see his boss towering over him. "Uh, good evening, Chief." His gaze darted between Ben and Monica before going back to Dana, who was filling a customer's drink order down the bar. Clearly, he was torn.

"Do you mind standing?" she asked Ben, then smiled shyly.

Ben raised one eyebrow—a really cool move she'd never seen him do—and she wondered if she'd laid on the sweetness a bit too thick. "I don't mind," he said. He turned sideways and inched his way between her and Edwin, facing her, standing *really* close.

Oh, boy. How was she supposed to keep from grabbing him when he was so close? And when—she inhaled briefly—he smelled so fabulous?

"What can I get you?" Dana asked, thankfully reminding Monica she and Ben were in a crowded bar, and she could not, under any circumstances whatsoever, attack him.

"Crown Royal on the rocks," Ben said, then nodded at her still-full glass. "You want another one?"

Why did he sound so smooth, so controlled? Something was up here. He always sounded controlled and in charge, but this was different. Mysterious. Seductive.

"Monica?" Ben asked, sounding amused. As if he knew he was such a big distraction. She flipped her hair over her shoulder nonchalantly and picked up her drink. "I'm fine, thank you."

Ben took a healthy gulp the moment Dana set his drink in front of him. Monica stared at her olives. Hair flipping was probably too flamboyant. *Okay. Calm down. Think of a conservative topic. Something serious and thought-provoking.*

"The decorating plans are gong well, don't you think?"

He stared at her. "Uh-huh."

"I'll give my presentation on the den and kitchen themes on Monday. Did you remind the men?"

His gaze dropped to her lips. "Uh-huh."

She swallowed and fought to keep her own gaze on his forehead. If she looked at his lips, she'd remember their kiss and then she might do something drastic. "I think everyone will like—"

"I don't want to talk about work."

"You don't?" Ben? Chief Work Ethic?

"I want to talk about us."

"Us?" Was there an us?

"You look lovely tonight," he said, his gaze roving over her with a thoroughness that heated every pint of her blood and scattered her coherent thoughts.

Still trying to assimilate this shift in roles, she angled her head. "Thank you."

"But something's different."

Yes! He'd noticed. *It's working.* "Really?"

"Your hair's flat."

"It's—" She narrowed her eyes. "I straightened it," she said sharply. "Don't you like it?"

He winced, gulped his drink, then ordered another. "Yes. Definitely. I love it."

"Then why—" She stopped. *Don't be defensive. Be demure.* She folded her hands in her lap and forced a serene smile. "You look different, too."

With a fresh drink in his hand, he smiled. "Really?"

"Kind of dark and dangerous and del—" Wincing, she managed to stop herself from saying *delicious.* Probably too bold and suggestive. "You look great."

He gulped his drink. "Thanks."

Her glance slid to his glass. Ben didn't strike her as a heavy drinker. It occurred to her that he was acting nervous. But then maybe he just seemed different because she was acting different.

He slid his arm across the back of her chair. She hissed out a breath and tried to ignore his proximity, the knowledge that his broad chest was inches from her back. His warm breath caressed her cheek. "You really think I look dangerous?"

She turned her head to meet his gaze, and her heart jumped. "Oh, yeah."

"You like dangerous men?"

She fought the urge to fan herself. "I'm crazy about dangerous men." She started to run her finger down her chest, realized that would *definitely* be too bold, and crossed her feet at her ankles instead. "Golly, Ben, danger is really swell."

He leaned back, staring at her as if he'd never seen her before. *"Golly?"*

Too much again. Annoyed with herself, she drummed her nails against the bar. Then, inspiration struck. "Do you like chocolate chip cookies? I make great cookies." *You* buy *great cookies, Monica,* she thought guiltily.

Ben tunneled his hand through his hair. He sipped his drink, then rolled his shoulders and leaned toward her, close enough that his breath stirred the hairs against her cheek. "I liked kissing you." He paused. "It was dangerous. And intense." He slid his hand over hers. "Unforgettable."

Her pulse raced. Could conservative clothes, flat hair and the promise of chocolate chip cookies really bring about such a change? In an odd way, she was disappointed. The real her wasn't good enough. But she waved aside her worry. *You're getting what you wanted. He's interested. He's practically drooling.*

"I'm wearing mousse."

Monica snapped back to reality. "You're...*what?*" His conversation was all over the map. As his face flushed, she glanced at his hair. It did look fluffier. Her fingers itched to rake through the inky strands, but she gripped the bar instead.

"Guess what else I did today."

His little boy enthusiasm was adorable. She'd known from the moment she met him that Ben could be a charmer if he wanted, and now she felt herself falling under the spell of that charm. "What?"

"I bought a hot car."

"You did?" He'd bought a hot car, and she was wearing boring clothes. This night was getting weirder by the minute.

"Yep." He reached into his front pocket, pulling out a set of keys. "Want to see it?"

You bet your— Damn, damn, damn. She shook her head. "Oh, I don't know, Ben. That sounds a little fast for me."

"Fast," he repeated. "Are you feeling okay?"

She was feeling stupid. Sensing the Crown Royal was responsible for his sudden non sequitur, she nabbed his keys. "I should drive."

The fact that he trustingly nodded, then paid their tab had Monica shaking her head in an attempt to jiggle the world back into focus. *I've just been picked up in a bar by Chief Kimball.* Strange? Definitely. But she wasn't about to argue with success.

They waved goodbye to Edwin and Dana, then swung by Jack and Skyler's table. The newlyweds were sitting on the same side of the booth, with Skyler practically in her husband's lap, gazing into each other's eyes as if they were the only people on the planet.

The cynical side of Monica wanted to roll her eyes, but another part of her, deep inside, was jealous. She hadn't really thought of men in a happily ever after, white dress and flowers way since the ninth grade. What was it like?

She made a mental note to ask her friend as she leaned across the table, propping her chin on her hands, and stared at the couple. It was still a good minute and a half before Skyler turned her head.

She jumped. "Monica. Good grief, you scared me to death."

Grinning, Monica straightened. "I'll try to avoid any more sudden moves."

Skyler's gaze slid from her to her brother. "I see you two found each other."

From behind her, Ben slid his arm around Monica's waist. "Finally."

"We're leaving," Monica said, relishing the warmth of Ben's fingertips brushing her hip. Her heart pounded in anticipation. "I'm sure you won't mind taking Jack home."

Jack slid his hand over Skyler's, and their wedding bands touched. "How 'bout it, *chère?*" he teased.

Skyler's eyes danced. "I'll get you home."

Watching them, Monica wondered if Skyler still trembled every time Jack touched her. And did she get that weird, anxious but excited roll through her stomach when she saw him? Of course, Skyler was severely in love, and Monica was—*analyzing one kiss and a couple dozen hot looks way too deeply.*

"Lunch on Friday?" she asked Skyler.

"You bet."

As Monica stepped back, she felt Ben's mouth against her ear. "If you lean over again, we might have to call the paramedics."

Turning, she linked her arm through his. "Don't worry, honey, I know CPR."

SKYLER FROWNED as she watched them leave the bar. "Why does my brother look like the bad guy in a Bruce Lee movie?

"Why does Monica look like a banker?" Jack countered.

Skyler glanced at her husband. She was glad Ben had gone to Jack for help. He loved being in the middle of their boisterous, sometimes messy family, and her brothers' acceptance meant the world to him. "Those two are making love much more complicated than it needs to be."

Jack smiled. "Didn't we?"

"I guess." She laid her head on his shoulder. "Should we butt in and help?"

"Let's give them a few days. Maybe they'll work it out on their own."

"If not, I'm sure I can reason with Monica."

Jack roared with laughter.

6

_____

BEN KNEW A HOT CAR when he saw one, Monica decided as she approached the sleek, black Corvette convertible.

"You've got great taste," she said, aiming the remote lock.

"I know." He spun her around, backing her against the door. He laid one hand on the roof and cupped the back of her neck with the other.

She'd barely acknowledged his intent before his lips captured hers. She melted against him, winding her arms around his neck. The scent and heat of him that had teased her all night filled her senses. His tongue slid against hers as if finding home. No timidity, no hesitation, but not the raw hunger of before. This was deeper, slower, more controlled and powerful.

The press of his muscled chest against her breasts had her throbbing above and below the waist. She tangled her fingers in his hair and pushed closer. The rough fly of his jeans met her thin silk blouse, teasing her, stoking the fire inside her.

He slid his mouth along her cheek; his teeth grazed her jaw. "You smell incredible."

She sucked in a breath as he nipped her neck. His forcefulness, confidence seduced her.

He slid his hands down her back, his fingertips caressing her lower back, then slid past her waist, along her backside. He groaned as he cupped her cheeks, pulling her against the hardness between his legs. Still, his lips moved against her throat.

She didn't know which sensation to grab on to first. She was rarely overwhelmed by anyone or anything, but as beads of sweat sprouted all over her skin and her heart raced in her chest, she grappled for stability. Curling her fingers into his T-shirt, she cheered the female instinct that had taken one look at Fire Chief Ben Kimball and said, *There's simmering sensuality. If he ever lets loose…*

A loud horn blasted through the air.

Ben jumped back. Running his hand through his hair, he glanced toward the street, where a teenager was hanging out the window of his pickup, holding the thumbs-up signal high. "I'm the fire chief. I can't be seen necking in parking lots."

That was the Ben Kimball she knew. Yet, she'd wanted him to loosen up, and he had. Oh, boy, had he. She opened the passenger's door and swept her hand out in invitation. "Welcome to my parlor."

As he ducked inside, she rounded the car, bouncing the keys in her palm. Maybe she should act a little more reticent about driving the car, but she'd pushed the June Cleaver routine a little too much, and she wanted her hands on that wheel. And on Ben.

She dropped into the driver's seat of the 'Vette, her mouth watering. Her Mustang was certainly a muscle car, but it was several years old, and any car fanatic man, woman or child bowed to the 'Vette as the ultimate in American sports car brilliance. She felt as if her butt was just inches off the road, and from the downward slope of the hood she could barely see the car's nose, but the black leather seat hugged her like a lover, and she nearly purred in satisfaction as she turned over the ignition.

Laying her head back against the seat, she reveled in the vibration. With Ben's kiss still pulsing on her lips, the sensation approached erotic.

The whirring motion of the top being lowered interrupted her thoughts. She glanced over, meeting Ben's glittering gaze. "Let's go," he said.

In March, the Georgia air could still be cool, but they'd been rewarded that day with mid-eighty degree temperatures, so the night air was balmy and refreshing, especially in light of the heat rolling off her body. She popped the car into gear, and they glided out of the parking lot.

She longed to floor the gas pedal and see what the powerful car could really do, but the last thing she needed was to get stopped by Baxter's finest with a strangely bold and unpredictable fire chief beside her, especially with his palm currently sliding over her thigh. "You move your hand any higher, we're going to get arrested."

He slid his fingers along the slope on the inside of her thigh. She sucked in a breath, her knees trembling and need for him pulsing through her veins. "I'll risk it," he said.

I'll risk it? When you got the man away from the office, he was really something. And, again, Monica was torn. She was drawn to the darkness and risk, but she missed Ben's reliable side. This Ben was about as predictable as, well, she was.

His fingers glided back and forth on her thigh.

Ah, hell, girl. Go with the flow.

She pressed her foot harder on the gas pedal as she pulled onto the main highway running through town. Her hair whipped around her face, and she laughed as she tried to tuck it behind her ears.

Leaning toward her, Ben's hand clenched her leg. He brushed the side of her neck with his lips. His mouth traveled higher, to the underside of her jaw, then to her earlobe. When his sank his teeth into the lobe, her hands jerked on the wheel, and the car swerved.

Heart racing, she corrected her steering. "Maybe we should slow down."

"I don't think we're going fast enough." So saying, he flicked his tongue against her ear.

She moaned. But she also pulled off the highway and onto a quiet suburban street. The possibility of being caught making out seemed less dangerous than flipping the 'Vette over a guard rail.

Ben didn't seem to notice. He slipped his other hand underneath her hair, cupping the back of her neck. His mouth grew hungrier, his breath hotter.

She fought to keep the car on the road, clenching the steering wheel with every bit of strength she possessed. She wanted to pull over, slam the car into park and straddle him, pressing the aching center of her against him, knowing he was the only one who could ease the torture. But the restrained need she sensed in him was equally as intoxicating. He wanted her. In fact, he seemed starved for her. The power and thrill of control made her want to laugh in delight.

As she halted at a four-way stop, he urged her head

around, capturing her mouth. Her tongued glided against his, seeking to entice him further, wanting to pull him completely under her spell, though she sensed she was the one falling. He smelled almost as good as he tasted, and she let go of the steering wheel to grasp the front of his shirt, kneading the soft cotton material rhythmically.

She sensed lights approaching behind them, so she eased off the brake, and the car rolled forward. "Ben," she gasped against his mouth. "I've got to watch the road."

Giving her one more hard kiss, he leaned back. But his hand didn't leave her thigh.

As she drove, Monica fought to clear her head. They couldn't keep this up in the car. She didn't really feel like going back to the crowded bar. His place? Hers? Did that seem too obvious, too forward?

With his fingers, he teased the inside of her thigh.

Worrying about forwardness was probably a moot point at this stage. So she headed for her apartment. She glanced at him out of the corner of her eye to find him staring hungrily at her profile. *Oh, my.* Having his intensity focused so completely on her was incredible.

But, as she pulled into a parking space outside her apartment, a suspicion wormed its way into her brain. She turned off the engine and looked at Ben. "Are you drunk?"

He rolled his glassy eyes. "No."

"How many drinks did you have with Jack?"

"One." He paused, angling his head. "I think."

Great. He'd downed two in the few minutes they'd

talked at the bar. "Before tonight, when was the last time you drank whiskey?"

"Mmm. Never."

"Never?" Damn, damn, damn. He was soused. That was why he'd been so forward and affectionate. The hair mousse and the 'Vette she didn't have any ideas about, and she doubted she'd get clear answers tonight.

She wanted him, but could she take advantage of him?

This demure business was exhausting on the conscience.

Her gaze locked on the series of buildings that made up her apartment complex. Each building had its own courtyard. Most held gardens, one housed the hot tub and gazebo, but hers contained the pool. She liked to sit beside it some nights when she needed to think clearly and didn't want any distractions. They could take the long way around to get to her apartment and walk through the pool area. Ben would hardly notice, and maybe by the time she reached her door, she'd know what to do.

She raised the Corvette's top, then slid from the car, locking the doors. She held out her hand to Ben. "Come on."

For the first time since they'd stopped, he glanced at his surroundings. "Where are we?"

"My apartment."

His eyes widened for a moment, then a sly smile came into the sparkling blue. "Lead on, darlin'."

Lord, he's so sexy! her conscious reminded her as she took his hand and led him along the sidewalk. All night they'd been heading toward the moment they were horizontal and sweaty on her silk sheets. She was vibrating in anticipation of exploring his body. But when they finally got down to it she wanted Ben clearheaded and fully aware of what was going on. If he woke up the next morning and either regretted, or, worse, couldn't remember their night together…well, Ben would think her retaliation against Wes was a mere warm-up. And after her temper was spent, Ben would never speak to her again, she'd regret losing it, she'd never have those awesome lips of his on hers again, she'd again never be subjected to his hot, blue-eyed stare… The entire mess seemed completely unproductive and avoidable. No, she decided sadly, tonight wouldn't be *the* night.

As she opened the iron gate leading to the deck, she could see the pool's glowing lights shimmering off the water. She led Ben into the courtyard, thankfully noting it was deserted.

All she had to do was convince Ben to bed down on her couch for the night, she decided. She really needed to spend the weekend on her firehouse presentation, anyway. In the morning, they could have a heart-to-heart about their feelings and discuss the rationality of their attraction.

She shook her head. *Discuss the rationality?* Hell, she *had* become June Cleaver. Maybe this whole night was too weird to complicate with sex.

"Skinny-dippin'. What a great idea," Ben said suddenly, then proceeded to strip off his T-shirt.

"You can't—" She stopped, her eyes bulging as she absorbed the sight of him shirtless. The peek she'd gotten last night hadn't done him near the justice he deserved. His broad shoulders seemed a mile wide, with muscles whispering along the tops, then developing into sleek biceps and forearms. The slight dusting of black hair on his chest arrowed down his lean stomach, disappearing into the waistband...

The waistband he was currently unbuttoning.

She licked her suddenly dry lips and glanced around the pool deck. They were still very alone, but given his slightly incapacitated state, she felt as though she should be the voice of reason. "Ben, we can't get naked in a public pool."

He continued unbuttoning his jeans. "Why not?"

She clutched a chair, her gaze locked on his fly, noting the really impressive bulge. Heavens, they could be so good together. Why did she have to question impulsiveness now? *He* was supposed to be the cautious one, she reminded herself. He was supposed to reign *her* in. "It's unsanitary?" she made herself say.

Shrugging with an obvious lack of concern, he tried to step out of his jeans but, realizing he still wore his tennis shoes, he sat on a lounge chair to remove them.

She groaned as he revealed firm thighs and demure white boxers. He had such a commanding presence she knew strength had to have been hiding behind his starched shirts and pressed ties, but she had no idea of the perfection of his lean, muscled body.

He tossed the jeans over his shoulder then stood, still wearing the boxers, but nothing else. He immediately crossed to her, yanking her into his arms. "You have on too many clothes."

She laid her hands on his bare chest, just above his dark brown nipples. His heart hammered beneath her palms. She was in big trouble. She didn't think she had enough honor to resist him.

He nuzzled her neck, his breath bathing her skin in heat. "I'll help."

She glanced down at the pool, then let her gaze drink in the whole, incredible length of him. The idea had merit.

"Or we could go like this." He leaned sideways, still holding tight to her waist, pulling her with him.

The split second before they hit the water, she remembered two things. Two things her desire-fogged brain should have realized, but it was...well, desire-fogged.

It was March. And the pool wasn't heated.

With her and Ben's combined weight, they dropped to the blue-patterned pool bottom like stones. Needles of pain stabbing her skin, Monica shoved off the floor, wondering if her new clothes were ruined. She broke through the water's surface, gulped air and screamed.

Loud.

In seconds, apartment doors around the courtyard burst open. Residents dressed in robes and slippers leaned over the railing as they stared at the pool. Beneath the balcony lights, she caught smiles and finger-pointing.

Ben! she thought in panic. Though her body felt like a heavy ice cube, she realized in a flash that if her neighbors recognized Ben he'd never forgive her for humiliating him. It hardly mattered that this swimming idea had been his. He'd been with her when it happened, and she knew she'd earn the blame. She didn't exactly have a clean track record when it came to embarrassing scenes with men.

As his shocked gaze met hers, she grasped his shoulder, forcing him back under the water.

"She's drowning him!" somebody shouted.

"I'm calling the cops!" another yelled.

Hell. Monica waved her hands. "We're fine."

Ben resurfaced, and she shoved his shoulder again. This time she didn't push him completely beneath the water, just enough that she could stand in front of him and hide him.

But of course the water was freezing, and he didn't want any more of his body in it than had to be, so he struggled with her. "Stay down," she whispered furiously.

"I-It's f-freez-zing."

She raised her eyebrows, water dripping off her eyelashes. "Really?"

He surged toward the pool's edge. "O-out."

Monica glanced up at her neighbors, noting no one had moved—though the guy three doors down from her had a portable phone in his hand. "Grab your clothes, and keep your head ducked," she ordered Ben as she levered herself onto the side.

Then, the night that had begun with such promise, and had even developed into fantasy, took a nosedive.

The barbecue grill, just ten feet from the pool's edge, burst into flames.

Frigid cold forgotten, Monica charged toward the grill. Ben's discarded jeans had ignited, the hem of one leg lying on top of the bright red coals. *What idiot had left behind this disaster waiting to happen?* Probably those college kids who just moved in one floor below her. They were always around the pool, cooking out and having parties.

Behind her, a neighbor shouted to call 9-1-1. Monica spun around, her gaze searching for something to hold water and pour over the flames. Heart pounding, she realized she had ten thousand gallons of water just a few feet away and no way of getting more than a handful to the fire.

A breeze brushed her body, and a bone-deep chill quivered across her skin. Her clothes. She grabbed the hem of her silk shirt, jerking it over her head just as Ben shouted her name.

She dropped the dripping wet shirt on the grill, and a satisfying sizzle resulted. Smoke billowed toward the sky.

Ben yanked her into his arms. "Don't touch anything! Are you okay?"

Clad in just her bra from the waist up, Monica's bare stomach brushed Ben's. She clutched him to her, reveling in the feel of his bare, damp skin, wondering how she could be freezing cold and burning hot at the same time.

Ben! Panic and worry reasserted itself. Skinny-dipping he might live down. But a fire? A carelessly heated grill that could have burned down an entire apartment building had it gotten out of control, plus getting caught with that wild O'Malley chick nearly naked?

She grabbed him by the arm. "We need to get inside."

"The fire—"

"It's out."

Still, he pulled away from her, grabbed his shirt

and dipped it into the pool. He wrung it out over the grill, then smothered the jeans thoroughly.

"Let's *go*." She grabbed his hand and pulled him up the stairs, ignoring the disappointed shake of her elderly neighbor's head. And slamming her door in the smug face of the guy who announced "the cops and fire department are on their way."

Leaning against the door, she paused a moment to draw a breath. Her whole body ached. Needles of cold and fear stabbed her skin where just moments before desire had warmed her soul. *Think, Monica, think.*

She looked at Ben, who seemed to be in shock. He stood just inside the door and stared at her. The vivid blue of his eyes stood out starkly from his almost-nude body. But still his gaze reflected heat. She glanced down at herself, realizing her bra clung to her curves, her nipples had puckered.

"The shower," she said, stalking forward. She grabbed Ben's hand and pulled him down the hall and into the guest bathroom. Giving in to desire now wasn't a bad idea. It was an absolutely horrible idea. The jerkface neighbor had called the *police,* i.e. Wes, and the *fire department,* i.e. everyone Ben knew and demanded respect from. She and Ben needed to be clothed, dried and feigning innocence within minutes. Otherwise, half the town would be speculating about their fire chief's competence by morning.

After flinging back the shower curtain, she turned on the water, wishing like hell she could enjoy sharing a shower with Ben. She clenched her teeth to fight back the vision of his hard, lean body pressed against hers as hot water rushed over them.

From behind her, his hands slid along her hips, his

teeth nipped her earlobe. "Mmm. You read my mind."

If she'd thought the icy water and a fire would snap him back to his normally cautious self, she was obviously doomed to disappointment. Didn't he realize his reputation was at stake here? She also cursed her volatile temper. Why had she retaliated against Wes? His cheating seemed so trivial now compared to the embarrassment Ben might suffer if they were discovered.

If? Hell, *when. The fire department is coming. Wes is coming.*

She'd withstood many disappointments and troubles in her life, but living with Ben's scorn wasn't something she wanted to consider. And that fear drove her.

"Get in," she commanded.

With a sensual smile gracing his lips, he followed her order, obviously not realizing they didn't have time for fun and games beneath the soothing spray. The law and Ben's men would be knocking at her door within minutes.

AS THE HOT WATER sluiced down his back, Ben grabbed Monica by her curvy hips and eased her back against the aching hardness between his legs. The woman drove him crazy. The icy pool and grill fire were unexpected developments, but nothing he couldn't deal with. His desire hadn't cooled a bit. And now he had her where he wanted her. He just had to get rid of his boxers and get her as naked as he was.

And he didn't have much time. When his men showed up, he'd have to give them a report on the fire. By then, he wanted full control of Monica's senses.

He grasped the edge of her sopping wet pants, then fought briefly with the button and zipper, his fingers clumsy.

"Ah, hell," he said, bracing his hands against the tiled wall. "You do it."

Her jaw dropped. "Ben, we have to—"

"Get closer." He wrapped his hands around her arms, his gaze traveling the length of her, noting her stiff nipples through the sheer fabric of her bra. His erection pulsed. He pushed her back against the tiled wall, then, after one long, needy look into her vivid green eyes, he laid his mouth over hers.

Part of him recognized he was acting against his personality, while another part sighed in relief that he was finally acting on his desires.

As the warming spray beat on their bodies, he tangled his tongue with hers, craving her response. She'd given him a lot of odd looks over the course of the night, she'd *acted* oddly all night, and he needed to reassure himself she still wanted him. She responded, sliding her hands up his chest, gliding her fingers into his hair. He reached down and slid his hands beneath her pants, cupping her backside. Her *bare* backside. He moaned against her mouth. Hell, she wasn't wearing panties. Just the thought made his erection grow, swelling to the point he wanted to forget restraint and responsibilities and just drive himself inside her. Then his fingers brushed fabric. He ran his finger along the edge of the fabric. *A thong.* Smiling, he wasn't surprised. The woman was a walking fantasy.

He fought with the button on her pants again. His

hands shook, either from the whiskey or the excitement, he wasn't sure. Finally, finally, he worked the button through its opening in the fabric, then pulled on the zipper.

And nearly fell over with the effort.

Desire pounded through his body. He wanted her. Had to have her. Bury himself inside her. And he couldn't get her clothes off. Frustrated, he grabbed the straps of her bra, shoving them down her arms.

She jerked back. "Ben, we have to—"

She stopped as he cupped her bare breasts. They were full and soft, with her nipples distended, as if straining for his hands. "Oh, man."

When her head dropped back, and as she arched her back, he flicked his thumbs over her nipples. She dug her fingernails into his shoulders. His heart jumped against his ribs. Watching arousal steal over her face, the way her body flushed beneath his touch, the way she gave herself over totally to the pleasure was a moment he'd never forget.

But then she suddenly straightened, her eyes popping open. She snatched the shower curtain back, peering into the bathroom. "Oh, hell," she said.

"What's—"

She waved her hand. "Shh. Turn off the water."

Confused and more than a little disappointed their shower was over, he did as she asked.

That's when he heard the pounding.

He shook his head to clear it. He'd drank more than he usually did, but surely not enough to have a headache already. The pounding continued, along with muffled shouting. "What's that?"

"The fire department. Probably the cops, too." She

leapt out of the shower, her sopping pants clinging to her hips, her breasts swaying. She unhooked her bra; the scrap of creamy fabric dropped to the floor. He swallowed hard. There were much more important things to see to besides pounding and the—

"Did you say cops? Fire department?"

"Yes," she said, shoving her pants and panties off her hips, down her legs, then stepping out of them, even as she grabbed a towel off the rack.

He was momentarily struck stupid by the glimpse of her completely nude body, those killer curves exposed to perfection. He knew one thing for certain— she was a natural redhead.

She wrapped one towel around her body, tucking the ends between her breasts, then another around her hair. "Stay here. Don't make any noise. Don't come out." She looked over at him. "Who's on duty at the firehouse?"

"Steve."

"What about Wes? Is he working tonight?"

His gaze jumped to her face. The genuine fear he saw there forced the misty fog shadowing his brain to lift. Fire department. Steve. Wes. Cops. Skinny-dipping. Fire. Witnesses. Public humiliation. He couldn't let the department and public know he'd been part of a careless fire. No matter that he and Monica had doused the flames, the implication of his carelessness would linger. His top-notch department, the respect he desired, would vanish into smoke. His father would never have been so irresponsible.

What had he done?

Monica didn't wait for an answer to her question. She opened the bathroom door. "Don't come out. No matter what you hear.'' Then she was gone, the door slamming behind her.

With regret and worry wobbling his knees, he sank onto the lid of the toilet. He'd managed being bad, all right. He'd bad-assed his way into disaster.

''Where is he?'' Wes asked from the other room.

Hearing his brother's forceful voice, Ben crossed to the door, pressing his ear at the crack, but he missed Monica's response.

''The man who helped you start that fire. The one you were trying to drown in the pool,'' Wes said.

Ben frowned. The fire was his fault, he'd thrown his jeans on the grill.

''The fire was an accident. A piece of cloth fell on the grill. It caught fire. I put it out. I didn't *start* the fire. Some idiot left the grill burning.''

''A piece of cloth? Steve says it's a pair of jeans, a woman's blouse and a man's shirt.''

Monica sighed loudly. ''My date took off his jeans—we were going skinny-dipping. The jeans caught on fire. I put out the fire with our wet shirts.'' Her voice was angry and sarcastic. ''Instead of interrogating me, you might try finding out who left that grill burning.''

A long pause ensued. ''There's still the matter of this drowning.''

''I wasn't trying to drown anyone,'' Monica said, sounding as if her patience had been pushed to the limit.

''I have ten witnesses who say otherwise.''

''Did you find yourself a body?'' Ben could imagine Monica crossing her arms over her chest and giving Wes her intimidating glare.

Wait a second. He could imagine Monica all right. Wearing nothing but a towel. In front of Wes. Jealousy surged through him. Was Wes looking at her?

Of course he is, you idiot. What man wouldn't look at Monica? Wes had said something about another woman, but he'd never known his brother to stick with a woman for more than a couple of months, and they all knew he wasn't reliable in the monogamy department. What if, at this very minute, his brother was making a move on his woman?

Unable to resist, Ben turned the doorknob, cracking the door. He saw nothing but the hallway wall. Damn. His imagination was supplying plenty of illicit pictures of the scene in the den. He could still hear them arguing back and forth, but he also remembered his and Monica's argument last night…and what the fighting had led to.

"…search the apartment," he heard Wes say.

Great. Just great.

"You're doing no such thing," Monica shot back.

"Get out of my way," Wes said, his voice hard. "For all I know, you've got some poor guy handcuffed to your bed back there."

"Get real, Wes. I haven't done anything to anybody—lately."

"I could arrest you, you know," Wes said, standing right outside the bathroom door. Ben could see the side seam of his uniform pants and a sliver of his gun belt. "Then we'll see who likes handcuffs."

"You wouldn't dare," Monica countered, though her voice shook.

"Watch me."

He couldn't let Wes arrest her. How had this night

gotten so out of control? All he'd wanted was to prove to Monica that he could be fun. That he could be like Wes. That Wes wasn't the only Kimball with an aura of danger and adventure. And, man, she'd responded beautifully. Hadn't he, just minutes ago, gotten her wet and naked?

Now everything had fallen apart.

While his younger brother laughed his butt off at his inept striptease—which led to a fire—and his ridiculous attempt to be exciting by skinny-dipping, Monica would realize what a nerd he was. She'd drop him like a hot potato. She'd kick him out of her apartment and her life.

But he didn't see what choice he had.

Swallowing his pride and relieved his father hadn't lived to witness the humiliation to come, Ben tossed a towel around his waist and pushed open the door.

7

"YOU'RE NOT TAKING HER anywhere," Ben said, ignoring the punch to his heart at seeing Wes and Monica standing so close together.

"Dammit, Ben, I told you to stay put."

He crossed his arms over his chest. "While you get arrested?"

She glared up at him, green eyes fired for battle. "I can handle myself. I don't need you coming to my rescue."

Now he'd gotten her pissed at him. Wonderful. He was so talented at seduction, he ought to give lessons. "Hey, don't snap at me. I wasn't the one threatening to arrest you."

"Wes wouldn't have arrested me."

Wes rocked back on his heels, looking as though he was loving every minute of the drama. "Oh, yes. I would have."

"Shut up," she and Ben said to Wes at the same time.

Monica's gaze came back to Ben. "Do you think I want to be responsible for embarrassing you? Causing you to lose the respect of your colleagues? Of the town?"

"Even if he hadn't shown up, it hardly matters. Your neighbors saw everything."

"They don't know who you are."

Wes's gaze was filled with admiration as he looked at Monica. "The story of how *you* got *him* to go skinny-dipping must be a doozy."

Monica shrugged. "I'm talented that way."

Beneath his frustration, Ben was in awe of her. She was protecting him. She had such passion for select things—and people—and he was honored to be among the chosen.

But he couldn't let her take the blame. "It was my idea," he said, then winced at the smile in his brother's eyes.

"You're kidding."

"No," Ben said, ignoring Monica's warning glare.

Wes's smile bloomed into a full belly laugh. "I love it! *Ben* skinny-dipping. And the fire?"

Ben's face heated. "When I got undressed..."

Wes held his stomach. "Oh, man." He nudged Ben. "Guess you managed better than fire drills and filing, after all. Didn't have much faith in you, really. Though when this gets out, no one's going to believe that part. Baxter's saintly fire chief is a closet skinny-dipper? A clumsy skinny-dipper who starts fires? I don't think so."

Monica poked her finger at Wes's chest, the tip of her long, silver nail looking lethal. "This may get out, but not through you."

Wes stepped back. "Hey, I'm not saying anything."

Monica smiled, but not sweetly. "I certainly hope not. Especially since we all have our little secrets, don't we?"

Even as Ben stiffened, Wes's eyes narrowed. "You wouldn't."

"Says the man who just threatened to arrest me."

What little secret? Something between Monica and Wes obviously. Ben stood silent, knowing he'd choke on his jealousy if he spoke.

Monica winked at Wes. "We sure wouldn't want your buddies at the station getting wind of your tendency to wear makeup and women's lingerie, would we?"

Ben stared at his brother.

Wes glared at Monica, his eyes icy. "Against my will."

"When this gets out, no one's going to believe that part."

Even as Ben acknowledged she'd thrown Wes's words back in his face, he finally saw the whole picture. And what a picture it formed. "How did you manage to get him into your lingerie?"

"I was pretty angry."

Ben smiled at her and realized how radically he'd changed his view of that night since he'd gotten to know her. At the time, he'd thought she was a nut for exacting revenge, now he found himself admiring her. Very few people got the better of Wesley Kimball, and obviously even fewer got the better of Monica. More passion—and strength.

Which made him all the more surprised to realize how much he'd missed her passion tonight. Navy and white clothes? Flat hair? Questioning him about his hot car? Saying things like "golly"? Where was the flamboyant Monica who wore skirts in mole-exposing lengths and whispered breathy, bold suggestions in his ear?

The communicator hooked to Wes's shirt beeped, distracting Ben from his thoughts.

"Lieutenant, you there?" the dispatcher asked.

Relief evident in his eyes, Wes answered back, "Here."

"We got us a brawl at a party on Ivy Road."

"I'm on my way." Wes sighed, backing away. "I love working Saturday night. It's been a thrill, guys," he said, waving as he scooted out the door.

"Make sure you send Steve and the rest of the fire department on their way. With no mention of Ben," Monica called after him, her tone ominous.

"Yes, ma'am," Wes called back, scooting faster.

As the door closed, Monica stared after him. "What did I ever see in that idiot?"

"I wouldn't mind understanding that myself," Ben said, trying to make the comment sound casual, as if he wasn't dying to know.

She turned her head. "This is a weird conversation to be having with you."

"It's been a weird night."

"Can't argue with you there." She pulled the towel off her head, and her long red hair tumbled out, the wet strands clinging to her skin. Her makeup was smudged; black rimmed her eyes. She'd never looked more beautiful.

He wanted to go to her, touch her with the flirting ease they'd found earlier, but his boldness had deserted him, leaving him contemplative—and underdressed. "I think I'll get dressed."

"Your clothes are burned on the grill."

He winced. "I don't suppose you have any sweats or…" he trailed off, his gaze sweeping her body. Nothing that covered those curves, that hugged her perfect waistline could possibly work for him.

Flushing, she glanced down at herself. "I'll see what I can find."

"If you don't mind, would it be okay if I slept on the sofa?" Her eyes widened, so he continued. "The, uh...dip in the pool sobered me, but the alcohol won't clear my system for hours. I'd rather not drive for a while."

She nodded. "Or I could drive you home."

He remembered thinking that she might be using him just to get her pride back after the breakup with Wes. If that was true, she was no doubt deeply regretting that idea at the moment. He was fairly certain bad-assed guys like Wes and Jack didn't start fires, drag their dates into a freezing pool, embarrass them in front of their neighbors and have the cops barge into their apartment. Excitement, maybe, but certainly the wrong kind.

He shrugged, not knowing how to make amends. "Sure."

They skirted around each other, then headed in opposite directions. Ben felt like punching his fist through a wall. He had to find a way to make it all up to her, but he had to know something first. "Why did you tell me about the lingerie and the makeup?" He paused long enough for her to stop in the doorway of her bedroom, then turn to face him. "You've kept the secret this long. You wouldn't tell the whole story now."

She lifted her chin. "I might."

"But why? The truth has the potential to embarrass you as much as Wes."

The caution in her eyes slid into tenderness. "I just couldn't bear to see him mock you," she said softly, then slipped into her bedroom.

Ben stood in the hall, wearing a stunned expression, a towel and soggy boxers, wondering helplessly if he'd just fallen in love.

MONICA GLARED at her makeup-smeared face in the mirror. "What's wrong with you? You're standing two feet from the man wearing a towel, and he wants to sleep on the couch."

With a damp washcloth, she repaired her face, grateful for the gift of waterproof mascara, then combed through her tangled hair. She had to admit Wes barging into her apartment and threatening to arrest her had put something of a damper on the evening, but as long as the lieutenant kept his mouth shut, no one would ever know who she'd been in the pool with, or whose clothing had started the fire. People would just roll their eyes and say, *Monica's out of control and smack in the middle of man trouble—again.* Ben's reputation was safe.

So, she wanted her hot date back. Tonight Ben had flirted with her, he'd *wanted* her, and she was very afraid that when the sun rose the odd spell he'd been under would be over.

She had to admit she was curious what had brought on the mood swing and change of heart regarding her. He'd obviously enjoyed their kiss last night, but had that really driven him to Corvette-buying and seduction? Skinny-dipping and a dangerously hot shower?

That kiss *was* pretty damn awesome. Look at the change it had wrought in her.

Then it hit her. Maybe he was doing the same thing. Maybe he was being wild for her benefit, just as she was acting conservative for his.

You said you wanted him to loosen up. Get the starch out of his shorts. He has.

But, she thought, wandering into her bedroom, it troubled her that his actions might be forced instead of genuine.

She'd felt off-balance in the role of the cautious one, though she'd certainly been right about the heat beneath his starch. And the man's body…she shivered in delight. Those shoulders alone could make a nun forget her vows of chastity. But then—

The hell with it. She flung open her lingerie drawer, wondering which would appeal to Ben more—the black satin camisole and tap pants or the blue baby-doll nightie?

Why should she care *why* he wanted her? She'd gotten what she wanted. A stable man. A man of respect, who respected her.

And with that, she chose the black. Surely Ben didn't want a conservative lover. She'd been at the demure business for *hours*.

How are you going to keep it up? her conscience whispered. *How long can you pretend to be something you're not?*

She shoved worries aside, digging into her closet for the matching ostrich-feather-decorated mules. In minutes, she had dried, fluffed hair, glossy lips and was dressed to stop traffic. But she strode back to the dresser, even as she started for the bedroom door.

She held up the blue nightie again. Maybe…

A knock sounded against the door.

"Come in," she said automatically.

Ben strode in. "Monica, I was thinking—" He ground to a halt as he saw her. His jaw dropped. He sagged against the dresser.

Her heart racing, Monica held up the nightie by its thin straps. "Let me guess…you prefer blue."

"I—" He blinked. "You—"

Had she shocked him into silence with her boldness? Was that a good thing? Or a bad thing? Dammit, she hated this uncertainty.

He still wore the wet, nearly see-through boxers. The outline of his erection was clearly visible.

Can't argue with biology.

Smiling demurely—quite a feat in a black satin camisole and tap pants—she dropped the nightie back in the drawer, then slinked toward him. She stopped just a few feet away, and recognized the intimacy of the situation, as if they'd both come home from work, looking forward to a quiet evening together. The picture of him making coffee in the big, gourmet kitchen she was building in her lake house flashed through her mind. The comforting steadiness of his hands as he stroked her cheek, then smiled with mischief at her idea of delaying dinner with seduction.

Irritated with herself for envisioning anyone besides her in her house, she flipped her hair over her shoulder, then slid her hands up his bare, muscled chest. "Blue?"

His throat twitched as he swallowed. "Ah, well…"

She wrapped her hands around his neck, then raked her fingers through his silky, black hair. "Am I making you nervous, Chief?"

"Definitely."

She brushed his boxer-clad hips with her silk-clad ones. "Good nervous, or bad nervous?"

His arm snaked around her waist, pressing her against him. "Oh, definitely good."

Aching need flowed into her breasts, into her stomach, then slid lower. "Yet you seem…uneasy. I'd think a guy like you would be used to being seduced.''

"Does Angie Malloy telling me in the tenth grade that she wore red panties count?''

Again, the easiness, the comfort of being with him slid through her. "Angie Malloy sounds like my kind of gal.''

An odd expression moved through his eyes. "Yeah. I guess she was.''

"That was some kind of scene earlier.'' Damn, why had *that* popped out? She was trying to get the romance back, not remind him how wrong everything had gone. But then, everything about their relationship was different than any other in her life. She felt comfortable having a discussion in the middle of seduction. It was absurd, but right. "If I hadn't shoved you under the water, trying to cover everything up...''

"Somebody might have recognized me.'' He stroked her back. "You've done a lot of protecting tonight. Of me. Aren't you worried about what people will say about you?''

She shrugged. "It hardly matters. People already think I'm wild and loose.''

"No, they don't.''

"Didn't you?'' She narrowed her eyes. "For all I know, you still do.''

He stroked her cheek, just as she'd imagined him doing in her vision. "I think you're vibrant and exciting.'' He paused as his thumb slid across her bottom lip. "Beautiful and sensual. And the most honorable person I've ever known.''

Her face heated. "Stop. I am not.''

"Yes, you are. You realized my brother was making fun of me and you leapt to my defense, regardless of how it make you look.''

She looked away. ''I was just tired of him being smug about the whole thing.''

With his index finger against her chin, he turned her to face him. ''You stood in front of me. No one's ever done that.'' He dipped his head until their lips were inches apart. ''No one's ever cared so much.''

Then his lips settled on hers and the passion, the heat and the raw need she'd expected arrived. His tongue tangled with hers, teasing and satisfying at the same time. Part of her wanted to stop him, to explain she cared, but just because he was the decent and honorable one. But their relationship didn't go deeper than that.

His fingers skimmed beneath her camisole, warming her back, teasing her sides, and she set aside everything but the chemistry bubbling inside her. As his mouth seduced hers, his fingers kneaded her back and his thumbs rubbed rhythmically against her rib cage. She clutched his neck, pressing her aching breasts against his chest.

The scent of him—spicy, clean, male—was shooting her heart rate higher, making her head swim. He kissed her as if he wanted to inhale her whole, as if he couldn't get close enough, fast enough.

Trailing openmouthed kisses against her throat, he gasped, ''Bed?''

Was he asking her permission, or its location? In answer, she let her head fall back as his mouth cruised lower, to skim the top of one breast.

He slid one arm behind her knees and the other behind her back, then the few steps to the bed. His gaze was a fierce blue and fixed on her face. The determination and hunger she saw there made her stomach tremble in anticipation.

When he laid her on the bed, he followed her down without breaking body contact. His hips pinned her to the comforter as his mouth's pleasurable assault shifted from her lips to her jawline to her throat. She groaned at the intimate contact of skin and the pressure of his hard, heavy body against hers. Her hips bucked. He pressed his hardness against her in answer.

Then he flipped them, and she found herself straddling him, staring down into that remarkable face of his, moaning as the silk tap pants provided little barrier to the hard ridge of flesh beneath her. She sucked in air through her teeth, arching her back as her body heated and throbbed and she rocked her hips.

He slid his hands beneath her camisole, cupping her breasts. "You look damn good sitting up there."

She braced her hands against his bare chest, rolled her hips again. "I feel damn good."

As their gazes caught, he smiled. An odd emotion shot straight to her heart, and she curled her fingernails into his skin, wanting to hold on to the feeling, hold on to him.

His thumbs flicked over her nipples, and she shoved aside the tenderness shimmering through her, forgot any emotion, save one.

Lust.

She stripped off her cami, then attacked the waistband of his boxers, wondering where the hell her stash of condoms was. He sat up, replacing his fingers with his mouth, and arrows of pleasure shot from her breasts downward. Her belly trembled, then tightened into a coil, winding her into a spell of desperate desire. All he had to do, she was sure, was touch her between her legs, at her soft, throbbing point of need, and she'd explode.

She wanted to slow down, to bring him with her to the peak, but she wasn't sure she was strong enough. The need to connect with him, to absorb him, pulsed through her blood.

With fumbling, desperate fingers she finally managed to yank down the waistband of his boxers. She wrapped her hand around the hot, rigid length of him, and he clutched her to him, then froze, his mouth open, gasping for breath against her chest.

"Condoms…back pocket," he said.

Keeping one hand wrapped around him, she shoved her hand beneath him, wishing she could fully appreciate the tight feel of his buns, then realized he didn't have back pockets. "Where?"

His gaze met hers, and pain like she'd never seen darted through his eyes. "In my jeans."

Burned. On the grill.

Not about to give into panic yet, Monica crawled toward the head of her bed, then reached into the nightstand drawer. Triumphant, she held a foil package between her fingers. Then she frowned. "Two. Only two."

With either a chuckle or a groan, Ben reached for her, pulling her back on top of him. "Greedy, are you?"

"Yes," she said as she ripped open the package— with her teeth. Once, twice wasn't going to be enough. Need for him clawed through her, demanding to be sated, and that was on top of the lust lingering in her system ever since she'd laid eyes on the man.

She wriggled off him. "Don't move."

He leaned back on his elbows, watching her kick off her shoes and strip off her tap pants. "I'm not going anywhere."

She pulled the condom from the package, then glanced down at his lap, noting his boxers were pulled down to just below his hips, his hardened flesh peeking over the rim of the waistband. Hell, she didn't have time to mess with any more clothes. Her knees were already trembling so she could barely stand. The coil of desire tightened. She bit her lip, wishing she could control herself, fighting for control, and finding none.

He continued to stare at her, his gaze hot. His hair was tousled from her fingers, his chest glistened in sweat.

Control be damned.

Straddling his thighs, she rolled on the protection, then lifted her hips and plunged over him. And the orgasm rippled through her, rolling and cresting through her body like the sea returning home. "Mmm," she moaned, dropping her head back.

He sat up, his strong arms surrounding her. "Did you— Are you—"

She wrapped her arms around his neck, laying her head on his shoulder as she tried to catch her breath. "Give me a minute here, Chief."

His hands cupped her face, and she gave him a dazed smile. He grinned back at her. "You're beautiful."

She wanted to be embarrassed about her enthusiasm, but he seemed so damn pleased with himself, she merely laid her mouth over his. She nibbled his lips lazily, glad she could explore a bit, now that the edge to her hunger had eased. He had great lips, she decided philosophically, just like every other body part he possessed. She could spend quite a bit of time exploring each one.

But then he lifted her a bit, twisting so she lay under him. His face hovering over her, his body still hard inside her, he pushed in, then pulled back. She arched her neck, her eyes glazing over as the pleasure rocketed back up.

"Again," he said, driving deeper. "And this time I want to watch."

It didn't seem possible, but the throbbing began anew. Even harder this time, more insistent. As he pushed in and out of her, their skin glowing with sweat, their bodies gliding against each other, her stomach wound into a complicated knot. She wanted him, but why did she have to want him this much? This didn't feel fun or light or simple. This was fierce, intense...beautiful. Like him.

She met him thrust for thrust. He never slowed or paused. His gaze never left her face. She forced herself to keep her gaze locked on his, even when she wanted to look away. He had amazing control and focus. She wanted to be pissed about that, especially since she had neither of those things where he was concerned. But the results were too incredible to argue with.

Her peak was churning toward explosion again. The energy bubbled through her, straining for release. Closing her eyes, she arched her back.

"No," he said, and she stared up at him. "Don't shut me out."

She lifted her hand, plunging her fingers into his hair—and held on.

Even as her completion bucked through her, he

threw his head back, his hips pounding against her, his body exploding.

And as she watched him lose control, finally, all she could think was how weak he'd made her. How would she ever build the walls again when he didn't want her anymore?

All she could do was regret she'd let him close enough to see her weakness.

Him.

"WHY AM I STILL HALF-DRESSED?" Ben asked, though with only mild concern.

"Hell if I know."

They lay beside each other, flat on their backs on Monica's bed, both wheezing and, he presumed, sweaty. He reached for her hand, noting her palm was damp. Both sweaty. While he was at it, he brought her hand to his mouth, kissing her wrist, then lightly sinking his teeth into the pad at the base of her thumb.

Her hand jerked. "You've lost your mind if you think you're trying that again."

Smiling, he rolled toward her. "I'll let you regain your strength."

Her eyes opened, her gaze sliding to his. "But should I? Do you really think this can work?"

Ben felt as if he'd been kicked in the gut. The serious expression on her face scared him. What had he done?

She pushed him back, then rose and snagged a red silk robe from the end of the bed. She turned her back to him as she slid into it. "Have we jumped into this too fast?"

Huh? Stunned, he watched her cross to the dresser, where she picked up a brush and began pulling it through her tangled locks. Her hand trembled, though, and her eyes, reflected in the mirror, were troubled.

"No, we haven't," he returned, not knowing what else to say.

Her distance was palpable. And not just in the physical sense. *She's pushing me away.* He felt it as surely as he felt the love for her coursing through his veins.

She couldn't do this. He'd finally found the courage to pursue her, to give in to the desire she inspired in him. He'd made a fool of himself all night for her. Drinking too much, coming on to her in public, starting a fire, skinny-dipping in her apartment pool. He could match her in excitement and abandon. He had to. He couldn't lose her when they'd barely begun.

Respect among his peers and the public he served had been paramount to him. He'd always vowed his father wouldn't have lived to be ashamed of him. But his reputation paled glaringly in comparison to his need for her. He could show her. He could have her. He just had to be smart. To remind her how incredible they were together.

Approaching her from behind, he took the brush from her hand, gliding it through her hair. He leaned forward so he could inhale the enticing scent of sex and perfume rising off her skin. "I think you're terrific. I think we're perfect together." He brushed her hair to the side, exposing her neck, so he could press his lips against her warm skin. "I think making love with you is…perfect."

She leaned into his caress. Her hands clenched on the lip of the dresser.

He slid his tongue around her earlobe. "I know you want me."

She moaned, reaching behind her to link her hands around his neck.

He parted her silky robe, his hand cupping one breast, his thumb flicking over the tip. His blood simmered as her skin flushed beneath his touch. Her nipple puckered, and he squeezed briefly before he continued his slow, measured strokes.

Don't move too quickly. Remind her how much she enjoys your touch.

And he smiled at the memory of her climaxing at their first intimate connection. He'd fallen a little more in love with her at that moment, and he wondered how many more moments like that lay in their future.

Endless, he decided, sweeping his tongue down the side of her neck, *if I just make the right moves.*

"Look at us in the mirror," he said, parting her robe so just the inside edges of her breasts and a slice of her stomach were reflected. Watching her gaze follow the movement of his hands, he slid his fingertips between her breasts, past her rib cage, her belly, then disappearing beneath the mirror's gaze into the softness between her legs.

She was already wet for him. Biting back a groan, he fought against the pulsing need between his own legs.

"We match each other."

"It's chemical," she said, though she leaned back against him.

It's so much more than that. He rubbed his finger up, then down, then sideways, as slowly as he could force himself, across the nub of flesh vibrating in sexual need. "Mmm. I know something about chemistry."

Her hips bumped his. "Paramedic training."

His fingers were slick from her body, and she wanted to talk about work. "No." He pressed his advantage by pinching her clitoris between his thumb and forefinger.

She gasped.

"If you're really interested, I've got some text-books—"

"You are so totally dead when I get my breath back."

Smiling, he released her, but just the most sensitive part of her. The rest of her body, he explored shamelessly with his hands, his mouth, his tongue. The warm sweetness of her skin he breathed in like a man deprived of oxygen. The curve of her from breast, to waist, to hips, he absorbed with a moan. The woman was so ripe and built for pleasure he could hardly believe the twist of fate that had brought her to his doorstep.

She spun suddenly, her green eyes full of fire and anger. She jabbed her finger against his chest. "You can't make me want you."

He captured her finger, sucked it into his mouth. "Oh, yes. I can."

Her head dipped, her forehead brushing his chest. "Damn."

He slid her hands around his waist. "Don't move," he said, echoing her command from earlier. Hoping the desire held long enough, he shucked his boxers. Wet, they were damn binding at the moment. He parted her robe, pressing his hardness against her stomach, tucking his hands at the base of her spine. "Don't you feel the steady stream of need flowing through your veins?"

Her head jerked up. "Just get on with it and kiss me."

He obliged her with an ease and tenderness he was sure she hadn't expected. He slid his lips against hers, tasting, enjoying, then seducing her surrender. He liked having her panting and needy and suspected very few people ever penetrated her air of casual distain. Like him in the beginning, they were intimidated by her sharpness, intelligence and seeming lack of vulnerability. How many people ever really paused to consider the woman beneath the body and the surface confidence?

She covered her vulnerability with a sly smile and sometimes outrageous behavior. And each time he uncovered a layer, he was more and more entranced.

He dropped to his knees, kissing her stomach. "Admit how much you loved the skinny-dipping."

She tangled her hands in his hair, massaging his scalp with her fingernails in a way that made his whole body rigid with desire. "It was fun...before I hit the water."

Fighting back a wince, he dipped his tongue into her navel. "You loved it."

"Well, I—" She sucked in a breath as his tongue dipped into, then beyond the curls at the juncture of her thighs. "You're really good at that."

He swept his tongue down the length of her. She clutched his shoulders, her breath coming in short bursts. When she trembled on the brink, he tumbled her onto the bed, then took just a moment to roll on protection.

He lifted her hips. "We're going to need at least a dozen more." Then, he plunged inside.

Her warmth and sweetness surrounded him, taking

his breath. He fought to keep the rhythm controlled and easy, praying he could hold on long enough. She clutched his arms, her face a mask of tension and pleasure, her head tossing against the comforter.

"Lucky for us…I've got a whole box in the car," he whispered in her ear just as her climax pulsed through her, squeezing him, bringing his own completion with sharp thrusts and ecstasy singing through his muscles.

HE DUG INTO THE BOX twice more before the first light of dawn peeked through the blinds. He explored her body thoroughly, but figured he'd made little headway into that complicated, female mind of hers.

As he kissed her shoulder and slipped from her bed, he wondered if he really had any prayer of holding her to his heart.

8

MONDAY MORNING, Ben paced his office. He had to go out there soon. He'd have to face her.

What should he say? How should he act?

He'd called her yesterday, leaving a message on her answering machine for her to call him back. She hadn't. Why hadn't he stormed over to her apartment, demanded she see him?

Because, in the light of day on Sunday, he'd analyzed their night together—and realized Monica had been more than a little different at the bar. She'd really acted strange. *I don't know, Ben. That sounds a little fast for me.* She'd actually said that after he'd told her about his Corvette.

Monica was worried about *speed?*

But then he went back to his own thoughts and desires. When he'd first met her, he'd complained about her flamboyance, even as he sensed he was attracted to her fire. He coveted that fire. A fire that had seemed oddly doused on Saturday night.

Why had she been so different? Had his influence somehow affected her?

He should be happy at a toned-down version of Monica. Hadn't that been his chief reservation about them together? But he wasn't pleased at all about the change. He wanted wild, unpredictable Monica back.

Then again, maybe it was a temporary thing. Maybe she'd just been in a different mood.

And what about him? He couldn't take her skinny-dipping everyday. He *definitely* couldn't start any more fires. He had a professional reputation to live up to, not to mention the legend of his father. That mousse had made his scalp itch, and the Corvette sucked down gas like crazy.

His plan to be bad and dangerous—like Wes—had worked, but could he really keep up with her? The old her, that is?

One thing was for sure—worrying was getting him nowhere. It was time to be bold. And dangerous. Again.

He'd better charge the fire extinguisher.

"Hey, Monica, heard you had a pool party over the weekend. You inviting me next time?"

In the middle of preparing for her design presentation, Monica attached a computer cable to the overhead projector. Hoping not to betray her conflicted thoughts about her "date," she smiled wryly over her shoulder at Phil. "Only if you bring the water wings."

Phil's round face flushed as he walked around the cables snaking across the firehouse's den floor. He rounded the long folding table holding her equipment and stopped next to her.

She'd enjoyed getting to know Phil, the firehouse's chef, over the last couple of weeks. He was warm and easy to talk to, making her feel as if she was part of the firehouse, instead of just a temporary interruption to their routine.

"Hot date?" Phil teased, nudging her.

She'd known keeping Saturday night under wraps would prove impossible, but at least she could start the ball rolling on the version she wanted floating around. Between her love life and the Kimball brothers, she might be a better press agent than a designer. "A little too hot. Some idiot at my apartment complex left a barbecue grill lit, and my date's clothes caught on fire."

Phil grinned. "Heard the clothes weren't on anybody when they flamed up."

Monica blushed. "Well, we'd been planning to go skinny-dipping…" As Phil's smile broadened, Monica saw Ben heading toward them. "Shh. Here comes the chief. I'd rather he didn't hear about my weekend plans."

Nodding, Phil stuffed his hands in his pockets. "Not gonna be easy. The whole town's talking about it." He scooted off toward the kitchen.

Great. At least no one would believe Ben had been her swimming partner, so his staid reputation was safe. She didn't see how another exaggeration could hurt hers.

"Morning," Ben said. His gaze locked on Monica's, the heat direct and unmistakable.

Her stomach fluttered. Her knees weakened. But when her heart sighed, she knew she was in big trouble. She'd gotten his attention by being someone she wasn't. Her plan had worked. Now what the hell was she going to do? She couldn't wear boring clothes forever.

"Ready for the—" He stopped, his gaze sliding over her from head to toe. "What are you wearing?"

Already out of sorts, the frown on Ben's face did little to comfort her. She wanted to snap her response, but remembered to plaster a demure smile on her face. "It's new."

"It's beige."

She ground her teeth. "I thought you liked beige."

"On walls." His gaze swept her again. "Even your shoes are beige. It's…different."

"You don't like it."

He shook his head. "No, I do. You're—" He moved closer, his voice lowered. "You look fantastic in anything. Especially nothing."

She went hot all over. She had to get back to the presentation before she grabbed him. "I just need a few more minutes of setup here, then when Edwin arrives with the fabric samples, we can—"

He leaned closer. His lips nearly brushed her cheek. "I don't want to talk about Edwin."

She stepped back, but the table stopped further retreat. Heavens, he smelled good. And that uniform. *Oh, baby.* Knowing the muscles hidden by his pressed white shirt had her nearly moaning in longing. Could the scent of starch actually be considered erotic?

"Really?" she squeaked out.

He closed the distance between them. "I want to grab you and run out of here." His breath stirred the hairs at her nape. "Your silk sheets are calling us. Can't you hear them?"

"But we have responsibilities. The presentation. The mayor's coming."

"Later. Right now I want you."

His boldness excited her, nearly as much as his restraint had tempted her in the beginning. But she found herself disappointed in his attitude. Men were coming to the firehouse on their day off to participate in the voting. They couldn't inconvenience all those people just to satisfy their needs.

You wanted him to loosen up. He has. Oh, yeah, he was so loose, she half expected him to melt into a puddle.

She also questioned herself. Two weeks ago would she have grabbed his hand and run with him? She'd always been daring, but was she selfish? Would she have put her own needs ahead of responsibilities? Did Ben think she was the kind of person who would?

She wasn't sure, but she knew she couldn't indulge herself today. Not even for Ben.

Her gaze connected with his. A smile spread across his face. His electric-blue eyes seemed to burn clear to her soul. A challenge. A promise. She swallowed hard. "Ben, we can't—"

"Good morning, Chiefette," Edwin announced as he strode into the room.

Angling his head, Ben stepped back. "Chiefette?"

"Don't ask," she muttered, then glanced over at her assistant, silently thanking him for his timely interruption. At least they had a busy day ahead of them to keep her mind off of Ben. After the presentation, they had supplies to buy—away from the firehouse. Until she got her balance back, she needed distance from Ben. "Did you bring the fabric samples?"

Edwin patted a folder tucked beneath his arm. "Right here."

"Great. Let's get started." She risked a brief glance at Ben, noting he'd banked the sensual fire in his eyes, though only by a degree or two. She fought for a professional tone. "Chief, can we continue our discussion later?"

His lips tipped up in a half smile. "Count on it."

As he turned and strode away, Monica couldn't help watching him go. He had an awesome butt. Maybe, if she rushed the setup, she could lure him back to his office... She shook the thought away.

Being demure was a damn heavy burden to carry.

"I've got great news," Edwin said, his face beaming.

"Yeah?" She could use some great news.

"Dana and I have a date Friday night, and Collins Paint and Hardware is upping our discount to twenty-five percent."

Despite the turmoil of her personal life, Monica gave Edwin a high five. At least somebody was happy.

"THANKS TO EVERYONE for taking time out of your busy schedules to see the progress we've made with the firehouse's new design."

As Monica began her presentation, Ben pulled his gaze from the mayor, who'd obviously just left an interactive a.m. showing of *Blue Hawaii*. Wincing, he decided his boss should have stuck with the black leather. Those white clam diggers were a picture-perfect example of taking an obsession way too far.

Speaking of obsession... Would he have really raced out with Monica? He wasn't sure, but tempting her had felt amazingly powerful. Being bad could be fun.

He watched her lean against the table, her long legs— Hey, wasn't that skirt a little long, too? It covered her knees.

"I also want to take this opportunity to thank my assistant, Edwin Collins." Monica gestured to Edwin, who sat in the front row. "He's been invaluable in getting data processed for this demonstration, as well as a source of creative ideas.''

A polite smattering of applause followed this announcement. A few people even looked impressed. Another reason Ben couldn't help but love her.

She'd given Edwin confidence.

"You have an important decision to make here today," she continued. "For the past two weeks, you've watched the changes being made to the sleeping quarters and offices. Now, the living and dining areas are yours. Remember these changes will shape the firehouse for years to come. Those who come after you will enjoy the comforts and practicalities *you* decide on. I've worked with firehouses for years, and I'm impressed with the unique opportunity your chief has given you.''

Her gaze met his in that moment. His heart pounded at the questions he saw in her eyes. She'd seemed uncomfortable with him this morning. And definitely surprised by his silk sheets proposition. The Ben she'd first met certainly would have never said that, and he would have been a tight-ass if she'd made a similar suggestion to him.

Knowing her, loving her, had changed him.

Not all his boldness was pretend. She'd given *him* confidence as well. He'd always admired his father's confidence and had always assumed it stemmed from his work, but maybe not. Maybe the swagger in his step, the quality that had made so many people respect and admire him, had come from his personal relationships, the confidence that he loved and was loved in return.

"To begin," Monica said, breaking into his thoughts as she flipped on an overhead projector, displaying a three-dimensional picture of the den. "We have the Southern Plantation House."

A murmur of pleased surprise moved through the crowd.

"We have elegant but comfortable sofas and love seats, with clawed feet and wooden accents. I've included wooden rockers for the porch outside, oak cabinets and floors in the kitchen, wide-paneled ceiling fans, and a fully stocked entertainment center."

As the program rolled on, and with the 3-D effects giving the sense of actually walking through the completed rooms, she commented periodically on color selections for paint and wallpaper. Nothing fussy, just the overall sense of Old South charm and tradition.

She moved through the other two options—the Sports and Modern plans. Most of the men sat forward when she mentioned the pool table and recliners, with heat and massage and a cooler in the armrest, contained in the Sports plan. Ben stared in rapt attention when she showed the steel and black-accented, state-of-the-art features of the Modern plan.

But as she wrapped up the presentation, he could tell there was a problem.

There wasn't a clear-cut winner of the three choices. Small arguments broke out around the room. As still shots of the rooms continued to flash, Ben groaned.

"I know this is a lot to consider," she said. "But I'm open to discussion for ways to make everyone comfortable and—"

She broke off as a commotion rattled down the hall leading to the front door. Everyone in the audience turned toward the noise which sounded, oddly enough, like a grunt—an animal grunt. Bernie was around somewhere, but he was more of a barker, so who—or what...

"Heel, Penelope!" came the sharp call from the hallway.

Ben rose from his chair but hadn't taken more than two steps when the voice and, he assumed, Penelope, strode into view.

All three hundred-plus pounds of her.

PENELOPE PRANCED into the room, lifted her fat neck—highlighted by a diamond-studded collar—and oinked.

Monica blinked, then refocused. Nope. No mirage. There definitely was a giant, pink, *leashed* pig in the firehouse den.

Her handler, a bearded, gray-haired man in overalls, waved. "Hope we're not late. Had to get Penny's bath in this morning."

Ben rubbed his temples. Poor man, Monica thought. He tried so hard to keep the fire department running smoothly and professionally. And in return he got Edwin and his accidents, an Elvis-obsessed mayor for a boss and pigs in the living room.

Snickers rippled through the crowd, but Penelope and her owner seemed oblivious. They ambled farther into the room then, spotting Monica at the podium, they switched direction and headed toward her. Chin raised as she walked, the pig's spiral tail wagged, her hindquarters swayed, her shoulders shimmied.

Penelope knew how to work a room.

"You through with your presentation, ma'am?" the man asked.

Still watching Penelope, Monica didn't know what else to do but nod.

"Great. If you'll just set that projector on the floor, I'll show y'all Penny's new trick. She's been workin' on it for weeks. Just couldn't wait to do her part as a citizen of this great town of ours."

As the man turned away, Monica held her questions, and, with a little more effort, her humor. After she unplugged her equipment, setting everything on the floor, she caught Penelope sniffing at her shoes. Her cold, mushy snout brushed her ankle. Monica stared down at the pig, who lifted her head and stared right back. "Watch the fabric, Penny," she said quietly. She'd never get pig secretions out of linen.

Penelope sat on her wide haunches and grunted.

"Chief?" the man called. "You ready for us to get started?"

Ben managed to release himself from his frozen, stunned state and stalk to the front of the room. "Harold, what are you doing here?" he asked quietly, his gaze darting to the audience, no doubt at the mayor specifically, who looked confused by the interruption.

"Pig lab," Harold said, setting a metal step stool on the floor. "Look what I taught Penny."

"Harold—"

"Up, girl."

In a blink, Penny ambled onto the stool, then laid her hoofs on the edge of the table, pushing her considerable weight forward until she stood on the table top. Now practically nose-to-snout with the animal, Monica blinked in surprise. And took a big step back.

Penny tossed her head, then lay down and rolled over onto her back.

Ben groaned. The firefighters clapped.

Harold beamed. "Whadda ya think? That's some cooperative patient, huh, Chief?"

"Harold…"

"Now, I know you want to get started, so I'll just stand over here." Harold winked. "She'll feel more comfortable if I'm nearby when she goes under."

Ben leaned over Penelope, close to Harold, keeping his voice low. "The pig lab is next month." He was careful to keep the conversation out of earshot from his men.

"Oh," Harold said. "Shoot."

"And we do the procedures at the hospital."

Fascinated, but a little unnerved by the whole turn of events—why did they need to go to the hospital, and what exactly were they going to *do* to Penelope?—Monica leaned over Penelope on the opposite side from Ben. "What's pig lab?" she whispered.

"We use pigs for the paramedics to practice their skills. They put in chest tubes, collapse the lungs, then inflate them. Pig organs are very similar to human ones, so the uh…*patient* performs a valuable community service."

Personally, Monica wondered if someone had informed Penelope of how extensive her contribution to the community would be. "Uh-huh."

"Harold, did the mayor make all this clear when he drafted you into this job?"

"Sure. He said you needed a good, strong pig." He patted Penelope's tummy. "Penny's the best I got."

Ben sighed. Looked at the floor. Then looked at the ceiling. Finally, he looked directly at Harold. "I think the mayor intended for you to volunteer one of your pigs destined for the—" he lowered his voice further "—bacon aisle."

Penelope lifted her head and grunted.

Monica patted her shoulder.

Harold gasped. "But, but... Penny's won the Georgia State Swine Beauty Pageant four years in a row. She eats at my kitchen table. She sleeps at the end of my bed."

Ben grasped Harold's shoulder. "I think we should limit her community volunteer activity to riding in a convertible in the Independence Day parade."

His heart in his eyes, Harold glanced at Penelope, then Ben. "Thank you, Chief."

Ben simply nodded.

Watching the simple, compassionate way Ben dealt with the pig farmer made Monica's heart quiver.

She was forced to admit that their connection went way beyond the physical. But what had their wild night together really meant to *him?* Clearly, he was physically attracted to her, but was that all he felt? She'd just wanted to prove she hadn't lost her appeal to men, but now this one man meant more than her personal quest.

But did he want her, or the woman she'd been pretending to be?

Harold patted Penny's hoof. "Let's go, girl."

Monica could have sworn irritation slid through the pig's eyes before she rolled over her considerable girth and stood.

Harold guided her off the table, then they both strolled out of the room.

"Ah, Chief," someone in the crowd called out, "there goes our lunch."

Ben's face reddened, and Monica instinctively darted around the table and stood in front of him. "Sorry about that, folks. I had this wild idea about some outdoor landscaping and starting a vegetable garden for Phil.'' She smiled and hoped she looked suitably embarrassed. ''Phil, I'm sorry to say you won't be able to make that wild truffle salad. Penelope doesn't like to get her snout dirty.''

A collective chuckle rumbled through the room at this preposterous explanation, but the men were no longer looking at Ben, so she didn't really care how stupid she sounded.

''Now, let's have some discussion about the three themes you saw, so we can take our vote…''

''YES, MR. MAYOR,'' Ben said, staring across his desk at his boss. ''I'm sure I can work everything out. Ms. O'Malley is extremely competent.''

At decorating. At everything else, she was both incredible and confusing.

Of course Ben stamped out these thoughts as the mayor rolled on about the mix-up of the pig, the garden—which the mayor didn't recall approving—and the complete stalemate of the voting. Since the alternative of Monica's silly truffle explanation was the pig lab—which made the mayor himself look bad— Ben kept silent on that issue and fought to explain the voting, which had been his idea.

He tried not to think about the possibility that this morning's fiasco would run in the newspaper alongside the article Fire Chief—Closet Firebug and Skinny-Dipper!

Being bad certainly came with risks he hadn't prepared himself for.

''I'm sure a compromise can be reached,'' he said to the mayor.

''How?'' Worked into a frothy lather now, Mayor Collins stood, then paced, waving his hands wildly, the white clam diggers flapping against his calves. "We can't have the kitchen looking like *Star Wars* and the den like something out of *Gone With the Wind*."

"Moni—I mean *Ms. O'Malley* is very skilled at these things. I'm sure she can meet everyone's needs." He barely resisted slapping himself on the forehead at the double meaning in his words.

"Oh, I never should have let that *Californian* handle this," the mayor moaned. "But aren't those legs of hers incredible?"

Ben ground his teeth to keep from dropping his jaw.

"She reminds me so much of my wife. Let me tell you something, Chief—a confident woman is man's greatest treasure and his biggest weakness."

Ben had been prepared to argue and defend Monica, so this admission surprised him. Hell, he and the mayor had something in common. Who knew? "Yes, sir."

"Women drive you crazy, distract you from business, interrupt your schedule. They can talk you into or out of anything they please. And damned if they aren't the most wonderful creatures ever invented." The mayor paused, linking his hands behind his back as he paced. "And if you find the right one...well, God help you. And God bless you."

Having his confusing feelings explained so concisely and eloquently by the *mayor,* of all people, left Ben speechless. If he wasn't sure he loved her before, he sure knew now.

But she'd spent the night with the fun, wild side of him. Would she would want the side of him that tended to overwork and obsess over regulations and training?

Wes broke rules. Monica laughed at them. Ben set them.

He could relax more, probably needed to, and he'd enjoyed the freedom and abandon of Saturday night, but he didn't think he could completely let go of his need for order. Just how much of himself was he willing to compromise for love?

Frustrated, he redirected his attention to the mayor.

"Now, Chief Kimball, I expect you'll work this out." The mayor knit his bushy eyebrows, but he hardly pulled off the stern look in his Hawaiian-print shirt and pants that didn't reach the tops of his shoes. "I'm bringing the city council by in a few days to inspect the work, so I'm sure you'll have everything under control by then."

Ben started to massage his temples, then realized this grand compromise was something, ultimately, that Monica would have to apply her design expertise to. And while he felt completely unsure about their personal relationship, he had no doubt about her design skills. "Sure. No problem."

Mayor Collins glanced at his watch. "Well, I'm off. Keep me—"

Someone rapped on the door.

"Come in," Ben called.

The door opened, and Monica strode in, her hips swaying gently as she moved. "Am I interrupting?"

Ben stood, though his mouth had dried to dust, so his reply was delayed. The mayor graciously filled in, though Ben noticed his gaze swept Monica's figure before he found his own voice. "Not at all, Ms. O'Malley. I was just leaving." He crossed to her, grasping one of her hands in both of his. "Terrific presentation. I was just telling the chief how confident I am that you can work out this little disagreement on the theme."

Ben raised an eyebrow. *Little disagreement?*

Mayor Collins released Monica, then scooted to the door, giving them both a backhanded wave. "See ya! And don't forget my favorite band, The Metal Heads, are performing a fifties revival concert tonight. They'll be taking care of business. I'm sure you will too." He laughed at his joke, then left the room.

Still staring at the closed office door, Monica propped her hands on her hips. "*Little disagreement?* The man turned four shades of purple during the voting."

Despite the mayor's fussiness, the pig's interruption and the doubts he had over the woman currently glaring at his office door, Ben smiled. They really did think so completely alike sometimes.

He extended his hand toward the chair in front of his desk. "Have a seat." When she did, crossing those spectacular legs demurely at the ankle, he returned to his own seat. He had her alone now, and just as soon as the design problem was settled, he was going to remind her how good they were together. "I'm assuming you have a plan cooking to settle this voting issue."

Her gaze shot to his, her eyes narrowed with suspicion. She was no doubt debating how he could have guessed her intentions so quickly and easily. Then she gave him a bland smile—the same one she'd had on her face so often the other night, the one that had him again wondering what was up with her. "Naturally."

"Care to share? The mayor's rather anxious."

"The voting line was clearly drawn with the Southern Plantation and Sports themes on opposite sides. I'm going to meld those two together. A few voted on the Modern theme, but that was obviously to please you, since everyone realized it had been drawn specifically for you."

"Had it?" he asked. The room was black and silver. Clean and plain.

She folded her hands in her lap. "Of course. Couldn't you tell?"

"It was a little stark." He paused, watching her carefully. "And plain."

"Maybe so. I probably should have added some plants."

"Is that how you think of me? Stark and plain?"

Her eyes widened. "No."

"The other night, the night of Edwin's trash can fire..." *The night we kissed for the first time. The night that changed my life forever.* "You said I needed to quit inhaling the starch in my shirts. Was that your colorful way of telling me I'm too stiff?"

Her gaze remained locked on his, and worry danced through the green depths. "No. Well, yes." She bit her lip. "You've loosened up quite a bit the last few days."

He stood, watching her eyes widen as he walked around the desk, then leaned back against the battered wood. Their knees nearly brushed. "And do you like me loose?"

She clenched her hands together. "I guess." She sank her teeth into her lip again, and his groin tightened with need. "You surprised me this morning, though. You weren't really serious about running out before the presentation, were you?"

He was tempted to say yes, but he couldn't really imagine he'd have gone through with it. His sense of responsibility toward the firehouse was too great. "No." He leaned forward, stroking one finger along her thigh. "But I'd do almost anything else for you."

Her dazed eyes blinked. "You would?"

He gripped her hand in his. "Have I told you yet how incredible Saturday night was?"

She shook her head.

"I can't tell you the last time I let myself go, not worrying about work or what people would think or what would happen later." Frowning, he angled his head. "Though I'm a little worried we might find ourselves in the newspaper. Your neighbors saw us— they called the police, the fire department. There's a public record, and so forth. I'm not sorry about anything that happened between us, but I'm sorry you might be dragged into a public scandal."

To his surprise, she laughed. "Ben, nobody's going to believe *your* jeans started that fire, or that *you* were skinny-dipping with me."

"Well, of course they will. I was there."

She pointed at herself. "*I* was there. With a dark-haired, half-naked man. I can guarantee you, you're not at the top of their list."

The last thing Ben wanted was to be humiliated in his hometown newspaper. These people considered him the direct descendent of their greatest hero. He had a family reputation to uphold, one he'd handled easily until he'd met Monica. He wished he could resent her for the predicament they found themselves in, but he'd taken those steps with his eyes wide open. He'd wanted to prove he could be exciting. To her. And maybe to himself.

But Saturday night he hadn't considered what people might say about *her,* and for that, he was regretful. "Of course I'm on top of the list. I was there," he repeated.

"Even if you walked into the newspaper office and declared you'd been my illicit lover, they wouldn't believe you." She squeezed his hand. "You're the most honorable man in this town. No one would believe you'd spend time with the likes of me."

Ben wondered how he could be complimented and outraged at the same time. "What do you mean the likes of you?"

She released his hand and rose, walking away from him. "Look, Ben, like it or not, I'm different than you. I'm an outsider, for one thing. And my temper tends to get the best of me at times, and I haven't had the greatest luck in maintaining a low-key reputation. People will never associate us."

"They didn't have any problem associating you with my brother."

Glancing over her shoulder, she looked at him. "No, I guess not. He's just as hotheaded as I am."

Ben bit back the fury trying to overtake him. Wes again. Wes suited her. He didn't.

He'd always anticipated falling in love one day. And now that the emotions had slammed him over the head, he loved the one woman he couldn't be sure about. Was he just a substitute for his brother?

He considered the times she'd defended him—to Wes, then again today, in front of the entire population of firefighters. She cared. She had to. But he didn't see tenderness in her eyes now, he saw uncertainty.

And knew exactly how lousy that felt.

He walked toward her, then slid his hand beneath her hair, cupping the back of her neck. As he laid his lips on hers, he saw the uncertainty in her eyes change to need. Her arms encircled his waist, and she held on as if he was her only anchor in the storm of desire. She wanted him. He just had to show her how much more they could have.

"How about dinner tonight?" he asked against her lips.

"I have to work," she murmured, then flicked her tongue across his bottom lip. "I should have worked this weekend."

Even as the clawing need for her infused his body, worry kept interfering. He couldn't give her time to consider their relationship too much. He wanted her a slave to her desire for him until he could figure out what to do, but his work schedule was horrible this week. Well, he'd just have to find excuses to invite her to his office for…consultations. "I have to stay here tomorrow night and fill in for someone. How about Wednesday?"

She smiled. "Let's try out the hot tub this time."

9

LATER THAT AFTERNOON, Monica set the last gallon of chocolate-colored paint on the counter. "Edwin, grab some paint sticks," she called over her shoulder.

Checking her list, she was pretty sure they had all they needed for the painters to start in the morning. At least something was going right on this confusing day. And since she couldn't keep her mind on work for more than two minutes without thinking of Ben and obsessing over the intimacy of their relationship, she checked the list yet again.

She and Edwin had made the decision to go largely with neutral paints—the firefighters seemed more interested in recliners with coolers, heat and massage than wall shades anyway—and let the furniture add the distinctiveness to the themes. Actually, a single theme. Now known as Southern Plantation Sports, which sounded a lot more like a sporting goods store than a design concept, but she couldn't find the energy to care. She couldn't find the energy for much of anything, actually.

She was brooding. And since she never brooded, especially about relationships, she was mad at herself for brooding.

Every time she looked at a paint swatch, she considered her lake house and whether that color would suit her day in and day out. Then she caught herself thinking she should ask Ben his opinion. Then she caught herself picturing him in rooms in her new house. *Then* she caught herself picturing him and her in various positions in rooms in her new house.

Why couldn't she put him out of her mind for five blessed minutes?

Edwin set the paint sticks and a gallon of Silver Sage—for Ben's office—on the counter. "This is the last of it."

Silver Sage was a great color for a bathroom, she decided, envisioning the silvery green in one of the her guest rooms. She could get some eggplant-shaded towels to contrast. Wouldn't Ben look great with an eggplant towel wrapped around his hips after they'd made steamy love in the shower?

Hell, here I go again.

Ben wouldn't be playing water fun in her Silver Sage bathroom, or wearing any towels in there. Her house was still months from completion. Ben wouldn't be around then. Well, he'd be around town, she guessed, just not around her.

And *that* made her want to lay her head on the counter of Collins Paint and Hardware and cry her eyes out.

"Will that be all Ms. O'Malley?" the clerk at the counter asked.

Monica handed Edwin her list. "Double-check that, will you?"

"You ought to try a hot tub next time. I've got one."

It took a few seconds for Monica to realize the clerk's comment was directed at her. She glanced up at the man, who she'd never seen before today, and noted the sleazy smirk on his thin lips. While she'd been teased by several people about the fire and the skinny-dipping, she was appalled this guy thought he had the right to say anything so rude to a customer. She was so shocked, she stammered out, "Pardon me?"

The guy leaned on the counter and gave her what she imagined he considered a come-hither look, but actually came off oily and disrespectful. "It's a little cold for the pool, but I bet we could heat things up real quick. Without the grill."

Bleck! Who was this creep?

Before she could tear into him, Edwin stepped in front of her. "I think you're speaking inappropriately to Ms. O'Malley. Apologize. Immediately."

The clerk gave Edwin a dismissing glance. "I'm sure the lady doesn't mind. And you'll have to wait in line, buddy." He smiled. "And I'm sure it's gonna be a long, long line."

Pain, anger and embarrassment all raced through her veins. She'd fielded insulting idiots before, but no one so blatant and ugly before. She was literally shocked into silence. Every snappy comeback and equally insulting return froze in her throat.

So when Edwin punched the guy dead in his face all she could manage was to shift her gaping stare to him.

As the clerk raised his hands to his split lip, Edwin grabbed the paint. "Tell your boss to put this on the account of Edwin Collins." He smiled menacingly— who knew Edwin could be threatening? "He knows me well. I'm his cousin." Then he calmly escorted Monica out the door.

EDWIN BOUGHT HER a drink at the restaurant at the end of the block, and she found herself pouring out the whole story of the fire and skinny-dipping and even her uncertainty about her feelings for Ben. The fact that she was revealing anything about her personal life to *Edwin* felt more than a little strange. But then she hadn't felt normal since the morning she walked into the firehouse and smack into Chief Benjamin Kimball more than two weeks ago.

"Sounds like you're in love with him to me."

She choked on her wine. "Oh, you are so completely off base."

Edwin shrugged, stirring his Shirley Temple with a cherry stem. "Just the fact that we're having this conversation tells me you're not feeling quite yourself, that you're worried about him. You tried to protect him and probably can't stop thinking about him. Sounds like love to me."

Edwin perceptive? Who knew?

Monica glared at him. She didn't like that he'd made a valid point—several of them, in fact. And she refused to acknowledge the trembling in her stomach was fear. "I don't fall in love."

"Have now," Edwin said simply.

Monica absolutely refused to consider the idea.

"You'll figure it all out eventually. Me, I knew I loved Dana the first time I ordered a Shirley Temple, and she smiled and said she loved cherries. I mean you wouldn't believe some of the looks and remarks a guy gets for liking a fizzy lemon-lime beverage mixed with cherry juice." He shook his head sadly for these small-minded folks. "And since you helped me overcome my fear and ask her out, I'm returning the favor."

"I would have preferred a nice bouquet of flowers."

Edwin angled his head, as if considering the idea. "No, this is better. You'll see."

She sincerely wanted to strangle the cheerful, goofy man.

"Now about that nincompoop in the store... The chief and the mayor need to know about the incident at once."

"No." Monica shook her head. "No way. Ben will tell the mayor the skinny-dipping was his idea, and the whole story will get out. I won't have Ben's name whispered about town. People can't know the fire chief *started* a fire. No, I won't risk the respect he's earned."

"Monica, he has to know."

She leaned forward. "*No.* Not over some insignificant creep who works at the hardware store."

"Not anymore he doesn't. The minute I get home, I'm calling my cousin."

She noted he didn't promise to keep the incident to himself, but she knew Edwin would respect her wishes.

He laid his hand over hers. "I'm sorry he hurt you."

"It's okay. He didn't." But because he had, and she hadn't expected him to, she squeezed his hand. "I can't believe you punched him."

Edwin grinned. "Pretty good jab, wasn't it? The chief's been sparring with me the last couple of weeks. He says it will improve my reflexes."

Ben was a gem, no doubt about it. He complained that Edwin wasn't qualified to be a firefighter, but then he took time to help him.

"You're thinking about him again, aren't you?"

Her face heated. "I am not."

Edwin drained his drink with a loud slurp through his straw. "I think you should name your first child Edwin."

GIVING IN TO THE COWARD she had no idea lurked in her body, Monica systematically avoided Ben for nearly two days. She didn't want to face her feelings, and she didn't know how much longer she could be June Cleaver.

When she arrived home from work Monday night, she ignored the suggestive answering machine message from him about what they could do on their date Wednesday night. Then, when he cornered her in the hall the next day, she told him she'd fallen exhausted into bed and hadn't gotten the message. She'd slunk off with the excuse of supervising the painting and managed to sneak out of the firehouse at the end of the day while he was giving a miniseminar on extension ladder maintenance.

But on Wednesday afternoon, her luck ran out.

"Monica!" came the stern command from down the hall.

She was in the kitchen supervising the installation of the new dishwasher. She sighed, stuck her pencil behind her ear, and walked to the end of the hall. Ben stood just outside his office. "Yes?" she asked, trying her best to look distracted and annoyed at being interrupted.

"I need to see you."

She held out her hands. "Here I am."

He crossed his arms over his chest, looking so commanding she wanted to lean against the wall for support. "In my office. Now."

She shivered. The man knew how to give orders. And as she walked past him and inhaled his spicy scent, she could think of a couple dozen illicit orders she'd be only too happy to comply with.

He closed the door, then leaned back against it. "Couldn't find another excuse to avoid me?"

Since he'd obviously seen through her stammering, asinine excuses of the last two days, she didn't see the point in defending herself.

What would she say? *Edwin thinks I'm in love with you, and you don't even like me—at least not the real me. You're respected and admired. I'm propositioned by smarmy hardware store clerks.*

Pretending a boldness she didn't feel, she sat on his desk, crossing one leg over the other and swinging her foot. "You called, and here I am, Chief. Let me guess, you don't like the chocolate."

The anger left his face, and his brow furrowed. "What chocolate?"

"In the kitchen."

He pushed away from the door, then walked toward her. "Phil made chocolate cake?"

She grinned, as if she had no idea she'd intentionally confused him—and, more important, distracted him from whatever confrontation was surely on his mind. "No. the chocolate-colored paint."

He stopped a few feet from her, waving his hand, dismissing the kitchen walls. "It's fine. Frankly, I hadn't noticed the paint. Which actually is your—"

"You should. These painters work by the room, you know. If you're not happy, you need to let me know."

He raked his hand through his hair. "I'm not happy, but it has nothing to do with paint."

Uh-oh. Distress was written all over his face. A major emotional chat was on his mind. But, cowardly as it was, she wasn't ready to face a deep discussion. And she hated seeing him upset, knowing she was the cause. Knowing her fear and uncertainty had driven her to avoid him.

Maybe that's why she was shocked as hell when he grabbed her.

He pulled her off the desk and into his arms. His mouth captured hers, demanding, seducing her response. Instinctively she returned his passion. She wanted him to forget how much trouble she was, about the worries of finding himself in the newspaper linked with the town scandal magnet, about the future and the past. She wanted to remind herself how much he wanted her, and delude herself into thinking he always would.

Sliding her tongue against his, she reveled in the heat spreading through her veins. No one had ever made her feel like he did. Needy and so full of desire that the rest of the world just fell away, but also comforted and protected. No matter how often she tried to tell herself she shouldn't get used to him, she wanted to anyway.

She relished the pressure of her breasts against his chest and buried her hands in the silky hair at his nape.

Aching need pulsed between her legs. How had she lived without his touch for the past two days? For the past ten years? Then his hands were busy unbuttoning her prim suit coat—another one in beige—and she pushed aside the questions. Instead, she reveled in the sensations he could give her.

He set her on the desk, shoved her jacket off her shoulders, then cupped her breasts, his thumbs skimming her nipples through her thin bra. She dug her nails into the back of his neck and let her legs fall open, pulling him against the juncture of her thighs. His hardness, pressing against the sensitive center of her body, felt glorious. She nearly laughed aloud at the pleasure.

Then, suddenly, he jerked back. "Hell, what am I doing? This is serious."

Fear and longing swamping her, she reached for his hand. "You're damn right it is."

He stepped back, and the loss of his warmth chilled her. When his gaze met hers, she saw anger. "Why didn't you tell me about that idiot in the hardware store?"

Her heart struck her ribs, and she let the question hang in the air, her mind racing for an excuse and her body trying to adjust to being denied its needs. Then she looked away, cursing Edwin.

Ben grabbed her chin, turning her face toward him. "He's lucky Edwin got him instead of me. I'd have put him in the hospital." He stroked her cheek with his thumb. "He hurt you," he said softly, with regret.

She didn't want to believe the tenderness in his eyes, instead, she melted into a puddle of mush. "No, he didn't."

"The whole town's gossiping about you skinny-dipping, about the fire. Why didn't you tell me?"

She shrugged. "It's not important."

He shook his head. "It is. But sharing your thoughts with me, that you were embarrassed and scared and angry—don't deny it, Edwin told me— you couldn't do. I want to know why."

Just how much of that had he guessed and how much had Edwin really told him? She was going to strangle the little interfering—

"And don't even think about blaming Edwin. He was right to come to me. Hell, this is my fault." He rubbed his temples. "Do you know how guilty I feel about causing all this mess?"

She hadn't considered his need to take on the responsibility for their night together. Frankly, because she'd never known anyone who would. Well, she'd really screwed this up. She stood, then walked toward him. "It's not your fault." She raised her hand, tapping his chin. "It was worth a little scandal. And one more won't affect me."

He turned his head, kissing the underside of her wrist, then capturing her hand in his. "I'm telling everyone I started the fire and that the skinny-dipping was my idea."

She narrowed her eyes. "Don't."

"Why? Are you embarrassed for people to know you were with me? I know I'm not Wes, but I'm pretty sure I'm capable of passion when I need to be."

She jerked her hand from his grasp, turning away. "Don't be ridiculous. Of course you're not Wes. Who'd want you to be?"

"You?"

"Hell no, I—" Something in his tone brought her head around. Beneath the anger and confusion and all the other muddled stuff between them, she recognized an emotion she'd become intimately familiar with the past few days.

Fear.

And for the first time, she looked at her former relationship with Wes from Ben's perspective. All he knew was that she'd dated his brother, she'd caught him cheating on her with another woman, and she'd retaliated with the whole merry widow–handcuffing thing. Then she'd appeared in his life, flirting and dragging him into intimacy with her. She remembered just a few days ago, when he'd mentioned Wes. He'd said no one had trouble associating her and Wes.

Was it possible he was weirded out by the idea of her and Wes together? Since she'd never considered Wes any grand passion, she hadn't really examined the comparison too closely. But the men were brothers. And, on the surface at least, she and Wes did seem more in tune. They were both headstrong, dangerous and wild at times.

And ever since Saturday night Ben had been headstrong, dangerous and wild.

She whirled to face him. "What kind of car does Wes drive?"

He shrugged. "Some sports car."

"A *Corvette?*" she pressed.

"I think so," he said, clearly hedging.

Aha!

"You've been comparing yourself to him. Comparing, hell, you've been acting like him." She said it with a kind of strange wonder she fully understood, since she'd been doing the same thing. *Maybe he doesn't want me to be someone I'm not either.* "That's what the skinny-dipping and urging me to run off with you before the presentation was about."

His flushed face was all the proof she needed.

"Ben." She grabbed his hands out of a deep-seated

need to touch him, to reassure him. "I'll admit, when we first met, I thought you could stand to loosen up a bit, but I don't want you to change for me. I certainly don't want you to be like Wes.

"I never wanted him the way I do you. You're—" she paused, meeting the vivid blue of his gaze, the words scratching their way to the top of her throat "—special."

Surprise shot into his eyes. Then wonder. He pressed his lips to hers. "Thank you. I needed that. And thank you for coming—well, charging—into my life. You reminded me I don't have to be tough, regimented Chief Kimball all the time."

"My pleasure."

He kissed her forehead, drawing her against his chest. "I'm still telling everyone the truth about the skinny-dipping and the fire."

Stamping her foot, she jerked her head up, glaring at him. She hadn't told him all that to distract him. She'd admitted what was in her heart.

Well, hell. "Everyone will know about us!" she blurted out.

"I don't care. I don't know why you do."

"I don't. But you can't—" She stopped, hesitant...*extremely* hesitant to put the truth to words. She'd rarely acknowledged her reputation to herself, much less anyone else. Then she figured she didn't have anything to lose. *Except Ben.* And somehow she trusted he'd be the one person who wouldn't care.

She swallowed. She looked him dead in the eye. "You can't be linked with the town tramp."

His jaw dropped. His eyes widened. His hands clenched around her waist. "You're *not* the town tramp."

"The truth hardly matters. Everyone thinks so."

His blue eyes turned fierce, with an anger and sense of protectiveness that took her breath away. "No, they don't."

His stubbornness frustrated her. "Why are you doing this?"

"Because I love you."

"I—" She shook her head, even as her heart tried to jump its way out of her chest. "You—" She shook her head again. It wasn't possible. "Why?" was all she could manage to say.

He stroked her cheek. "Hmm. So many reasons. Your tender heart, your wit, your...legs." He kept his gaze locked on hers, and she really started to believe the words, crazy as they sounded. *Maybe he doesn't want me to be someone I'm not either.* "And let's not forget the night you defended me to Wes. No one stands in front of me. They stand behind me, expect me to protect them." He paused, his eyes gleaming. "Everyone except you."

Her heart hammered against her ribs. "Ben, I—"

The doorknob rattled.

As their surprised gazes darted to the door, it swung open. And before Monica could blink, Ben had pulled her around the desk, laid his hand on her shoulder and shoved her beneath it. She bit back a protest when she heard another voice in the room. Phil.

"Sorry to interrupt. I was—" Phil paused. "You okay, Chief?"

"Fine," Ben said, his voice creaky and unconvincing.

Monica poked him in the shin. She wasn't crouching under the desk to hide from Phil. It was ridiculous. It was—

I'm telling everyone I started the fire and that the skinny-dipping was my idea. I love you....

Vaguely, she realized Phil continued talking about schedules and reports, but she could barely hear him through the ringing in her ears. To her utter horror, tears flooded her eyes.

Ben had no intention of telling anyone anything. *Just shove her under the desk. Don't let anyone see you with That Woman.*

If her heart wasn't threatening to explode, she'd laugh at the idea of a man like Ben loving her. She'd known he'd never take her seriously. Not even when she'd tried to act serious.

She drew shallow breaths, trying to gain control of her emotions. What was wrong with her?

She heard the door close, then Ben's hand appeared at the opening of the desk. Blinking away the tears, she buttoned her jacket, then scooted out.

"That was close," Ben said, then grinned.

From somewhere deep inside she found the strength to glare at him, rather than burst into tears. In fact, fury surged through her veins. She shoved him backward. "Not worried about being seen with me, huh? You were just about to announce the skinny-dipping was your idea, right?" She jabbed her finger in his chest, ignoring the hurt and confusion on his face. "Don't insult me."

"Good grief, Monica," he said, stepping out of her reach—good thing, too. She was tempted to slug him. "I was only trying to protect you. You weren't dressed."

She narrowed her eyes. "Look, *Chief.* I didn't ask you for anything. I never expected promises and undying love." She paused, lowering her voice, gathering steam for her tirade, familiar with turning hurt into anger. "But I won't be lied to. And I won't be pushed in the corner, swept under the carpet or shoved under a desk."

His eyes pleading for understanding, he laid his hands on her shoulders. "It was just instinctive. I didn't want you to be embarrassed."

She shrugged off his touch. "*I* wouldn't have been. What about you?"

"I—" He paced away from her. "I'm in charge around here. I have to maintain a certain level of respect. We shouldn't have been making out in the middle of the workday."

"Well, telling everyone about the skinny-dipping and fire won't help your respect much, will it?"

He sighed. "I suppose not." He stared at her over his shoulder. "But I'm still doing it. It's only right. I won't have people talking about you that way."

She headed for the door. "Don't bother. It won't change anything."

"Dammit, Monica. Don't walk out on me."

Ignoring him, she turned the knob. "Bye, Ben. It's been fun." She blew him a mocking kiss, closed the door, then walked away with her head held high and her heart broken.

SHE'S JUST MAD, Ben told himself for the millionth time as he stared at the setting sun outside his office window.

And, by damn, he was mad, too. At himself. At her.

He'd tried to protect her by pushing her under his desk, but he should have realized she wouldn't see it that way. Beneath all that sass, Monica was very vulnerable. And she sure as hell wouldn't hear that from him either. She was so prickly, and hotheaded, and—

And he wanted her more than he wanted to draw his next breath.

And now, hours after she'd left, he'd begun to question himself. Was his motivation to protect her reputation, or his own?

He spun away from the window, not wanting to face the answer. He had to do something. He couldn't just stand here and wait for her to come around. She wouldn't. Would she?

How would he know? When he'd spilled his guts, she'd just stared at him like he'd suggested they jump off the roof. In fact, the only positive statement she'd made had been about Wes. She'd didn't want Wes and didn't want him to be Wes. Ben was *special.* Of course, she'd probably describe Edwin and Phil and Bernie as special.

What a mess.

He snagged his keys from the top drawer of his desk. He had to find her, make her confess her feelings, make her understand his.

When the door opened, he glanced up to see Edwin walking into the room. "What's up? I'm on my way out."

"Sir." Edwin's posture was so stiff Ben was tempted to see if a steel rod held up his spine. "I need to talk to you. It's a personal matter."

He really didn't have time for this, but he held out his hand, indicating the chair in front of his desk. "Have a seat."

"I'd rather stand, sir."

Puzzled by the formality in Edwin's voice, Ben

propped one hip on his desk and inclined his head. "Fine."

"I should have come by earlier." He shoved his hands into his pockets, his eyes narrowed behind his round glasses. "But I was afraid my temper would force me to do something rash."

Ben started to laugh, but realized quickly Edwin wasn't kidding. He was major-league pissed.

Fists clenched at his sides, Edwin took an aggressive step forward. With Ben sitting they were almost eye-to-eye. "When Monica left she was crying."

Ben's heart dropped to his feet. "She was?"

"She said you'd had an argument. She tried to act mad, but I could tell—" He stopped, looking down.

Ben's heart lurched. He'd hurt her. "You could tell what?"

Edwin's furious gaze met his. "I could tell her heart was broken."

Regret coursing through him, Ben let his head drop back. "Oh, damn. I really messed everything up, didn't I?"

"I'd say so. Respectfully, sir, I'd like to call you out."

Ben stared at Edwin. He'd never heard the old-fashioned term outside of the movies. "You want to fight me?"

He raised his chin. "Unless you'd prefer pistols at dawn."

With a painful, self-depreciating chuckle, Ben shook his head. "I don't have time to fight you, Edwin. I've got to figure out how to get Monica back."

"Making her cry is not the advisable solution, sir."

"You're probably right."

"Why don't you tell me what happened?"

Though seeking advice from Edwin would have seemed absurd a few weeks ago, Ben acknowledged nothing would ever be like it was. And Edwin had spent more time around Monica than anyone. Maybe he could offer insight into her feelings.

At the conclusion of Ben's story, Edwin angled his head. "You're thinking you need to prove your feelings to her."

Ben paced in front of the window. "But how? An ad in the newspaper? A billboard on Main Street?"

"Those planes with banners are pretty cool."

"She'd think all that was hokey."

"Probably." Edwin paused, considering, then said, "Have you ever thought about just telling her how you feel?"

Ben threw up his hands in frustration. "Hell, man, I tried that earlier. Look where it got me."

"Try harder. Make her understand."

"If I could just redo this afternoon—prove to her she's the best thing that ever happened to me. I'd never be embarrassed by her. I love that she's outrageous and unpredictable. She's helped me tap into a side of myself I didn't know existed."

"You have been smiling more lately, sir."

His mind racing, he paced faster. "My sister used to always tell me the Kimballs all have wild impulsiveness in their genes. Then she'd look at me and say how grateful she was that one of us was practical and predictable. But those wild genes have been taking over a lot lately. I'm feeling the need to do something unpredictable."

"Don't forget the mayor and the city council are coming tomorrow to check the progress of the renovations."

Ben ground to a halt. He smiled. "Perfect." He headed to the door. Noting Edwin wasn't beside him, he turned, waving his hand. "Come on. We've got to find that banner paper."

10

MONICA STOOD ON HER DECK, staring at the moon's reflection glistening off the lake. She could hardly believe how quickly the house was coming together. It wasn't just a frame of wood and concrete anymore. It was taking shape into the dream she'd imagined for longer than she could remember. It was strong, beautiful and permanent.

She'd made the decision to build something lasting in her life, and she had. Maybe that's what had led her to Ben.

"Now what the hell am I going to do about it all?"

The moon, not surprisingly, didn't answer.

Turning, she walked through the back door and into the kitchen, which was lit by a single, generator-powered lamp. The deserted construction area, scattered with sawhorses, dust and abandoned equipment, looked cold and lonely. Much like this house would if she didn't have Ben to share it. She'd ordered the tile for the kitchen earlier—in chocolate—and wondered if he'd approve.

Leaning on the bar, she propped her chin in her hand. Well, she'd finally figured out she loved him, and he'd said he loved her in return, then he'd shoved her under a desk rather than be seen with her.

What's wrong with this picture?

So maybe he had been trying to protect her, and

maybe Phil finding them half-dressed and panting wasn't the ideal way to announce their relationship to the world. She could see that, she supposed.

The big question for her was simple. She'd spent the last week trying to be someone else. So who did Ben really love?

She had hoped he'd seen beneath the beige suits and flat hair to the real her, that he'd been as confused by her sudden switch in personality as she had his. She'd been able to see beyond the bold and dangerous qualities to still love the whole man. Was there any chance he could do the same?

He shoved you under his desk. How's that for an answer?

But she knew he'd never lie to her or betray her. If he said he was going to tell the truth about skinny-dipping, he was. If he said he loved her, he did.

She just needed to find out which version he'd fallen for.

Glancing at her watch, she headed out the door. She hoped Skyler had some flat shoes she could borrow in the name of love.

THE NEXT MORNING Monica took one more look at her reflection in her car's rearview mirror. She winced, then shrugged. This love business was heavy in the sacrifice department.

She stepped out of the car and ran smack into Skyler.

Her friend held out her arms, as if to block Monica's path to the firehouse. "I can't let you do this."

Monica sighed. She wasn't up to another argument like last night. Who knew her tiny, blond friend could be so stinkin' ornery? "What are you doing here?"

"Stopping you from going through with this crazy plan."

"Move, Skyler." When she just stood there, Monica stalked around her.

Skyler darted to the firehouse door, blocking it with her body. "You *stole* those shoes from me. Take them off."

Monica glanced down at the navy patent flats. She winced again. "Did not. You said you wouldn't speak to me ever again if I left with them." She glared at her friend. "So, I repeat, what are you doing here?"

"Monica, please. Be reasonable."

"When have you ever known me to be reasonable?"

Skyler bit her lip. "Well, never. Though you did wear that purple taffeta bridesmaid's dress in my wedding."

Monica reached for the door handle. "A slip that will never be repeated."

"Ben's going to hate this."

"Let's hope so."

"Just tell him how you feel."

"I will. Right after I get his reaction to—" She stopped, staring at Skyler. "You're afraid he won't notice, aren't you?"

Skyler bit her lip.

"Worse, you're afraid he *wants* me to be June Cleaver." Truthfully, Monica was somewhat nervous, too. But she didn't see any other way to learn the truth.

While Skyler was distracted with her thoughts, Monica jerked the door handle and bumped Skyler out of the way with her hip. She rushed inside on her friend's wail of protest.

She stalked down the hall, then crossed the den, noting the Welcome Mayor And City Council banner. Ignoring the strange looks she got from the firefighters, including Edwin, she blew past them and the city statesmen, giving them all a backhanded wave. She paused only when she reached Ben's office door, where she drew a bracing breath before she knocked.

"Come in," Ben called.

She walked in and forced herself to keep moving until she reached the center of the room, directly in front of his desk. Her heart pounded like crazy as he raised his head.

His surprised gaze met hers as he stood. "Monica, you're here—" He angled his head, staring at her oddly. *"Monica?"*

She held up her hand and managed a nervous, wane smile. "Present."

He walked around the desk, then around her, slowly, his blue gaze seeming to measure and evaluate every inch of her body from head to toe. Finally, he stopped in front of her. He crossed his arms over his chest. "Okay. What are you up to?"

"Up to?"

"What's the costume for?"

"Costume?"

She glanced down at herself—the high-collared white cotton shirt, the double-breasted navy blazer, midcalf-length, navy wool skirt, navy stockings, flat shoes. She winced a third time. She recalled the sparing makeup on her face and the bun—yes, the *bun*—she'd twisted her hair into, and winced yet again before she forced herself to look directly at him. "It's the new me."

Ben goggled. "It's the— What?" Then, suddenly,

his eyes narrowed. "Last Saturday night you wore that strange banker costume, too."

Hope made her heart race. "Uh-huh."

"And you said 'golly' and that my Corvette was too fast."

"I did, didn't I?"

"You were trying to act conservative." Understanding and wonder lit his eyes. "Just like I acted wild for you. You were conservative for me."

"Yep."

He scowled. "Stop it—immediately."

She smiled and threw her arms around him. "Damn, I love you."

"You— What?"

She brushed her fingers through his hair. "I love you, Ben Kimball."

He wrapped his arms around her, and the pleasure and happiness in his eyes was stunning. "You know, five minutes ago I would have said I'd kill to hear you say those words. But I have to tell you, seeing them come out of your *unpainted* lips…it's a little frightening."

"I completely agree." She leaned into him, covering his mouth with hers. As the familiar heat rolled through her veins, she breathed in the scent and taste of him. He tasted of coffee and mint, and his spicy cologne made her head swim.

"I'm so sorry about yesterday," he said next to her ear, then trailed kisses along her jaw.

She angled her head to give him better access, sucking in a breath when his teeth nipped her skin. "I know. You were trying to protect me."

"And myself." He cupped her cheek, then kissed

her lips. "But no more. I have a question, then a surprise for you."

Wrapping her arms around his neck, she pressed her body against his. Why were they talking *now?* It had been so long since she'd touched him. "Later."

He groaned, holding her hips against the hardness between his legs. "You are going back to normal soon, aren't you?"

She stared up at him. "You're sure you hate the outfit?"

"Yes."

"You hate the hair?"

"Immensely."

She could feel a smile working its way to her face. "You hate the shoes?"

He glanced at her feet. And winced.

"Thank God." She yanked the pins from her hair, tossed off the blazer, unbuttoned the top three buttons of her blouse, kicked off her shoes, then crossed the room to pull a pair of navy and white check-patterned heels from her bag. "Those shoes were killing me."

She walked toward him, relieved to note her natural sway was back with the shoe substitution. Then she gave him a long, deep, powerful kiss. "I really love you," she said breathlessly when she came up for air.

"I love you." He tangled his hands in her hair. "You're going to drive me crazy. Happy, but crazy."

"Count on it." She ran her thumb across his bottom lip. "And since you hated me trying to change, I have a request."

"Anything."

"When I go back to being the wild, impulsive one, could you be the steady, predictable fire chief again?"

He raised his eyebrows. "But it's been fun, hasn't it?"

"Frankly, I've had a little too much fun the last few weeks. I wouldn't mind some quiet. How do you feel about flopping in front of the TV with a bowl of popcorn?"

Even as laughter slid into Ben's eyes, a loud crash reverberated through the room. The very foundation of the building shook.

Ben jerked her away from the windows and exterior wall, forcing her into the far corner of the room, protecting her body with his.

When the rumbling finally stopped, and Monica remembered to breathe again, she peeked over Ben's shoulder. "Oh, my."

Ben turned, staring at the gaping hole in his office. The windowpane and glass lay in scattered shards across the floor. And the nose of a pickup truck sat in its place. Edwin's truck.

Shouts reverberated in the distance. The alarm sounded. Someone pounded on the office door.

He held Monica against his chest, assuring himself she was all right. He was going to wring Edwin's clumsy neck when he got his hands on him.

Then, in that odd moment of stillness, the idea hit him. People were about to descend on them like ants on a sugar cube. Firefighters, the mayor, the city council—they were all just outside the door.

He tore off his tie, then started on his shirt buttons. "Mess up your hair. Untuck your shirt."

Monica gaped at him. "What?"

He untucked her shirt himself. "You don't look like you've been caught in the middle of an illicit liaison."

"Well, gee, Ben, I think we've got bigger problems than getting caught making out in your office again."

"Can you make that skirt shorter in the next thirty seconds?"

Monica planted her hands on her hips, flinging out her hand to gesture at the ruined window. "Do you see the truck?"

"Yes." He raked his hands through her hair, scrubbing the strands until they fell in a sexy tumble around her face. "Remind me later to give Edwin a promotion." He dropped his shirt on the floor.

More pounding on the door. "Chief? Are you in there? Are you okay?"

Ben grabbed Monica's hand and tugged her toward the door, noting she wasn't nearly undressed enough, but she'd have to do.

"I hope you're planning to explain all this to me later," she said.

"You'll understand in a minute." As he unlocked the door, though, he heard the crunch of glass from behind him. The mayor—sporting his Vegas Elvis white glittery jumpsuit today—the city council and half the on-duty firefighters alternated between astonished looks at him and Monica and the truck. Pleased as punch with himself, Ben flung open the door, then yanked Monica into his arms.

Jack was the first man through the door. "*Mon Dieu*, Chief, I thought I was going to have to bust the door—" His gaze raked them from head to toe. "But you seem…fine."

More firefighters rushed in, with Skyler stumbling in behind them. "Ben, Monica, are you all—" She stopped, staring at them, then the clothes scattered carelessly on the floor. "I'm getting a real sense of déjà vu here."

The mayor stomped toward Ben. "Chief Kimball, what the devil is going on?"

Ben did his best to look guilty and embarrassed. "Uh, sorry, sir. We, uh—" He glanced down at Monica, who looked as though she couldn't decide whether to laugh or punch him. He made an attempt to straighten her clothes, then snagged his shirt off the floor and shrugged into it.

Mrs. Markenson, one of the ultraconservative council members, stepped forward, crossing her arms over her chest. "I think you'd better explain yourself, Chief."

"I guess so." Grasping Monica's hand, he cleared his throat. "I'm afraid my behavior lately hasn't been as exemplary as you should expect from your fire chief. I've been distracted at work, I caused a mess of confusion by accidentally starting a fire." He broke off at the mayor's angry expression, then quickly added, "But I put out the fire, too. I dragged Monica into the pool to skinny-dip, and—"

"That was *you?*" the mayor asked, obviously skeptical.

"Yes." Ben thought he saw a hint of admiration in the mayor's eyes. Of course, this was the man who'd changed the library's winter bake sale fundraiser into a lingerie fashion show starring his buxom wife. But the mayor did have to answer to his constituents, and Ben regretted his actions might cause the man grief from the more conservative citizens of Baxter. "And now today I'm afraid I got…carried away again. But, well—" he gazed down at Monica, brushing an errant strand of hair off her beautiful face "—it's love."

Her face flushed and her green eyes widened, then love, pure and strong, filled those eyes, and he finally felt his world right itself. He hoped she fully understood how she completed him, how much he loved the flamboyant, outspoken, honorable person she was. And how he'd stand with her, in front of her or behind her as long as he lived.

"So, on that note, let's all go into the den." Ben wound his way through the firefighters, briefly patting Edwin's shoulder as he headed for the door.

"What about the window? The truck?" the mayor protested.

"We'll get to that eventually. This is important." He waved his hand in an impatient, come-along gesture. "Follow me, please, people."

"What are you doing?" Monica said in his ear as they strode down the hall.

"Work with me, sweetheart. I have a plan."

"Does this grand plan of yours have us getting naked anytime soon?"

He grinned down at her. "All in good time."

"Just so you know I'm getting impatient."

Ben—quickly—assembled everyone in the den. "First of all, we need to give Monica, and her assistant Edwin, a big round of applause for the terrific work on the firehouse." After the applause died down, he added, "Though it looks like my office might need some work now."

Several people chuckled, and a red-faced Edwin stepped to the front of the crowd. "Uh, Chief, about that…"

"Later, Edwin, later. Help me with the sign,

okay?'' Each grabbing an end of the Welcome Mayor And City Council sign, they tugged, revealing the sign behind it.

Marry me, Monica.

He dropped to one knee beside her, holding out his hand toward Edwin, who dropped a jeweler's box into his palm. He heard Monica's quick, indrawn breath as he flipped open the lid to reveal the teardrop-shaped diamond inside. Looking up, trying to memorize the stunned, tender look on her face, he clutched her left hand in his. ''Will you marry me?''

Her eyes shimmered with tears, reminding him of his thoughtlessness yesterday, and why he'd vowed to keep them from falling from now on. And, speechless for once, she simply nodded.

He slid the ring on her finger, and everyone clapped and cheered as he rose to kiss her softly, but thoroughly. She was really his. Forever. No matter how wild the ride became, he knew he'd always remember the simple sweetness in her eyes, in her kiss.

When he lifted his head, he smiled down at her, his heart full of joy.

She punched him in the stomach. ''I look terrible. If anybody takes pictures you're in big trouble, Chief.''

Edwin stepped in front of them. A broad grin on his face, he held up the camera Ben had asked him to bring. ''Smile!''

MONICA LEANED against the kitchen counter, smiling as she watched the mayor try to drag Mrs. Markenson onto the dance floor.

''If there's a fire, I don't know how I'll be able to

get them in the truck,'' Ben said from behind her, sliding his arms around her waist.

She turned to face him, linking her hands behind his head. ''Just keep an eye on Edwin.''

Smiling, Ben shook his head. ''Poor guy. He went by the jeweler to pick up the ring this morning, forgot it in his truck, so he went outside to grab it and knocked the gearshift on his way out. He stood there, watching the car roll down the hill and into my office. But when he looked in and saw we were all right, he ran for the mayor and town council.''

''And gave you the perfect opportunity to tell everyone about us.''

''I'm thinking I could find a way to make him an honorary captain.''

She shook her head. ''Sorry. I'm hiring him to be my assistant.''

Ben raised his eyebrows. ''We may have to negotiate that.''

Thinking of all the sensual ways they could bargain, she threaded her fingers through his hair. ''Oh, I hope so.''

He leaned his head toward her, but she pulled back. ''I have some issues to settle first.'' And as she looked into his bright blue eyes, the words she couldn't find earlier came to her. ''You stood up for me,'' she said, shaking her head in wonder. ''It was the most amazing, loving, selfless thing I've ever seen.''

''See how I felt the night you stood up to Wes for me?''

She had a very good idea. And that sense of protection was an aspect of their love she would always treasure.

She gazed down at the sparkling diamond on her finger. "I'm high-maintenance, you know."

"I know."

"And I spend a lot of money on shoes, makeup and clothes."

"I figured."

She met his gaze. She wanted him so much, could see her dazzling future just on the horizon—and it flat-out scared her to death. "We're both really independent."

"I know."

"And stubborn."

"I know."

"My house is the only thing I've ever wanted permanently in my life until you. Do you really think I have what it takes for the long run?"

He laid his forehead against hers. "Yes. You've always had commitment, darling, you were just waiting for the right man to come along to share it with."

Hmm. She liked that rationale. "You're the right man."

"Definitely."

"That picture of us is going to wind up in the newspaper, isn't it?"

"Probably."

"Then kiss me and remind me why I don't care."

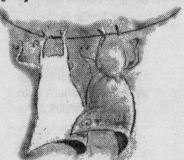
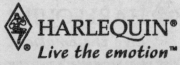

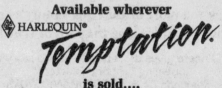
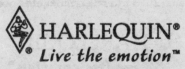

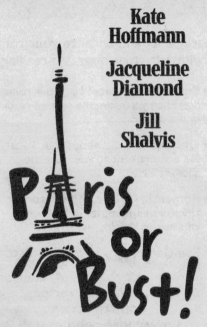
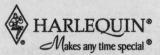